AMERICAN FAMILY

AMERICAN FAMILY

A Novel By Robert Crooke

iUniverse, Inc.
New York Lincoln Shanghai

AMERICAN FAMILY

iUniverse books may be ordered through booksellers or by contacting:

iUniverse
2021 Pine Lake Road, Suite 100
Lincoln, NE 68512
www.iuniverse.com
1-800-Authors (1-800-288-4677)

ISBN: 0-595-33565-9 (pbk)
ISBN: 0-595-66970-0 (cloth)

Printed in the United States of America

This book is for my father and for my son.

What you have done for the least of these, my brethren, you have done for me.

—Mathew 25:40

The foregoing generations beheld God and nature face to face; we, through their eyes.

—Ralph Waldo Emerson, *Nature*

CHAPTER 1

It was easiest for my Grandfather Hank to love things that were most like himself and—as much as anything—he loved this house, which he built in a secluded spot along the Hudson River in 1929.

When we were kids, my sister Liz and I spent a lot of time with him here and, even then, we understood its nostalgic influence. It reminded him of Ireland, he often said, and of a girl he'd grown up with, there. She was the daughter of a wealthy landlord who lived in a great, fieldstone mansion set on a hill overlooking endless meadows, in which my grandfather's family had worked for generations. The landlord's daughter and Grandfather had been childhood playmates, and as they got older, some deeper attraction bloomed, he said. Then, one summer day when they were 15, something happened that seemed to haunt him for the rest of his life.

"We're standin' outside her father's house this one day," he would say, usually after a few drinks. "She asks me what I want outta life, so I tell 'er, 'to be rich a' course.' An' she says, 'is that *all*?' 'An' marry *you*,' I say. She gets a funny look on 'er face and tells me ta' come inside the house. She takes me up to the highest window in the place and we look out on her father's estate an' all. 'Everything ya' see is *his*,' she says. And I'm lookin', sayin' nothin'. So, finally she says ta' me, 'do ya' understand what I mean, Henry Gannon?' An' I tell 'er 'it's sure a lovely view from up here.' And a' course she thinks I'm daft, so I laugh. An' then I say, 'you can see all the way to Cork City.' And she looks over m'shoulder an' says 'so you can; not much of a city though, compared with Dublin.' An' I have to tell 'er 'I wouldn't know.'"

We called this "the window story" in our family, and there were several versions of it, often conflicting, but always told with the same palpable sadness.

Once, he even claimed the girl had accepted his brusque proposal, until her father heard about it, and packed her off to a boarding school up north.

Of course, he wouldn't tell any version of the window story if Grandmother was listening. Instead, after describing the landlord's stone mansion, which he so clearly admired, he'd talk bitterly about how politics and the church had ruined Ireland, especially the south, where boys like him were destined for hard, predictable lives serving others. And I doubt Grandmother cared for her grandchildren hearing about that, either.

I also doubted that this girl—if she existed—ever had considered his offer, since the window story was so clearly about being told "no." And it confused me to hear Grandfather say he'd put up this house with a large, fieldstone structure in mind, because it's a simple white, wooden cottage, modeled after the Dutch homesteads that once were as plentiful as elms along here. But, whatever the flaws in his memory, there's no doubt he chose a beautiful spot—a rolling piece of hillside above the river in Garrison, New York, 50 miles north of Manhattan.

What I try to remember, now, is that he gave this cottage to my father at a time when our family needed help. And if I'm troubled by my own memories of this cold and drafty old house, I have no further doubts about Hank Gannon.

He was an ambitious, 17-year-old kid when he first arrived at Brooklyn's Red Hook harbor on a cold November day in 1910. His brother had arranged a job for him at a small, Irish-owned brokerage house in New York, and they started him as a ticket runner down on the Exchange floor. But he was already studying for his broker's license five years later. And then one Sunday, walking with friends in Prospect Park, he met my grandmother, Libby McGrath.

She was from a somewhat genteel family of Dublin teachers and civil servants, and I've often wondered what they ever saw in each other, so different were their politics, their views about raising children, the uses of money. Even their common heritage and religion were expressed in distinct ways. But I've come to think that each relationship is its own unsolved mystery. And it's enough to say that, if there was a common thread binding them, it was America itself.

They married in 1916, and Grandfather was soon put in charge of a special division at his brokerage, where he dealt in speculative bonds and made a small fortune. In 1928, just when it looked like making money would go on forever, he abruptly sold his share of this business back to his bosses who thought he was crazy. But as the markets crashed within the year, he was putting his earnings into Manhattan real estate, and undeveloped land along the Hudson, at bargain prices.

Grandmother Libby had been a schoolteacher when they met, but made her own abrupt change when she decided to become a truancy officer, visiting cold water tenements on the Lower East Side, trying to convince abandoned mothers that school would save their children. She got active in the New York Democratic Party because it supported this kind of social work. And she canvassed the tenement wards for Al Smith's presidential campaign. But when that hope ended bitterly, the best Hank Gannon could say to his heartbroken wife, was: "What did I tell ya'?"

The story goes that she wouldn't speak to him for weeks. And to patch things up, perhaps, he had an agent buy her a large brownstone on Prospect Park West, while he busied himself overseeing construction of this cottage.

Grandmother continued working all through the 'Thirties, helping poor children and teaching her own to see the world with empathy. She started bringing her oldest son, Joe—my father—on her tenement visits. And every summer, she had five or six unfortunate children stay with them here in Garrison. But Hank Gannon was never comfortable with the intrusion of poverty on his own escape from it. He took to staying in Brooklyn during those summers, widening the rift in his marriage and nursing his intolerance, which a talent for making money had somehow fostered.

"Now, *Tom*," my father would say, if he were here. "Try and have a little more sympathy for people." Of course, he'd be right, which only makes it all the more ironic that his life would have inspired anyone's resentment. I could say that good men always have enemies, but that's too simple. What hurt him was an implicit faith in people who didn't always deserve it. And I was one of them it turned out.

So, whenever I'm tempted to divide my relatives or even the world into simple groups of good and bad people, I try to remember my father, and the part of myself that was least like him. He believed, as his mother did, that even a world like ours could be changed, not merely endured. Yet, being here again reminds me of a time when it seemed crazy to think that way. I don't really know if the path I've followed in the years since then would be something he'd understand. I only know that I rejected the path of bright lies far too late.

And on the last Monday in May 1954, I had no idea how late it was, as I awoke from a light sleep thinking of April Stannard, who lived across the river in a red brick, Georgian mansion. We were 17, and I was in love with her in a way that made everything else about my life seem vaguely out of date. Lying in bed, gazing up into the shallow ceiling of my cramped, third-floor bedroom, I could actually feel myself outgrowing my family's home.

Our property on the rustic east bank of the river was big and sprawling, but still only half the size of the Stannards' 40 manicured acres on the west side, where real estate prices had "gone through the roof since the war," according to Grandfather. And the Stannards' mansion—35 rooms and an intricate web of hallways and staircases to connect them—was not merely bigger than our cottage. It seemed to represent a different life lived in a different world.

I rolled out of bed and stood up, hitting my head hard against ceiling plaster. My little brother, David, rustled in his bed across the room, and I held my breath for a moment, before stepping quietly to a small window below the shallow roofline. I bent down and gazed west across the river. There was a thin wash of light turning the ancient brownstone cliffs into gold along the summit a half-mile above the water, and the first rays of sunlight reflected in the windows of buildings on the bluffs. Fog still drifted up from the riverbank on our side, distorting the great valley's width, and obscuring the river's quiet motion.

This was the highland valley of Cole and Church paintings, of Cooper and Irving romances—the American "Garden of Eden." But I fancied myself a student of cool historical fact, and had been struggling to write a term paper about one—Benedict Arnold's plot to betray George Washington and help the British capture West Point, which I could see from my window. And there were a dozen books filled with facts about Arnold scattered beneath my bed. Yet, oddly, he had eluded me.

As my breath clouded the windowpane, I wiped at it, and noticed my father emerging from the mist below. Returning from his morning swim, he seemed calm and even happy, as he walked up the steep hillside toward the house in his long, white robe.

I stepped back and quietly opened a drawer in the large, oak dresser my brother and I shared. Grabbing a pair of navy blue shorts and a red tee shirt—my running uniform from St. Paul's School—I quickly dressed. I tried not to think of the trouble that was coming over my unfinished term paper, but nothing relieved the guilt I felt about my parents' sacrifice to give me such an expensive education. St. Paul's was a prep school for Catholic boys from mostly wealthy families. It had been founded in 1820 by a group of English Jesuits who'd come all the way from Pennsylvania to build it, by hand, on the Hudson's western cliffs near Highland Falls. You had to pass a difficult test to get in. And graduates generally went on to the better universities, and professions that served the circles of influence in America.

I found a gray, West Point sweatshirt at the bottom of the drawer and pulled it on. I put on sweat socks, leaning my head against the ceiling for balance. I grabbed my shoes, glanced once at my brother's quiet bed, and crept from the room. I glided across the polished wood of the top-floor landing and, as silently as the creaky stairs allowed, descended past my sisters' bedrooms and the guestroom, where my grandparents slept.

I paused in the living room and saw my father sitting just outside the windows, calmly, in a whicker chair on the porch. His eyes were closed and his chest subtly rose and fell beneath his robe. In profile, his handsome face seemed young and ruddy from exercise. His graying brown hair was still wet and looked dark; and his powerful arms were comfortably folded in front of him. For a moment, it was easy to think of him as the 15-year-old boy who'd saved his brother and sister, Donald and Grace, from drowning in the river one summer day in 1932.

I tiptoed into the kitchen at the rear of the house and sat down to put on my shoes. The table was littered with weekend papers, my parents' *New York Times* and *New York Post*, and Grandfather's *Journal American* and *Daily Mirror*. Tying my laces, I half-heartedly read Winchell's account of the latest Hollywood figure to testify about his friends at the House Committee on Un-American Activities. There were big headlines about Senator Joseph McCarthy's latest hearings—he was claiming Communist infiltration of the U.S. Army now. And there was a story about a plan that President Eisenhower had to build a massive highway system, linking every one of the 48 states across the continent—one nation, indivisible—with a single, endless road.

The *Post* had just published a story claiming that the New York parks commissioner, Robert Moses, was spending millions refurbishing Riverside Park from West 72nd to 125th Street, stopping abruptly at Harlem's southwest border. And my father and grandfather had argued about this the day before.

"*They* deserve a park, too," Father said about the mostly black people who lived between 125th and 145th near the river, where no park had ever been built.

"It's throwing good money away, spending it up there," Grandfather sniffed, as Father's jaw tightened. "And those Reds at the *Post* publish this tripe just ta' cause trouble an' upset the coloreds."

I stood up, glancing once more at the scattered papers. It was clear something was haywire in America; fear and anger hung over everything like cold rain. Even reasonable people seemed afraid. And there was so much exploitation of fear in the newspapers and radio, and television, and movies—in the government itself—that you could hardly tell any more what was true and what wasn't.

I walked slowly on my rubber heels, keeping the spikes in front from clicking on the floor, heading toward the kitchen door at the rear of the house. I paused near the alcove beside the door, and glanced in at the bottles of beer and soda stacked in wooden cases. Cans of pork and beans, packages of hamburger and hot dog buns, and large tins of potato chips were stacked on shelves. On the floor near the beer and soda cases were the empty burlap bags, which Grandfather had used to haul dozens of Blue Point oysters from Brooklyn on a large block of ice fitted into a metal tub in the trunk of his Ford. All of this, plus the oversized bowls of potato salad and coleslaw, steaks, and lobsters, which Mother had packed away in the spare refrigerator, was for my parents' Memorial Day party.

Our closest neighbors, the Wilsons, and our friend Edith Neumann, who owned a dress shop in Cold Spring, were coming. My mother's parents were expected, as were some of my parents' old friends from Brooklyn, and a few people they'd recently met in Garrison. Donald and Grace Gannon had sent regrets; but most people who knew us understood how important the day was.

My father and his good friend, Arthur Spencer, one of the richest black businessmen in the country, had a new project to develop affordable housing on a rundown section of St. Nicholas Avenue in Harlem. They'd submitted a proposal, received encouraging signals from the City, and planned to discuss financing today with some of Father's richest clients—clients who'd actually left his law practice two years earlier, but seemed ready to return. My father needed this deal, because we were broke. He hadn't worked much in two years, and he'd been forced to liquidate all of his real estate investments to cover our expenses. We'd even had to sell our home in Brooklyn—which is how we'd come to live in Garrison eighteen months earlier.

I left the silent house, leaning hard on my heels down the wooden steps from the kitchen door to the sloping back lawn. Direct sunlight still hadn't reached our side of the river, and I felt the crunch of half-frozen dew on the grass, as the thin leather tops of my shoes grew moist. My breath frosted as I started jogging down into the mist that hid even the tallest pines and oaks, thirty yards above the shoreline. I kept my strides short at first, digging in with my spikes, leaning back to avoid slipping. But the downward slope took over, and I gathered speed as if flying in a cloudbank. And when the tree line suddenly appeared out of the mist, there was no way to stop. My heart raced as I leapt and landed on soft needles and fallen leaves inside the wet shelter of the trees. I smelled pine, and rotting oak and onion grass. And my face and hair dripped.

I started running again, slowly, through the ribbon of damp forest above the river, jumping over rocks and fallen tree trunks. A spooked deer buck snorted, suddenly, and bolted past me out of the mist. His large, brown-yellow eyes glared. His body turned in one direction and his head bent in another as he sprinted by on adrenaline, snapping off branches with his antlers. He charged uphill and then turned quickly, bounding into the fog ahead, hooves popping on half-buried shale until he was gone.

I continued south, and the tree line widened into thicker forest and dense overgrowth. I found a narrow pathway and followed it, picking up speed again, down the final thirty yards of rocky incline to the base of the hills where the New York Central tracks traced the river. My spikes dug into cinders as I moved south along the rails. Waves lapped against a narrow lip of muddy sand and rock, just yards away, beneath the fog. Dead perch and shad, churned up by one of the large tankers that plied the river, rotted in the mud.

When I heard the sound of Manitou Falls ahead, I slowed again, because the tracks went over a slippery wooden trestle there. Soon, the air tingled with spray and my jog became a walk as the falls emerged from the fog. I saw the great stream of water rushing off a ledge on the mountain's face fifty feet above, and dropping into a pocket cove just inside the trestle. And above the ledge, shining faintly through the mist, was the white glow of the sun starting to rise over the eastern hills. Several hundred yards farther up the mountain were the ruins of Beverly House, where Benedict Arnold and his wife stayed in 1780, during his brief summer tenure as commander of West Point. And this was the cove where he kept a small boat that he used to escape down river, when his plot was uncovered.

I walked across the wet trestle past the falls, and resumed running, following a path that climbed the steep hills above the tracks. I pushed myself hard, digging into the rocky footing with my spikes, leaning into the forty-five-degree angle of the hillside. I was drenched beneath my sweatshirt and my lungs ached. My legs throbbed. My throat was dry, and the air grew warmer as I neared the first hill crest a half-mile up. Finally breaking through the mist, I stopped, as rays of sun washed over me. I bent down with my hands on my hips, and sucked oxygen into my burning lungs until the dizziness faded.

When I could stand straight again, I looked upriver at the gleaming ramparts of West Point. A concert and fireworks display were taking place that night on the parade ground, and we'd heard that the Army's old Civil War cannons might be fired off into the valley at the end of the show. The *Highland Times* had run something about the creation of Memorial Day in 1868, to honor the Civil War dead, "though the day now honors fallen Americans from all wars." Nevertheless, the oldest Civil War veteran, a gentleman of 105 who'd served with the Maine Regulars, was to be the concert's guest of honor.

Finally, I looked down river several miles and could see April Stannard's home on the high western cliffs south of the bridge. A bit of its red brick shell was visible through the trees. Eight white portico columns guarded the front door and a shimmering green lawn ran from one side of the house to a line of hedgerows along the bluffs. A brilliant white tent had been raised for a party the Stannards were hosting; and it covered nearly all of the lawn between the house and the hedges.

I'd met her five months earlier, at the annual Christmas dance of the New Amsterdam Club. A schoolmate of mine named Georgie Keller had invited me to go as his guest. So, on a cold Saturday night between Christmas and New Year's, we took the train from Garrison into the city and walked up from Grand Central Station on Park Avenue to the Waldorf Astoria.

On that windless December night, the lights of Manhattan seemed to drift into a tide of winter stars flickering in the endless sky. Our lips and noses, and the tips of our toes and fingers were frozen numb within minutes as we waited near the hotel to catch a taxi. The cab we finally got had a lousy heater, and there was heavy holiday traffic heading uptown. And by the time we reached 70th Street and got out, we were deeply chilled, even beneath our coats.

We paid the driver, ran west on 70th, and entered the club through large oak doors at its main entrance between Park and Madison. A giant fireplace burned brightly in the crowded entranceway, which was carpeted with a faded Oriental rug. After checking our overcoats, we walked across the polished marble floor of the huge lobby, where the walls were ringed by oil portraits of the Dutch and English governors of old New Amsterdam and New York. At the back end of the lobby, we waited on line at the elevator bank with scores of other well-dressed young people.

Georgie and I pushed into a crowded, wood-paneled elevator, and waited, as a few more kids squeezed in after us. I noticed the car had a domed, gilt ceiling and a shiny brass plate near the door, with *The Otis Co.—1885* stamped into it. When the door closed, an elderly man dressed in a maroon uniform with gold chest buttons and epaulettes set the lift in motion.

"Looks like an usher at Radio City," I whispered. Georgie laughed and heads turned in the silent compartment.

We stepped out on the tenth floor, and squeezed forward in a tide of boys and girls toward the massive ballroom. Dance music grew louder as we reached one side of the room and stood for a moment.

Suddenly, Georgie shouted. "Hey, Tom…you want a drink?"

"Sure. A Coke?"

"They usually have punch at this thing…an' somebody usually spikes it."

"You go ahead, Georgie. I'm in training…you know?"

He smirked. "You're such a friggin' teetotaler, Gannon." Then, he disappeared into the crowd.

I waited at the edge of the dance floor, listening to the orchestra, watching couples dance in a swirl of black, white, red and blue. All around the room, young men and women talked and laughed in interlocking groups of established familiarity. And hanging on the walls above them was another set of portraits—men in modern business dress—bankers, industrialists, recent senators, and even presidents.

On the opposite side of the ballroom there was a bracket of French doors, through which I could see a rooftop terrace and, beyond it, the city lights. A string of tiny electric holiday bulbs, glowing like silver and gold stars, traced the doorframe, and the motion of dancers on the floor, and the glow of the chandeliers above, reflected in the glittering panels.

I first saw her standing near the doors with three other girls. She was beautiful, standing in profile, speaking quietly to her friends. Suddenly, as if distracted by a thought, she turned and looked at me. She was even more beautiful straight on. I was embarrassed at being caught staring, and I wanted to turn away, but her expression held me. Her blond hair fell in long, thick waves to her shoulders, which were bare above her muted, red-satin gown. A single string of pearls wound around her neck in a perfect circle. Her earrings were pearls as well.

One of her friends said something to her, and she turned briefly to smile and reply, before turning back toward me again. For a moment longer, we stared at each other. Then, subtly, so imperceptibly that I might have imagined it, she nodded and half-closed her eyes.

"Here's your Coke," said Georgie, handing me a bottle, and taking a satisfied slug from a large Dixie cup in his other hand. "I think there's rum in this."

I nodded. "Do you know that girl?"

"Who?"

"Over by the doors…in the red dress."

He took another slug and peered across the floor. Suddenly, he came to attention. "You don't mean April Stannard?"

"Who *is* she?"

"*That girl*…in the red dress…the blond."

"You know her?"

"Her father's one of the wealthiest men in America…*that's* who she is. Guys kill themselves to date her, but she rarely goes out…except with her friends."

"She doesn't have a boyfriend, a girl like her?"

"She went to school in Paris last year…I heard she was dating some older guy in his twenties…some artist…but her father put the kibosh on it and brought her back."

"So…she's not seeing anyone…now…"

"What do I know, Gannon? Go ask her yourself." He took another gulp. "Get in line."

"I *am* going over. You coming?"

"Naw." He smiled, sipping his drink. "I'll watch from here. This should be good."

I squeezed across the dance floor and reached the group of girls and intro-duced myself politely to each one. As I met Martha Bradley, and Claudia Radc-liffe and Penelope Potts, I could see in the corner of my eye that the girl in red was smiling at me. When I finally turned toward her, the smile had faded and she was staring at me with brilliant green eyes. Suddenly, a bit of her smile returned, as she said her name. "April…Stannard."

"Would you care to dance, Miss Stannard?" I cringed at how I sounded. She smiled at her friends and they smiled back. Then, she stepped away from them and reached for my hand.

As we walked out to the dance floor, she glanced at me. "You're so *polite*," she said, with a casual laugh.

"I'm sorry."

"No…it's nice."

We stepped toward each other. I put my arm behind her back and felt her hand on my shoulder. And we began dancing as the music stopped.

"Oh," I said, stepping back awkwardly.

Couples came and went on the crowded dance floor, and she frowned at me. "What's wrong?"

"I wasn't paying attention…the music…I'm sorry…"

"They'll play another," she said, brightly. Suddenly, the orchestra began a foxtrot. "See?"

And then, I laughed out loud at myself. She laughed, too, as we grabbed each other again and followed the music. As we danced, she asked me questions about school, and my family and where I lived. At one point, she smiled wearily. "I saw you standing with Georgie Keller."

"We're schoolmates," I said. "He's a member...I mean...he asked to me come. He says he knows you."

She scrunched her nose and frowned, and then nodded. "I know Georgie. I bet you aren't very *close* friends..."

"He's all right," I said. She smiled again.

We made our way back, and April introduced a young man who'd joined her friends. "Tom...this is Rowe Bradley...Martha's brother."

"Hello," I said, shaking his hand. "Tom Gannon."

"Hi there," he replied. Then, as the girls began talking with each other, he spoke to me in a studied tone of voice. "Where do you prep, Tom?"

"I go to St. Paul's..."

"Oh! I'm Choate. What year?"

"Third."

"Right! Then, you must know Dickie Thorndike and Beaver Simms...they're great friends of mine."

"No...I..."

"Mmmm," he muttered, with a searching expression. "Who's in *your* crowd, then?"

"You know what. I think we're talking about a different school. I go to St. Paul's in Highland Falls...near where I live..."

"Really," he said, nonchalantly. "Huh."

I heard Penelope whisper to Claudia, "where's Highland Falls?"

April scolded Penelope. "You've *been* there."

"I have?"

"Our *summer* place...up in the valley..."

"Oh. *That's* Highland Falls?"

"We have a summer place there," April said, turning to me. "I know where your school is...it's pretty close to us actually."

Martha focused her eyes on me. "So, where are you travelling this summer, Tom?"

"Travelling?"

The group was silent then.

"Listen," said Claudia, finally. "What's the deal with this *Catcher in the Rye*? I'm still trying to finish my term thesis on it…I just don't get the point of it."

"That's a funny book," said Penelope.

"I thought it was a bore," said Rowe. "I mean, that kid who tells the story…what a pain in the ass…he's supposed to be nuts, isn't he?"

"Depends on your perspective," I said. Now, everyone turned and stared at me.

Rowe frowned. "Yeah? What do you mean?"

"He *could* be crazy, and that's why he can't fit in, or…it's what he sees that's crazy…the hypocrisy I mean, all around him…it's too much for him…too much to bear or ignore…and *that* makes him sick…crazy if you like…"

Martha interjected. "So, what's the difference? He ends up in some mental hospital…doesn't he?" I smiled and nodded a little, but didn't answer. So then, Martha turned to April. "What do *you* think?"

"I think…I agree with Tom," said April, smiling at me.

The group was quiet again.

"Nice to meet you, Gannon," said Rowe, suddenly grabbing Claudia's hand and starting toward the dance floor. As they walked away, I heard them whispering, and then Claudia laughed.

"Hi," said a new voice.

I turned and saw Georgie standing next to me. "*There* you are," I said.

He reached out his hand to Martha. "George Keller. I don't believe we've met."

"Martha Bradley," she said in a businesslike tone, allowing him to shake her hand.

Then, he looked at Penelope.

"Penelope Potts," she said, forcing a smile.

"Hello, Georgie," April suddenly said. "How've you been?"

"Oh, fine," he answered nervously. "You were in Paris, I heard."

She smiled and nodded and then turned to me. "Another dance, Tom?"

"Sure." I grabbed her hand.

Georgie looked at Martha again. "Would *you* like to dance?" When she shook her head, he turned quickly to Penelope, who shrugged and glanced at Martha for help. But Martha turned away and gazed out through the glass doors.

"All right," Penelope said, walking past Georgie toward the dance floor.

At nearly midnight, we all went down to the lobby together and April gave me the check stub to retrieve her coat, while she said goodnight to her friends.

I brought back her coat, and after helping her on with it, we walked out through the big oak doors. A fleet of yellow and red taxicabs waited in line at the curb, pumping white exhaust into the frigid night. I walked down the steps with her to a cab and opened its door.

She leaned toward me and kissed me quickly on the lips. "Where's your *coat*?" she said. Then she grabbed my hand and pressed a small bit of paper into my palm, before jumping in and giving the driver a Park Avenue address. I closed her door, and as the cab pulled away, I stood shivering on the sidewalk for a moment longer.

Back inside the club, waiting on line to retrieve my overcoat, I remembered to look at the paper clutched in my fist.

Georgie and I barely made the last train out of Manhattan. And as our half-empty car began rolling down the cavernous tunnels beneath Park Avenue, he asked me for details. I showed him the notepaper April had given me.

"You got her *phone number*? Lemme see that. That's a *Manhattan* exchange."

"She told the cabbie to drive somewhere on Park."

"Wow. You know...they have a summer place up near school, on the cliffs...just south of the campus. There's a big stone wall on three sides, and lots of trees around it. You've probably passed it a hundred times and didn't know it."

"I guess so."

"My parents went to a cocktail party there, last year" Georgie paused and shook his head. "April Stannard...the *golden* girl."

Our train sprinted out of the long underground and then northwest, into the dark outskirts of the city. From the window, I could see the dark river and the running lights of a steamer carrying coal. House lights on the distant shore flickered faintly through the trees, and grew less frequent from minute to minute.

When we reached Garrison, it was one-thirty in the morning and there were no cabs waiting for us, so we called the number for Highland Taxi printed above the public telephone inside the station. As we waited, keeping warm next to the old steam boiler, I asked Georgie to tell me everything he knew about her.

"First of all," he said, "her mother's family came over on the friggin' *May-flower*. And her father's family...the Stannards...weren't far behind. I mean, these are the people who *founded* the New Amsterdam Club."

As Georgie displayed his formidable knowledge of this family, I began to understand his amazement. Charles Lyman Stannard was the descendant of bankers who'd moved through American history—in and out of presidential cabinets and ambassadorships—with the same fluidity as their investments in the great industries. There was a U.S. Senator or two in their lineage, but Stannards preferred personal appointments to elective office, Georgie said. And as we rode home in the taxi, I remembered reading something in the *New York Times* about Charles Stannard being named to a board of financial advisors to the President.

I called April a few days later, and she invited me to a New Year's Eve party one of her friends was giving in a large apartment on Fifth Avenue above 60th Street.

And throughout the evening, she held onto my hand as she introduced me to more of her friends. Once or twice, I sensed sarcasm in a glance not meant for me to see, and in a silence held too long. But I reserved judgment, perhaps afraid that sensitivity to unkindness confirmed its accuracy. Then, as midnight approached, we stood near the living room windows, watching ice skaters on Wollman Rink and the flickering traffic on Fifth Avenue far below. Suddenly, people started counting down to 1954. The Guy Lombardo Orchestra struck up *Auld Lang Syne* on a television somewhere in the crowded apartment, and we kissed again and again.

CHAPTER 2

❀

My older sister Liz sat in the living room with Grandfather, watching a midday news report. Her morose expression lightened, only briefly, when she saw me come down the stairs. I sat with them, and listened, as a reporter described the interrogations of witnesses that were now a daily television event.

"Wisconsin Senator Joseph McCarthy makes his case…alleging Communist influence in the Army. A controversial figure since Nineteen-fifty, when he told a group of West Virginia Republican women that hundreds of Communists worked in the State Department, McCarthy achieved national prominence at the Republican convention two years later."

Footage appeared on the screen, showing McCarthy at the podium, speaking in his odd monotone.

> '*One* Communist in a defense plant is *one* Communist too many. *One* Communist on the faculty of one university is *one* Communist too many. *One* Communist in the State Department…would *still* be one Communist too many.'

"But last autumn, McCarthy claimed US Army Intelligence officers had covered up 'a Rosenberg-type spy ring' in the Signal Corps Unit, at Fort Monmouth, New Jersey." The reporter was talking into the studio camera now. "Secretary of the Army Robert Stevens has challenged these claims…many say with President Eisenhower's backing. And so, the Senator commenced public hearings to prove his charges. The hearings continue tomorrow in Washington, and will be broadcast live over this television station beginning at ten AM.

We now return to our Holiday Movie Matinee, *Yankee Doodle Dandy*, starring James Cagney."

Grandfather looked away from the television screen and muttered, "give 'em hell, Joe." Behind the lenses of his wire-rimmed glasses, his eyes seemed wet and angry. "God damn Communists…"

"In the Army?" I said, incredulously.

"Not *just* the Army," Liz said. "In the State Department, colleges, defense plants…and Hollywood, of course. Should we check under the beds, too?"

"You kids can fool with this all you want, now…but ya' don't know what yer' talkin' about…just like yer' father…and yer' none of ya' smart as ya' think…with *all* your fancy schoolin'. Now keep quiet. I'm watchin' Jimmie Cagney. *That's* a man for ya'."

Liz rolled her eyes and frowned at me. "When are we leaving?"

"About two o'clock?" I said.

"Okay…but you better make it back in time to help out."

"I know…I know. I'll be back…"

"April too?"

"I don't know…maybe."

"Is that the Stannard girl yer' goin' ta' see?" Grandfather blurted, keeping his eyes on the screen

"Yes," I said.

"You know she's not a Catholic, don't ya'?" He laughed wickedly.

"Could be worse," I whispered.

Liz smiled with dramatic sarcasm. "Something's worse than being a *Protestant?*"

"She may be a *Communist!*" I said. Liz laughed.

But Grandfather wasn't amused. "Aghhh…it just said on the TV…there's a Rosenberg-type spy ring in Monmouth."

I suddenly thought of that hot day last summer, when Liz and I heard the news that the Rosenbergs had been executed at Sing Sing, for passing atomic secrets to Russia.

Liz sighed. "Grandpa…that was a miscarriage of justice…at least it was for *Ethel* Rosenberg."

He scoffed. "Ah fer' chrissake…those Jews had more sympathy for Russia than their own country. They were *Communists*…just like a *lot* a' Jews."

"You mean like Roy Cohn?" Liz said, angrily.

"Wait here."

He quickly got up from his seat and went outside to his car, which was parked in the gravel just below the front porch. We heard him open the trunk. Moments later, he returned with a dog-eared magazine, which he held up so we could read the cover—it was a 1939 copy of *Social Justice*, a magazine once published by the disgraced radio priest, Father Charles Coughlin. There were head notes for articles that claimed "Wall Street Jews" had caused the 1929 stock market crash, and that warned America to stay out of a war with Germany. One headline flatly stated that "Nazi persecution of Jews is excusable" since it "opposes Communism."

As Grandfather slumped back in his chair and tossed the magazine onto the nearby coffee table, Liz and I glanced at each other, shocked—having heard about such hateful ideas, we'd never imagined a member of our family would take them seriously.

We got up then, and headed down the hall toward the kitchen. I leaned close to Liz and whispered. "He's been drinking already."

She nodded and whispered back. "Grandma had a big fight with him...didn't you hear it?"

"I was out running."

"Well, they were at it...slamming doors...yelling...crying. She's still in the guestroom...reading."

We stopped just inside the kitchen and glanced back through the hallway at our grandfather, who watched the flickering screen, mesmerized by simplistic Hollywood patriotism. Then, Father came in through the back door wearing smartly pressed tan slacks and his favorite blue golf shirt, the one I'd given him this past Christmas. He smiled when he saw us. "Seen your grandfather?"

"In the living room, Dad," said Liz, pointing down the hall.

"Okay, thanks," he said, walking past us. A moment later, we heard him speaking to his father in a low voice. "Say, Pop...this St. Nicholas Avenue deal..."

"What about it?"

"I was thinking...it's odd there haven't been any *other* bids for that property...it's three months since *ours* was announced."

"Well...I don't know, son. Real estate's an unpredictable business..."

"So...you're saying you haven't heard of any other parties being interested in that site...none of your friends in real estate have mentioned anything?"

"Nope."

There was a brief silence then, until we heard Father again. His voice sounded angry. "What is this?"

"What?"

"*This*! This magazine; haven't I told you about this before? Get rid of it. I won't *have* it in my house!"

After another brief pause, we heard Grandfather's sarcastic reply. "So it's *your* house, now, is it?"

At one o'clock, the Spencers' sleek blue 1954 Oldsmobile crunched up the driveway and their fifteen-year-old daughter, Laureen, waved from a back window.

Arthur Spencer was a transplanted Midwesterner. The son of a railroad porter and a domestic servant, he learned business in night school while washing dishes at a diner near the Chicago Board of Trade five days a week. After returning from The Great War, he sang in the black vaudeville circuits, and made his first real estate investments—two south-side nightclubs. But once Repeal took effect, he sold the clubs to some mobsters, tried his hand at bank-rolling movies with all-black casts, and finally moved east with his wife, Hazel. By 1933, he'd acquired some choice Harlem properties at deflated prices, and, over time, became well known across the social, political, and business boundaries that separated Harlem from "downtown." Lately, he'd been renewing his interest in show business, buying several Harlem nightclubs, plus a theater on 125th Street, which Father had helped him acquire.

The Olds came to a quiet stop below the porch, and Laureen jumped out. Her yellow sundress swirled like a soufflé around her long brown legs, as she slammed the door with a twist of her body. She smiled and hugged Liz as her parents emerged, slowly, from the car.

Hazel was a short, heavy woman, whose weak heart had kept the Spencers from having more children. She was well-educated, the daughter of a minister who'd run a mission for alcoholics in Kansas City, where Arthur's vaudeville company had frequently played. They were married in her father's church, in 1927. And today, she looked as if she'd just come from church, in a blue dress and wide-brimmed blue hat with a white band. She held a dozen white roses wrapped in pink paper across one arm and two green bakery boxes in the other.

Arthur wore his customary dark, pinstriped suit, white shirt with a high collar, and a dark blue tie. He preferred Homburgs, but today, he held a brown straw fedora in his big hands.

Liz and Laureen ran inside the house giggling at some private joke, and Arthur shook Father's hand as he gazed down the valley. "I love this spot, Joe."

Mother kissed Hazel and told her the roses were beautiful. Then, she took the flowers and the bakery packages inside, while Father and I started slowly toward the rear of the house with our guests. From a window in Liz's bedroom, I heard the HiFi playing a new Chet Baker record.

> They're writing songs of love, but not for me.
> A lucky star's above, but not for me...

Father put his arm through Hazel's, and she leaned against him, as they walked down the grassy hillside toward the picnic table near Mother's twin magnolia trees. Arthur walked with me and told some vaudeville jokes. He seemed extremely happy. When we reached our picnic spot beneath the trees, Arthur and Hazel sat in wooden, folding chairs as Father glanced at me. "You handle the drinks, Tom." Then, he hurried back to the house.

Bright sunlight filtered through the white and purple magnolia blossoms. The branches swayed in a warm breeze rising from the river, carrying voices. David and our little sister, Mary, were playing hide-and-seek in the woods above the riverbank. I opened a large ice chest and Arthur peered in. He chose a beer. Hazel saw the pitcher of Mother's lemonade and asked for some. And as I served the drinks, perspiration formed on my forehead and rolled in beads down my back beneath my starched white shirt.

Mother's parents—Phillip and Alice Brent—soon arrived, and Arthur hauled his large body up from his chair. I glanced at my watch, and Hazel noticed, and smiled. I waved, and the Brents came down the hill with the comfortable strides of country club golfers.

Grandfather Phil was shorter than Arthur, but made an equally imposing figure. His silver-gray hair was thick and he wore gray slacks, a blue blazer and a pink, Oxford shirt. His blue and red college tie was done in a perfect Windsor knot. Grandmother Alice's light gray skirt and jacket flattered her lean figure. She wore gold seashell earrings, a pearl white silk blouse, and brown Papagallos raised slightly at the heels. A bit of natural gray mixed with her lightened brown hair. Her face was tanned, and remarkably soft.

I shook Grandfather Phil's hand and kissed Grandmother Alice on the cheek, while offering them something to drink. They asked for Cokes. Pushing my sleeve up and reaching deeply into the ice chest almost to my elbow, I paused, feeling a pleasant numbing chill in my right arm. Finally, when my head began to ache, I yanked my arm out, gripping the necks of two wet Coke bottles.

"Where are your mother and dad?" said Grandfather Phil.

"Up at the house," I said, feeling dizzy as the chill in my arm melted off. "They'll be down soon…"

"Oh, Tom," he said, "we brought a case of wine…I wonder if you'd help carry it out of the car later?"

"Of course."

"Good lad." He smiled. "Will your dad's parents be joining us?"

"Oh, yes. They came yesterday…stayed overnight."

The Brents glanced at each other.

"How is Hank feeling, these days?" said Grandmother Alice.

"Fine, I guess."

"And your grandmother?"

"Fine, too." I popped the tops off two sodas and they thanked me with their gracious, Southern smiles.

Phillip Brent was from Annapolis, descended from an English Catholic family that had come to Maryland in 1650 under the Calvert Proprietorship. Alice Hastings, whom he'd met while at college in Philadelphia, was the daughter of a circuit judge from Chadds Ford. Phillip Brent was now a partner in the engineering firm that built and maintained the New York State reservoir system, and the Brents lived in a granite townhouse on East 65th Street. They also owned a Stanford White-designed summer home in Southampton.

As they sipped their Cokes, I thought about the long-standing animosity between my grandfathers, which had started with the construction of Rockefeller Center of all things.

The project had begun on the eve of the Depression and though the Rockefeller family self-financed, they did issue minority shares to lay off risk in the first few buildings. Grandfather Phil's engineering firm oversaw site excavation, and he and his partners were invited to invest. Grandfather Hank, flush with cash to spend on real estate then, also tried to invest, but was rebuffed. He never got over it.

"I'm a shanty Irishman ta' them Rockefellers," he once said to Father. "Money's not good enough to sit with theirs at Chase National Bank or the Radio City. And they with their grandfather, a ruthless article…which is fine with me…but they *forget*. And the *old man's* father…nuthin' but a quack elixir salesman and bigamist, from the Ohio backwoods."

"Calm down, Pop," my father said, reminding him that two members of Grandfather's old brokerage firm, both Irish Catholics, managed the lease on one of the buildings. But Grandfather only seemed angrier then.

I pulled another Coke from the ice chest and gulped half of it.

Grandmother Alice smiled as she looked up into the white-purple branches. "Your mother's magnolias are blooming late."

I nodded. "It's been a late spring."

There was polite talk about the suddenly warm weather, Frank Sinatra's comeback, and the odds of another Yankees-Dodgers World Series. Finally, in the inevitable custom, the women and men paired off. Hazel and Grandmother Alice arranged chairs together under the trees, facing the river. Grandfather Phil suddenly turned and stared at Arthur.

"How are things on St. Nicholas Avenue?" he said, his voice having lost its casual tone. "I understand you're acquiring the old arena, now, too."

"Well, yes." Arthur had a curious smile on his lips. "But...*that's* not public."

"The City asked our firm to look over the water and sewage plans you filed."

"I see. Well...what do you think?"

"The engineering makes sense. Joe's involved, too, I guess?"

"You bet...done all the legal work."

Grandfather Phil looked tense and uncomfortable. "You know, of course...the arena site used to be a stable...carriage horses...that sort of thing."

"Fifty, sixty years ago," Arthur nodded.

"Won't have to dig deep to reach the manure under the foundation."

Arthur's laughter boomed. "Never thought of that!"

"But...you may find the shit goes deeper than you expect..."

Instantly, Arthur's smile disappeared. He glanced at me standing a few feet away, and could tell I was listening as I sipped my soda and pretended to stare out at the river. Suddenly, Grandfather Phil turned and waved. "Come here, Tom." I walked three strides and reached them. They looked around to make sure that their wives were pretending not to listen, and then Grandfather looked directly at me and raised one finger to his lips. "This is *real business*...understand?"

I nodded.

"What are you getting at, Phil?" said Arthur, urgently.

"You're going to have problems with that project," he said. "I just hope you and Joe will *think*...before getting involved again, in something that's more trouble than it's worth. Joe, especially...now that he's getting back on his feet."

"It's a simple, affordable housing scheme, Phil...in *Harlem* for goodness sake."

"I'm not talking about construction problems, Arthur..."

"Then *what?*"

"*Your site*…it's the southern end of the avenue, above 125th Street…a few blocks from where you had the trouble two years ago." Arthur nodded in grim silence as Grandfather Phil continued. "Well…you're going to have trouble again. People are saying the City Planning Commission 'green-lighted' your proposal too quickly. I've heard Bob Moses is pulling support for your bid…"

"Why would he do that?"

"Who knows? He's *always* wanted to run an elevated highway along 125th Street. Maybe he's decided your project won't help him…or maybe, he's just decided he prefers the *other* project…"

"*What* project?"

Grandfather Phil frowned. "You hadn't heard?" He seemed annoyed at Arthur. "A group of investment bankers has teamed up with some Texas oil types. The bankers were targeting the arena site for over a year…on the QT. But they needed more money."

"For what?"

"Television studios and offices. Apparently the networks are willing to pay top dollar for space *anywhere* in the city, now…they've run out of downtown space. Anyway, I hear they're going to make a big announcement…soon."

Arthur muttered sourly. "So, they'll announce a TV network is paying big money for the site, but the fact that they'll get ten years worth of tax deferrals…that'll be in the *small* print."

"And that's *business*, Arthur…you know it."

"All right…what if we don't bid on the arena, if that's where these folks want to put up studios? We'll just tell the City they can have it…we'll be content to build our housing up the block as planned."

Grandfather Phil shook his head and frowned. "If one of the networks goes in there…you don't really think they'll let you have low-income housing a few doors away, do you…with their advertising agencies and sponsors coming and going?"

"But…the Mayor…he *likes* our project."

"Sure. It's the kind of urban renewal he campaigned on. He might even take your side, but *this* is Bob Moses' game. Come on…he's the City's Construction Coordinator…runs the Mayor's Slum Clearance Committee…*and* the Housing Authority…*and* controls the Planning Commission. There's too much money involved in this other project…these people supported the Mayor's campaign…now they expect something for it. You know what it costs to run for Mayor these days? I heard he spent three million dollars just on advertising. He doesn't have that kind of money." Grandfather Phil sighed and drank from his Coke, as Arthur looked out over the river. "I'm surprised you haven't been contacted."

Arthur glowered and shook his head. "First I've heard any of it…"

"Well, you'll *be* contacted…probably some aide to the Mayor, or someone attached to the Planning Commission. He'll be very polite…apologetic. He'll say 'something's come up' with the site or the paper work. There'll be a hold on federal housing funds, and you'll be faced with finding that money else-where…even if you *can*, you'll be seriously delayed…"

"But I *have investors*, Phil." Arthur's voice sounded angry. "They've put up good faith money; Joe has other people coming here today…we have signa-tures on preliminary approvals from the City. We're supposed to close with the arena owners next week."

"*Technicalities*…the City wants you out. They'll negotiate a kill-fee. If you don't fight them…they might even offer another site…"

"Where…on a barge up the river?"

"I know how you must feel, Arthur…"

"We're talking about human beings, Phil, families…low-income sure, but they work, pay taxes, vote. That's who's gonna live in our apartments…use the community center we wanted to put where the arena sits. There's a *housing shortage* in the city…"

"I know, Arthur."

Arthur sighed and shook his head wearily. He looked into Phillip Brent's steely eyes. "How do you *know* all this, Phil?"

"There have been conversations between our senior partner and the City. I wasn't invited to the meetings, but I have friends at the Planning Commis-sion…so I know what went on. They're going to build a television studio. That's that. If they can't pay you to go away, I'm afraid they'll find some other way to do it. It won't matter whether you get the Mayor on your side or not…"

"What if we refuse? Fight for our legal rights…go to the newspapers?"

Grandfather frowned and shook his head. "You're not dealing with crackpot community groups like two years ago. Have you forgotten what happened with that theater project…those filthy accusations against you…and my son-in-law? Well, *these* people would do the same thing…and more. Once that started again…the Mayor wouldn't even return your calls."

As Grandfather Phil finished his Coke, Arthur stared out over the river. Finally, he turned back and said, "does anyone know you're giving us this advice?"

"No one sent me, if *that's* what you mean." Arthur frowned and nodded helplessly, as Grandfather continued. "I'd rather not be having this conversation, Arthur, but I'd be wrong to keep silent. I'm concerned for Joe and his family...yours too. You've been a friend to my son-in-law...I admire that, but let's face it; he's a little headstrong. We know how things work...you and me. There's always another project..."

Arthur suddenly raised his hand to make Grandfather stop talking. "Phil...I understand."

Just then, a cannon shot boomed out from West Point, startling us.

Grandfather Phil spun around and looked across the river. "What the..."

"It's the old Army cannons," I said, pointing to the gray smoke floating off the top of the cliffs. The sound rumbled down the valley and faded like a fast-moving thunderstorm. Faint cheers rose up miles away. "They're practicing for the concert," I said.

CHAPTER 3

"How are you, Joe?" said Grandfather Phil, forcing a smile.

Father shook his hand and glanced at Arthur. "You tell him about the arena?"

Grandfather's smile dropped and Arthur nodded gravely. My father turned to me, then, with a confused look. I had to turn away.

"Joe, we have to talk," said Arthur, suddenly.

But Father ignored him and stepped closer to me. His after-shave lotion mixed with his body smell in the growing heat, and his slacks were softening at their creases. "Tom?" His voice was inquisitive; he put his arm over my shoulders. "Aren't you heading to the Stannards'?"

Grandfather Phil nodded approvingly. "Still seeing that girl, then, eh?"

I replied to both questions with a weak smile and looked at my watch. It was nearly one-thirty.

"We have another guest, Tom!" It was Mother, smiling in the dappled shade in her flowing, white sundress. She held one hand above her eyes and pointed toward the house. When I looked, I was surprised to see the headmaster of St. Paul's coming down from the crest of the hill where he'd parked his MG convertible. "Go up and *greet* him!" she said.

Father Jonathan Stevens was a Jesuit priest, who'd come to St. Paul's in 1949, after publishing a book called *Liberal Education and Modern Society*. We were given copies to read during my freshman year, when the book was already in a second printing. His updated preface described an "atmosphere of uncertainty," which he'd found upon arriving at the school, and this, he wrote, reflected the "general lack of certitude plaguing America today." He had big plans for "a new" St. Paul's, and often spoke of them as he walked the campus with a confident demeanor that comforted students and parents alike, and probably explained his skill in raising funds among the wealthier alumni.

He'd never come to our home before, but his easy stride and broad smile suggested otherwise. He wore a tan suit, a blue Oxford shirt, and a St. Paul's School tie. His thick black hair, dark eyes and olive complexion resembled the looks of Tyrone Power.

We met and shook hands halfway up the hill. "Glad you could come, Father."

"It was nice of Mom and Dad to invite me, Thomas." As we started back down together, at a slow walk, he looked out over the valley. "This is lovely…"

"It is…isn't it?"

He smiled and nodded. "So. Ready for next week?"

"You mean the exhibition meet…at West Point." He nodded again. "Yes," I said. "We're ready."

"Excellent! A good showing *there* will be noticed…and our cross country team should compete seriously for the eastern prep title next *fall*…"

"I think so, Father, yes."

"Coach Bunning tells me he's recruiting some excellent freshmen. You and the other experienced boys will help him…won't you?"

"Of course, Father."

"Good. That's good." Suddenly, he stopped walking and leaned toward me in a confidential way. "I'll let you in on a little secret I've been discussing with the Parents-Alumni Association. I'm going to mention it to your mom and dad…I hope they'll get involved." He paused, and I waited. "I've asked Father McHenry, as history chairman, to help me choose a student who'll represent St. Paul's in a national honors seminar…at Yale University next spring."

"Really."

He smiled and nodded. "This program attracts the brightest students from the best prep schools in the country…they study American history, literature and philosophy for a month. Now…we're establishing a prize, the St. Paul's Award, which we'll give to the winner of an essay contest…that's how we'll choose the student who represents us each year. But only students with a certain grade average are allowed to compete, so…this will be quite an honor."

"Yes, Father."

"You're one of our best students, Thomas…and *history* is your best subject. I'm sure you'll qualify. You might start thinking about an essay topic…but…keep this under your hat for now…will you?"

"Of course." We started walking again.

"We'll talk some more about it…but…I should say hello to Mom and Dad and the other guests." As we neared the magnolias, he surveyed our small group and noticed the many, empty folding chairs. "I hope I'm not too early."

"Oh, no. People will come and go all afternoon."

"I see."

He stepped away from me and said hello to my parents. They introduced him to the Brents and Spencers and soon he was chatting with them all in his confident manner. I checked my watch again.

Suddenly, Father slipped away from the group and came straight for me. "What's wrong, Tom?"

I stared at the river. "Nothing…everything's just great…"

"You see…*that's* what I mean."

Turning my back to the guests, I whispered. "Didn't Grandpa Phil tell you yet…what he told Arthur?"

"Oh, sure. Is *that* what's bothering you?" He sighed in confident relief. "Tom, listen…your grandfather may have heard some things…but these big projects *always* have complications. If you were more familiar with business, you'd understand. And, I think it's probably time we talked *more* about business…and the world…the way we *used* to talk about history and literature…"

"We don't need a book chat." He looked at me, straining to comprehend my sarcasm. "Dad…he told Arthur there was *no way* you were going to win the bid on St. Nicholas Avenue…and that fighting things would only bring up those…*accusations* against you, all over again. Doesn't that *concern* you?"

Now, he frowned and nodded. For a moment, he seemed to understand. Then, he sighed and looked fiercely into my eyes. "Tom…I haven't spent enough time…with you *or* Liz…or any of you kids…lately…"

I shook my head angrily. "That's not it, Dad."

"And I'm sorry about it…"

"Don't apologize…"

"I understand you and Liz have your own friends…your own lives…I've been busy…your mother and I have had to make so many changes…moving here and all. It's disrupted us…been very hard. But we're seeing the light of day, now, and I promise…we'll spend more time together as a family."

"Dad…"

"I promise," he said again. I sighed, and silently nodded. "By the way," he said, oddly changing the subject. "Is everything going all right at school?"

"*What?*"

"School…how's it going?"

"Oh...*yeah*...great," I said. "Everything's...no problem. Just like you."

"All right, Tom," he said, with an exasperated smile.

Now, I felt like a heel. "Dad? Is there some way I can help you?"

"Well," he said with a hopeful sigh. "I wish you *could* be here today...help out with some of the investors...my clients...when they come."

I shook my head. "So...you're going forward with this, anyway?"

"You could entertain them with some of your little known facts of American history. People love those little items, especially the Hudson River stuff...and...*these* people would be good for you to meet...see how men do business."

I sighed in frustration. "*Jesus...*Dad..."

"I know, I know, you're going to see April."

"That's *not it*," I said angrily, as he stared at me. "Listen, Dad. I'll be back early...all right? Maybe I can help...then."

"Sure! Say 'hello' to the Stannards for us. We should have them over to dinner soon...I guess..."

"That would be nice."

"How're you getting there?"

"I asked Liz to drop me..."

"Oh." He sounded vaguely disappointed. Then, he turned to Mother, who stood a few feet away listening to the headmaster tell a story. "Mary...Liz is taking Tom to the Stannards'..."

Father Stevens turned smoothly from his conversation. "I'll be glad to drop you, Thomas. I'm heading back to campus soon..."

Mother frowned. "But you've just arrived, Father. Don't rush off."

"I'm on a tight schedule, Mary...though, I did want to discuss something with you and Joe...a new program at school..."

"That's fine. We'll discuss it...my daughter will get Tom to his date."

I waved to the headmaster. "Thanks anyway, Father." He smiled and resumed his story.

I glanced at my watch again, and heard Liz calling out to me. I looked up the hill and saw her standing with Laureen near the house.

"Say hello to April...Dear," said Mother.

"See you later," said Father, turning and walking back to his guests.

I started up the hill and noticed Grandfather Hank and Grandmother Libby leaving the house from the kitchen door. He'd changed into a clean white shirt and nondescript blue trousers. She wore a long, green print dress over her hefty body, and her white hair was pinned in a bun.

As we passed each other, Grandmother smiled weakly but Grandfather seemed preoccupied by his unsteady stride. He tried leaning against Grandmother, but she quickened her pace and pulled away, leaving him to skip unsteadily down the slope.

I turned and watched them head toward the others. I could see my parents talking and laughing with their guests beneath the magnolias, and David and Mary returning from the lower tree line. And I felt a dizzying, confusing anger, and sadness, like the burden of gathering heat.

"Are you ready?" Liz was waiting impatiently near the Buick with Laureen. I hurried toward them, swallowing emotion with a gulp of warm air. "Tom?"

"Yeah…"

She and Laureen exchanged glances and shrugged. We all jumped into the front seat together, with Laureen in the middle. Liz and I quickly rolled the windows down, and she turned on the engine, and then the radio. Laureen reached forward and twisted the knob rapidly through a distorted stream of voices and music, until hitting a particular station.

She leaned back as a deep-throated announcer spoke from the dashboard. "Now two members of the group are leavin'…to join the Ink Spots. Sonny plans to replace 'em and go back in the studio…but nothin's clicked since they had the hit on *Crying In The Chapel* last year. So…say a prayer and keep 'em in your thoughts. Sonny asked me to tell you that…specially you gals out there. Meanwhile, here's the one that started it all for 'em…in 'Forty-eight, before the car accident…and all the bad luck. It's still *my* favorite…with Sonny Til on lead vocal. The Oh…re…oles…"

> *Does she love me? It's too soon to know…*
> *Can I believe her when she tells me so?*

Liz and Laureen laughed as the car moved slowly down the driveway. I tried to ignore them as warm air from my open window hit me in the face.

> *Is she foolin'? Is it all a game?*
> *Am I the fire or just another flame?*

And as my family's house shrank away in the little side-mirror, I closed my eyes and leaned back in my seat.

Laureen poked me in the ribs. "Cheer up."

Liz smirked. "He's *loooove* sick."

"Be quiet," I muttered. They laughed again.

Liz reached the end of the driveway and paused to look both ways, and then she turned right, heading south toward the bridge. The car's suspension felt soft from the heat, and we seemed to glide over the pavement's imperfections like a boat on calm water.

In minutes we were at the blinker and turning onto the bridge. I saw the three large chain-links hanging from the iron plate, embedded in the rocky crag at the east entrance—all that remained of the great chain Washington had hung across the valley, to keep British ships from approaching West Point.

Liz groaned. "Look at this!"

"Holiday traffic," Laureen sighed.

A line of cars extended from the tollbooth on the western side all the way back to the middle of the bridge. As Liz slowed the Buick down, I watched her concentrate on her driving. For some reason, at this moment, she reminded me of Father, and I was overcome with a rush of sad affection, as confusing as my anger was, moments before. Beyond her open window, I could see almost ten miles down river to the City of Peekskill on the east shore beneath the bright sun. We came to a stop and waited for the lead cars to slip through the tollgate one-by-one. As they did, Liz pressed the gas lightly and we crept forward.

Laureen lowered the radio. "*So…who's gonna be* at this party?"

I glanced at my watch. "Lot's of different people."

"Most of 'em pretty horrid," muttered Liz.

I looked at her again. "What do you mean by *that*?"

"Oh, come on. That Martha Bradley…her insufferable brother?"

Laureen looked at me with confusion.

"A month ago," I said, "April had a swimming party, and Liz came. That was the *first* and *only* time she met our other friends…"

"*Your* other friends!" Liz snorted. "Look! April…is *very* nice…but I don't get it…because the rest of that bunch…are *assholes*."

"You sound jealous," I said.

"Of *what*?"

"And judgmental."

"Maybe…but *you* give them way too much credit."

"Rowe thinks you're cute."

"Who?" said Laureen.

"He means this boy…his name is *Rowe*," Liz said. "Can you believe it? Rowe Bradley…*Maaatha's* brother…"

Laureen chuckled and turned to me. "So, how come *we're* not invited?"

"You *were*," I said, staring forward.

"Really?" said Laureen, with surprise.

"Ask *her*," I added.

"I didn't wanna go, Laureen," my sister said, lowering her voice.

"Why not?" Laureen replied.

"Because *she's* the snob," I said. "That's why." There was silence in the car then. Finally, my anger got the better of me again. "You know…you should get outta that house more often, Liz. Go get a *boyfriend*."

"Screw you!"

Laureen suddenly grabbed us each by our legs and held on. "You know…it's a beautiful day…our fathers are about to do something that'll make money for both of 'em…*and* help people at the same time…so…come on…"

I stared at the stalled traffic in front of us. "Yeah. Sure they are."

"What are you talking about?" Liz demanded.

"When you get home…ask Dad and Arthur what Grandpa Brent just told them…about their St. Nicholas Avenue deal."

"What *about* it?" Laureen said.

"It's in the shitter!" They seemed shocked. "It's not gonna happen," I added bitterly. "There's another project the City likes better."

Liz snapped the radio all the way off and stared through the windshield. I could tell that Laureen was confused by the anger between my sister and me. How could she understand what we'd hardly realized ourselves—that each member of our family had been pushed to a personal breaking point that couldn't be expressed, except in blunt emotions like anger, faked good humor, and hope. And as we sat suspended in silence above the valley, with bridge traffic jammed in front and behind, and the brilliant sun beating down on us, I thought of all that had happened.

When Father graduated from Brooklyn Law School in 1949, Grandfather Hank made a few phone calls to some Wall Street people he still knew. Father did a little tax work for these men and won their confidence. They referred him to their friends and associates and, within a year, he'd built a thriving practice.

Toward the end of 1950, he was able to move out of space he'd been renting from one of his law professors. He established his own office in an elegant building on Carroll Street, not far from where we lived. By then, he was handling the merger of two mid-sized brokerage firms, and helping an investment bank develop a Manhattan rail yard for a new office building. He'd also helped a famous soft drink company find 200 acres of land in Westchester for its new headquarters.

He often worked directly for the chairmen of these companies, finding inventive loopholes for them in the tax laws, and they loved his ideas. He encouraged them to invest in residential development, which was exploding in the suburbs. And he also started structuring mixed-use developments, combining residential and commercial space with open land on big parcels in Westchester, Long Island, New Jersey, and Connecticut. He got Hank Gannon and Phillip Brent involved in several of these investments, too, and everyone made money.

But my father was also his mother's son. During 1950 and '51, he ran a special program to help Brooklyn's Puerto Rican immigrants learn the details of "statutory citizenship" and their rights in dealing with the Long Island potato and sod farmers who hired them as laborers.

And then, in 1952, he got a call from a Harlem investment syndicate that wanted to buy and refurbish an old vaudeville theater, at the corner of Broadway and 125th Street. The theater's previous owners had gone bankrupt, and the City was holding the property in lieu of unpaid taxes. The Harlem businessmen planned to take over the building and produce legitimate shows and jazz concerts.

But a group of local residents opposed this, claiming it would introduce undesirable elements into the neighborhood. In public hearings, they demanded that the old theater building be condemned. And their attorneys and public relations men presented studies that said a park was needed in that location.

Father took the case on behalf of the businessmen. He pointed out that the City ought to do what it had long resisted—extend Riverside Park 20 blocks north from 125th Street. When he made that argument, he got support from liberal newspapers that claimed the racism behind the gap in Riverside Park might also explain opposition to the theater. The coverage suddenly galvanized support for the theater among other residents in the area, including one well-organized Jewish civic group.

The hearings, street protests, and court testimony went on for months. Hundreds of people were present when Father made his eloquent argument for the theater at the final hearing. The *New York Times* editorialized in favor of the theater, and published a big story when Father won the case in U.S. District Court.

The *Times* had a picture of Father standing outside the Federal Court Building downtown. He wore a gray suit, with his shirt collar opened and his tie loosened. He looked tired but happy, and his face shone with a broad smile. His clients—a dozen black men in dark overcoats and Homburgs—who all looked old enough to be his father, surrounded him. These no-nonsense businessmen were smiling, too, and one of them, Arthur Spencer, had his arm over Father's shoulder.

The next day, an attorney named Gerry Moran, who'd represented the local opposition groups, called a news conference and said that Arthur and Father should be investigated for "subversive affiliations."

Moran claimed Arthur was a man "of dubious background...who has consorted in the past with Reds in show business...people who have been barred from working in the entertainment field. Spencer, and his attorney Joseph Gannon, apparently will stop at nothing to support these subversives...including building a theater for them to perform in, over the objections of honest, hardworking Americans in a respectable neighborhood."

Immediately, the *New York Times* printed another editorial, calling these accusations "worse than obscene." The *New York Post* took a similar view, but other papers gave credence to the accusations, which Father denied in many interviews. The furor finally subsided a week later, and it seemed that there would be no further trouble. But some of the neighborhood people who'd sided with the businessmen were affiliated with the now discredited Progressive Party, and its 1948 presidential candidate Henry Wallace FDR's former Vice-President. When this was reported, everything changed.

Father started getting phone calls from his other clients. They told him they understood and supported his right to do "any kind of work" he wanted, but that these were "complicated times." They said they were worried about the publicity; their families and customers were concerned. Even the Democratic Party was distancing itself now from the old Progressives, they said. And before the month was out, every one of them had resigned from his law practice.

There were costly libel suits, letters to Congressmen and Senators, and even a meeting with the head of the Manhattan FBI office. Nothing helped. Meanwhile, Father could get no work except for some things that Arthur arranged. And so, we'd finally run out of money. By the time we'd moved to Garrison, even most of our old friends from Brooklyn had stopped calling us.

My parents managed to join the Highland Country Club near the cottage, hoping some business might arise from making new friends. Liz and I volunteered to get part-time jobs, and transfer to the public high school in Highland

Falls, but our parents would hear none of it. Their one concession—we'd now attend our prep schools a bit more economically, as day students. My sister and I knew the facts of our parents' finances. And so, there was no way to explain how they were managing country club fees, or tuition at St. Paul's, and at The Mount, the exclusive school for Catholic girls that Liz attended in Pough-keepsie. We finally decided that Mother's parents were lending her money. But of course, she'd never admit it to us; she wasn't the kind of woman who could tell the truth to her children and lie to her husband.

Then, Mother suggested she get a job. With her degree from Columbia Teacher's College she could work in a local elementary school, she said, just as she had in Brooklyn, while Father was finishing law school. "It would only be a temporary thing, Joe," she assured him.

But he smiled, and said, "be patient, Mary, things will turn around soon." And for some reason, she didn't argue.

Finally, after two years of this, Father came home one evening and sat us all down in the living room. He said he'd reached an understanding with the attorney, Moran, who'd made the false accusations. He said Moran had sent a retraction around to the newspapers that very evening. And then, he smiled wearily.

But what appeared in the papers over the next several days was a small news item, buried within the folds near the Obituaries, far from the front pages where the original stories had been.

And even that night, as Father told us his news, we'd sat together waiting in vain to feel relieved. When our parents went to the kitchen to have sandwiches and beer, Liz and I stayed in the living room and put the television on. I leafed absently through a copy of *Life* magazine as Liz held Mary on her lap; David sat on the floor directly below the screen.

At some point, I heard Mother speak in a soft voice to Father in the kitchen. "Are we going to be all right, now?" At first, there was no reply. But then, I heard him sobbing, and heard her frantic footsteps as she hurried to close the door between the kitchen and the living room. I looked at David, who'd turned from the television and was staring down the darkened hallway at the closed kitchen door. Then, I looked across the living room at Liz. Mary was asleep in her arms, and Liz was looking down and stroking her hair. Only when Liz looked up at me, a moment later, could I see the tears that streamed from her eyes.

CHAPTER 4

As I stood in the sun below the Stannards' front portico, I could hear orchestra music rising on breezes from the valley side of the house. I breathed in, deeply, as if it were possible to inhale the joy that seemed to float in the bright spring air.

I bent down and looked at Liz. "I'll call you when I'm ready. Or…if April comes, she'll drive me."

Laureen smiled weakly and nodded, but my sister, with her hands gripped on the wheel and her face forward, waited only a moment before gunning the gas. The Buick lurched away with a screech of tires, and sped back down the entrance drive.

In a large meadow to the west, beyond a row of ancient pines, young men in white shirts and black trousers parked cars in neat, back-to-back rows. A lengthening stream of vehicles wound slowly into the bright field, and guests walked a narrow footpath through the trees back to the house.

"Please come in, Mr. Gannon."

I turned and saw John Jennings, the Stannards' butler, in a dark blue suit looking down from the portico. He held his right hand to his forehead, shielding his eyes against the glare of sun off dark pavement.

Quickly scaling seven marble steps, I followed him across the wide porch and into the house. And as the massive front door closed behind us with the solemnity of a bank vault, I remembered what Mrs. Stannard once said, that it had been carved by hand from the trunk of a single oak tree, felled in the Adirondacks in 1880.

Sunlight streamed through a ceiling window, onto an ancient marble statue—a Roman maiden on a granite pedestal—set in a shallow pool at the center of the vestibule. With a water jar balanced on one shoulder, she gazed downward and water trickled from the jaws of a brass wolf's head embedded in the granite.

"Miss Stannard asks that you wait here." Jennings pointed to a Romanesque settee upholstered in pink, purple and white silk.

"Will she be long?" I said, sitting down.

"Presently, sir."

He disappeared into the shadows of the main hallway, and my eyes wandered. Just inside the door, there were two stone vases painted with scenes of Roman athletes. A polished silver disc, the size of a dinner plate, leaned on its edge against the flat stone surface above the door. The disc was an oversized coin of the ancient world, filigreed, and minted with the double faces of Janus.

I glanced at my watch. It was past two-thirty. Leaning back against the wall behind the settee, I could feel the muffled sounds of the orchestra throbbing faintly in the thick stone.

Water trickled endlessly into the pool, and I gazed up at the placid maiden. The angle of bright sunlight through the ceiling window had subtly changed. Now, refracted light-rays washed down her body and into the gleaming pool, spilling out across the floor almost to my outstretched feet.

Two months earlier, on a bright Sunday morning, I'd met April's train in Garrison and we'd trekked into the hilly woodlands above the station. The forest overflowed with birds moving north. We saw rabbits and raccoons; copperheads rustled in the deep brush. And a herd of deer, which had gathered near a stream fifty yards off the trail, nervously watched us pass.

By noon, we reached a spot where the forests opened into wide meadows that stretched beyond sight. "It's about two miles more," I said, pointing across the sea of billowing grass.

"Okay." She smiled and uncorked the small thermos of cold water she'd brought with her. She offered me a drink.

I shook my head. "You first."

She sipped and breathed deeply. Then, I took her thermos and drank, as she wiped her face with a linen handkerchief.

We rested for another minute before pushing out into the fields. For half an hour, we waded through meadow grass up to our faces. Larks and blackbirds flew up and circled until we'd passed. Gradually, we could feel the air grow moist, and soon, we emerged onto the narrow, sandy shoreline of Lake Manitou.

The lakefront was sheltered from the March breeze by tall grass, and the midday sun glowed brilliantly in the silent sky. We stepped to the edge of the water and knelt. I told her to put her hand in to feel the uncanny warmth. "There's a hot spring in the center of the lake," I said.

At first, she touched only the surface. Then she smiled. "It's *amazingly* hot," she said, gazing out over the lake, drawing her hand back and forth, making wider and deeper ripples with her fingertips. "Do many people come here?"

"Depends," I said. "You can't drive in, and it's such a long walk from the highway…you could be here for hours without seeing anyone."

"Let's go in," she said.

"What?"

"*Go in!*" She pulled her hand back and tugged at my jacket. "*Come on.*" Then she stood, turned away, and shed her clothes in seconds. Without a word, she waded into the warm water, and I watched as her body and then her hair slowly disappeared below the surface. A moment later, her head bobbed up again and she laughed out loud. "What are you waiting for?" I stripped off my clothes and tossed them near hers on the bank. Then I quickly waded in. She watched me for a moment before turning in the water and swimming farther out. I dove forward and swam after her. When I reached her, she grabbed for my hand beneath the surface and we kissed. "How did you find this place?" she said.

"Liz and I used to come here…when we were younger…"

She smiled and seemed happy, but pensive "I wish I knew Liz better. Do you think she'd come to a swimming party…if I asked her?"

"I guess so…why?"

"Get to *know* her," she said. "Aren't you listening?" She moved her arms and legs rapidly under the surface in the warm water. "Besides…you really love her…and…"

"Who…Liz?" I said. She stared at me pensively. "We haven't been getting along very well, lately," I confided.

"Older sister…younger brother."

"I guess."

"Wish *I* had a brother," she said.

For a moment we floated. "Is that…how you think of *me*?" I said.

"*What?*"

"Like a…brother…or something?"

She frowned. "Why…because I'm not self-conscious with you?" She paused for a moment. "You know…I had an odd feeling when we met…that I'd seen you, or met you before…or I'd been thinking about a person I'd made up in my mind and suddenly…there he was. And the more we talked, the *more familiar* it seemed…we had the same memories…somehow. I don't know how else to say it…but *that's* how I feel about you." I frowned and nodded, as she leaned her head back to get sunlight on her face. "The air is *cold*," she sighed.

I grabbed her hand and pulled her out into the deep center of the lake, where steam rose off the surface. "This is where the hot spring comes up," I said.

Bubbles tingled at our feet, and rose along our bodies, before popping all around us in the chilly air. We bumped together, and she felt soft and slippery-smooth against my legs. Strands of hair fell across her cheek, and I pushed them back and kissed her again. She smiled vaguely and pushed away, leaning back and floating with her body just beneath the surface, gazing distantly into the white sun.

"What's wrong?" I said.

"*My parents*," she sighed. "They're not letting me go back to Paris…in the fall."

"Oh," I said, secretly happy. "That's…what you want?"

"I'm interested in *painting*, Tom…you know that." She paused, and then imitated her parents with uncharacteristic sarcasm. "'*What would you study there…painting? That's no education.*'"

I laughed. "Whadda they want you to do?"

"Pick any school in America…as long as it's one of these five or six…you know." There was a sharp edge in her voice suddenly. "It's okay to study the *history* of art…but not *painting*."

"You don't need to go *anywhere*…to be a painter…do you?"

"I suppose not. It isn't really the point."

"All I'm saying is…go to school, but paint! They can't stop you." As she listened, she smiled in an odd way that seemed to say how innocent of her life I was. "You're sure you want to go back to Paris…just to paint?" I said.

She stared at me. "What's *this*?"

"Well…because…Georgie Keller told me…"

"Georgie Keller! What would *he* know? That little shit…he once tried to…*grab me*…in dancing class. Did you know that?"

"What?"

She nodded and laughed. "I said 'George Keller…I wonder what your mother would say.'" She smiled with satisfaction. "*That* got through to him."

"Ever met his mother?" I laughed.

She smiled again. "Formidable woman."

"*I'll* say."

"So…what *did* Georgie tell you?"

"That your father *made* you leave Paris. Because of some artist."

"Oh." And for a while, she said nothing more. Then, she sighed and shook her head. "I suppose I shouldn't have to tell you any of this…but, well, you're a big boy."

"I don't need to know…I…don't really care."

"Oh, *not at all*," she said with a sarcastic laugh. "You started it; so now, shut up and listen." She paused to get a breath, as if she needed a deep one. "His name was Laurent. And yes, he was a painter. I liked him, I suppose, because he was older…and he encouraged *my* painting. He asked me to model for him, too, and…I got caught up in it…the idea of a twenty-five-year-old man, wanting me to pose…was exciting…I guess. Naturally, he wanted me to…sleep with him. He couldn't understand why I wouldn't. After all, there I was, with my clothes off. What could be simpler?"

"So…you *didn't*?" I said, stuck on one thought.

"It's funny…everything changed when I started modeling for him. Everything…he never even mentioned my painting again. Anyway…my father heard what was going on…I'd told Martha, and she let something slip about it, accidentally, to her mother. Naturally, *she* told *Mister* Bradley and *he* called Daddy." She shook her head and sighed. "He sent Laurent a very threatening letter. Laurent showed it to me…Daddy wanted the painting destroyed. He sent an agent to see Laurent in his studio about it…the agent paid him, and watched Laurent burn it in his fireplace. The thing was…by the time my father forced me to come home, I'd already broken off with Laurent."

"Because he took the *money*," I said.

She frowned and shook her head. "Because no *real* artist allows anyone to destroy his work."

We floated for a while longer and then swam back to shore. Coming out of the water, jolted by the March air, we were shivering in seconds. She wrapped her arms around herself as droplets rolled down her body. Her water-darkened hair lay flat on her head. Her lips were blue, and her skin looked as cold as marble. I put my arms around her and began rubbing her back. She rested her face on my shoulder and, after a moment, we kissed again.

Suddenly, we fell onto our clothes. The clothing was hot against our bodies, and lying under the sun inside the sheltering grass warmed us a little. At some unconscious moment, my body began to press against her soft stomach. When she noticed, she sighed, and pressed herself hard against me. Her long, smooth legs tangled in mine. I could hear our breathing, faster and faster, and then she pulled me on top of her. Her legs moved apart beneath me, and I pushed. Moments later, her body shook, relaxed, and shook again. She was covered in sweat. Suddenly, I breathed in violently. It shocked her, and she put one hand on the back of my head, pressing my face against her chest, and as I breathed out slowly against her skin, she whispered. "Shushhhhh."

I glanced at my watch; an hour had passed in a moment's consciousness. She lay beneath me, half-asleep. Our stomachs felt glazed together, skin to skin. The sun had moved beyond the center of the blue sky and we were half in shadow. "We better go," I muttered.

"All right." She held me tightly, pressing against me for a moment longer. Finally, we rolled away from each other and stood up. As she reached for her clothes, I was suddenly embarrassed; something more vulnerable than naked-ness had been revealed and it confused me. I looked away. Then, standing apart with our backs to each other, we rapidly dressed.

Our walk back to Garrison was mostly silent, and by the time we reached the station it was late in the afternoon. Shadows covered the station house and the tracks along the river, and it was truly cold.

We waited for twenty minutes until the next southbound arrived. We walked down the platform toward the front of the train, and I wondered if she felt the same sense of nameless loss that I felt. I was afraid to let her go, now, but the train was waiting. We kissed quickly and she started up the metal steps of the first car. Stopping on the top rung, she turned to look at me with a sad expression. "I *love* you," she said.

"I love you, *too.*"

Then she turned and was gone quickly inside the car. I waited on the plat-form until the train disappeared beyond the bend at Manitou Falls, and then I took a cab home in the dark.

"Tom!" I rose toward the sound of her voice, feeling her hand on my shoul-der, pulling me toward the flattened light at the surface of the lake. And as I opened my eyes, her face appeared in the watery shadows. "You were sleeping."

My vision cleared, and I realized that she was standing over me. I struggled to my feet and glanced at my watch. It was after three o'clock. Direct sunlight had passed beyond the ceiling window, and the vestibule seemed dusky and cold.

"I'm sorry," I said. "Didn't sleep well last night…"

"No, *I'm* sorry…making you wait."

I stared at her white, cotton dress. There was a thin, leather belt around her waist, and her elegant brown shoes matched it. Her hair was combed back in thick golden waves, and held behind her ears with a white ribbon. She smiled and kissed me. Her face felt hot and damp.

"Are you all right?" I said.

"I'm fine."

"You seem…you look pale…"

She waved her hand with assurance. "My parents want to talk with us before we go out to the party."

"What about?"

"I'm not sure." She stared hard into my eyes. "Something's wrong," she said. I shook my head. She pressed me. "I can see it in your face. What *is* it?"

"It's something…I've just heard." She kept staring at me. "…To do with my father's business…another setback."

"Tell me what it is…"

I glanced at my watch again, and sighed angrily. "I don't know exactly what's happening," I said. "I just need to get home soon. They have all these people coming and…now…"

"Is this like that other thing you told me about…that theater?"

I nodded. "It won't be…if my father and his partner will just do the sensible thing…there doesn't have to *be* a problem."

She smiled wanly. "I'm sorry, Tom. I'm not sure I understand."

"Why don't you come back with me?" I said. "We'll see most of the fireworks from my house and…even hear the music…over the water."

She frowned and shook her head. "My parents expect *me* with *them* at the concert…they're having a group of people, too; friends and business associates." I nodded. "Daddy gave me two tickets…maybe I'll just ask Martha. When do you have to leave?"

"I don't know; an hour, maybe?"

Suddenly there were footsteps coming toward us from the hallway. A moment later, Jennings appeared. "Miss Stannard! Your father wants you. He wants to see you and Mr. Gannon right away…"

"Yes, Jennings…I know."

"He said to come see him…in the library…right away, Miss."

"We'll be there in a minute," April said, with a frustrated sighed.

"I'll tell him, Miss." He spun on his heels and hurried back into the long hallway.

She moved closer again and pressed her face against mine, holding me tightly. I felt her lips and warm breathing against my cheek. Her skin was hot and damp beneath the cotton of her dress.

A few moments later, she led me to her father's library. Her parents weren't there. I gazed across the large room, which had several chairs and small sofas in its center, and walls lined with elegant mahogany shelves filled with ancient and modern books. Some were bound in rich, unflawed leather. Others were covered by paper jackets, as bright and perfect as the day they'd rolled off the presses. In one section, a cache of ancient-looking parchment scrolls was protected in a glass cabinet. And on one wall, there were two vertical windows that looked out onto a private lawn and the swimming pool. Suddenly, she raised her arm and drew a wide arc in the air. "All the wisdom of the world," she smiled.

"They're beautiful," I said, walking slowly along the stacks, astounded by first editions of Twain, Hawthorne, Melville, Emerson, Dickens, Austen and Tolstoy, Henry James and Edith Wharton, Hemingway, Fitzgerald, and Faulkner. There were Dryden and Pope translations of the ancient epics, and a mid-17th Century edition of Shakespeare. And there were priceless, hand-printed copies of Chaucer and Dante, and the ancient Greeks and Romans. Time had nearly stopped in this room.

"This is a fraction of his collection," she confided. "The rest are in a warehouse on Madison Avenue."

I kept gazing around the room. "What does he do...change the display every year...like a museum?" She looked into my eyes and smiled, quizzically, nodding. Then, she reached up to a small book and removed it. When she handed it to me, I saw that it was *Catcher in the Rye*. "I've never *seen* a hardcover version of this," I said.

She smiled warmly. "Weren't many printed, I guess."

I leafed through the first few pages and came to an inscription:

April—I shouldn't have really signed this book or anything, because now you'll think you <u>have</u> to read it and all, and that's pretty boring. But thanks for talking with me. And remember, most of what you need to know in life you already do. The trick is don't forget it, or trade it in for all the crap they'll be telling you.—Jerry

"This is to *you*," I said, impressed.

"Oh," she replied. "Daddy took me to a party at the Plaza Hotel, a few years ago; he was signing them for everybody."

"Really," I said. "What was he like?"

She thought for a moment. "Happy…and sad."

"Did your father see what he wrote to you?" I asked.

She smiled faintly, and nodded. "He thought it was funny." Suddenly, she turned and scanned a section of shelves that seemed devoted to female authors. "These are mostly mine," she said. "Edith Wharton was an obsession when I was fifteen. Last year…I found this…in Paris." Reaching high, she pulled down Simone de Beauvoir's *The Second Sex*. "I showed it to my father when I came back. I don't think he liked it. Do you know her?"

I shrugged. "Sartre's girlfriend…"

She smiled and then whispered dramatically. "They were saying in Paris…she's been sleeping with Richard Wright…"

I smiled and scanned the shelves again. "You know…I don't see *Native Son*." She suddenly frowned. "Or *Invisible Man*…are they in the warehouse?"

Her face seemed oddly blank. "Uh…I don't think so."

"Ah! They're here…finally!" It was her father. We turned toward the library door and saw him, and her mother, smiling graciously. Charles Stannard was a tall thin man, whose most prominent facial features were his pale green eyes. His thinning, black hair was slicked straight back on his head. He wore fine, charcoal gray slacks and a brilliant white shirt without a tie, and the solid gold buttons of his navy blazer glittered.

Constance Stannard was as tall and thin as her husband; a pleated, pink blouse and gray, summer skirt down to mid-calf accented her angles. Her tinted blonde hair was tightly coifed and her facial features were sharp and acute, like the rest of her. "Let's sit down," said Mr. Stannard, pointing to the chairs and sofas in the middle of the room. "Shall we?"

April grabbed my hand and guided me to one of the small sofas that faced another one just like it. As her parents walked toward us and sat down on the facing sofa, I could see Mrs. Stannard noticing the natural way in which April had arranged this pairing off. Then, as April moved close to me and leaned against my shoulder, with her hand on my knee, her mother's eyes widened.

"April!" she said, embarrassed.

"Oh…Mother," April smiled

Mr. Stannard turned to his daughter and changed the subject. "Now…will Tom be joining us at the concert tonight?"

"No, sir," I answered. He looked surprised. "My parents are entertaining some friends and business acquaintances. I'll need to be getting home soon."

"Ah. I see. Family comes first."

"Yes…sir."

"Good. Now tell me something…Tom…would I have read about your father in the newspapers…in the past few weeks?"

There was silence in the room, then. I paused before answering. "You…might have, sir." I felt April's hand squeezing my knee.

"Something about an old real estate development," he said, with uncertainty in his voice.

"Yes, sir. My father was involved in a theater project…two years ago…as attorney for the developers."

"That was it," he said, smiling, nodding briefly toward his wife, who stared straight at me without apparent emotion. "A group of investors," he continued, "from Harlem, wasn't it?" I nodded. "And there'd been a bit of trouble about it…"

"A dispute with some local residents…yes. Ultimately, the project went ahead."

"I was spending a lot of time in Washington, then. Some *political* accusations were made, I believe…"

"That's been resolved," I said. "Though…you'd hardly know it from the recent articles."

"The point seemed clear enough…to *me*," he smiled.

"I hope you're right, sir."

"This man," he said, "Moran…retracted the accusations…isn't that right?"

"The trouble is…sir…it's much easier to *make* accusations than take them back."

"What do you mean?" asked Mrs. Stannard suddenly. They both stared at me, now, waiting.

"Accusations create an impression that's hard to dismiss," I said, "even when they're *false*."

"Interesting," said Mr. Stannard. "Well…here's what I wanted to say. I'd like to meet your father some time soon. Do you think we could arrange that?"

"Yes, sir."

"Like you, I'm distressed by the character assassination that goes on these days…the unpleasantness of it. It's wrong, I think…though…none of us should be naïve enough to believe there aren't people trying to pull this country down…destroy us, as a nation. But, once people are shown to be good citizens, why, that should be the end of it."

"Yes, sir."

"Now, Tom," he said, glancing briefly at his wife. "I want you to speak to your father, and let him know that Mrs. Stannard and I would like it if he, and Mrs. Gannon, came to dinner. Can we do that?"

"Of course. My father said the same thing today…about having you and Mrs. Stannard to *our* home." I glanced at her and she nodded with a faint smile.

"Let's sort it out, then!" he said, clapping his hands together and holding them. "We'll have *them* here first."

"He'll want to know why you asked about his theater project," I said

He seemed transfixed by another thought, but suddenly smiled again. "You must know that I'm involved in investment banking. Our bank raises capital for corporations to use in their domestic and overseas expansion, acquisitions, and development projects…real estate. Mrs. Stannard and I also run a family foundation, which invests in real estate on a *charitable* basis. And…it seems to us, that your father has expertise in just these areas. We're always looking for good new ideas. We prefer working with people whom we know…personally. I'd like very much to talk business with him…*if* he's interested, that is."

"I'll tell him, sir."

"*And* if there are no further stories in the newspapers," said Mrs. Stannard pointedly.

"Mother!" April said, angrily, as Mrs. Stannard continued staring into my eyes, making her point clear.

"Tom," said Mr. Stannard, more diplomatically. "What Mrs. Stannard simply means is that…we want to know your parents better. Knowing you, we believe, I mean we assume, they are fine people…the sort of people we like to work with, and who can help us…particularly in our charitable endeavors, which are very important to our family. But we don't want public attention drawn to ourselves…or our charities…unnecessarily. And we just can't have *bad* publicity."

"Sir…I understand."

"Good," he said, smiling, and clapping his hands on his thighs.

"Can we go, now?" April suddenly interjected. "I promised Tom he could meet Mr. Littlefield."

"Oh?" said Mrs. Stannard. "You're interested in history, then."

"Tom's the best history student at his school!" April said proudly, as we stood up.

"That's not true," I said to Mrs. Stannard, embarrassed. She smiled.

"Joshua Littlefield, the Civil War veteran," said April's father in a wistful voice. "Amazing old gentleman. Superintendent Mackenzie sent him over from the Academy, with some officers. I think they're on the south side of the marquee."

"So…we're gonna *go* now…all right?" said April.

"Certainly," he smiled, as Mrs. Stannard nodded next to him.

We walked across the nearly empty ballroom as afternoon sunlight glowed beyond latticework doors, facing the east lawn. The doors were open, and the music and voices drifted in from the lawn.

At the back of the ballroom, Jennings gave orders in a quiet voice to a corps of uniformed servants—black men and women, dressed in black and white. He stood at a long banquet table stacked with china, and rows of sparkling silver and glassware, and silver chafing dishes, each with a small round candle flickering beneath it. On smaller tables there were circles of exotic cheeses, and cold salmon and lobster on silver beds of shaved ice. A dozen waiters queued up to get drink orders filled at the makeshift bar in one corner. Jennings heard our footsteps on the wooden floor and briefly nodded.

I intercepted a waiter rushing by with eight crystal glasses of champagne balanced on a silver tray. Lifting a glass, I gulped the champagne. His eyes widened as he watched me. April's head jerked around and a smile broke over her lips. I placed the empty glass back on the tray, and the waiter hurried out to the party. April shook her head and grabbed my hand.

We stepped out onto the limestone patio and gazed across the lawn. Hundreds of guests talked and laughed in groups that gathered and dispersed, like whitecap waves on a green sea. Other people relaxed around black iron lawn tables, under canvas umbrellas, that fluttered like buoy flags. Near the hedgerows along the cliffs, more guests gathered in the late afternoon sunlight in their spring blazers, pastel-colored shirts and dresses, and wide-brimmed hats. And from beneath the tent, stretching fifty yards across the immense lawn, there was a rushing whisper—the sound of many voices together.

Acrid champagne taste clung to the back of my throat, and I felt a pleasant detachment, suddenly. Everything seemed to be leaving me—drifting away like ripples across the surface of a pond. April gripped my hand with a constant intensity, and I could feel that her palm was warm and moist. I could see a small film of sweat on her upper lip, though the spring air was cooling as the sun passed over the mansion behind us.

We descended the patio steps to the crowded lawn and walked toward the tent, which was open all the way around. I could see inside, now, to the dark mass of people, some standing, and many more sitting in imprecise rows and circular clusters on hundreds of folding chairs. We ducked under the tent and immediately found her friends sitting together in a semi-circle.

Penelope Potts noticed us first and she smiled, waving her hand high above her head. "There they are!"

"Hello, Gannon," said Rowe Bradley, reclining in his chair, his legs stretched out on the trampled grass, and his right arm slung over Claudia Radcliffe's shoulders. When Claudia smiled, I raised my hand in a polite wave.

Martha Bradley was chatting quietly with a well-dressed man, who was about five or six years older than the rest of us. They looked up, briefly, and nodded at April, before returning to their conversation.

Penelope addressed the group, but looked at me. "Lovely day!"

I smiled back at her. Rowe and Claudia glanced at each other.

"Claudia," I said, "did you ever turn that English paper in?" She frowned, glanced at Rowe, and looked back with a confused expression. "You know...*Catcher in the Rye*."

"Oh, *that*," she said. "Yes."

"So...what was the verdict?" I asked. She looked twice as confused, now, turning again to Rowe for help.

"She got an *A*, Gannon," he said.

"No!" I shook my head at Claudia. "I mean...*your* verdict...on Holden Caulfield?"

"Nuts," said Rowe, with arch finality.

Claudia nodded in agreement. Then, her expression changed, as she saw something she didn't like in mine. "I got an *A*," she asserted, with a hint of annoyance.

"Congratulations," I said, without bothering to cut the sarcasm.

Suddenly, Penelope jumped in. "Tom...have you seen your friend, George Keller, lately?"

"Isn't he *here*?" I said.

April shrugged. "His parents are...I think..."

"Then, I don't know, Pen," I answered, with a smile.

"Martha!" said April. "Do you have plans this evening?" Martha glanced at the man next to her. "Because I have these tickets...you know...for the concert...Tom can't go with me...he's got to leave soon."

"Oh?" Martha said, looking at me, now, as the slightly older man held her hand.

"My parents are having a party, too," I said. "I need to get back soon." I felt April squeezing my hand.

Martha looked uncomfortable, as she glanced at April. "Actually...Lan asked me to go...with *him*..."

"Oh!" April said. "That's nice...we'll probably sit in the same row, anyway." Martha smiled.

"I'll go," offered Penelope.

"You will?" said April. "Thank you, Pen." Penelope smiled warmly at April.

Rowe snickered. "Good ole Pen. Done her good deed for the day."

"Stop it!" Claudia slapped his shoulder and laughed.

"Are you two going?" I asked.

"Uh...no," said Rowe, glancing at his watch. "I'm heading back to school tonight." I nodded. "By the way, Gannon, how's your sister?" Claudia frowned at his question.

"She's well," I said. "She's home with our parents..."

"Say 'hello' for me...will you?" He sounded disappointed.

"I will."

"Well...we're looking for Mr. Littlefield," April said, conclusively. Their faces were blank. "I'll catch up to everyone later..."

"Seeya, Gannon," said Rowe. I raised my hand in a wordless wave to the group.

April pulled me away. "Insufferable," she hissed, as we pushed through the crowd. "I'm starting to really dislike those two."

"Oh," I said, "they're just...who they *are*..."

"Exactly."

"Who was that *other* person...with Martha?"

"That's Lanning Eliot...he's a bright young man...works with my father, now, at the bank."

We headed toward the south end of the tent and the deeper we pushed into the thick crowd, the hotter the air seemed under heavy canvas. It was slow going. The chairs had obviously been set up in rows and there'd been aisles, but this order had broken down in the ebb and flow of guests. We had to walk completely around one group of five couples, people in their early 40s, who sat bunched together, completely unaware that their chairs were blocking the makeshift aisle.

"But what does it *mean*?" said one woman, as April and I squeezed through.

"It's a Supreme Court decision," replied the man next to her. "Brown versus Topeka."

"*About time*," said another woman.

"So...you want colored boys in school with *your* daughter?" a third man said.

"Is *that* what it means?" said the first woman.

"*Technically*," said another man in the group. "It's mostly about *public* schools..."

"*Oh*," said several relieved voices together.

"...In the South," the man added, while behind him, a black waiter held up a large tray and stared impassively into the crowd. Suddenly, the man turned in his seat. "Oh! The drinks are here!"

A few moments later, I noticed the familiar faces of Bill and Dot Keller, Georgie's parents. They sat in another ragged circle of guests, and I waved as we advanced toward them. They smiled quizzically, as if surprised to see me. And as April and I pushed by, I recognized Bill Keller's voice in the crowd. "McCarthy's just gone too far, this time. This Army thing...Ike's had enough."

Someone responded. "Eisenhower never defended Marshall, when McCarthy attacked *him*."

"Ike's too smart," said Mr. Keller. "He plays it down the middle...let someone else defend the liberals...and let *McCarthy* do the dirty work...hounding them."

Over the group's laughter, someone else retorted, "People still take McCarthy seriously."

"No one with any brains," said another voice.

"No...McCarthy served his purpose," said Mr. Keller. "Nixon, too..."

"Who do the Democrats have in 'Fifty-six," someone said. "Stevenson, again?"

"Good luck!" said Mr. Keller to more laughter.

As we reached the south end of the great tent, I felt fresh air and saw daylight. I looked at April. "How are you feeling?"

"Okay." She nodded with determination, looking pale.

"Let's get some fresh air," I said.

"Good idea." A moment later, outside the tent, she sighed. "Oh! That's better."

"We'll stay here a minute," I urged. She nodded.

As we stood outside the tent, I noticed Andrew O'Leary, the father of another schoolmate. He was dressed in a dark blue blazer and a white golf shirt. A group of police and military men stood around him and there was a dark blue American Legion armband on his sleeve. He was a minor celebrity in the Highlands. The owner of a successful real estate and construction business, he'd been a hot baseball prospect at Peekskill High, and in American Legion ball, before the war. But he'd lost his right leg when the Navy cruiser he was serving on exploded in Leyte Gulf.

When he saw me, he stopped talking to his friends. We stared at each other without expression for a moment, and then I looked away. I disliked him, ever since he'd almost come to blows with Father over some political argument a few years earlier, outside Wilson's Cigar and Newspaper store in Cold Spring.

I assumed he was here looking for votes and money. He'd been elected to Congress from the Highlands district in 1948 and '50, but narrowly lost in '52, when a moderate Democrat from Hyde Park ran against him with Mrs. Roosevelt's backing. Failing to be part of the national Republican landslide that year must have been embarrassing, and his reelection campaign was in full swing. From what I'd read, his platform consisted mainly of questions about the incumbent Democrat's patriotism.

O'Leary was rumored to be a financial backer of *Red Channels*, the sleazy newsletter that kept a record of people accused of Communist sympathies, particularly entertainers. His generosity to St. Paul's was also well known. Of course, it was widely assumed among us boys that he'd been beating his son Andy Jr. violently for years, but this had never been acknowledged openly by the adult community.

Suddenly, I heard Mrs. Stannard's voice. She was standing just beneath the tent, giving an order to a waiter. When she looked up at April and me, she nodded in our direction, briefly noticing our clasped hands. Then, she looked away, as Jennings came up and whispered in her ear.

"April!" It was her father again. We spun around and saw him standing about 30 feet inside the tent, surrounded by a small group of people who stared gravely at us. He waved and we joined him. "Have you met Mr. Little-field, yet?" he asked.

"No…we haven't found him," April said.

"Follow me!" Excusing himself from the encircling group of guests that suddenly included the curious Kellers, Mr. Stannard turned and walked quickly with April and me right behind him. Once outside, we followed him toward a small man who sat in serene detachment on a black iron lawn chair. He was so small that he looked like a boy with his feet dangling above the grass. But as we drew closer, I saw that his face was ancient.

"Mr. Littlefield, may I introduce my daughter, April, and her friend, Tom Gannon?"

The old man looked up and smiled. "Pleased to meet you," he said in a high-pitched voice. The skin on his hands and face looked like water-stained parchment. He wore an old blue Civil War tunic, with a single row of shiny brass buttons running up his chest. The buttons were etched with American eagles, which years of polishing had dulled into soft impressions. He had a red bandana around his neck and wore a straw boater with a navy blue band. I smiled as I noticed his soft, white tennis shoes.

Several Army officers stood by, chatting quietly among themselves, and having a casual smoke.

Mr. Stannard gave the old man a respectful bow. "These young people have been reading about you, sir...in the newspapers." The old man continued to smile, but said nothing. Finally, Mr. Stannard stood up straight. "Well...I must see to my other guests."

He turned and walked toward the tent, and I saw Andrew O'Leary limp toward him with his right hand extended. Mr. Stannard stopped, looked at the offered hand, and hesitated. Then, they shook briefly and O'Leary talked rapidly, as if trying to sell something. They were too far away for me to hear them. When O'Leary finished, Mr. Stannard gave him a brief reply and disappeared beneath the tent folds. For a moment, O'Leary seemed to be thinking hard about something. Then, he also disappeared into the tent.

CHAPTER 5

"How does your father know Andrew O'Leary?" I whispered to April.

She asked the old veteran to excuse her for a moment, and then she looked at me, frowning. "The Congressman?"

I nodded. "He's here, today."

"Oh…I don't know…Daddy knows everybody. Why?"

"No reason…forget it," I said.

But she could see concern in my face. "What *is* it?" she pressed.

"Did he mean what he said inside…about talking to my father…I mean about business?"

"Yes!" She kissed my cheek. "He doesn't *have* hypothetical conversations, Tom. If your father is having some sort of difficulty with his business…maybe mine can help."

I sighed and nodded. "As long as there's no more bad publicity…"

She frowned again. "*That's* my mother talking."

"I think she…*suspects* about us," I said.

"What…that look on her face?" April muttered. "That's her trying *not* to think about it. It's *one* confrontation she doesn't want."

"So, this is your beau?" interjected Mr. Littlefield, with a dry laugh.

"He is!" April grabbed my hand and turned to the old veteran. "He's my beau." Then, she smiled at me again. "Mr. Littlefield was telling me about his trip from Maine."

"They wanted to get me up in an aero-plane," he said. "But I told 'em I had to take the train up to Portland air base from Blue Hill anyway, so…might as well stay on the train the whole way."

April laughed. "They sent a special train from West Point, with a private car that General MacArthur used."

"That must have been exciting," I said.

He answered me with a nod.

"I told Mr. Littlefield you're a history scholar," said April, "and probably have all sorts of questions about the Civil War." She smiled broadly. The perspiration was gone from her upper lip, but her face was pale.

"What would you like to know, boy?" The old soldier's voice was pitched in a child's register.

"I'm not sure I qualify as a 'scholar' sir, but I *am* interested in history."

"Me too," he said. "Go ahead...ask me somethin' if you want...no need to be shy about it..."

"Well, sir. It's just so interesting to meet a person who's as old as...well, I mean, who actually lived during the Civil War..."

A smile crept across his thin, dry lips. He seemed amused by our curiosity, or our politeness. "Joined in 'Sixty-four, near the end. I was just past fifteen, then."

"I wonder what people *really* thought in those days," I said. "I mean...did you join to free the slaves in the South...save the Union? That's what the books say...but *you* were *there*."

His yellowed, watery eyes stared. "I might have had some notion about them things. My mother nearly tarred my fanny when I told her I was goin', though."

"You lied about your age," I said.

He smiled and shook his head. "Didn't have to. Joined up in the Hill-Toppers Division. We was drummers and pipers for the Maine Regulars." His smile faded suddenly. "There was quite a few of us my age, then, boys...to play music and keep up the men's courage." He paused. "It's been so long a time, now, you see. I mean...we think we know why we set out to do somethin'...but then, we learn things as we do it. Lookin' back...it's hard to remember which was which."

April knelt at the old man's feet and reached for his hand. He looked at her and smiled, perhaps remembering another girl and some long-faded moment. He looked up at me again.

"This whole idea about the Union, well...it's like folks talkin' 'bout loyalty to the government now days...it *was* in the papers...Mr. Lincoln made a point of it. But...in them days...the state you come from meant *everythin'*. Your *state* was your country."

"So, it was state's rights that led to war...*not* slavery," I pressed.

"Son...it's hard to separate 'em...*slavery* was the issue men like John Brown was fired up about." The slightest crack of weariness entered his voice, and he paused.

"Did you ever meet John Brown?" April asked.

"Oh Lord, no. But...we knew folks who knew his people in Litchfield...Connecticut. Met Mr. Emerson, though. He *admired* Mr. Brown."

"Ralph Waldo Emerson?" I was amazed.

He smiled and nodded. "Mother took me to hear him speak at the Unitarian Church, up in Concord, when I was fourteen. Took us three days to get there from the farm. But she wanted me to hear him."

"What did he say?" I asked.

"Said it's a man's duty to break the law...if the law's *immoral*. You children say you know your history?"

"Probably not like *you*, sir." I wanted to hear as much as he'd tell.

"Did you know there was slaves in the north for generations? They had slaves in New York and New Jersey...even parts o' New England, into the late Eighteen-twenties, because...the first abolition laws didn't much help them that was born *before* a certain date." I nodded, and glanced at April as she shook her head in amazement.

"Did you know people who owned slaves...in the north?" she asked.

"We knew folks who remembered them times. You wouldn't get much talk about it, though. Up where we were, you didn't see many Negroes when I was a young boy. A few Negro men actually owned farms around our state, but not many...they stayed to themselves. If there *was* others around...you wouldn't see 'em...'cause they'd be runaway slaves...people up north was startin' to help 'em, then."

"You mean the Underground Railroad," April said.

"That's right. You had John Brown raisin' Cain...Mr. Emerson speakin' out. And others...Miss Harriet Tubman, Mr. Frederick Douglass...that newspaper man in New York State here...Mr. William Garrison...other folks, too." His voice cracked and he paused again. "You see...the states had compromised again in Eighteen-fifty...lettin' California in as a free state...but only if they all agreed that harborin' runaway slaves in any state meant breakin' a law of the whole Union. So, now, *this* was the law...the Eighteen-fifty compromise so called...that Mr. Emerson said was 'immoral' and should be resisted."

"Did *you* help runaway slaves?" April asked.

He grew silent, then, and leaned back in his iron chair. He took off his straw hat and fanned himself a few times before putting it back on his yellowed skull. Just then, one of the Army officers started toward us. April let go of his hand and stood, as the officer came up behind the old man and spoke in a terse, vaguely southern voice. "We don't want to you to be imposed on, now, or tired out."

"Nonsense!" The old man never looked up. "I'm enjoying my chat with these young folks."

The officer frowned. "Can I get you anything, then?"

"Wouldn't mind some lemonade, if they had it."

"I'll see if we can find you some." The officer stepped around the old man's chair and stood very close to April and me. He spoke as if to raw recruits. "Don't you tire this old gentleman. He's got a long night ahead of him."

Then, he went looking for a glass of lemonade. April and I stared at the other two officers, who were several yards away, smoking cigarettes, staring back.

Mr. Littlefield gazed out over the valley. "There was *one* man…a runaway. This was…Eighteen Fifty-nine…I was ten…livin' with my mother in Blue Hill. I had chores to do each day before school…tendin' the cattle…milkin' 'em and lettin' 'em out to graze in the meadow over the bay…"

"Where was your father?" April said.

"He died o' fever soon after I was born, Miss. Never knew him…except for what Mother told me…she said he was a fine man and she missed him…she said I missed him too, but didn't know it. Mother would say things like that, you see. Anyhow…this one particular mornin' out in the barn, I see this big heap o' somethin'…lyin' in the corner of a stall, half-covered in hay. At first I thought a cow had calved overnight, but there wasn't a cow near it, and…it was a pretty large thing for a new calf, anyway. Then…it started movin' and a man jumped up…big colored man, don't ya' know. Scared me half ta' death…till I saw he was more afraid than I was. He had on some overalls and an old shirt…a dirty old floppy hat. He had a coat with no sleeves…and his *shoes*…well. But the sorriest sight of all was the look in that man's eyes. He kept starin' at me, and lookin' all around. I told him it was just me…and I wouldn't tell. I asked him if he was hungry…said I could give him some of the cow's milk, or some griddlecakes mother'd be makin' for breakfast. He seemed to calm down a bit, then…said I was a kind boy. It was odd to hear the way he spoke…formal…like an educated man. I told him I should let Mother know he was there…he got nervous again. But I told him not to be."

The Army officer suddenly appeared with a glass of lemonade, and he handed it to Mr. Littefield. "We'll need to be leaving in a few minutes, sir. We're expected at the Academy by six for dinner. The Superintendent is having you to the Officers' Club and then…the concert."

"All right with me," Mr. Littlefield replied. The officer nodded politely and walked back to the others as the old man raised the glass of gray lemonade to his thin lips. His hand shook, and a large slice of lemon bobbed against his mouth as he took a long sip. "That's good," he sighed. After a moment, he looked up at April. "This is *your* home?"

"Yes."

He smiled at her. "You know…you're a pretty young thing." She smiled in embarrassment and looked at me. The old man looked at me, now, with a broad smile. "I bet you tell her that all the time, right son?"

"I do. I tell her that…all the time." April slapped my arm.

He cocked his head in a conspiratorial nod. "Better finish up…I guess." He took another sip of lemonade, and placed the glass down on the seat next to him. April knelt again to listen. "This runaway stayed with us for a month. He was sick the first week. He'd been tryin' to make Canada, which is only 'bout ninety miles from Blue Hill…and he'd come all the way up from Geor-gia…travellin' mostly at night…most o' the way hidden below bales o' cotton on river barges…eatin' maybe twice a week. Once he started feelin' bet-ter…he'd get up each mornin' to read from our Bible. He said he'd been a house servant on a big plantation near Savanna…and was able to read books in that house from time to time. He was taught to read and write as a boy by the family that owned him. He knew Shakespeare and Homer and I don't know what all else. I'd head out to school each day, but keep quiet about things, you see…b'cause…even then, there was *some* folks might inform the authorities…'cause o' the law and all…and the bounties they could collect on runaways…or for just turnin' *you* in for harborin' one. Each afternoon, I'd come back from school…and we'd all read in the house together after supper. I'd show him how my readin' was from one of my schoolbooks…and he'd have me read out loud from the newspaper, too. He told us stories from the books he knew…and stories 'bout his people who come here in chains…in the bot-tom o' boats, from West Africa. Then, late one afternoon…it was real quiet in the house when I got home. I saw Mother sittin' at the table…knittin'. She was…somber. It was almost dark outside…but she hadn't even lit a lamp, yet. I asked her where Will was…that was his name. She said he'd had to get on…leave for Canada…and I'd just barely missed him. It was too dangerous for him to stay any longer, she said. Then…she gave me a long letter he'd left me. It said how he was sorry he had to leave so suddenly…but would never forget us…Mother and me. He told me to take care o' Mother, and keep up with readin'…and he said God would bless us. I guess he was right about that, but…I never saw my mother so sad as that day."

"*That's* why you went to the war," April said. Mr. Littlefield smiled at her.

"Did he make it to Canada?" I asked.

"Don't know, son. I *believe* he did…"

"All right, that's enough," grumbled the Army officer, standing very close behind the old man again. "We really do have to get back to The Point, sir."

Mr. Littlefield paid no attention. He was staring down at April. "You feelin' all right, honey?"

"I don't know," she gasped. "I just…feel…dizzy." She was breathing rapidly. "Maybe it's the heat."

I knelt down and put my hand on her back. She was sweating again, and very hot. "You don't feel right," I said.

She turned to look at me, but didn't answer. Instead, she smiled briefly. Then, her face hardened in a glazed stare, and her eyes widened, as she slumped on the grass at the old man's feet.

The officer helped me put her down on the soft grass. I kept her head raised, and I asked a waiter to get her parents and call for a doctor. I said her name but she didn't respond. Mr. Littlefield seemed shocked.

"Let me try first aid, son," said the officer.

Suddenly, I heard Mr. Stannard's voice in the crowd that had gathered around us. "Move away…everyone…*please.*" The officer immediately stood and walked behind Mr. Littlefield's chair. I laid April's head down gently on the grass, and got up, as her father and another man pushed through and knelt down beside her. Mr. Stannard put his hand on his daughter's forehead. "This is Doctor Simon," he said, referring to the other man. The doctor reached into his pocket and pulled out a white, ammonia capsule, which he cracked open and waved under April's nose. She groaned.

Mrs. Stannard arrived, and knelt down next to her husband. "Is she all right?"

"I think so," he said.

"Oh, Dear, please wake up," said Mrs. Stannard.

"Richard's got her coming 'round," he assured her.

"Let's see if we can get her up," the doctor said. I stepped forward to help, but Mr. Stannard moved on his knees, putting his body between his daughter and me.

"I'll help you, Dick." He reached down and slid one hand under April's back. "You take her on one side; I'll take the other." She seemed vaguely aware of what was happening but her knees wobbled as the men struggled to get her up. "Put your arms on our shoulders," her father said.

She tried, but couldn't get her arms high enough, and finally gave up.

"Let's just get her inside, Charles," said the doctor.

"Yes, Dick."

They lifted April off her feet and cradled her in their arms. Quickly, they moved through the parting crowd with Mrs. Stannard following them.

I glanced again at Mr. Littlefield and he nodded to me with his hat in his hands. Then, I followed the Stannards and Dr. Simon, as they skirted the tent and hurried across the lawn toward the house. They hustled her up the patio steps, and quickly to the ballroom doors, where Jennings stood with a grave expression. I bounded up the steps as the men disappeared with April into the ballroom. Mrs. Stannard paused to say something to Jennings, before following them. I hurried across the patio and stepped inside. As my eyes adjusted, I could see Jennings off to my left, but the Stannards and Doctor Simon and April were already gone.

"How is Miss?" asked the Stannards' chef, who stood near Jennings, shaking his head. "She must eat better…this girl," he grumbled.

"I'm to call the guests in…if you're ready," Jennings replied. Then, he stepped out onto the patio where scores of guests stood, peering through the open doors, murmuring to one another. I could see many more guests standing on the lawn, curious to know exactly what had happened and why it was that the band had suddenly stopped. "Dinner is served…ladies and gentlemen," Jennings announced. And after a polite hesitation, masses of guests moved toward the house.

I retreated to a spot near a large, latticed window. The lawn was covered in shadows, now, and the white canvas tent was an immense gray thing, somehow out of place, as if a cloud had fallen from the sky. People filed in and formed a line along the banquet table, picking up plates and silver, and moving forward from one chafing dish to the next, at each of which a black serving man stood at attention. As some guests began heading back outside with filled dinner plates, more people entered and got on line. The party resumed in a subdued way. The swing band played a moody, semi-classical piece, and the afternoon continued its slow fade as I waited in the darkening ballroom.

Some time later, Jennings broke into my distraction. "Would you care for something to eat?"

I turned from the window. "Thank you…Jennings…I couldn't…"

"I could have a plate made up for you, and brought over…we could find you a quiet place in the study."

I shook my head. He nodded, and walked back to the banquet table, as a house servant began turning on bulbs in four large chandeliers. Suddenly, an electric twilight filled the ballroom and I remembered to look at my watch. I was shocked to see it was past five o'clock.

Ten minutes later, Charles Stannard emerged from the shadows of the front hallway. He saw me standing alone near the window, and hurried across the dance floor. "Doctor Simon says she's fine…for now," he confided, when he reached me. "She's entirely conscious, a bit embarrassed, I think. She wanted me to tell you that she's all right."

"Does the doctor know what happened?"

"He's not sure…she fainted from the heat, he thinks, or exhaustion. He asked her when she'd eaten last…she couldn't recall taking a thing all day." He paused and rubbed his chin hard with his fingers. "On the other hand…she may be coming down with a…spring flu. Her temperature is elevated slightly. But, no cause for alarm…her mother is with her. Dick…Doctor Simon that is…may want her at the hospital tomorrow…"

"*The hospital?*"

"For tests…she'll be fine tonight, he says. He'll see how she feels after a good night's sleep. There'll be a nurse with her."

"May I call tomorrow…to see how she is?"

"Of course." He glanced at his watch. "Your parents will be expecting you. Do you need a lift home?"

"That would be kind of you, sir…"

"Not at all."

"You're sure there's nothing I can do to help?"

"I think we're set, Tom. You go ahead out front…wait for Lawrence. He'll bring the car around." He put his hand on my shoulder. "Don't forget our little talk."

"No, sir."

Then, as he slipped into a nearby study to call the chauffeur, I noticed April's friends standing together across the ballroom. They'd been watching Mr. Stannard speak with me, and now, Martha Bradley hurried over.

"Tom, how is she? What did her father say?"

"She fainted…they don't know exactly why…"

"The doctor is with her?"

"Yes. He told them it may be flu…or the heat…"

There was a skeptical look in her eyes. "She hasn't eaten all day, right?"

I was surprised. "That's what she told them."

Martha exhaled a forceful sigh, and stared at the floor for a moment. Then, she looked at me again in a challenging way. "Are you going to see her?"

"They're sending me home, now. I'm s'posed to call tomorrow. I guess I'll see her then…unless the doctor puts her in the hospital…"

Martha stared angrily. "Does that sound like the flu to you?"

"Well…"

Suddenly, she gripped my forearm and squeezed it tightly. "Listen to me. Don't let them…" She paused.

"Don't let them what?"

"She loves you, you know." Her eyes gazed fiercely into mine. "If *you* love *her*…don't lose track of her *now*."

"What does *that* mean?" I said.

But she pressed her lips together tightly and released my arm. Then, she turned on her heels and walked back to the others.

I hurried through the front hallway past the staircase that led to the upper floors. I continued out through the dark vestibule, and past the marble maiden staring into trickling water. I opened the front door and stepped out onto the portico to wait for the car. The door closed firmly behind me and I glanced at my watch. It was five thirty.

As I waited, I glanced across the property and noticed a black couple coming toward the house from the field where the cars were parked. A small crowd, including some of the parking lot boys, surrounded them. The man walked with a pigeon-toed gait and wore a milk-white shirt with a blue tie, and elegantly pressed camel-tan slacks. The woman seemed to glide next to him in her crème-white, spring dress. They looked like a couple in a magazine advertisement for expensively casual, California fashions.

Then, as they came closer, I understood the excitement. It was Jackie Robinson and his wife, Rachel. They came along the driveway near the house, and Robinson noticed me watching from the top step of the portico. He waved to me. "Hello, there!" I waved back, and tried to smile politely. Mrs. Robinson smiled. They were such an attractive couple, vibrant and alive, moving with unconscious grace. Suddenly, Robinson paused. "Any Dodger fans here, today?" The small crowd broke into laughter, and his wife smiled her pretty smile.

"Not sure how many, Mr. Robinson," I said, raising my hand. "*One*...at least!"

"Good for *you*, son...if there *are* more, we'll find 'em...otherwise...we'll just have to convert some Yankee fans, I guess!" The crowd laughed again.

Then, he said something to his wife, who nodded as they moved past me, followed by the others. Moments later, I heard polite applause from the party guests on the lawn, and it occurred to me that these were the only black people I'd seen here today—not counting the waiters.

The Stannards' forest green Bentley pulled slowly up in front of the house and I ran down the steps to meet it. The chauffeur got out and opened the rear door.

"Hello, Lawrence."

"Sir."

He waited for me to get in, and then closed my door, and got behind the wheel again. We were separated by a mahogany partition that went from the gray carpeting to the gray cashmere roof lining, but I could see him and most of the windshield through a wide, open window in the partition. He shifted into gear, and started down the long black driveway toward the entrance of the estate. I leaned back against the leather seat and stretched my feet out. I felt nervous and tired.

"Are you comfortable, sir...with the air conditioning?"

"It's all right, Lawrence. I like the cold."

I closed my eyes and let the motion of the car take over. After ten minutes, I felt us slowing down and I opened my eyes again. We'd reached the west entrance of the bridge, and Lawrence was steering the Bentley into the east-bound toll barrier. There were almost no other cars heading in our direction, but westbound traffic was jammed from one end of the bridge to the other.

"All going to the concert, I imagine," said Lawrence.

"How will you ever get back?"

"Oh, I'll get through."

He stopped in the gate, and his window slid down with an electric hum. The guard leaned out and Lawrence flashed him a badge on the inside flap of his wallet. When the guard saw it, he nodded and waved us on. I leaned back again and closed my eyes. In ten minutes, I'd be home. I tried to get myself ready, but I couldn't stop thinking about the look on Martha Bradley's face.

CHAPTER 6

I saw only two cars parked near the house. Their familiar shapes glowed in the porch light. Beyond the river, a fiery orange sunset covered the bluffs and the silver shadow of an almost full moon was ascending in the southeast, as the cool mountain air of evening settled in.

Down near the magnolias, three men talked in whispery voices. But another voice drew me along the crest of the hill behind the house until finally, standing under the bright kitchen windows, I realized it was Mother's radio. An announcer was earnestly muttering about the wonders of Lucky Strike cigarettes.

Suddenly, my mother appeared in one of the screened window frames. A moment later, Hazel Spencer came and stood near her.

"What will you do with all this food, Mary?"

My mother looked down in grim concentration. "I wish you'd take some…"

"Of course we will. It's just…there's so *much*, child…"

My mother slowly nodded her head.

"And now…a lovely recording Frank Sinatra made on August Eleventh…Nineteen Forty-seven…in Hollywood. You'll remember this…"

A lilting flute melody piped from the radio and Mother stopped to listen, gazing through the window above my head.

> *It's not the pale moon that excites me…*
> *That thrills and delights me…oh no…*
> *It's just the nearness of you…*

She was lost in the music as she stared at the horizon unaware of Hazel's troubled glances.

> *It isn't your sweet conversation...*
> *That brings this sensation...oh no...*

I turned away from the house and hurried down the slope as the song drifted in the air.

> *It's just...the nearness...of you...*

The magnolias were silent shadows in the dusk. Father, Arthur and Grandfather Hank sat more or less together beneath them, but stared in different directions.

Father noticed me first. "How was *your* day?"

Surveying the empty chairs along the hillside, and then slumping into one, I answered with a loud sigh. "Strange." But he smiled, oddly, as if he hadn't really heard me.

Suddenly, Grandfather snorted. "Strange is it? Ya' shoulda been *here*."

"*Pop*," my father said.

"Dad...where *is* everybody?"

"The Brents went back out to Long Island," he said. "They had a dinner engagement at their golf club. Edith Neumann was here this afternoon...you just missed the Wilsons. Grandma Gannon went to lie down...she wasn't feeling well."

"It's not what the boy meant."

Father ignored Grandfather. "Your mother and Mrs. Spencer are doing a few things in the house. They'll be down..."

"Where's Liz?" I said.

"She and Laureen went in to get sweaters," Arthur interjected. "Your little brother and sister, too...it's chilly now the sun's gone down."

"Didn't anyone one *else* come?" I said.

My father turned away and stared into the valley, but Arthur looked at me with a mournful expression and silently shook his head.

And so, I sat with them in their silence, as the distant sunset faded and bright stars emerged in the vast spaces between pale clouds, like moths on a dark screen.

Eventually, there were female voices on the crest of the hill. I looked back toward the house and saw Mother, Hazel, Liz and Laureen coming down together, chatting softly, the kitchen windows glowing behind them. Liz held

David's hand and Laureen held Mary's. Mother carried a large blanket folded in her arms. The children and the girls wore thick sweaters and sweatshirts. Mother had one of Father's khaki zipper-jackets over her dress, and Hazel's heavy suit was now perfect for the evening chill.

I glanced at my father watching my mother and his other children coming down to meet us, and I felt a cold-hearted anger that nothing could suppress.

Mother bent over and kissed Father on the lips. Then she stepped away and unfurled the blanket, allowing it to settle on the grass. As Liz and Laureen sat down quickly on the blanket with David and Mary, Arthur pulled an empty chair up for Hazel.

Mother turned and looked at Father. "When does the show start?"

He smiled weakly. "Any minute, I guess." I could see them staring at each other in the gathering darkness. Then, he roused himself from his chair, kissed her on the cheek, and walked down the slope a short distance. He looked west and glanced at his watch. "I've got seven forty-five, Tom; what have *you* got?"

"Same."

"Good," he answered. "Everyone see those large buildings on the cliffs, over there?"

"Yeah," David muttered. Liz and Laureen giggled and Mary fidgeted.

"We should hear music, soon, from the parade ground on the other side of those buildings. I'm sure we'll get a great view of the fireworks, too…just watch the sky over there."

Father stared west for another moment before coming back and grabbing a chair, which he placed next to Mother and me. When he sat down, she reached for his hand and held it in her lap.

Grandfather Hank had fallen asleep in a chair near the picnic table, and he began to snore. Suddenly, everyone laughed.

At a few minutes before eight, the US Army orchestra started tuning up. We could hear them astoundingly well from our perch across the valley. Then, after a brief silence, the concert began with Dvorak's symphony, *From the New World*. And as the music filled the valley and drifted with the winding river, peaceful night descended on our distant slope.

An hour later, after the symphony and a brief intermission, the orchestra changed tempo with a string of military marches and old waltz melodies, and the adults had a contest to see who could name each tune first. But no one could beat Arthur; he named every new song after a note or two.

When the concert ended just before ten, the sky was an ocean of stars with the moon straight above us. Army searchlights scanned the western sky, and the parade-ground lights glowed on the horizon.

Suddenly, there was an explosion. "Oh, look!" Liz shouted, pointing to a Roman candle falling from its arc like a green shooting star. We laughed and clapped as the roar of the West Point crowd echoed on the water, and another rocket lit the sky and quickly fell in red trail streams. And then, the sky exploded in a storm of red, orange, blue and green. Each new rocket was like a new star born in a spray of light, followed by the sound of its birth.

The show went on for thirty minutes, and the explosions came faster and faster until one final, thunderous burst formed a red, white and blue American flag. We heard applause along the river, now, and cheers from the academy crowd. But the beautiful skyrocket flag couldn't hold together, long; it soon faded in a burnt-out sheet of red.

Finally, the old Army cannons went off one by one along the ridge, ten of them spitting bright orange bursts in smart order, and making an unholy racket.

As the rumbling echo of the last shot faded in the valley, I looked at my watch, reflected in moonlight—ten thirty. Window lights were coming on in the academy buildings, as cadets returned to their rooms, and the bridge down river was already jammed with the lights of east-bound cars. Upriver, an old Gilded Age love song played on someone's antique Victrola, or perhaps it was an orchestra on some village green.

I suddenly thought of Charles Stannard and I turned to tell Father what he'd said to me, earlier. But Father's chair was empty. He'd gotten up, unnoticed, during the fireworks, and had walked down the hillside. Now, I could see him standing below the magnolias, gazing west. And as Arthur rose from his chair and walked down the slope toward him, my father turned and smiled at his friend.

I climbed the stairs with David, and waited, as he stripped to his underwear and slid under his bed covers. When he was settled, only his face was visible against his pillow. He stared at me. "Tom?"

"Yeah, buddy?"

"Nobody came to our party."

"A few people did…"

"Don't people like us no more?"

"*Any more*…listen, Dave…lots of people have Memorial Day parties. So…maybe some of Dad and Mom's friends decided to go to their *other* friends' houses. Ya' know?"

"Dad was real angry, today…"

"Oh, yeah?"

"He had a big argument with Grandpa Hank out in the garage. And he yelled at Mom. Then he took the car out for a drive…you know how he does…when he's *real* mad?"

"You mean *angry*. Why were they arguing?"

"I don't know."

"Did you ask Liz about it?"

"Yeah."

"And what did *she* say?"

"'That they were probably fighting about *you*.'"

"*Me*?"

"About you shoulda been here with *us*…not some other party…"

"Oh. Well…I should have come home earlier…I just got caught up and delayed…anyway,…I bet Liz was sad…about the party being such a bust and all."

"Yeah…"

"All right, then…*you* get to sleep…school tomorrow…"

"Yeah…"

"You want the light left on?"

"Okay." And almost that instant, he was asleep.

I kicked my shoes off, wearily, leaning with one hand against our dresser. I looked once more at my sleeping brother, turned off the bedroom light, and started down to say 'good night' to the Spencers. When I passed Liz's room, the door was closed and I could hear her talking to Laureen inside. At the bottom of the stairs, I found myself in darkness. Grandfather had already gone off to bed, and no one had thought to put the living room lights on. The porch light was off now, too.

Waiting for my eyes to adjust, I realized I could hear Father and Arthur talking softly on the porch just outside the screen of the open front door.

"I'm gonna *dissolve* St. Nicholas Development Corporation," Arthur whispered, urgently. "No arguments."

"Oh, Jesus…don't," Father whispered back, forcefully.

"No. I'm pulling us out. We cut our losses and move on. After what happened today, I can see it isn't worth the fight."

"Arthur…you'll lose thousands of dollars…your partners can sue you. As your attorney…I advise you…"

"If you want to *be* my attorney, Joe…follow my wishes." The two men sat silently for a moment before Arthur continued. "There's a reason people didn't come today. You can't deny it. They're afraid to be associated with you…*with us*…and we're in no position to start some big public fight over this arena, or anything else. Your father-in-law gave it to us straight…that old bastard, Moses, will hold up our housing funds indefinitely…we'll be easy targets for threats and accusations again…I don't care for myself, understand. But *you* can't afford it, and *I* won't be responsible."

"Arthur…what about those people living in broken down buildings on St. Nicholas Avenue…our hopes of *changing* that neighborhood?" There was another silence. "Wait a few days, Arthur."

"For what?"

"Until I get back from Washington, at the end of the week."

"No. I want to call the partners tomorrow morning, and tell them we're getting out…you tell 'em we're gonna compensate 'em for their outlay and their trouble…that we're negotiating with the City. And whatever costs we can't recover, we'll raise…if I have to sell another building to do it. And what the hell you goin' to Washington for?"

"Arthur…I may give a statement…to the Senate Investigations Committee."

"*McCarthy*?"

"Private testimony…with the committee's chief counsel…"

"Cohn."

"Probably…if I do it."

"Why didn't you *tell* me you got subpoenaed?"

"That's the thing, Arthur…*I* called *them*."

Beyond the silent porch, headlights flickered on the highway, and I could hear the faint voices of my mother and Hazel behind the closed kitchen door.

"Joe…"

"I can't go on putting my family through this. Moran's retraction didn't work…that press release of his was so soft, the papers hardly knew what to make of it."

"What more could he do, Joe? You want him to repeat every accusation about us…and dispute them one by one? There's nothing about us that should cause alarm for anyone…and *that's* what his release said. When did you decide this?"

"Today…well…I actually called the Committee a few weeks ago, when I was negotiating with Moran. I guess I didn't trust him to keep his promise. The FBI chief in New York suggested *two years ago* that I should testify…clear myself…of course, I rejected the idea, then. Anyway, the Senate staffers said I could come down and see them Thursday this week, if I had anything for them."

"If you're going down there to have your loyalty put on the record, you better remember something," Arthur said. "They rarely let it go at that. They usually demand you give them something…about somebody else."

"I know…I'm *giving* them a name…"

"You're *what*?"

"Gerry Moran."

"Christ all mighty!"

"Our friend Mr. Moran has a little problem in his *own* past…he was a leading member of the John Reed Club, at Columbia, when he was a student in 'Thirty-six."

"Who *told* you this?"

"My father obtained the information somehow…may have paid for it…I don't know how he got it. I don't want to know. But it's solid. I have Moran's transcripts with the official college seal…an old yearbook with a group photo in it…even a clipping from his college newspaper…"

"This is a dangerous game, Joe. You can't trust McCarthy. He's a drunk…a maniac. His staff people are worse this could all backfire. You're the lawyer, not me…but I believe I'm right in saying…once you give the Committee *any* statement, they can ask you whatever else they want and you *have* to answer, or be in contempt."

"All I can tell them is what I know, which isn't much," Father sighed. "I'm running out of time. McCarthy's just about finished politically…this Army investigation is the end for him. So, while he's still got the microphone, and some influence with the press…and public opinion…I need to act. His committee has press contacts that publish what he tells them to. And by cooperating…I get his staff to put out some better stuff in the papers about me…counteract this cloud over my name. *And*…Moran gets a dose of his own medicine."

"Joe…"

"I warned him. I told him we wouldn't rest until he fixed the damage he's caused us. *You* know how hard I tried in the courts…I couldn't get a judge to hear our case for two years…well, enough."

"Listen. If you want press clippings, we'll hire a PR man, Joe, but *not now*. For Christ sake, man, the last thing *you* need is your name in the paper again, connected with *this* sort o' thing. Give it a rest for a while. Maybe later, we'll have somebody go to the liberal papers for us."

"Who? The *Times*? The *Post*? They won't do anything about this. They can't."

"Joe, they *have*...I can show you the clippings from the theater project..."

"I mean *since* the accusations..."

"They did that, too...don't you remember? But it's *old news* for them, now, Joe..."

"It didn't seem like old news today. No...even the liberal papers have been running scared...I can't wait any longer for them to grow their balls back."

"You want to know who's running scared? Roy Cohn. You don't need him. I've been hearing whispers around New York...he's looking to bale out on McCarthy. He's trying to start a private law practice in Manhattan..."

"What sort of clients?"

"Corporations...investors...real estate developers...the usual thing. Cohn sees the end coming, and McCarthy self-destructing...*everybody* sees it Joe. Why don't you just give this information to the FBI, and let *them* do the dirty work? Better yet, let your father give it to them."

"That won't clear *my name* with the public, Arthur."

I could hear Arthur sigh. He sounded frustrated and angry. "Ya' know, Joe...in a few years, people are gonna look back on all this witch-hunting and scratch their heads...they won't be able to figure out what the fuss was. Our kids don't understand it, even now. Don't give in to creeps like this, and beg them for your name. I'm telling you, these men have nearly ruined the coun-try...and *that's* what people are gonna remember...that...and the names of whoever cooperated with them. Don't do it, Joe."

"Arthur...why are we in business? To do something about the way citizens are treated when they have no resources or powerful friends."

"Of course, but...I still say we wait..."

"For things to change by themselves? They won't. We have to *make* the changes."

"Joe. It matters what we do in this world...I mean, what *methods* we use to get along. Success...failure...*they* don't make the man. It won't matter if you succeed by this committee's rules Joe, because they're corrupt. No matter what happens...you cooperate with 'em, you've lost..."

"No…I've put it off too long, already. My family can't afford this price they're paying for my…*integrity*." There was a long silence again. "Besides, if we walk from St. Nicholas Avenue now, *that'll* be our reputation. Then…it's just that easy for another bunch of thugs to run us off the next project. *Think* about *that* Arthur."

"It's getting late, Joe. I ought to be heading home…I'll go see about Hazel and Laureen…"

"You're welcome to stay the night…"

"Thanks just the same, Joe. We'll be going."

My eyes opened, suddenly. Moonlight shone through my bedroom window. A speeding train clattered along the river. Throwing off the bed covers and sitting up, I thought about April. I held my watch up to the moonlight. It was four in the morning.

I got up and went to the window. Through the screen, I could see the moon far out in the western sky, and its bright light shining over the river onto our hillside behind the house.

As I breathed in the fresh air, I suddenly noticed a man standing near the tree line above the riverbank. It was Father. He stood very still, with his back to the house, watching the river through the trees for several minutes. Finally, his arms moved out to each side, and I could see that he was holding his white robe open. The robe fell to the ground and he stood a moment longer, naked, in the moonlight at the bottom of the lawn. Then, he walked down toward the river.

CHAPTER 7

❀

I could hear my father's voice in waves of receding sleep. A door slammed somewhere, and I was awake. I sat up in bed and felt a warm gust of air through the open window. I thought of April and checked the time—it was five to seven, and I needed to catch the Highland Bus Company's morning express in an hour.

Briefly wondering if I'd imagined seeing my father walk toward the river during the night, I crept to the bedroom door, allowing David a few moments more of his own dreams. But as I closed the door behind me, and started quietly down the hall to the bathroom, Grandfather Hank's edgy voice came up the stairwell from the living room.

"Yer' gonna forget this deal now, eh?"

"Arthur wants to pull out," Father replied.

"Makin' sense for once. You tell the committee…it'll show good faith."

"Wait. I thought the deal was…give a statement about this man…"

"Sure, but…"

"But nothing!"

"Son, you been down for two years already…you need ta' start makin' some money, with people who want ta' do *business*…not this nonsense you're involved in. Ya' folla?"

My father laughed sarcastically. "*What people*…the ones we invited yesterday?"

"That's right! We been hurt enough…associatin' with this colored man. Don't ya' *see* that, Joe?"

"All I see is a friend, Pop…to me, and my family. And I don't know what you're so resentful of…I'm just trying to make a success out of doing a few good things…"

"'Course *you'd know* about success!" Grandfather scoffed. "*You* take responsibility for changin' the world, for Chrissake. It ain't that *easy* bein' a success. If it was…everybody'd *be* one."

"Well," my father sighed. "I know it flatters people to think their accomplishments are unique…"

"*What?*"

"*Everybody* needs help, from time to time, Pop…*nobody* succeeds alone! What did *you* find when you got here…open arms? I don't think so! You found you didn't speak the right way, or go to the right church. Your *brother* got you a job. Then, you caught a wave…and rode it in…played the market…got out in time…with skill and luck. But the *fact* is you were *helped*…the whole way…*your brokerage* took the risks…not you. *You* invested *their* money. Now…*you* don't wanna make room for people working *their* way up? Who d'you think you *are?*"

"I made somethin' o' myself…that's who."

"Sure…fine…you feel no responsibility   no gratitude?"

"To what? Somethin' wrong with bein' rich, now?"

"No! I'd like to see *more rich people*…all the *advertising* we do for it."

"Agh!! You wanna just *give* it away…to some coloreds and spics."

"Pop," my father sighed. "We're investors, looking for a profit like *any* businessmen. You're saying it doesn't count if we're not doing it for the right people."

"No! I'm sayin' nobody ever gave *me* a goddamn thing I didn't earn! My brother Mike hadn't got me that job…I'd of got one otherwise. These other friends o' yours can't do the same…too bad. An' I don't want to talk about this no more. See? Can't do no more for ya'. Keep talkin' this stuff; don't even bother about that committee. And this Spencer…he's no friend, either. He's the reason you're *in* trouble!"

A door slammed again, and then there was silence. My hand shook, gripping the hallway banister. Suddenly, I heard Liz's bedroom door open. I looked down and watched her come out onto the second floor landing in her nightgown. She stood there for a moment, listening in the silent stairwell, and then she turned and went back to her room.

I knotted my tie and pulled on my blue blazer with the red and gold crest of St. Paul's School on the left breast pocket—a book and golden torch, and a Latin motto: *Amor Cognito Vincit Omnia.* "Love of knowledge surpasses all."

With my leather school bag under one arm, I went to David's bedside and shook him by the shoulder. His body jerked. Then, he rolled over on his back; his eyes popped open.

"Time for school, buddy," I said.

"Is somebody yelling?"

"Everything's fine. Just get up. Okay?"

"*Awwww-right.*" He sighed and kicked his legs in frustration under the covers, and I knew he wouldn't fall asleep again.

When I got to the living room, Liz was sitting near the windows in her gray skirt and red blazer, waiting for her girlfriends to pick her up for the 10-mile ride to The Mount. She ignored me, so I walked across the room and stood at the windows, next to her chair. I saw that our grandparents' Ford was gone. I looked at my watch; it was ten minutes till eight.

"You heard them this morning?" I said. But she stared down at the carpeting, and wouldn't answer. "Liz, talk to me."

"You don't care," she muttered.

"What?"

"*You* weren't here, yesterday."

"Oh," I sighed.

"You didn't have to watch them…standing around with egg on their faces."

"All right…so I should've *been* here." I paused. "None of *your* friends came?"

She glanced out the window again. "They had things to do…with *their* families. Edith came for a while…thank god. I had *her* to talk to…and the Wilsons…"

"Look…someone's gotta get through to him. I mean…what does he think…going to that committee?"

She kept staring out the window until, finally, she spoke in a sad, dull voice. "He doesn't know *what else* to do…"

"Well, going down *there* isn't the answer."

"So *tell* him…"

"I *will*…a lot of good it'll do."

"Then don't."

"He got *himself* into this…now he's only making it worse," I muttered.

Liz sounded shocked. "You blame *him* for this?"

"That's *not* what I'm saying," I answered, angrily. "I'm just saying...why can't we live a normal life...like other people?" She sighed, deeply angry herself, now. "Can't he just do business straight...*for once*?" I said. "Always gotta be some *cause* attached to it? Lemme tell you something...*other* people do good things, and don't need to attract this bullshit attention to themselves."

She stood up, suddenly, as a car pulled into the driveway. She picked up her bag and walked quickly to the front door, but then paused to glance back at me. "What's happened to you, Tom?"

As the screen door slammed, I watched her hurry down the porch steps and get into the car with her friends. And as the car drove away, I was more confused than ever.

I looked at my watch—two minutes before eight. Suddenly, I heard my father's voice. "What's up, Tom?"

I turned from the window and saw him standing at the edge of the living room. The loose ends of his maroon tie hung from his open shirt collar, and he stared pensively.

"Nothing," I replied. "I was just going to school."

"Well, I'm driving to the city...let me drop you on the way."

"Oh...I was planning to take..." I heard the screech of brakes on the highway—my bus, slowing down just enough for the driver to see that I wasn't waiting. I heard him downshift and drive on. Now, I had no choice. "Sure...all right."

"Five minutes," he said, disappearing down the hall.

I pushed through the screen door, descended the porch steps, and walked around to the garage, a separate structure the size of a small barn on the south side of the house. As I swung its big door open, the hinges squeaked in the quiet morning air.

I edged inside, opened the passenger door of the Buick, and climbed in to wait. I glanced at Mother's grass-cutting tractor, parked near the workbench built into the wall on my right. On top of the workbench there were cans of motor oil and gasoline and house paint, and glass jars filled with nails and screws. Along the wall to my left, there were shovels, hoes, rakes, hammers and saws dangling from hooks. Suddenly, I remembered the first days and months of our move here.

Snowdrifts covered the landscape the day we arrived. Ice crystals hung along the edge of the upper roof and from the thin, bare branches of surrounding trees. And we quickly discovered how much work the old place needed.

During the first month, Mother fixed a hole in the roof and two trouble-some toilets, and then repainted every room. And the third floor, which had been built more or less as an attic space, was turned into a bedroom for David and me.

By the middle of March, the sun rose on a higher arc, and receding snow revealed the first green coming through wet, brown earth. That's when she bought the tractor from a local farmer and connected a grass cutter with giant blades to the back of it. Throughout the spring, we helped bale and haul away the wild grass her tractor mowed as she extended the small back lawn, and cleared woodland down to the tree line above the river. In doing this, she uncovered two wild magnolia trees hidden in the dense overgrowth. She was amazed. "Have these always been here…all these years, and we never knew it?"

We helped her plant seed for new grass, and to dig flowerbeds around the base of the house. And as she pushed the forest away, she discovered wild American blueberry patches on the north and south sides of the property. She stopped, then, and let the thick underbrush stay thick from the blueberries to the forest for acres on each side.

Father began taking the train into New York most days, to work for Arthur, who'd given him an office in one of his buildings on upper Broadway, because Father had been forced to break the lease on Carroll Street.

Old friends from Park Slope disappeared so completely from our lives, then, that it seemed as if we'd never known them. Even certain family members, like Donald and Grace Gannon, began to take care about how and when they were seen with us. But Mother's parents never stopped inviting us to Southampton, where Phillip Brent and Father would play golf, while Mother and Grand-mother Alice took us children down to the ocean beach below their house.

One rainy Saturday in May, that year, Mother and Father put on their best suits for a meeting with the FBI bureau chief in Manhattan. Father had talked with him several times already, but on this rainy morning our parents seemed strangely hopeful.

While they were gone, we began running around in the wet grass behind the house in our bathing suits. At some point, we noticed the immense pile of mowed grass near the house and started hurling ourselves into it, laughing wildly. The sweet, rotten smell of hay filled the air and clung to our bodies.

We pushed it higher, climbing the back stairs from the kitchen to the second floor landing, into Liz's bedroom and out her window onto the slick, black roof. We slid down the shingles on our behinds, and flew off the ledge, feeling airborne for moments before landing hard in the dank hay-pile. We made this trip again and again, tracking the grass and grass-smell with us, every step of the way, forgetting time in the ceaseless rain.

Our parents returned in the late afternoon, and Father seemed dumbstruck as he came upon his children, sprawled together on the back lawn. The neat pile of hay was gone, but its brownish tufts and clods were strewn everywhere. Staring at us, briefly, he turned and went inside the house without a word. But Mother seethed.

"I do not understand how a boy and girl of your intelligence could be so self-indulgent," she said, sternly, to Liz and me, after putting David and Mary into baths. "This world will *not* fall at your feet, you know…or be amused by your fancies…it's time you grew up. And don't *ever* endanger your brother and sister like this again…do you understand me?" Liz and I nodded. We'd never seen her this angry. "Put them to bed, when they've finished their baths." Then, she turned on her heel and disappeared behind the closed door of the bedroom, where Father had gone. And as Liz and I glanced at each other we knew, without being told, that there would be no further trips to New York to see the FBI.

At eight-fifteen, I looked through the rear window of the Buick, wondering what was keeping him. Facing forward again, I noticed the ladder rope hanging from the loft, where Mother had stored the extra furniture, lamps and carpets we'd brought from Brooklyn.

And in the corner beyond the left headlight, I saw Father's old golf clubs—the ones he'd used as a kid. Mother had gotten him a new set when they'd joined the Highland Country Club, but her best efforts to convince him to discard the old ones had gotten them only as far as this dusty corner. I could see moth holes in the blue, woolen head covers, as light from the rising sun grew stronger against a nearby window. And in the light, I saw a spider web between the clubs and the dusty window frame, and the husks of dead moths caught in the silky pattern.

I finally heard voices. My parents were standing together, just behind the car, now. Father was dressed in his dark blue suit and he carried a bag in each hand. Mother clutched the lapels of her white cotton bathrobe at her chest. Father said something that I couldn't quite hear.

Mother smiled weakly and responded. "So *this* is why we've sacrificed for two years…for you to go do *this*?"

He frowned at her and kissed her on the forehead. She stared at him for a moment, as if trying to see inside him. Then, she reached up and touched his cheek. Suddenly, they kissed again on the lips, and I turned away.

A moment later, Father came to the driver's side and opened the door. He hefted a small suitcase and his business briefcase into the rear seat. He removed his suit jacket and hung it by its collar loop from the little hook in the door-frame. Then he jumped in, started the engine and backed us out.

Mother waited near the garage door, and raised her hand in a tentative wave, as we made our turn toward the driveway. I saw her forced smile, but Father was looking straight ahead now, not at her. We reached the end of the driveway and turned south.

"So, Tom," he said. "Father Stevens told us about the Yale seminar." I nodded. "I think we'll contribute to his fund…"

"He's raising money?" I said.

He nodded. "Participating schools support the program *every* year," he said, "whether or not they have a student attending…"

"Oh," I said. "He mentioned something about a prize…"

"That's a scholarship, covering tuition and accommodations…it *all* has to be funded."

"Who runs this thing?"

"Some prep schools in New England started it…twenty-five years ago, I guess. Each school has one member on a board of trustees…they run everything. Father Stevens said he heard about when *he* was at Yale."

"Hhmm," I muttered, dispassionately, staring briefly out my side window.

"It's a peculiar arrangement," he added. "Most public schools can't participate, because of the funding requirement. The better private schools seem to have it to themselves…more or less." He paused, as if waiting for me to say something, but I stared straight ahead at the highway. We'd be reaching the bridge soon. "The curriculum is great, though…and it's a real opportunity for someone with your aptitude in history…literature." He paused again. "I'm assuming you'd apply."

"I guess."

"You don't sound too excited…"

"No…it's fine…"

"You know, Tom…you don't have to keep things so bottled up…*tell* me what's bothering you…it won't surprise me…I'm a big boy…so are *you*. We just don't live in a perfect world, and we don't make decisions based on what's perfect. We need to see what's good, and what's not so good, and go on from there. Now, St. Paul's is a good school…it has faults…there just aren't any *per-fect* ones."

"Dad…"

"Your mother and I think it's important that you and Liz have a…social connection…with *other* serious young people."

"We *know* that, Dad. We…appreciate…" I suddenly realized we'd driven past the bridge entrance and were heading south on Route 6, a winding section of highway that led down to the City of Peekskill. I looked at my watch; it was past eight-thirty. "You missed the turn!"

"I thought we'd take some time, this morning," he said, calmly. "If they give you any trouble at school…have them call me."

I sighed with obvious annoyance, but he was impassive at the wheel.

Fifteen minutes later, we reached the base of the mountain, where the highway moved across marshland dotted with scrub oaks and littered with refuse thrown from cars. Six tall factory smokestacks appeared in the haze above the old city a few miles ahead. A half-century earlier, those factories processed coal that was barged out to Manhattan, or to the iron mills in Troy and Schenectady. During the 1930s, the Hudson Electric Company retrofitted them as power generators, which meant fewer jobs for local citizens, but no less coal burning.

We continued south. Cheap row houses began appearing along the roadside. Built in the 1880s by the first factory owners, for their Irish and Negro laborers, they were now derelict buildings—an embarrassment to the local gentry. Poor blacks and a few whites still lived there, subsisting on federal home relief; and fires, not always of discernible cause, broke out often.

One mile outside the city limits, the highway forked. A left turn on Route 6 would take us into the downtown business district, but Father followed Route 9 south, across the wetlands and out toward the river along a small, tidal inlet called Lents Cove.

He turned off the highway and pulled into a cinder-covered area on a secluded point, where sightseers sometimes parked, and high school kids came at night to drink and make out. Somewhere nearby, I knew, Benedict Arnold's barque met a British sloop, and he made his narrow escape from George Washington's pursuing soldiers.

Father turned off the engine. Across the river, we could see Tomkins Cove and the mothballed fleet of liberty ships anchored there, about 200 oil tankers, cargo vessels, and troop carriers, left over from World War II. The U.S. Merchant Marines were responsible for guarding the fleet, and from time to time, you'd see them patrolling the cove.

Suddenly, Father confronted me. "I take it…you overheard your grandfather and me, this morning."

"I heard what you told Arthur last night, too," I replied. "On the porch."

"So, *this* is what's bothering you."

"Shouldn't it?"

"Yes," he said, in a voice that was strangely calm, almost relieved. "It should." He was silent for a while, and then pointed out toward the fleet. "D'you see that extra large ship there…in the center of the cove?" I looked, but didn't answer. "It's an old troop carrier…like the one I shipped out on in 'Forty-two." He paused and sighed. "Just kids…all of us…not much older than you and Liz. The oldest guy with us was about thirty." He paused again, contemplating some distant thought. "Career Army…not a Marine, like the rest of us…a *colored* man." He smiled. "The armed forces were still *segregated* then, and…it was a surprise…finding myself bunked beneath this guy…Charlie Peters…from California. But we got very friendly on our way out to Guadalcanal. We'd lie in our bunks most days, and shoot the breeze…it's funny what men tell each other, when they've got nothing else to do."

"I don't get it," I said. "What's this all about?"

Father kept on, as if he hadn't heard me. "You see…he happened to be in San Diego…on leave…when the Japanese hit Pearl Harbor. They announced over the radio that anyone in uniform should report immediately to the nearest installation…so Charlie stayed in San Diego, and got assigned to a cargo ship. The following June, my division arrived from South Carolina and they put us on *that* ship…the Navy'd turned it into a troop carrier. Charlie was still waiting for his orders to rejoin an all-Negro Army division that was headed for England. But somehow, his paperwork got fouled up…when we sailed, Charlie was still on board."

I shook my head in disbelief. "That sounds pretty stupid."

Father laughed bitterly. "They couldn't even stop to let him off at Pearl, because they were still digging out the harbor. When we got to Guadalcanal…the brass roused him off with everyone else. Before we knew it, we were making our approach to the beach in those god-awful LSTs. It was odd…no resistance from shore…no strafing…machinegun fire…nothing. We learned, later, that the Japanese knew we were coming for weeks, and pulled back…dug in. They had…I don't know…ten…maybe twenty thousand men in the countryside…around the airstrip…which, we were supposed to take."

"Dad…why are you *telling* me this?"

But he simply continued. "Charlie was with *my* group…maybe a hundred men…we got off the LSTs…waded in…proceeded across the beach into a line of palm trees…and settled in for the night…about a hundred yards from the water. It was about six o'clock. We put point men out…front and back…especially on the beach, to make sure the enemy didn't sneak up our rear. Just ahead of us was an open field…and there were Japanese troops sitting in a palm forest on the other side of it…about seventy-five yards away. They'd been watching us the whole time, and once the sun went down…they started firing…rifles at first…then grenade launchers…mortar. We were sitting ducks."

"You couldn't pull back to the beach?"

He smiled wearily. "Too wide open…besides, the Marines don't pull back, Tom. There was a bright moon, too, so we couldn't easily make it across the field. The problem was, we didn't have mortars or grenade launchers of our own…we were supposed to, but the stuff hadn't come in with us. We shouldn't have arrived so late in the day, either…it was all screwed up." He stopped talking and thought about something for a moment. "The Japanese kept at us…we had bullets ripping through the brush…grenades falling in and exploding…mortar shells…trees falling on us. It was chaos…our platoon leader, a lieutenant from Virginia…had been hit in the head…he was gone. Our top sergeant took a machine gun burst in the stomach, and was cut in half…literally…two pieces of him, lying in the brush ten feet apart. So finally, a group of us tried to advance across the field, carrying hand grenades and a few of those big Browning Automatic Rifles. The idea was to get as close to the palm forest as we could…do some damage…maybe push them back a little, or make them lay off for a while. There were about sixty of us…we left a few guys behind with the wounded and told them to radio for help. The Japanese spotted us about halfway across…or maybe they saw us the whole time and just waited…who knows? Anyway they opened fire…caught us in the field…it was worse than where we'd started. People were being hit…but we had no choice…*had* to keep crawling forward. We thought we were dead already, anyway. We crawled toward the enemy line, with no idea how many there were in that palm forest…knowing we'd have to start killing people, hand to hand, if we ever reached it."

"What about air support?" I said.

"No carriers nearby. A destroyer in the bay lobbed some shells in, when our guys called for it…but most of that landed too far inland. Then, they just stopped. That's when Charlie suddenly told me to get everyone back to the first position. He grabbed one of the BARs from a dead Marine and crawled forward about twenty yards…began firing into the Japanese line. He kept them occupied and came under extreme return-fire. As we crawled back, I saw him take one in the leg…but all the while he's shouting, and waving us back farther…and firing that Browning. By now, the Japanese were angry…and they lost track of *us* for a few seconds, while they concentrated on him. That was just enough to get our platoon back."

"And Charlie?"

He frowned and shook his head slowly. "Grenade landed on him. We saw it throw his helmet up in the air…and the Japanese fired at it…like skeet shooting. I remember the clanging sound when one of them hit it." Father stopped speaking and sighed. For a while, he stared through the steering wheel at the dashboard. Finally, he looked up straight again and gazed out toward the ships in the cove. "We hung on…for the rest of the night. By morning, they sent us reinforcements…and better equipment. Even at that…it took the rest of the next day to push the Japanese back. We took a lot more casualties…but the Japanese did, too…they finally retreated inland after dark, the second night."

"I've never heard you tell this before…"

He sighed. "Yeah," staring out at the ships. "We couldn't find anything of Charlie when we searched the field on the third day…not even tags. A few of us went to see the division officer about getting a citation for him…something his family could keep, to remember him. But the CO was tied up…rebuilding the airstrip…and we had no ID for Charlie…there wasn't even a record of him having been with us. We were told there just wasn't enough time to do the paper work…"

"Oh, man," I muttered.

"After I came home, in 'Forty-four, I tried for a few years to get Charlie a commendation. One or two of the other guys did the same…sent letters to congressmen…the war department…got a few form letters back. Turned out Charlie had no living family members to fight for him…and he wasn't in the Army's official paperwork…they'd just lost track of him…back in December…'Forty-one. All he had was a few of us guys from the platoon…sending out letters. One thing led to another in our lives then…careers…children…time went by…we all fell in love with living again…and…we just…let it go. Meanwhile, they'd given *me* a Silver Star…for saving the lives of about forty men that night…the ones I took charge of getting back across the field, while Charlie took the fire and saved us all."

"You have a Silver Star?"

"Not *any more*."

"Whadya' mean?"

"Remember that business trip I took to Los Angeles, a few years ago, when I was just starting my practice?" I nodded. "Well," he said, "I took the last day for myself and caught a bus down to San Diego. I paid a guy with a fishing boat to take me out into the harbor. I said a prayer for Charlie...and gave him his commendation...dropped the medal in the harbor, where I'd met him."

"Oh Jeez, Dad."

He stared at the anchored ships, and they looked like rows of metal tombstones in the morning sunlight. "I just hope...someday...you'll be able to understand why I *have* to go do this."

"Because of this guy...Charlie Peters?" I said skeptically.

"It's not just that...what happened to Charlie...it's what's wrong with this whole country, Tom. Thousands and thousands of men, just like Charlie, are trying to live honorable lives...willing to give everything...but they're invisible...it's as if they don't exist."

"But what can *we* do about it?" I said urgently.

"We have to try, Tom, because we're *all* diminished by it. That's what your grandfather doesn't understand."

"Dad...Liz and I know we didn't move up here just because we ran out of money...and all those things that guy Moran accused you of. We know it's because of our friends. They're the wrong color...and people don't like that."

"You're right," he said, nodding. "Just remember...those aren't different things. They're all part of the same unjust thing."

"We *know*! We remember the FBI agents watching the house in Brooklyn...following us to school...following *you* to work and Mother..."

"You never said anything about that."

"We *weren't* gonna make it worse...by complaining."

"I'm sorry, Tom..."

"But it doesn't matter, now! We've already survived it...we don't mind living up here. You and Arthur can find another project...the world won't end if you don't do St. Nicholas Avenue...how many other slum areas do you need? Take your pick! But...testifying to that committee..."

"I can't discuss that, now." Just then, two Merchant Marine guards cruised by in a small motor launch, leaving a dirty gray wake along the surface as they headed out into the river. Finally, they disappeared in the cavernous rows of mothballed ships. "I'll stay with the Spencers tonight and...if I go to Washington...it'll probably be tomorrow. I'll take the train from New York, I guess. I'll ask Arthur to have someone drive the car back home…so you have it while I'm gone. I should be back Friday. Then, we can talk some more." He paused again. "Try not to judge me so harshly, Tom…"

"Dad…"

"In fact, say a prayer…we can use it."

There were deep lines in his face. His eyes were tired and he was fixed on some distant thought. Briefly, I imagined that he was changing his mind, but his stare remained fixed and I recognized its determination. I looked at my watch. It was almost nine-thirty.

"We don't have to drive all the way back, Dad. Just drop me at the bus terminal in Peekskill…I'll catch a northbound." He looked at his watch, and nodded. He started the car and drove up the highway into town. When he stopped at the curb in front of the terminal, I jumped out and stood for a moment with my hand on the open door. Suddenly, I remembered I still hadn't told him about Mr. Stannard's offer to meet and discuss business. "Listen…Dad," I said.

"Huh?" His voice was vague and distracted, as he stared over the steering wheel. Then, he turned and looked up at me, quizzically. "What *is* it, Tom?"

I looked at him for a moment, and was about to tell him. But then, another impulse took hold and I wondered what the point was, because once his name hit the papers again, no one would want to help him. Finally, I answered. "It's nothing. Nothing important."

"You're sure?" he said.

"No…it's…nothing."

"All right." He smiled and shook his head.

I closed the passenger door and he continued smiling for a second. He waved and I waved back. Then, he drove slowly away from the curb and gathered speed down Main Street toward Route 9. I watched my father's car disappear around the final bend in the roadway that led out of town, curving toward the river.

CHAPTER 8

❀

I sat on a bench in the waiting area and listened for my bus to be called. After checking the departure gates along the rear wall, I looked around the terminal. A few people sipped coffee and smoked cigarettes at the sleepy luncheon counter, just inside the main entrance, and a tiny newsstand did modest business. I noticed four Bell Telephone booths near the benches, but the Stannards would think it was still too early for me to call their daughter.

Finally, looking down at the endless checkerboard pattern of the floor, I accepted how lost I felt—about to miss the deadline for turning in my history paper; and failing the course. Applying for the headmaster's Yale program would be absurd, but I hadn't the heart to tell my unsuspecting father. But there was a more chilling realization I could no longer deny; Liz was right—I had blamed my father for much of our family's troubles. And I knew my cold anger was the thing that had kept me from telling him of the Stannards' offer to help. I was ashamed at how easily this betrayal had occurred. I glanced again at the phone booths, and told myself that I could call him when he reached his office, in an hour.

I checked the gates again, and then noticed an elderly black man facing me on the opposite bench, reading the *New York Journal-American*. As he held his paper up, I glanced over a jumble of headlines, but was soon distracted by a little girl sitting next to him. She was about ten, and her resemblance to the old man suggested they were granddaughter and grandfather.

They were dressed for an important destination. The man's plain, brown suit was neat and unwrinkled, and he wore a burgundy bow tie, a brown straw hat and steel-rimmed glasses. The girl's blue dress floated on a sea of white crinoline and her hair was intricately braided, with blue bows woven into the rows.

Suddenly, she glanced down the bench to her right, where a boy of about her age was making faces at her. He was dressed in a crisp white shirt and gray slacks, with his light brown hair slicked and cut short around the sides, accentuating the perfect roundness of his head. His big blue eyes bulged again, and he made another horrid face. The girl smiled.

As the old man continued reading, the girl started inching away from him, sliding along the polished oak bench. When she neared its midpoint, the boy jumped up and met her. He sat down. And for a moment, they stared off in opposite directions. Finally, the boy turned and whispered something in her ear. As she listened, her legs swung beneath the bench, and her patent leather shoes barely touched the floor.

She opened a small, plastic purse and took out a stick of Juicy Fruit chewing gum. Resting the purse in the blue folds of her lap, she carefully ripped the gum in half, and gave a piece to her new friend.

"William!" The boy turned to look at a young woman standing where he'd been sitting alone, moments earlier—his mother probably, back from the ladies room or the ticket window. She was young and very pretty, and wore a gray spring suit and a tiny, black velvet hat. And the expression on her face mixed panic and surprise. "Give that back!" she demanded.

"Awww!" he groaned, arching his body, as the little girl's legs hung, motionless. Then, the boy stubbornly gripped his gum and stared at the woman.

"Give it *back*, I said. You'll spoil your appetite." But the boy stared her down. "Come here, *this instant!*" she ordered.

By now, the elderly man had looked up, clearly surprised. He folded his newspaper down on his lap, and removed his eyeglasses. He seemed to be looking past the children toward the woman, because she quickly averted her gaze and sat down, angrily. A moment later, she glanced at her thin, silver wristwatch and then looked impatiently toward the gates. Reluctantly, the boy handed the gum back and the girl accepted it.

The PA system squawked. "New York City bus...now boarding at Gate One...Manhattan bus!"

The young woman rose in obvious relief, and reached for her black velvet handbag. But as she briefly turned her back to the children, the boy grabbed the gum and shoved it into his shirt pocket. The girl smiled, as he jumped to his feet and ran quickly to the woman, who clutched his arm and shook him.

The old man extended his right hand and called to the girl. "Isabel...come here, child."

She slid off the bench and watched the boy being dragged toward Gate 1. Then, she walked back to the old man and sat down next to him. As he pushed his newspaper into the corner of the bench, and wrapped his right arm over her tiny shoulders, she rested her head against his chest. A moment later, she noticed me watching and quickly looked away.

The PA squawked again. "Attention passengers! The northbound bus...scheduled to depart from Gate Three at ten o'clock...is delayed for approximately thirty minutes. Again...the ten o'clock bus...making stops at Highland Falls, Cold Spring, Beacon...and...Poughkeepsie...will be delayed approximately one half-hour. Please listen for further announcements."

Confused passengers were already lining up at the information window, so I walked to the gate and peered into the dim, hazy garage. The air was ripe with diesel exhaust and there were three drivers in gray uniforms, and a fourth man in mechanic's overalls, staring gravely at the bus parked down-ramp. Suddenly, the mechanic disappeared behind the massive vehicle as one of the drivers started up the ramp toward the gate.

As he neared, I stepped back to let him pass through. "What's the problem?" I asked.

"Flat tire," he said in a wary voice, as if he'd been asked to disclose a national defense secret. He stopped and pointed to the crest on my blazer. "What kinda jacket is that?"

"It's a school jacket," I said.

"Oh yeah?"

"St. Paul's...in Highland Falls."

He nodded and strode briskly into the lobby. I watched as he headed toward the luncheon counter. He was probably no more than 21 or 22, maybe working his first real job after high school and possibly a stint in the service. I couldn't think why, but he seemed familiar.

The PA squawked again. "Newburgh bus...now boarding...Gate Six."

Travelers were lining up at Gate Six and I noticed that the old man and the little girl were among them, holding hands near the front. This time, when the girl saw me looking her way, she stared back calmly.

I decided to get some fresh air, and as I neared the main entrance, I saw the young bus driver again. He was leaving the luncheon counter with four cups of steaming coffee balanced in a little cardboard box. As he passed, on his way back to the garage, he smiled at me. "Should be ready to go by ten-thirty!"

Outside the terminal, I watched traffic moving east toward the rotary below the Lutheran Church, and west toward the Route 6/9 fork. The warm, humid street seemed stifling, suddenly; sweat rose on my forehead, and trickled down my back under my blazer. I thought for a moment of my father, driving stoically to Manhattan, but I forced him out of my mind again. It was the only way to keep my own self-loathing at bay until I could reach him.

A sanitation man in white pedaled by on his tricycle with a steel barrel attached in front, and brooms and shovels vibrating in the barrel. I noticed, now, how littered the sidewalk and gutter were with red, white and blue confetti, and the red and white paper poppies of the American Legion.

Removing my jacket and slinging it over one shoulder, I walked east on Main Street. Cars were parked headfirst into meters on both sides, and the dark green meter-heads on silver sticks were like endless rows of tin soldiers. Men and women hurried into office buildings, banks, insurance companies and department stores, all dressed in suits, almost everyone with a hat. And the buildings conformed to their own pattern—mostly two or three stories, and either red brick or cement.

But there were also two large granite office buildings on the south side of Main. One was the Hudson Electric Building, across from the terminal. It had been erected in 1934, and at eight stories, it was a noble structure. Its facing was dulled by decades of factory soot, and on its roof was a neon sign, whose soft blue glow could be seen from miles away though not from the street below.

Farther east, I stopped at the Arcade Cinema and looked across the street at the other large building in town—the four-story O'Leary Brothers Building. Built in 1946, it housed O'Leary Development Co. and O'Leary Realty Inc., a subsidiary run by Andrew O'Leary's older brother Tony. The brothers collected pricey rents from their many other professional tenants, while keeping the top two floors for themselves.

I glanced up at the marquee—a John Wayne double feature—*The Sands of Iwo Jima* and *They Were Expendable*. The Arcade showed a lot of re-issued westerns and war films like these two. But I remembered how a booking of *High Noon* had been cancelled in 1952, because its writer had recently admitted to being a Communist Party member ten years earlier. This writer had told HUAC all about himself, but balked at giving the names of others he'd seen at party meetings in Hollywood; so then, he'd been blacklisted in the movie business.

When the theater manager cancelled *High Noon*, he told the newspapers it was "a phony western anyway, written by a phony Red." He was supported—some said instigated—by the Peekskill posts of the American Legion and Catholic War Veterans. The *Peekskill Evening Sentinel* ran an editorial in favor of the ban, and also printed a photo of the manager shaking hands with Congressman O'Leary in front of the Legion Hall. O'Leary posed for the picture in his Legionnaire cap; five or six younger men stood in the background, smirking.

Glancing back at the O'Leary Building, I noticed a man and woman emerge from a side entrance at the far end of a long alley. They started toward Main Street, and I realized instantly who the man was. He walked with a limp and had a copy of the *Journal-American* folded under his left arm. The dark-haired woman with him looked about 25, and she wore a tight yellow skirt and white cotton blouse, that emphasized her voluptuous body.

As they stopped to talk on the opposite sidewalk, I moved back under the marquee until I reached the cool glass of the locked theater door. I couldn't hear their conversation, but I could imagine it. Mr. O'Leary leaned over and whispered in the girl's ear, and she smiled, glancing the other way, missing his vaguely contemptuous expression. Suddenly, he stepped away from her, and they parted without ceremony.

The girl strolled a short distance to a brand new, red Ford convertible, parked in one of the O'Learys' private, curbside spaces. It had big, white-wall tires and the top was down. The hazy morning sun highlighted its racy, red interior and its gleaming, enamel-white steering wheel. As she leaned toward the car and opened the door, she kept her knees locked, and her skirt stretched like yellow skin across her rear end. She slid herself in behind the wheel, legs last, and casually pulled the door closed again. Then, she started the ignition and watched Mr. O'Leary casually limping east.

She put the car in reverse, backed into the street, and drove after him. As he stopped in front of the Legion Hall, she honked her horn and waved. He waved briefly before jerking his right hand back to his side, and glancing up and down Main Street.

When the convertible disappeared around a corner, Mr. O'Leary unfolded his *Journal-American* and examined it for a moment. Then, he tucked it under his arm again, spun around on his good leg, and ambled into the Hall. Immediately, I ran out from under the marquee and sprinted back to the terminal.

Pushing through the revolving door into the now bustling lobby, I glanced at the busy newsstand, and then squeezed through the crowds toward the waiting-area, hoping the old man had left his *Journal-American* behind. And when I saw the disheveled pile of pages jammed into the bench corner where he'd sat, I dropped my bag and riffled through the sheets, searching for a particular page.

Finally, I found what I'd unconsciously noted but somehow ignored earlier, while watching the old man read.

Investment Group Makes 11th Hour Bid For Harlem Site
City Receives Second Offer Worth $125 Million
Peekskill Developer Is Key Player in New Deal

My eyes jumped from paragraph to paragraph. The story mentioned a Wall Street-financed development group, and named two Texas oil magnates who'd recently joined them. A member of the New York City Planning Commission was quoted, saying their "bold new bid deserves careful consideration."

The story mentioned the mayor's campaign promise to rejuvenate neighborhoods like St. Nicholas Avenue in southwest Harlem. The St. Nicholas Development Corp.'s $55 million bid was briefly described—low and middle income residences and a community center, set off by a strip of parks on the west side of the avenue. Arthur and Father were mentioned by name, but not quoted. Several Harlem residents, including an uptown member of the City Council, said they preferred "the Arthur Spencer proposal." But the story brimmed with excitement over the new bid:

Andrew O'Leary, president and owner of the lower Hudson region's largest real estate development firm, is said to have made a significant financial commitment to the Wall Street group pushing the new plan.

The former Congressman from Peekskill refused to confirm this, but sources say he was a key broker in recent discussions between Wall Street and City officials. These sources say O'Leary Development Co. will serve as construction supervisor if the project is approved by City Hall. O'Leary, a Republican, is campaigning to win back his House seat. If successful, he would need to comply with Congressional rules that prohibit members from engaging in commercial ventures. It is expected that O'Leary's brother and partner, Anthony, will be named on the deal contracts.

The City Planning Commission, in a press release, said: 'however the bidding works out, there will be dwellings on the site. The $125 million bid is mainly for construction of modern TV studios and office space, but includes a daring pro-

posal for high rise apartments with Hudson River views along the west side of St. Nicholas Avenue.'

I heard the squawking announcement for my bus. It was ten twenty-five, and across the wide, crowded lobby, I could see the blinking light above Gate 3, the final boarding signal. I glanced at the telephone booths, and then my watch, and then folded the newspaper into my schoolbag. I hurried through the crowds past the gate, and into the dim garage. The driver was already closing down the baggage compartment along the side of the bus. I ran down the ramp and stopped outside the bus door, breathlessly waiting for the driver to come and take my ticket. As he turned and approached, I saw that it was the young driver from before.

"Made it...huh?" His smile was friendly, but businesslike.

"Just." I breathed a deep sigh.

"That's a small enough bag to keep on your lap...or you can put it in the overhead railings...if you want."

"Thanks," I said, handing him my ticket and stepping up into the bus.

He followed me up, slid into his seat, and released the door brake with a loud hiss as I walked to the rear. The bus was filled with passengers going as far north as Pougkeepsie, but I finally spotted an empty double-seat across from the toilet, and quickly sat down by the window, placing my bag next to me.

The driver put the bus in gear and drove the massive vehicle forward through the slot, making a tight left turn onto a narrow ramp that traced the interior wall of the hazy garage. The heavy bus moved swiftly, making tight turns around girders with the agility of a trained circus elephant. I could already feel the air conditioning system starting to work.

Soon there was daylight ahead, and the bus swooshed out of the garage into an alley behind the terminal. The driver made a quick left, drove alongside the terminal for a few hundred yards, and came to a stop sign at Main Street.

As we paused, I noticed another bus parked halfway up on the sidewalk to our left. At first I assumed it had broken down but, then, I saw the driver standing in the street, with two other people—the grandfatherly black man and the little girl. The driver was furious, making aggressive gestures toward them as they stood close together and stared at him. From the windows of the parked bus, the shocked passengers gazed down at the one-sided argument.

Suddenly, the little girl looked up at our bus and immediately recognized me staring at her from my window. I waved, and her eyes grew large and she began to cry. I felt like a fool. A police car arrived and our driver began his turn.

As our bus picked up speed heading west on Main Street, I rose from my seat and walked forward. Near the front, I could see the driver's face in the big round mirror above the windshield, and his eyes following me. When I reached him, I held tightly to the nickel-plated safety bar beside his seat and shouted above the droning engine.

"Did you see that bus driver, back there…arguing with two passengers?"

"Yeah!" He looked straight ahead at the road.

"Any idea what the problem is?"

"See the cop pull up?" he shouted.

"Yes."

"He'll handle it…"

"But what do you think the problem was?"

"Son…go back to your seat now…or I'll have to stop *this* bus."

Then, he jerked his head around and glared at me; I knew I'd better listen. But something held me for a moment longer—a sudden chilling memory of his face and this particular expression. He was one of the young men standing with O'Leary and the Arcade Theater manager in the newspaper photo, when *High Noon* was banned.

I made my way back, staring at garish posters above the baggage railing—pitches for beer and liquor, cigarettes, candy and soda, movies and Broadway shows—and even one about the dangers of walking in the aisles while the bus was in motion. Collapsing in my seat with a frustrated sigh, I looked up absently and saw an ad sponsored by the American Legion.

It showed a typical American family—husband and wife dressed in suits, with unquestioning expressions on their bland, white faces; and beside them, a dutifully smiling son and daughter. They seemed to be walking toward the reflected glow of some bright future not visible on the poster, while dark storm clouds receded behind them. But on closer inspection, I saw that they weren't normal clouds. They were the mushroom crests of A-bombs, and woven into the billows of each cloud were the words—"Disloyalty," "Subversion," and "Communism." And a line of print below everything said: "**Vigilance Keeps America Free.**"

The bus moved swiftly north on Route 6, up out of the Peekskill basin. I knew that the St. Nicholas Avenue project was lost for my father and Arthur, no matter what they did. I glanced at my watch—ten-forty. Father would have reached Manhattan by now, and seen the papers, I thought.

I could smell the odor of the motion-roiled toilet across from my seat, and I began to feel sick from the smell, and the motion, and the cool, artificial air with its diesel taste. I gagged suddenly; alarmed passengers turned and stared. "Oh god, this kid's gonna puke," their angry faces said. But I looked away from them. And my eyes burned as I struggled against tears, staring out the window through my own pale reflection into the hazy morning glare.

Two weeks earlier, Father McHenry had asked me to meet him in his cramped office on the fourth floor of St. Paul's main building. It was late in the day when I arrived to find his office empty, the door wide open. I waited a few moments in the hall, and then went in and sat down, quickly noticing the stack of student papers leaning precariously at one corner of his messy desk.

Most of my classmates considered McHenry the oddest individual they'd ever met. He was a Dominican, working in a school run by Jesuits, and he was definitely off the beaten track. Some days he'd come to class unshaven, maybe hung over, and he'd assign a quiet reading. Then, he'd stare out the window, or riffle through the mysterious legal documents he always carried in his over-stuffed briefcase. On other days, he'd arrive on waves of energy and launch into discussions of interesting but obscure points not found in the textbook. Students couldn't figure out what he wanted from them, and this irritated them. Nevertheless, he was Department Chairman, and his honors class in American History was required for graduation.

As I waited, I looked around at the framed diplomas and citations on his walls. He'd studied history at the University of Paris and economics at Cambridge. He'd been teaching since the 1930s, first at Cambridge, then Harvard. He'd moved to the Foreign Service School at Georgetown in 1945; several framed magazine clippings mentioned the scholarly papers he'd produced there, for the Truman State Department. One of the papers examined the Marshall Plan's effect on US-Russian diplomacy, and became a noted book in 1948. That was the year he'd been hired by the headmaster who preceded Father Stevens.

He finally arrived, out of breath and apologetic. After closing his door, he reached into his briefcase and extracted a batch of student papers, which he added to the already precarious pile on his desk. Then, collapsing in his chair, he stared at me with fierce blue eyes.

"Mr. Gannon," he finally said, "why do you suppose Benedict Arnold is the worst villain in American history?"

"He betrayed the Revolution."

"As simple as that?"

"*And* George Washington," I added, "the Revolution's patron saint...*his* mentor." McHenry nodded, as I continued. "So, regardless of his motives, or how cheaply he was treated by the other Colonial generals...Arnold seems ungrateful and vindictive."

"And Washington's good character only *compounds* the negative view of Arnold..."

"That's not how I'd put it, Father." The priest looked puzzled now. "How can a man be compared against a saint?" I said.

"What do you mean?"

"Historians have difficulty putting Arnold's treason in a context outside of his character...at the same time, they generally *underplay* Washington's flaws."

"What flaws?" he demanded.

"His obsession with loyalty...for one."

"*Obsession?*"

"With spies and spying...and loyalty...yes. Washington searched constantly to uncover spies and traitors, and employed spies of his own..."

"Mr. Gannon...Colonial America was all uneasy alliances...shifting loyalties...the Revolution heightened this uncertainty. The revolutionaries had a cause...but no *nation*, really. Imagine cutting yourself off from your family's homeland and background...from the solace of the past itself. Even the nation they *would* eventually create would be based on an untested idea about man's essential rights and freedoms...not the familiar, tribal affinities of Europe. Washington's suspicions were...understandable...I think."

"It's a problem, though, Father...America never resolved those early uncertainties...its fear of betrayal...attack..."

"Support that statement."

"Just read the papers," I said. The priest stared with intense concentration, as I continued. "You said the United States was based on a new idea, that made it different from European nations, where citizenship was basically a fact of history and background...*tribal*, you said. And...you said the United States was more of an *ideological nation*...based on a new idea, you said. So then, citizenship is something that needs to be *demonstrated*...by adherence to this *idea*. The problem is...any dissent from the idea...is treason, by definition...strict adherence becomes the definition of loyalty."

"You're painting with a pretty broad brush..."

"Maybe...but that's exactly how our history portrays Benedict Arnold...*and* George Washington. One is the ultimate symbol of disloyalty to the revolution, and represents the chaos of dissent. The other is the symbol of benevolence...sainthood, deceived by Arnold...an officer close to him...symbolically, his favored son."

"Dragging Freud into American history, now, Mr. Gannon?"

"I'd say Sophocles, Father...Aeschylus."

"All right, all right, Mr. Gannon. Why not Milton, while you're at it? But...are you trying to make a case that Benedict Arnold was merely a prodigal son...*not* a callous traitor?"

"I'm not sure, Father. Maybe that's my problem in coming to terms with him. I'd hoped to go beyond simplistic definitions...*traitor*...what does it really mean in Arnold's case? The books say his motives were personal and petty. But he *had* political beliefs...he published them. He felt that the Revolution had been corrupted, by business interests and military graft, and rash alignments with other European nations...like France. *And* he believed England wanted peace."

"Yes," said McHenry. "But the best scholarship shows Arnold to be an immature idealist, who reacted childishly...both to compliments *and* insults. He was a courageous field general, but politically inept...too ambitious for his own good...though, I grant you...ambition did not distinguish him from other officers in the Continental Army."

"But Father...it just seems the word *traitor* gets us nowhere if it blocks discussion...and thought. Traitors...dissenters...can provide a useful perspective on the causes they betray...and besides, most of them believe they're entirely justified."

"That doesn't absolve them, Mr. Gannon...isn't there an *objective* truth?"

"I don't know, Father. I started this project hoping to find a *new* truth...reassess history's verdict about Arnold...*and* Washington."

"Yes...but a reassessment based on what?"

"The *Revolution...itself...*"

"Ah!"

"What did Arnold actually betray? From reading...I see the extent to which the American Revolution *was* incited...and financed...by businessmen, planters and shipping investors, who wanted freedom from England's authority...mainly over their *commercial* interests...including the highly developed commerce in Negro slaves."

"Yes," said McHenry. "Go on."

"At the time of the Revolution, there was growing disfavor in England about slavery and trading in slaves...influential members of Parliament were trying to curtail it..."

"England was a slave-trading nation, Mr. Gannon."

"*But*...in Seventeen Seventy-six, attitudes were changing..."

"Not just in England," he countered. "Many signers of the Declaration of Independence hoped to see the end of slavery..."

"So they said. But the Revolution ended...the Constitution was ratified...with *incentives* for slaveholding. England moved on."

"What's your point, then?"

"That the English might have done, in North America, what they did elsewhere concerning slavery...but the Revolution prevented it," I said.

"Speculative, Mr. Gannon...interesting, I suppose. But disingenuous, obscuring Arnold's treason by discrediting what he betrayed...after the fact, no less?"

"Father, *you* said the United States was founded on a new idea of man's essential rights and freedoms! Were all men free in Colonial America...*after* the Revolution...even now?"

"Mr. Gannon, I've encouraged you all semester, but had no idea you would take your thesis in *this* direction. I believe Benedict Arnold owned slaves himself, and I'm unaware of any statement he may have made about dissatisfaction with the practice. Now...even if he had, you can't persuade me to overlook his vindictive self-interest. You can only fail in an argument that rests on having the United States Constitution declared a fraud...slavery notwithstanding."

"I know, Father. I realize that. I thought I had a way to compare Washington's America with our own time...and see the Revolution in a truer light...and maybe Arnold in a different way. But...I guess I can't...so, I'm stuck."

"Mr. Gannon," he suddenly said, with a concerned expression. "How would you compare Washington's time with our own?"

"Well...I was gonna compare Washington and Eisenhower." McHenry nodded, listening. "Each rose to the presidency after achieving a great military victory, which is enshrined in the nation's heart. Each presided over a government that permitted blacks to remain enslaved...the modern equivalent of slavery being discrimination, segregation. Then, there's this endless search for Reds, spies, subversives...you could argue it's not that different from Washington's endless search for spies and traitors...his fear of disloyalty across the land. So...it's really the same culture of racism and suspicion. If I can't judge Arnold against what he betrayed, including its hypocrisies…why *must* I judge Washington primarily on the basis of that same cause…just because he defended it? It's a double standard…don't you see?"

McHenry stared at me and sighed. There was a pained expression on his tired face now. "You've wasted your intellect following this negative tack…but I'm more disturbed by how bleak you find the world, at your age…how lacking in moral purpose."

"Do you know my father?" I said.

"We've met…"

"I mean by reputation…the things that are said about him?" McHenry seemed uncomfortable, suddenly. "You don't have to deny it, Father…they've been published in the papers!"

"I'm aware of *certain* things…yes," he said.

"Well…you become a little cynical when that happens to your father."

"I wouldn't be so sure that everyone believes those claims, son. What I know of your father…he's a good man. Benedict Arnold, on the other hand, was not. He betrayed Washington who only helped him…rewarded his success at Ticonderoga and Saratoga…his valiant attempt to take Quebec. Washington's inner circle of officers wouldn't accept Arnold. They were aristocrats…he was a tradesman's son. But his treason only validated their petty snubs and hypocrisies. He played into his rivals' hands. At his lowest spiritual ebb, his aristocratic second wife…and her Loyalist father…that family…the Shippens of Philadelphia, poisoned his mind. They encouraged his resentments, and suppressed his better instincts. What's more…as suspicious as Washington may have been, he was shocked by Arnold's betrayal…heartbroken. Mr. Gannon…tell me this…if you wrote your paper and compared Eisenhower with Washington, you'd need a current figure to compare with Arnold…"

"Yes," I said.

"Are you suggesting that it would have been your own father?"

"That's my problem," I replied. "The more I've read, the less I've understood Arnold. He disappears from the pages as I read about him. I don't know *who* to compare him to."

"But maybe you *do*…maybe your reading led to a conclusion you hadn't anticipated. Research often presents this problem. So…if not your father…then *who*?"

"I said, I *don't know!*"

"Mr. Gannon…I'm *only* asking a question."

CHAPTER 9

Anne Drummond, the headmaster's secretary, smiled as she rose from her desk behind a large wooden counter in the Main Office. "What happened to *you*, this morning?"

"Miss Drummond," I said, "my father needed help with a family matter."

"Oh? Nothing serious, I hope."

"No. He said you can call him about it."

"Really." She was confused, and concerned, as she leaned on the counter and scribbled my name and the time in her big attendance ledger.

Most of us boys were in love with Miss Drummond, a very pretty woman of about 30, from Brookline, Massachusetts, educated at Radcliffe. She had long, chestnut brown hair and a way of making her traditional clothing seem beyond fashion. It was considered generally odd in those days for a woman of her age to be unwed, but this only seemed to add to her mystique. There was a rumor around school that she'd planned to marry a man who'd been killed in the war. All I knew was that she treated us with the patience most women reserve for favorite sons; but, if compassion is the result of a broken heart, then maybe the rumor was true.

I could tell that beneath her concern this morning was uncertainty about what to do. I looked at the big black and white wall clock—three minutes till eleven—and could think of nothing but getting to a phone.

The door to the headmaster's private office opened suddenly behind her, and Father Stevens walked out holding a large folder. "This can go back into the Yale file, Anne."

"Of course," she said taking the folder. "Mr. Gannon has just arrived," she added.

"Really?" He glanced at the clock.

"Because he was helping his father with something," she said in a neutral voice.

He frowned. "Is everything all right, Thomas…at home?"

"Yes, Father," I said. "Do you need a note or something?"

The next-period warning bell started ringing throughout the building. It was two minutes till eleven, and the halls suddenly echoed with laughter and conversations of boys coming in through the main entrance and climbing the stairs.

"Well, no," he said. "Let's not stand on ceremony. Your next class is…"

"American history…Father McHenry."

"Just go. As long as you're assuring me everything's all right, we'll forget the tardiness. Sounds like…it couldn't be helped."

"Yes, Father." I started backing away from the counter, thinking I could quickly make it to the telephone booth inside the main entrance.

But, suddenly, Miss Drummond whispered in the headmaster's ear, and he nodded emphatically at her. "Oh, yes…of course." He looked directly at me again. "Wait, Thomas…Coach Bunning called Miss Drummond earlier…he needs to see you urgently. Can you meet him in his office? I'll talk with Father McHenry and explain you've been detained…"

"What's it about?" I said.

The headmaster and his secretary looked at each other, and back at me, and then smiled as the period bell rang in three brief bursts. "I believe he wants to discuss the vote…for team captain," the headmaster said.

I quickly walked along the ancient hallway, out the main entrance, and down the old stone steps, grooved in their center by the shoe leather of many Catholic boys over many decades.

I hurried across the quadrangle, as the chapel bell finished its eleventh gong. Several students late for class raced across the lawn to the main building. They wore the black academic robes of seniors in their final semester. They laughed as they ran, with their robes, loose ties and unbuttoned blazers flying.

Beyond the library, the science building, and the residence hall where most of our professors lived, the field house was another five minutes' walk.

At the end of a stone path that cut through a cluster of oak and ash trees, I reached the crest of a hill above a series of grassy slopes that descended in a valley. And at the bottom of the valley, the enormous new St. Paul's field house sat next to the football stadium. From the hilltop, I could see inside the stadium—our clay track an orange oval, around the lush green field.

St. Paul's students had played football back on the quad from the mid-1800s, but a real football pitch was laid out here in the valley when the school joined the Northeast Prep Association in 1919. Then, in 1947, with construction and financing from O'Leary Development Co., the stadium was built. The adjoining field house, which replaced a much older one, was another gift from the O'Leary Brothers. And according to Georgie Keller, the field house or the stadium would soon be named after Andrew O'Leary in recognition of his generosity.

I jogged down to the field house and entered through giant, sheet-glass doors. Avoiding the big red and gold school emblem embossed on the lobby tiles, I passed trophy cases filled with silver cups, old team photos, framed newspaper stories, souvenir footballs, basketballs, baseballs, and track and swimming ribbons.

Skirting the hockey rink on one side, and the indoor running track on the other, I pushed through a double door into a long hallway of athletic offices and locker rooms. Coach Bunning's office was at the very end of the hall, and his door was open. But I detoured at the home team locker room, where a pay telephone hung from the wall just inside the entranceway. Checking first to make sure I was alone, I lifted the receiver, dropped a nickel, dialed and waited.

"The Stannard residence."

"Jennings, this is Tom Gannon. I'm calling about April. How *is* she?"

"Good morning, Mr. Gannon. I haven't seen Miss Stannard today, sir. She's…resting. Mr. and Mrs. Stannard are just here…waiting for the doctor. Let me ask if she's taking calls…"

There was a muffled silence over the line as I waited. The operator came on and asked for another nickel. I dropped one in. Finally, a second receiver was picked up on the open line, and Jennings hung up with a click.

"Hello?" It was April. Her voice seemed distorted and flat. "Is that you…Tom?"

"Yes! How *are* you?"

"Fair," she said. "Did you know I'm going to the hospital?"

"Which one?"

"Grace-Episcopal. For tests…don't worry."

"When?"

"This afternoon…my father's waiting to hear from Doctor Simon about a bed."

"Do they know what's wrong with you?"

"That's what the tests are for."

"I'll come over…"

"What…*now*?"

"Sure."

"You're in school…aren't you?"

"I can walk to your house from here in fifteen minutes; less if I run."

"No…you can't…I'll be leaving soon anyway…"

"I'll come to the city then…*after* school."

I heard the click of another phone on the connection and voices in the background. Then, the line clicked shut again.

"Tom?" she said.

"What?"

"I love you…"

"I love you, too."

"But I have to go now…"

"I'm coming to *see* you tonight," I repeated.

"Okay…goodbye." The connection abruptly disengaged. Finally, when I heard the drone of the dial tone, I hung up. I could hear voices, growing louder and then fading in the hallway outside the locker room door. I looked at my watch. It was eleven-twenty. I picked the receiver up again and dropped another nickel in. I dialed home. My mother answered after two rings.

"Mom, it's me…have you seen the *Journal-American*?"

"The St. Nicholas story," she said. "Yes. Well no, I haven't actually *seen* it. Liz called when she got to school and read it to me. I don't have a *car*, Tom."

"No…of course," I said.

"I've had the radio on…there's been a brief news report about it."

"Does Dad know?"

"I imagine he does. I called the Spencers and spoke with Hazel. Arthur had already left for the office to meet your father. She said it's in *all* the papers."

"No one's talked with Dad?"

"He hasn't called me…I'm *sure* he's seen it…it looks pretty bleak, don't you agree?"

"Yes," I said.

"It's a pity," she sighed. "The people in that neighborhood have so few advocates."

"Grandpa Brent told Dad and Arthur all about this, yesterday. It's no surprise." Mother was silent. I looked at my watch. It was eleven twenty-five. "Do you think he'll still go to Washington, now?"

"I don't know, Tom."

I waited for her to say more, but she didn't. "Mother..."

"Hhmm?" She sounded distracted.

"April's sick..."

"What do you mean?"

"She fainted yesterday, at her parents'...I haven't had a chance to tell you..."

"We're your *family*...Tom!"

"I know, Mother..."

"We've had that girl to our home...I don't understand you sometimes..."

"You're right..."

"Do they know what's wrong...should I call Mrs. Stannard?"

"They really don't know anything; yet. I just spoke with her...they're taking her to the hospital for tests..."

"What should we do...which hospital?"

"Grace-Episcopal...I'm going down there, after school."

"I see. Did you say she...fainted?"

"Yes. I better call you later...see if you've heard from Dad. I need to tell him something..."

"Do you want to leave a message, in case he calls?"

"No...I'll tell him myself..."

"Well...he should be with Arthur...at his *new* office, remember, in the theater building."

"Oh...right."

"Naturally, I don't have that number, yet...they've just moved in. You could try Information...now listen to me, Tom...you must tell us the minute you hear something about her. Do you understand?"

"Yes."

"When will you be home?"

"I don't know. I may go see Dad after the hospital...as long as I'm there, anyway."

"Really...things are as pressing as that?" I didn't answer. "Don't leave me in the dark, son."

"No...I promise."

I hung up and went to a sink inside the dressing room and turned on the cold water tap. I put my hands under the icy stream and then brought them up to my face, pressing the cold wetness against my eyes. Grabbing a clean, white towel from the stack on a nearby dressing bench, I dried my face and hands.

"Coach!" I rapped my knuckles on Mr. Bunning's open door.

"Ah…Mr. Gannon. I'm glad you're here." He was coming from a storage closet on one side of his office suite. I stepped in and he smiled formally, closing the door behind me. He pointed toward the large desk in his inner office. "Let's sit down."

Asa Bunning was a legend whom Father Stevens had lured from retirement following his long career as the track coach at Princeton University. He'd set three national sprinting records of his own at Princeton, and competed in the 1900 Olympics; and he was a pillar of the clubby establishment that ruled American track and field.

I sat down in front of his desk, as he stepped around to the other side, and eased himself into the black, leather cushions of his big wooden armchair. Leaning back, with his long legs stretched out beneath the desk, he folded his arms across his stomach and stared at me with chilly blue eyes.

"The ballots for team captain are in, Mr. Gannon. Your teammates have chosen *you* for this honor…for the cross-country season, next fall." I was surprised. Even though I'd recently become the team's best distance runner, I was not its most popular member. "I wanted to speak with you about this," he added, "*confidentially*."

"Sir?"

"Three *other* juniors were passed over, including two who've been on the team longer than you…I believe I'm right about that…I was just checking the archives…"

"I didn't run freshman year," I said. "*This* is my second full year on the team."

"Yes. And my concern is for your three teammates…none of whom has anything like your physical ability…your chances of attracting the interest of college coaches. I think you'll even find yourself being offered scholarships, soon."

"I will?"

He nodded. "Now…your teammates will apply to college early in the fall, as *you* will…and distinctions, like being named captain, add weight…particularly at the very *best* universities."

"Was it a *close* vote?" I asked, still surprised.

He frowned. "Two shy of unanimous."

"Well. I voted for one of the *other* juniors…"

"I would *hope* so."

"It's amazing, though," I muttered. Mr. Bunning continued staring at me, his eyes narrowing beneath an increasingly furrowed brow, and his lips pressed tightly together. "So, what you're saying is…you want me not to accept?"

"I can't *tell* you to do that, son."

"Then *what*? I don't understand."

He sighed, frustrated. "You'll be running winter track and spring track next year, after the cross country season. At least, I'm counting on you for that." I nodded. "And colleges will come looking for *you*. And…you'll have two *more* opportunities at being voted captain. Even if, for some reason, you don't happen to win in those votes…why…we can see to it that…um…an adjustment is made."

I was more confused, now. "You mean…you'd just change the votes to whatever you want?"

He cleared his throat in a slightly embarrassed way. "You don't *need* this, Mr. Gannon…not nearly as much as your teammates do."

"I don't know what to say, Coach." We were silent for a moment. "Can I think about this?"

"How long do you need?"

"I don't know…a day…two days?"

He sighed and sat up straight in his armchair. "There's a real responsibility presented here. I'm just wondering whether you're up to it." I nodded inconclusively, trying to conceal my irritation over his clearly paradoxical challenge. "There is actually hard work involved in being team captain," he said. "Besides acting as a role model for your teammates, and representing their interests at meets…*I'll* need your help…representing the school in our recruitment of new runners." I nodded, but said nothing. He removed a large, brimming file from a drawer, and placed it solemnly on the desktop between us. He pressed his right hand down on it. "I've scheduled meetings with some of the more promising boys and their families. I'll need you to attend, and host these families when they tour the campus…starting in the next few days, and continuing through the summer."

I nodded. "All right."

He leaned back in his chair again and looked me in the eyes. I returned his wordless gaze. Then, he surprised me again. "Are you passing all your courses?"

"I *believe* so," I said, as he frowned, skeptically. "I'm having some trouble in history…"

"Yes?"

"But I'll resolve that."

"You must…or you can't serve as captain."

I nodded.

I got to history class on the second floor of the main building with fifteen minutes left in the period. McHenry stared sourly, as I slipped in and hurried to my desk.

Across the room, Georgie Keller looked at me with his head hidden behind another boy, and he silently mouthed the words: "Where the *fuck* have *you* been?" I ignored him, and pulled my history text from my bag. Placing it on my desk, I opened to the page where everyone was, and then looked toward the front of the room. Father McHenry was still staring at me.

He finally resumed what he'd been doing—a review of the weekend reading assignment. He snapped at two boys in quick order, when their mute responses to questions made it clear they hadn't read the chapter.

Now, McHenry surveyed the silent rows and caught Andy O'Leary Jr. in his gaze. "Ah! Mr. O'Leary…I know that *you* have read chapter twelve. I'd like to discuss the key battle outlined in the chapter. I'll allow you a moment to gather your thoughts…I'm *depending* on you, O'Leary."

"Yes, Father," Andy said.

McHenry put his copy of the textbook down on his desk, and walked across the front of the classroom to the open windows along the far wall. He stood there, with his back to the class, staring out onto the quad.

I looked over at Andy. He was a small, fat boy with a passive disposition. More than once in the three years we'd all known him, Andy had taken long absences for what was given out as measles, chicken pox or respiratory infections. But the strange marks we noticed on his face or behind an ear, when he came back to school, weren't the usual signs of those familiar conditions.

As McHenry stared out the windows, and the class leafed in dull silence through the pages of chapter twelve, I thought of an early September day at the beginning of our first term at St. Paul's. A bunch of us boys had been changing for gym class in the student locker room, and as we insulted each other, in boisterous, common nakedness, it was noticed that Andy remained in a corner, staring at the floor, fully dressed.

"Hey, what's the problem, O'Leary," somebody called out. "Forget your jock again?"

"He doesn't even own one," another voice jabbed.

"Doesn't *need* one," a third voice added.

Laughter rose in the locker stalls, as Andy reluctantly removed his blue blazer and put it down on a nearby bench. He pulled off his shirt and trousers, and then, as he stood there his underpants, with his back to us, we saw the sickening, purple and black bruises on his back and his stubby, fat legs. Some of the bruises seemed fresh; others looked as old as birthmarks. The boisterous locker room fell silent, then. And for days, not one of us was able to speak about what we'd seen.

Father McHenry turned from the windows and walked back to his desk. He checked something quickly in his textbook, and stared across his silent classroom. Then, he walked slowly down the aisle toward Andy, stopping inches from him. The room, which in one moment had seemed foggy with teenage lethargy, now seemed charged with animal tension. I prayed that Andy had read the chapter.

Father McHenry had a thick and muscular frame, like a boxer, and he stood ominously, with his hands on his hips. The thick, white wool of his Dominican robes touched the front edge of Andy's desktop, and the crucifix and rosary beads hanging from his belt clicked against the wood.

Andy slowly turned his head and gazed across the room at the iron-framed windows, as a humid breeze gusted and died.

"All right, then, Mr. O'Leary," said the priest. Andy turned back from the windows and stared down at his open textbook. "The Battle of Yorktown Heights has been called a turning point in the War for American Independence. This view is held by many scholars, and our textbook concurs…in some detail…in chapter twelve…"

"Yes, Father."

"*So*," the priest said. "Please describe the circumstances of this pivotal event."

"…Battle of Yorktown Heights?"

"Yes, Mr. O'Leary," said the priest. "The Colonial Army meets a large British force led by Lord Cornwallis…ringing any bells?"

"Battle of Yorktown Heights?"

"You're repeating yourself, Mr. O'Leary." McHenry's determined voice now visibly melted Andy's veneer of composure. I felt embarrassed, and then angry, watching Andy's confused face inches from the white blur of his interrogator's robes. I could see Andy's left foot shuddering. "I'm waiting, Mr. O'Leary." But Andy could only shake his head. "What are you saying…haven't you *heard* of this battle?" Andy looked up at the priest for a moment, before laying his head down on his desk, and slowly bringing his arms and hands up over the back of his head. "What is *wrong* with you, Mr. O'Leary? Sit up in your seat!"

"Leave him alone!" another voice suddenly demanded.

"Pardon me?" McHenry spun around sharply, and fixed his gaze on the sullen classroom. "I won't put up with this, gentlemen. I won't hesitate to make things uncomfortable for every single one of you, unless the individual who called out behind my back stands up, right now, and addresses himself to me." Slowly, I stood up. "Mr. Gannon?" His face showed extreme surprise.

"Father," I said, "Andy didn't understand your question…"

"That's quite apparent…"

"…And I'm pretty sure no one else did either."

"Really! Why is that?"

"It made no sense."

I could hear attempts to stifle laughter in the rows.

"You're trying my patience, Mr. Gannon."

"There *was* no Battle of Yorktown Heights," I said.

Now, shrieks of laughter and piercing whistles rose from the other boys. Andy raised his head and turned to look at me.

Father McHenry was shocked and embarrassed as he began to comprehend his mistake. "All right," he said, "you can sit down, now."

But I refused to sit down. "There *was* a Battle of *Brooklyn* Heights in Seventeen Seventy-six. *That* was a stunning victory for the British, though…until Washington escaped to New Jersey. But there was no battle at *Yorktown Heights*. I assume you mean the little village across the river from here. I've never read of Lord Cornwallis being this far north. Have you?"

"Sit down, Mr. Gannon." The priest was angry.

"Maybe what you're thinking of, is another place entirely," I added with sarcasm, as thirty-five boys held their breaths. "In Seventeen Eighty-one, there *was* a Battle of Yorktown…*in Virginia*, which more or less ended the Revolutionary War. Cornwallis spent a lot of time in Virginia and the Carolinas. Ringing any bells?" The class shrieked with laughter. "Of course *you* said Yorktown *Heights*…maybe you were confusing the two…or confusing Yorktown Heights with *Brooklyn Heights*…Cornwallis was there, too, supporting General Howe…but, well…*who knows* what you were thinking. Who *ever* does?"

The shocked priest simmered in anger. "Are you quite finished?"

"Yes…I'm finished. Just leave Andy alone."

McHenry stared at me, calmly, as I sat down at my desk. He pressed his lips together and nodded with relief. I looked over at Andy, who stared back at me in great surprise. Slowly, he allowed the smallest hint of a smile to emerge on his face.

But the priest wasn't finished. "Perhaps we should address your dissatisfaction with my class, Mr. Gannon. Gentlemen...I apologize for my lapse in memory. Mr. O'Leary, I apologize...I *meant* Yorktown, Virginia." He glanced at Andy and then back at me. "But...Mr. Gannon...I thought St. Paul's was a place where scholars became *gentlemen*. We seem to have failed, with you. Perhaps we're ill equipped to satisfy so challenging an intellect as your own. I must speak to the headmaster about your dissatisfactions. Naturally, I'll need to speak with your father, too."

The chilled silence returned to the classroom. I looked across the aisles at Georgie Keller's shocked and reproving face. The bell rang to end class, and Father McHenry abruptly packed his books and papers into his briefcase and walked out. I got up from my desk as groups of boys surrounded me, grinning, punching my shoulders and slapping my back.

"What the fuck was *that*?" said Georgie, standing nearby.

"You saw what happened," I said, as he gazed in awed confusion.

Andy O'Leary moved through the crowd of excited boys and held out his hand. I grabbed it, and he seemed about to say something, but finally, he shook his head, let go of my hand, and left the room.

Above the buzzing of my classmates, and the noise of students moving in the hallways, I heard the chapel bell begin its ponderous sequence of twelve gongs across the quad outside. My classmates gathered closer and pushed me out the door into the hall, heading to our final classes before lunch. As we shuffled and merged into the larger stream of boys, my confrontation with McHenry was described all around me. The group began splitting into smaller groups, heading in different directions. I hurried upstairs to the third floor and along the hallway, toward my English class. For a moment, I stood outside the classroom, as other boys hurried inside, grinning and patting me on the back as they passed.

The class bell rang, but I walked a few more steps to the end of the third-floor hallway and looked out the large window there, struck by a sense of absolute emptiness. I could see all the seniors who had no noon classes. They were walking across the quad below, or gathering into groups and sitting on the grass with their robes and blazers off, and the sun on their faces.

During my last class of the day, I was summoned to the headmaster's office. Anne Drummond handed me a sealed, blue envelope addressed to my father.

There was a note inside, she said, from Father McHenry. "Is everything all right, Tom?"

"I guess so," I replied.

I noticed the door to the headmaster's office was open, and I could see Father Stevens sitting at his great mahogany desk. Suddenly, he looked up from the papers scattered before him, and he gazed at me with a look of great concentration. When I looked back at Miss Drummond and smiled, she frowned. I turned and walked out into the ancient hallway.

CHAPTER 10

❀

I climbed the runway beneath the stadium and came out into the empty stands. Down on the track, 13 runners sprinted past the quarter-mile mark and continued, on as Mr. Bunning's voice echoed across the football field. "Fifty-nine seconds!" I hurried down to the field level and jogged across the track to the infield. The coach glanced up as I approached, and then, he looked back at his stopwatch. "Nice of you to join us, Mr. Gannon."

The sprinters and field-event guys snickered, as they stretched on the grass, nearby. I tried to explain. "Sorry, Coach. I was called to the headmaster's office." He stared at his watch and said nothing. "How many half-miles have they done?"

"They ran a slow warm-up," he replied, turning to look across the infield at the runners struggling along the backstretch. "This is their second…it's *supposed* to be all-out." He sniffed as he watched them. "Loosen up and get in the next one. Maybe *you* can get them going."

I sat on the grass with the other guys, their smiles confirming that my flare up with McHenry was no longer news. As I stretched my legs, I watched the runners coming up the home straightaway led by Jimmy Pauling—a popular junior, who'd gotten my vote for team captain.

"One fifty-nine, seven," the coach yelled, as Jimmy lunged past the finish line, followed closely by the others. "Keep moving. Walk it off!"

The tired runners staggered down the track and their strides shortened. Some stayed on the track and walked with their hands on their hips; others wandered in wide, breathless circles on the infield grass. Jimmy came over to me and bent down with his hands on his hips, breathing heavily.

The coach barked again. "Don't stand around! You go stiff on me...you're useless." The word "stiff" drew raunchy laughs from the boys on the infield, but the coach wasn't amused. "Distance men...I'll see you on that starting line in three minutes! Sprinters! You're wanted across the track...shot-putters, discus men, high jumpers! You should be warmed up by now...go start your workouts."

As the rest of the boys began heading for different points around the stadium, I got up and walked with Jimmy. He glanced at me and asked, "you wanna lead the next one?" I shook my head. He glanced back at the coach, who was occupied for the moment, watching his team disperse. "You think he'll make us do more than six of these?" he whispered.

"Who knows?" I sighed. "This isn't conditioning. It's a competition workout...and the season's *over*."

"It's about the exhibition at West Point, next week. He wants us to look good against the Plebe team, because he invited some of the boys he's recruiting, and their parents, to come watch us." I nodded. "Listen. I heard about you and McHenry. What happened?"

"He was bothering O'Leary."

"Be careful," he said, as I frowned. "I'm serious. Look, I know what's going on with O'Leary...but he's gotta say something. If he just keeps denying it, he can't expect the rest of us to play guardian angel..."

"I know, but Jim...McHenry was in one of his moods. Somebody had to stand up to him. I didn't think about it...I just did it."

"Everybody knows McHenry's fucked-up, Tom...but...I've never seen him act in a really *cruel* way..."

"You weren't there."

"I know...I've just never seen that..."

Suddenly, the coach shouted. "Pauling...Gannon!" We walked back and joined him near the starting line. "So...who's in charge here?"

"Jimmy's gonna lead this one," I said.

He scowled and stared at Jimmy. "I want a better pace."

Jimmy nodded. "We'll do better."

"Listen, Coach," I said. "About this morning." He looked at me, gravely. "Make whatever move you think is right...for the team...and I'll back you."

A thin smile crept across his lips. "Good. Let's gather 'em up." He turned and bellowed across the infield. "All right, gentlemen...back on the line!"

Jimmy and I stepped out onto the orange, clay track and waited for the others to join us. Across the infield, the high jumpers leapt over their horizontal bar into a sand-filled pit. Shot putters heaved twelve-pound cannon balls into brief arcs that ended with quiet thuds. Discus men spun in their tight circles and hurled, while the sprinters did fifty-yard bursts—all under the watchful gaze of Mr. Bunning's young assistants.

Suddenly, Jimmy muttered, "I heard something else, too."

"Heard what?" I said.

"You *know* what." I turned to look at him, but he glanced down at the track, and whispered. "Thanks, Tom."

As the other runners stepped onto the track behind us, I looked out over the stadium roof. A bank of dark clouds was moving east, blocking out the hazy afternoon sunlight.

I turned to Jimmy. "I can't *do* this."

"What?"

"I've gotta get going." I spun around and quickly walked off the track, and continued up into the stands, scaling the steps toward the exit ramp.

From behind, the coach's voice boomed out. "Gannon...hey Gannon! Where are *you* going?"

Reaching the top step, I turned and looked back. "I'm sorry, Coach! Something's come up...I've gotta go *do* something!"

"Je—zuz Christ! What next?"

The bus from Highland Falls stopped at Broadway and 165th Street at six o'clock. I got off and walked west to Grace-Episcopal, a complex of medical buildings arranged like a university on a giant piece of urban real estate, blocks long, overlooking the George Washington Bridge.

I reached the main building—a gothic skyscraper looming in the overcast—and I hurried through the entrance doors and across its quiet lobby toward the desk. Three well-dressed receptionists looked up, suddenly, in unified horror. Quickly realizing my breach of propriety, I went back to the end of the shortest line of visitors.

As the line crept forward in brief steps and endless pauses, my eyes adjusted to the dim lighting and I noticed writing on the wall of a hallway leading to the elevators on my right. Slowly, the writing became clearer and I realized it was a list of benefactors, artfully engraved in the polished surface, so that the names seemed to emerge from within the marble itself. Between several Roosevelts, and Mrs. Arthur Thiebault, I saw the names of Mr. and Mrs. Charles L. Stannard.

At last, it was my turn to approach the desk. Leaning against it, gripping the edge of its smooth wooden top, I barely controlled my impatience as I spoke to the prim, middle-aged receptionist. "April Stannard?"

She stared. "Your name and relationship to the patient?"

"My name is Tom Gannon…I'm a close friend."

Instead of writing out a little blue card for me, with April's room number on it, she frowned, pressed her thin lips together, and reached for a telephone. She quickly dialed two digits on the rotary and waited, with her head down, until someone answered. Then, she turned away from me and whispered into the phone. A moment later, she straightened up and glanced at me, still listening. "Yes," she nodded, "I understand." She hung up, stiffened her back, and looked at me, gravely. "The patient is under restriction."

"What does *that* mean?" I said.

"Do you understand the word *restriction*?"

"But how do you mean it? Do you mean *quarantine*?"

"I didn't say that."

"Then *what*?"

"The hospital has placed a *procedural restriction* on…that patient…"

"I can't see her."

"That's correct."

"Visits are restricted…"

"Correct."

"*All* visits…including family." She nodded firmly. "Close friends, third cousins removed…"

"Young man…"

"Or is it just *me*?"

"Are you trying to be funny?"

"Do you see me laughing?"

"Step aside."

"I just want to know why I can't see my girlfriend, Ma'am."

"Next please!" She angrily looked past me.

"Wait a minute!" I pounded my fist down on her desktop and she recoiled, shocked. "I need to know how she is…"

"Next person in line…step up. Please!"

Just then, two uniformed security guards appeared and stood on either side of me. As relief broke over the receptionist's face, one guard spoke in a challenging voice. "There isn't going to be trouble, now *is* there, son?" I turned to face the guards. Abruptly, they put their arms over my shoulders and began urging me toward the entrance doors.

"What *is* this!" I shouted.

The guards then pinned my arms behind my back, tangling them in their own, strong forearms. Visitors gasped, as the guards hustled me back toward the entrance. Suddenly a man's voice echoed across the lobby.

"Officers…please…this isn't necessary." The guards stopped, but maintained their hold on me as they turned and looked toward a dim alcove to the left of the reception desk. Moving quickly toward us out of the shadows, was Charles Stannard. "Gentlemen, *please* let him go."

Reluctantly, the guards loosened their grip, and as they did, I jerked my arms away with a violent force and stepped back.

"Hey! Hey!" the guards barked, moving toward me again, and pushing their fervid faces at me. People on the visitors' lines seemed confused and upset. Some were muttering, angrily.

Mr. Stannard pressed his hand firmly against my back. "Let's all calm down. Tom, please come with me." A moment later, Mr. Stannard and I sat on a couch in the corner alcove. The guards stationed themselves at a respectful distance, and faced the lobby with their feet planted and their hands clasped behind them. "You *must* control yourself," he pleaded.

"Sir. Tell me what's going on."

"The press is now aware that my daughter is here." He paused and stared hard into my eyes. "Reporters have called our home…and the hospital. Apparently my family's name, or my associations in business and government, have…encouraged them…to make entertainment of this."

As he spoke, in a harsh whisper, I was struck by the realization of hearing him for the first time, not as April's father, or even the figure from the social and financial pages of newspapers he claimed to loathe.

"I'm sorry sir; I didn't know."

He nodded and continued. "We stopped a news photographer only an hour ago. We discovered two reporters…young women mind you…posing as friends of my daughter, trying to obtain passes, and to get upstairs to see her. Can you understand why we've asked the hospital for heightened security?"

"But, sir…surely no one thinks *I'm* a reporter. Look how I'm dressed…this is a school uniform." He briefly smiled at this. "I *told* the woman at the desk who I was."

"I know," he said, nodding. "I spoke with her on the phone…and I was coming down to see you. These people are simply trying to do their jobs. I would have thought the last thing you wanted was a picture of my daughter in tomorrow morning's tabloids…"

"But how *is* she? Can't I see her?"

"She was awake most of last night…and she spent all afternoon being examined and tested. Now, we've given her something to *help* her sleep. We can't disturb her, Tom. Do you understand?"

"Yes, sir."

"Good."

"So…what *is wrong* with her?"

"We still don't know, I'm afraid. There are more tests scheduled. The medical staff are working hard to ease her discomfort and…it's *our* job, now, to stay strong…for *her*. Do you see?"

"Yes, sir."

"Now. You must promise not to speak about this with anyone…outside your family."

"Of course, sir. Who would I speak to?"

"Reporters are everywhere, it seems, masquerading as friends."

"May I call her?"

"A card would be best, Tom. Send it to our home…will you? Not here…we're asking that of everyone…to keep the flow of attention away from the hospital."

"All right."

"Now, son." He suddenly seemed nervous. "I wanted to ask you something else…about your father…"

But he stopped abruptly and stared out toward the lobby. The look on his face drained of all expression. I turned and saw Mrs. Stannard, standing near the security guards.

"Are you ready, Charles?" she said, in a blank voice. "We *must* go."

Mr. Stannard seemed annoyed. "In a *moment*." I looked at him, and then again at April's mother. She'd already turned away from us and was gazing out into the lobby. There was an awkward silence, now. Finally, I stood up, and Mr. Stannard whispered. "Remember…what I asked of you, Tom." I nodded and turned to say something polite to April's mother. But she was gone.

I caught a downtown Broadway bus and got off at 125th Street. It was seven o'clock, and the sun was dipping below the overcast, shining through breaks in the western skyline, casting beams of amber light from the rooftops to the streets of southwest Harlem. Heavy traffic moved slowly on Broadway, beneath the elevated platform of the A-train, while shafts of sunlight through the tracks cast a checkered pattern over the street.

The marquee above the Broadway entrance to Arthur Spencer's new theater promoted an all-star jazz concert opening in two weeks. Dizzy Gillespie's band was headlining, and a long queue of ticket buyers stretched from the box office to the corner, and then west on 125th.

As I started west, a trumpet and saxophone began a slow, Be Bop improvisation on *Laura*. The music was coming from an open apartment window somewhere on the block. People on line looked up, suddenly. Others smiled as they came down from the El and walked home. An old man came to the doorway of his fruit and vegetable store, and listened, with his hands in the pockets of his long, white apron.

When I reached the entrance to the theater offices, I stopped to listen for a moment longer, and I noticed a small crowd gathered across the street. There were people in the open windows of apartment buildings, staring down at the crowd, as the music played. Most of the people on the street, and leaning from the windows, were black.

At first, I thought they were all music lovers, like me, but then a large Cadillac ambulance came up the street from Broadway with a cherry red light pulsing on its sloping white roof. It stopped near a fire hydrant, and two men in white suits jumped out. They pulled a stretcher from the rear door, and then, the crowd parted and revealed a young black man sitting on the edge of the sidewalk, with his feet in the gutter and his face in his hands. His brown suit was dirty and disheveled, and his tie drooped, and his thick, bushy hair was wild.

"That boy ain't been right since he come back from Korea," somebody said.

"He was on the junk before he went," said another voice.

"Not like this."

The stricken man tried getting to his feet, but the ambulance attendants gently pushed down on his shoulders and prevented it. A few people staring from the windows laughed. The attendants placed their stretcher on the sidewalk behind the man and coaxed him into lying back on it. Once he had, they quickly secured him with leather straps and hefted the stretcher back into the ambulance.

After locking the rear door from the outside, they jumped into their seats and slammed their doors. A brief burst on the siren signaled the bystanders to back off, as the ambulance pulled away from the curb and headed west.

An ancient black woman called down to the crowd from her third-story window. "Where they takin' 'at boy?"

One man on the sidewalk removed his hat and looked up at her. "They'll go on up to the VA Hospital, Miz Bailey. Near the Stadium."

The old woman scoffed. "All the way ovah thah?"

"Well, they're not takin' 'im to Grace-Episcopal," said a voice.

There was chilly laughter in the crowd for a moment. I noticed that the jazz musicians had stopped playing. Then, the crowd dispersed on the silent street.

I stepped into the theater building and walked down a dark, narrow hallway toward a bank of elevators. Examining a glass-encased digest of tenants on seven floors, I saw that the top three accommodated Arthur Spencer's realty management and leasing companies, and his theatrical investment firm. The first four were mostly leased to companies that seemed to be theatrical agencies and music publishers. A few offices were leased to individuals—show business lawyers and accountants I assumed, or even writers and composers.

When the elevator doors opened on seven, I stepped out and gave the receptionist my name and asked for my father. She pressed a button on her phone console and smiled. "Won't be a minute."

Almost immediately, Arthur appeared. His dark blue suspenders pressed tightly against his white shirt on each side of his tie, which was loosened at the collar. His sleeves were rolled up and he looked tired.

He shook my hand and said, "come in, Tom." He ushered me down a hallway lined with offices, in which well-dressed men and women conducted meetings, and talked on telephones. Arthur noticed me glancing at my watch and smiled wearily. "This is real estate," he said. "It's not a nine-to-five business."

We reached a private office suite where Arthur's secretary, Arlene Baker, sat at a wide desk behind a large typewriter and a flickering telephone console. The door to Arthur's office was open, and I could see his desk and several empty chairs inside. A large window behind his desk had a panoramic view of the Hudson River and New Jersey.

The door to my father's office was closed. I stared for a moment at his name, printed in black letters outlined in gold, on the opaque glass in the upper half. Then, I looked at Arthur and Arlene. "Is my father here?"

Arthur put his arm over my shoulder and guided me into his office. He pointed to a big leather couch and then stepped back to the doorway. "No calls or interruptions, Miss Baker." She nodded, and then looked in at me with a worried expression, just before Arthur closed his door. I sat on the couch, as he pulled a chair up close to me. "We haven't heard from your father all day, Tom. When was the last time *you* saw him…or spoke with him?"

"This morning…around nine-thirty…he dropped me at the Highland Bus terminal."

"*Peekskill?*"

I nodded. "It's a long story…we drove down there together…I'd missed my bus…he wanted to talk…"

Arthur glanced at his watch and shook his head. Then, he stared at me hard. "We were supposed to meet here at eleven, this morning. He never showed up…"

"He told me he planned to stay in the city, tonight," I said, "with you and Mrs. Spencer."

"That's right."

"Maybe he went straight to Washington."

"Why would he do that, son?"

"So he wouldn't have to hear any more arguments about it?"

"I don't think so," Arthur said, pausing, as if considering my suggestion anyway. Finally, he sighed and shook his head again. "No. He doesn't ignore business appointments. If he'd gone to Washington, he'd be there, now. Somebody would have heard from him…your mother, at least."

"Maybe the car broke down or he…had an accident."

Again, Arthur shook his head. Then, he hauled his large body out of his chair and stood above me. "I've already called the State Police…and the New York City Police. No accidents have been reported…no broken down Buicks." He turned and stared at the window behind his desk for a moment, with his hands on his hips. When he turned back and looked down at me again, I could see a deep anger in his eyes. "What were you doing in Peekskill? Your mother thought he was driving you to school."

"He wanted to talk…"

"About what?"

"I don't know…Washington…St. Nicholas Avenue…his…*beliefs.*"

"Did he mention Andrew O'Leary?"

"No."

"Charles Stannard?"

"*No!*" I could hear the surprise in my own voice.

Arthur's expression was skeptical. "Are you sure?"

"He *didn't* say anything about Charles Stannard…it's just…you mentioned his name, and it made me think about something." Arthur's face froze as he waited for me to tell him what. "Mr. Stannard asked me about Dad…at his party, yesterday. He asked me about your theater here, and the controversy over it." Arthur sat down again and began nodding at me, urging me to continue. "He said he wanted to speak with Dad and…maybe do some business…"

"Is *that right.*" Arthur's sarcasm was so bitter it shocked me.

"He said his bank…and some foundation his family runs…are looking for real estate opportunities and maybe…he and Dad might have some common interests…"

"What 'id Joe say about it?"

"I haven't told him." Arthur's eyebrows arched in surprise. "There wasn't time last night," I explained. "Or…this morning…"

"*Wasn't time?* It took fifteen seconds to tell *me.*"

"It…it slipped my mind, I guess…until it *was* too late, and…this morning…we got off the track." The sound of my voice was something outside of me now, distant and impersonal, the voice of a stranger telling a lie. "I tried…I just couldn't…I don't know why." My head was spinning, suddenly, and I could feel my lips tremble.

"It's all right, son. It's all right. We'll find him." He leaned forward and put his long arm out, gripping my shoulder hard with his large right hand. "He'll turn up…"

"No." As I looked at him, I could feel tears rising in my eyes. "That's not it," I said. "I *didn't* try to tell him." Arthur looked surprised. "I didn't *want* to tell him."

His hand relaxed at my shoulder, suddenly, and then dropped away. He leaned back in his chair and stared at me. "Why not?"

"I was…angry, I guess…"

"*Angry?*"

"About…what he's doing."

"You mean *testifying*…in Washington?"

I nodded. "*Everything*…how it would all look in the papers…again."

He sighed. "You're being awfully hard on your old man…"

I took a deep breath and tried to explain. "I *thought* about telling him, when he dropped me at the terminal. I thought…'maybe I can help him…maybe if he got involved with somebody as influential as Charles Stannard, he wouldn't have to waste his time on projects the City doesn't want…or talking to that committee in Washington…or trying to get back clients who aren't worth his time.' But then, I didn't. Arthur…I just let him go." My lungs burned as I breathed out. The tears in my eyes felt like acid.

"Well. That's quite a burden to carry, son…quite a thing." He paused, staring at me. "But…it wouldn't be the *first* time a son kept a secret from his father. Now, let me tell *you* something. I don't know exactly what business Charles Stannard has in mind to discuss, but I doubt your dad'll be interested."

"Why not?"

"He's not that crazy about Charles Stannard…*or* the people he does business with…O'Leary for one. Your father *despises* O'Leary."

"They're in business *together*?" I said.

Arthur laughed, coldly. "Stannard's bank has just become a big investor at St. Nicholas Avenue…"

"Oh, God…"

"And he's probably lent the O'Learys whatever *they've* invested in the project. You didn't know they were tied up together?"

"No! I didn't. Nobody told me this." I sighed in growing recognition of the world I'd mistaken for a dream. "So…*that's* why O'Leary was there yesterday…at the Stannards' party."

"You certainly keep a lotta things to yourself, boy…"

"I noticed them talking…I'm sorry. I didn't think enough about it."

Arthur scowled. "You thought they were maybe chatting about the weather?"

"No…there were *hundreds* of people there. I must have thought the Stannards…you know…being who they are…invited *all sorts* of different people…especially someone running for Congress. They're both Republicans…I guess I thought O'Leary was asking for a contribution…"

"Probably was," Arthur said. "Stannard's contributed to his campaigns *before*…and has money tied up in O'Leary projects. When I saw the papers today, I said to myself, 'they're together on *this* project too, I bet.' So, I made a few calls and confirmed it. I'm told *Charles Stannard* is the heavy new player behind the scenes…*not* the Texas oil men…and *definitely* not O'Leary. *He's* just a front man…no matter what the papers are calling him." Arthur sneered. "'*Inside broker*' my behind."

"Who told you this?"

"I have a few friends on the City Council."

"But I don't see the point…why does Mr. Stannard need a front? I mean…what's the big secret? It's pretty clear the City wants to put up TV studios. Everybody *loves* the idea…it seems."

"What's happening to me and your father is a dirty deal…a bait and switch. We were dangled out there by the Planning Commission to get these big boys to finally commit…now that they have…your dad and I are having the rug pulled out from under us. But there's gonna be some bad publicity…some City Council members from up in *this* neighborhood are about to start asking questions. Like…what do TV studios and luxury apartments have to do with the Mayor's campaign promises…about fair housing? Someone could charge discrimination, and then, it's all in the papers…see? Stannard wants his name out of it…that's where O'Leary comes in."

"O'Leary *wouldn't care* about charges of discrimination?" I said.

Arthur smiled. "Wouldn't hurt him…with *his* constituency. Tom…listen. Real estate isn't about buildings and land. What it's really about…aside from the money, I mean…is influence. Real estate determines just about everything that's important to people…where they live…who they live near…who they don't…what sorts of businesses are allowed…where the highways go in…the railroads. And it's about how blocs of voters are bunched together or split apart…how communities and whole states are laid out and managed…controlled, really. Y'understand?"

"Sure," I nodded. "I think so."

"Well. The O'Leary Development Company is known in the business for finding barely legal ways to keep choice real estate away from *colored* folks…keepin' us *out* o' places where *white* folks live. It's done up there where *your* family is…it's done on the other side of the river, too…where the Stannards live…"

"As an organized *thing*?"

He laughed. "You've got a lot to learn. Charles Stannard has given hundreds of thousands of dollars to O'Leary's campaigns in the past. Ask yourself 'why?' Why is he that interested in supporting a local Congressman…with a voting record that puts him with the worst racists and segregationists on Capitol Hill?"

"What you're *really* saying is…*Mr. Stannard* is a racist."

He nodded gravely. "Some ways worse than O'Leary, because he's such a phony about it. Stannard believes he's some kind of aristocrat…because his people came here before the Revolution, and decided all this was just for them, and their descendants. It's nonsense. The Stannards don't really have anything on your *mother's* family. Come to that…*my* family got here 'bout the same time *his* did, 'course…they came on the wrong boat." I nodded. "But to a man like Charles Stannard…the rest of us are just tenants…"

"My father's never said anything about this to me."

"He *knows* how much of a shine you've taken to Stannard's daughter. Maybe he's just hoping you'll figure things out for *yourself.*"

I stared back at Arthur for a moment. "Or maybe...*that's* what he's been trying to work up the courage to tell *me*." Arthur frowned. "But why would Stannard make a big thing of talking business with Dad?" I asked. "He *must* know Dad's reputation...what you and Dad think of him."

"Of course, but he's no dope. He might think it's good public relations to do a few community-minded projects...take the sting out of any claims of discrimination in the *big projects* he cares about. And if he had someone like your dad working for him on that...a man with a solid reputation with...well...*colored people*...he might think he can hide behind Joe...like he hides behind O'Leary. So...he hedges his bets on *both* sides of the street. *And*...maybe he thinks your dad would come cheap, right now..."

"Arthur...I saw O'Leary in Peekskill this morning...after Dad dropped me off..."

"Did he see *you*?"

"I don't think so. He was...distracted...reading the *Journal-American*. I guess we know why."

"We have to reach Joe," said Arthur. "What I think is...he's off by himself somewhere, thinking all of this through. I'm sure he's seen the papers by now...and maybe he's having second thoughts about Washington. I sure *hope* he is, but we need to find him. He needs us."

"What do we do?"

"You better call home...see if your mom's heard from him, yet. Here...use my phone."

Arthur left me alone in his office with the door closed. I sat at the edge of his desk and dialed. As I waited for the long-distance connection to Garrison, I stared out the window. It was seven-thirty and the sun was below the horizon line. Orange-red rays glowed above the brown palisades across the shadowy river. Headlights flickered on the West-Side Highway.

After thirty seconds, the connection still hadn't gone through. I heard only hollow, popping noises. Just as I thought of hanging up and re-dialing, the number rang.

"Hello...who is it?"

"It's me, Mother. I'm here with Arthur."

"Have you seen your father?"

"No...there's been no word from him."

"Have you been to see April?"

"They wouldn't *let* me see her. Her father...spoke to me. They're doing more tests."

"Charles Stannard just called *here*."

This surprised me. "What did he *want*?"

"To speak with your father. He said it had to do with business. I told him your father is travelling...that I expect to hear from him before the evening is out. It's something about running the Stannard family's foundation..."

"He mentioned that to me, *too*, Mother."

She was silent for a moment. "Well...I don't think your father ever would. He doesn't think Charles Stannard is a very nice man...to put it bluntly. I'm sorry to tell you that, Dear."

I heard the popping noises again. "This is a bad connection," I said.

"What will you do, now?"

"Come home, I guess. I'll have to take the train...the buses stop running from Manhattan at seven."

"When you get to Garrison, take a taxi from the station."

"All right."

"Do you have enough cash? Arthur will lend you some if you need it..."

"I'm fine, Mother."

We hung up and I slid off Arthur's desk and walked to the door. As I opened it, I saw Arthur and Miss Baker standing close together. Arlene clutched a handkerchief, and her eyes looked red.

Arthur's broad, dark face was ashen. "We just had a call from the State Police," he said. "They found your father's car."

"Just the car?" He answered me with a grave nod. "Where?" I said.

"Off the highway, south of Peekskill, near Lents Cove...a secluded spot, they said..."

"Where you can see the old Liberty Ships?"

"You *know* that spot?"

"It's where we were...this morning."

"They found the car about an hour ago," Arthur said. "Locked...no keys inside or anywhere. They said they're getting a court order to pry it open. I'm going up there. I've called for my car to be brought around...you want to ride with me?"

"Yes!"

I looked back at the darkening window beyond Arthur's desk, and breathed in deeply for a moment, before walking to the phone and dialing my mother again.

CHAPTER 11

❀

Arthur turned his car north on Broadway, skirting the El buttresses and slipping past slower traffic. We sped through the intersections until a red light caught us at 140th Street. It was past eight o'clock now; night had fallen completely. I gazed up at the aging art-nouveau apartment buildings lining the thoroughfare and saw people in the bright frames of oversized windows. Most of them were black people, moving from room to room below high ceilings in a flickering world above the dark street, so far away that they seemed like the off-speed actors in silent films.

The light changed and we sped north again. Broadway became Route 9, and we followed it out of the city. Droplets of rain began to spot the windshield. They seemed to freeze against the glass in the headlight glare of oncoming cars and the rhythmic reflections of lampposts. There was a storm front moving across the valley far upriver, and I could see the silent pulses of lightning in the distant sky.

Arthur lit a cigarette. Then, he turned on the radio as smoke enveloped us and he twisted the dial through band music, past *Sergeant Preston* and *Our Miss Brooks*, finally reaching a news station. He turned on the windshield wipers and opened the fly-window half an inch on his side to let the smoke out. And we listened for some mention of Father.

"In Geneva…peace talks stalled after reports that Vietminh forces are moving south. Secretary of State Dulles expressed U.S. opposition to the incursion, during his meeting with representatives of France, Britain, China, and the Soviet Union. The French delegation left the session in protest, when Dulles mentioned the debacle at Dien Bien Phu, and criticized what he called

- 125 -

'Europe's taste for capitulation.' Secretary Dulles also warned the Chinese and Russians against intervening in Vietnam.

"In Washington...Wisconsin Senator Joseph McCarthy heard more testimony in his committee's investigation of alleged Communist influence in the U.S. Army. The Army's Chief Counsel, Joseph Welch, again criticized the entire proceeding.

"In Atlanta...President Eisenhower addressed Baptist Church leaders, and mentioned the recent 'Brown vs. Topeka' court decision on public-school racial equality. Without endorsing the decision, Ike said the Supreme Court had spoken, and that he was sworn to uphold the Constitution. Southern Democrats *and* Republicans continue to criticize the decision as an overreach of authority on states' sovereignty. The President's spokesman said Ike will spend the next few days relaxing at Augusta National Golf Club.

"Hollywood...spokesmen for screen star Ava Gardner confirm her separation from Frank Sinatra is final. The actress is currently shooting a film with Humphrey Bogart in Spain, and is looking for a permanent home there. Sinatra, who won an Academy Award this year for his comeback role in *From Here to Eternity*, was unavailable for comment. He's said to be preparing for release of a new film, in which he plays a disgruntled former Army sniper, plotting to assassinate the President with a high-powered rifle from the window of an ordinary building in a southwestern town.

"On the local scoreboard, the Dodgers beat the St. Louis Cardinals, four-to-three, at Ebbets Field, on Jackie Robinson's eighth-inning solo homerun. Robinson once again declined to speak with reporters and..."

Arthur snapped the radio off in frustration and lit another cigarette. "They just don't get it," he muttered. I turned and looked at him. "They want to see *gratitude*," he explained. "Jack won't give that to 'em."

"Do you know Robinson?" I asked.

"I've met him. He's a gentleman...a good man."

"*He* was at the Stannards', yesterday."

"So?"

"Well...from what you say about Charles Stannard..."

"Son. How many *other* colored people were sashayin' around on that lawn?"

"None...actually...except for the waiters."

"Jack Robinson's a celebrity," Arthur sighed, staring straight ahead. "The *exception* that proves the rule. Now mind, I'm not criticizing *him* for that. He's a hero to colored folks, and can do whatever he wants to. Besides...he's a Republican...more or less..."

"He *is?*" I was surprised.

"Sure. Oh, he's voted Democrat in the past…just as I've voted Republican, from time to time…but party politics isn't Jack's thing, anyway. He's taking on the whole racial question wherever he sees the power is. He's not gonna work at it from the bottom, or the outside. He's determined to be accepted…*now*…not later. In fact, he *assumes* it, which is what gets *some* folks mad. So, whether he gets invited to the Rockefellers' or the Roosevelts'…or the Stannards'…he'll go."

"You think…he shouldn't?"

"Well…let's just say I *care* about *Jack*. I don't know how he did it, those first years with the Dodgers…the vile insults and names he was called out on the field. And some o' those redneck morons, from St. Louis and Cincinnati, slidin' into him at second base with their spikes up…itchin' for a fight. More than once, I saw him cut on the legs pretty badly…and on purpose, too…and worse. And he'd just turn away, and walk back to his position, pounding his fist into his glove, and telling his pitcher to 'play ball.' Jack's carried a lot on his shoulders…for a lot of other folks. So…if I find any fault with him, it's got nothin' to do with goin' to some party." He paused, and we drove for a moment in silence. "You knew Jack appeared before HUAC as a cooperative witness didn't you…back in 'Forty-nine?"

"I guess I heard something about it," I said, remembering a bit of old newsreel.

"It was big news," Arthur said. "I don't think he wanted to go, but…he felt he had to, I guess…colored man in *his* position. He gave them a statement against Communism, but said he cared mostly about *discrimination*…the bleak lives of colored people in America…which, he thought Communists only cared about when it suited their purposes."

"Sounds like a very *careful* statement," I said.

"That was fine…as far as it went, I guess…if you're *going* to cooperate with that committee…which, I don't think he should have. But, like I said, Jack works to be accepted by the powerful. He thinks that'll help him change things…for colored folks. He'll learn."

The rain was falling heavily when we reached Lents Cove. Arthur pulled his car off the highway and followed my directions along the tree-lined, cinder path toward the edge of the river. We could see the glow of bright lights through the trees, as we neared the spot where Father and I had parked that morning. The rain had turned cinder dust into muddy paste, and the tires began spinning as the Oldsmobile fishtailed.

"Jesus Lord," muttered Arthur.

Instantly, I recognized our Buick in the distorted headlight glare. Its doors were open, and there were men with flashlights sitting or kneeling on the front and rear seats. There were many more men standing around the car. All but two wore police uniforms. Two State Police cruisers were parked with their headlights and searchlights trained directly on the Buick and, out in the cove, two small boats moved back and forth with bright floodlights shining from their prows, scanning the water.

The policemen stared, as Arthur stopped near the water line and turned off the ignition. Three more State Police cruisers and an unmarked car sat next to us with their headlights shining onto the cove. The police boats were moving farther from shore, now, directing their searchlights over deeper water. And in Tomkins Cove across the river, the silent shadows of the mothball fleet were like a cityscape without lights.

Arthur and I got out and walked toward the Buick. I noticed its interior roof light flickering down. The rain grew heavier, suddenly, and several troopers opened umbrellas and held them over an officer who seemed to be in charge. Rainwater poured off the umbrellas and the starched brims of the troopers' hats. The two men in business suits were drenched, and the ground was a mass of puddles and black mud. The wet-cloth smell of Arthur's overcoat hung in the air, now, and water trickled over the curled brim of his Homburg. I felt cold water squeezing around my toes, and my school uniform was soaked.

"Who are *you?*" barked the State Policeman whom the others protected with their umbrellas.

Arthur looked straight into his face and pointed to the Buick. "This is my partner's car. And *this* is his son."

"You're Spencer?"

"That's right," said Arthur, holding out his hand.

The policeman looked at it for a second before grabbing it in a perfunctory shake. "Captain Roy Blanchard," he said, "State Police. We spoke by phone today. Commander Hardin says he knows you."

Arthur nodded. "We go back. He helped me organize a basketball camp for city kids in Newburgh, a few years ago."

Blanchard nodded in the direction of the search boats. "Well, can you help us with any o' this, here?"

Arthur shook his head. "No. This is…unexpected." The cop frowned and nodded again. "You're convinced the cove is the place to look?" Arthur asked.

Captain Blanchard glanced at me before answering. "Well, his car is here…isn't it?"

"But what's your thinking?" said Arthur.

"I'll tell you what…it doesn't look like robbery…or homicide." Blanchard glanced at me again before continuing. "We found his things in the car…his business briefcase…packed suitcase…suit jacket laid out neatly on the back seat. The car was locked. We haven't found the keys. It's possible he parked here and went for a walk, but had some trouble. This is a tricky piece o' river and people do fall in…did you know that? People go out walking, get distracted, lose their footing, and then…well…"

"My father's an *expert* swimmer," I interjected.

"What's that?" said Blanchard.

"A champion swimmer…"

"*Champion*? Of what?"

"He was a top swimmer in high school…"

"*High school*?" Blanchard's smile was condescending. "Twenty…twenty-five years ago?"

"He stays in shape," I asserted, "He swims in the river all the time."

"Oh he does? In this river?"

"That's right. He once saved his brother and sister from drowning, near Garrison, when they were children. Their raft floated away and he swam out and caught them…held onto them,, for *hours* in that current, until he got them to shore. He's a good swimmer, Captain."

Blanchard frowned and shook his head. "Even still…that's a long time ago, son."

"My father didn't drown…he knows everything there is to know about this river."

Arthur suddenly interrupted us. "What about fingerprints?"

"We've dusted," said Blanchard, still staring at me. "I'd like to hear more about your father's swimming habits, son…"

Arthur kept at him. "Outside?"

"Outside and in…it was the first thing we did when we got here." Blanchard seemed annoyed suddenly that he was not conducting the questioning. "That was before the rain started."

"And you found nothing?" Arthur pressed.

"Nothing much…a couple clear sets…and…lots o' smudges." Blanchard turned to one man sitting inside the car. "Jerry, that was *two* new sets o' prints you picked up, right?"

"That's right, Captain," the man replied in a muffled voice while rooting beneath the front seat.

Blanchard turned back to Arthur. "I presume one set will be Mr. Gannon's…"

"And the other will be mine, probably," I added.

"Oh? When was the last time *you* were in the vehicle?"

"This morning."

"You were in the car with your father, this morning?"

"Yes."

"Anyone else?"

"No."

"Where was this?"

"Right here," I said. "Where we're standing."

Captain Blanchard stared at me. Then, he traded looks with several of the other policemen as I described the morning's drive to the cove and then into Peekskill. I mentioned being dropped at the bus terminal and watching my father drive toward the highway.

"And that's the last you saw him?" Blanchard asked.

"Yes."

Blanchard turned to Arthur again. "We looked through the papers in his briefcase. He was intending to give some testimony in Washington this week, from what we gather." Arthur listened in silence. "Is that where he was headed, today…Washington?"

"He was expected at my office in New York, this morning," said Arthur. "Like I told you on the phone."

"So what's this testimony about, then?" But neither Arthur nor I answered as Blanchard's gaze moved back and forth between us. "*Look*," he said, "I have to ask these questions…but I'll wait. Let's see what we come up with, when we drag the river."

"You think my father drove up here and jumped in the river?" I said angrily.

Blanchard glanced at the other cops again. Finally, he turned and smiled at me. "I don't think I said that, son…did I?" I shrugged. "Like I said, we'll explore the Washington angle. Tomorrow, we'll call the Senate Committee and ask why they wanted to see him. In the meantime, we've asked federal authorities in on this." At that, Blanchard indicated the two men standing near him, dressed in business suits. They were FBI agents. They stared blankly at Arthur and me, as Blanchard finished his thought. "I think we have to explore the *possibility* at least, that he was…under some pressure about this testimony."

"He called *them* to testify," Arthur muttered. "It was *his* idea…"

"Oh?" said Blanchard in a flat voice.

"And he didn't jump in the river," I repeated.

"All right, take it easy," said Blanchard. "I said we have plenty of accidents along here…"

"If he *had* fallen in," I added, "he'd have been able to swim out again."

Blanchard frowned. "And that's…because…he was a champion swimmer in high school…and saved his brother n' sister…right?" I shook my head angrily as the two federal agents glanced at each other. Suddenly, Blanchard tried to change the confrontational mood. "Look…first things first. We have to find…see if we find anything. Maybe he fell in, maybe he didn't. Maybe he had a heart attack and *couldn't* swim." He paused and looked at me hard. "Maybe he just left the car and walked away. And just maybe…he met someone else here, and left with that person. Give us a chance to try and find out what happened, son." I nodded. "We'll drag in the morning, then we'll talk some more. Now, maybe you two can leave us alone and let us do our jobs. Before you leave, though, give our man here samples of your fingerprints. He can take 'em in one o' the cruisers. You aren't compelled to, of course. You can consult a lawyer first, if you want, and come down to the barracks in the morning to give us your prints. But it's getting late, and *we* want answers as fast as *you* do."

"Just curious, Captain," said Arthur. "Were there any signs of struggle here…or in the car?"

Blanchard frowned. "No. We noticed a lot o' footprints in the cinder dust around here, when we arrived…just before sundown…but our guys didn't have time to get anything meaningful before dark. Then, the rain started. I'm not sure we would've learned anything, anyway. This is a kids' hangout…folks park here all the time to look at the ships."

"But you don't discount the *possibility* of homicide?"

"I discount nothing, Mr. Spencer."

"That's good," I interjected, "because my father never puts his jacket on the back seat, like you found it."

Suddenly, one of the federal agents leaned forward. "What's that, son?"

"The captain said my father's suit jacket was laid out on the back seat. He *never* does that. He *always* hangs his jacket on the hook, just behind the driver's seat."

"Interesting," muttered Blanchard. Again, I sensed his resistance to the idea that anyone might have harmed my father. I glanced at the federal agent, who asked nothing more, but nodded.

"What about the local police?" Arthur suddenly said. "I don't see anyone here from town."

Blanchard sighed. "This is a state matter…at present. We're on state property that the federal government leases. We'll be working with the Peekskill police and civil authorities tomorrow, when we start questioning in town."

Arthur turned off 9D and drove slowly along the soft, mushy gravel toward my family's house. The porch light was on, and the living room windows glowed. I could see that the front door was open behind the screened door. It was almost eleven o'clock.

As we neared the house, Mother came out onto the porch with Liz. Arthur turned off his ignition and got out of the car as I slid from the passenger side with my school bag. The rain had finally stopped, though everything was soaked and dripping. A thick, slow-moving fogbank covered the back hill, and the night air smelled like rotten burlap. The temperature was dropping and I shivered in the dampness.

Mother called to Arthur from the porch. "Any word?"

"Nothing yet, Mary."

She came down the steps and embraced him, but Liz stayed on the porch and looked at me. I smiled up at her sheepishly.

"Can you stay for a cup of coffee, Arthur," my mother said. "Something to eat?"

"Nothing, Mary," he said, holding her hands. "I should get back to the city."

"*Tom*," said Liz, suddenly, "your fingers are all blue!"

Arthur looked up at her. "We gave fingerprints to the State Police, hon." Suddenly, he pulled away from Mother, and said, "I'll get ink all over…"

"Oh, Arthur," she sobbed. He put his arms around her again, but kept his fists clenched.

Liz stared away into the fog behind the house. "Will you be able to drive home in this soup…Arthur?"

"Oh, I think so, child."

Mother wiped her eyes with a handkerchief she'd pulled from a pocket in her dress. "Maybe you *should* stay the night," she said, "and drive back in the morning, after this lifts."

"No, Mary…I need to be with Hazel and Laureen. They're upset enough, already." They kissed each other on the cheek. Then he nodded to Liz, glanced at me, and walked back to his car, where he paused with the door open. "We'll pray tonight, Mary."

"Yes, Arthur," she smiled, weakly.

Moments later, as his car headed toward the dark highway, I followed my mother and sister up the steps and into the house. I put my school bag down near the foot of the stairs and looked around the quiet living room. The television was on, with its volume turned low.

"Are you hungry?" said Mother. I frowned and shook my head. "Well, then," she sighed, putting the little handkerchief back in her dress pocket, and patting her thighs nervously. Suddenly, she began sobbing again. I put my arms around her and was shocked by the feeling of my mother collapsing against me.

CHAPTER 12

David whispered from his bed. "Is it thunder?"

"I don't know, buddy." I threw off my blanket and stood beneath the shallow bedroom ceiling, thinking. Quickly walking to our window, I pulled up the sash and knelt down as another explosion echoed in the valley. The wet hillside below the house was strewn with branches and fallen limbs, but the fog had dissolved overnight, and the sun was bright on the river.

Suddenly, I felt David's body against me, as he squeezed his head and shoulders under the window sash. Another explosion rolled up the valley.

"Hear that?" he said.

"Sure, buddy." I tried speaking without emotion, to protect him from my own unsettling realization—a police detail was working the river between Lents Cove and Tomkins Cove, firing blank cannon shots from the bows of boats. It was an old-fashioned method of retrieving drowned bodies, which I'd seen before on the river. Grandfather Hank called it "setting the lost souls free," a poetic description of a simple process that induced vibrations in the depths and usually worked only too well—freeing lifeless bodies in an indiscriminate tide of stunned turtles, dead fish and bottom silt. Over the years, I'd also seen police haul the river like fishermen with large nets and three-pronged anchors at the ends of long chains. I wondered, now, why they'd chosen cannons, considering the river's depth between the coves, and the unpredictable currents that could easily take a dislodged body down river and out to sea before it ever reached the surface.

David suddenly pulled his head back inside. "I'm gonna see if Dad's home, yet!" he said, racing across the bedroom.

"David!"

But he was gone quickly, as a wave of nausea washed over me and kept me kneeling at the open window, reeling from the sweet-rot smell outside. I clenched my teeth and gripped the windowsill; sweat rose on my forehead and rolled down my spine. Finally, three explosions in close succession rumbled up the valley and I came to my senses again.

My knees ached, as I struggled to my feet and walked slowly back to check my watch, which lay flat on our dresser. Eight-thirty—we'd overslept. Another cannon shot rolled in the valley, as I reached down to my school bag on the floor beside the dresser and pulled out Father McHenry's note. I placed the sealed envelope on the dresser and stared at my father's name, typed by Miss Drummond, on the pale blue paper. I touched the crisp letters with trembling fingers.

Mother sat quietly on the living room couch in her white cotton robe. A great pile of newspapers from New York City, and from several Highland towns, lay scattered on the coffee table near her. Liz sat across the room in the big armchair by the windows. Like me, she was already dressed—in blue jeans and an old shirt. David and Mary sat quietly on the floor below the television in their pajamas.

On the screen, the NBC announcer Dave Garroway sat on his own couch, with his back to a wall of windows. Curious people watched him from the sidewalk outside, as he chatted with a chimp dressed as a cowboy—checked shirt, cuffed jeans, fringed leather chaps and a wide-brimmed hat. The chimp held a six shooter cap gun In one of his elongated hands, and when he suddenly waved it threateningly at Garroway, the people on the street laughed.

"Anything in the papers?" I asked Mother.

"There's something about the new bid in most of these," she said, pointing to a copy of the *New York Daily Mirror*. Even from across the room, I could read the headline and story on its billboard-front page. Like the *Journal-American* story the day before, it described the $125 million bid for TV studios on St. Nicholas Avenue as a great victory for the City.

"Nothing about *Dad*?" I said. She shook her head; her face was blank.

Suddenly, Liz spoke up bitterly. "Did you *know* Charles Stannard is behind this other bid?"

"Arthur told me, yesterday," I nodded gravely. "The papers are saying it now?" Neither Liz nor Mother responded, so I walked closer to the coffee table and scanned all the newspapers before sitting at the edge of the couch. "How did we get the papers?" I asked.

"Your sister rode her bicycle into Cold Spring and got them at Wilson's," said Mother.

I smiled at Liz and said, "how did you carry them all?" She didn't respond.

"She found one of your old canvas bags in the garage," said Mother. "She hung it on the handlebars the way you did when you had that route...in Brooklyn."

"Good work, Liz," I said.

She stared back at me and spoke at last. "How's April...Mom said you couldn't get in to see her?"

"Yeah. They're doing more tests..."

Mother smiled weakly. "Why don't you call the hospital, Tom...maybe you'll get through now."

"You think so?"

She nodded. "Just don't tie up the phone."

After a moment to think about it, I rose from the couch and walked toward the kitchen. As I passed Liz, she turned away and stared out the windows onto the empty porch.

In the kitchen, I lifted the receiver from the telephone on the wall near the sink. I got the number from an Information operator and quickly dialed. A female voice answered after three rings. "Grace-Episcopal Hospital."

"Yes...good morning," I said. "I'm calling to check the status of a patient?"

"Name, please..."

"April Stannard..."

"*Your* name?"

"Tom Gannon..."

The operator paused. "I see that patient is under restriction on the Private Floor. Are you a relative?"

"A close friend..."

"One moment, please." She put me on hold. As I waited, I imagined she was checking with hospital officials or April's parents. I braced myself for the polite refusal. She came back. "I'm sorry...I just came on duty...our lines are very busy this morning...now, you asked me about..."

"April Stannard..."

"You're the friend..."

"Yes."

"I see...hold another moment." And she was gone again. This time, it took several minutes for her to return, and she seemed overwhelmed. "You know what? I'm just going put you through, please hold..."

"Oh…"

Instantly, I heard the sound of a room extension being dialed. Then, a long series of beeps, until the phone was answered.

"Yes…who is it?" It was April's mother. For a moment I couldn't speak. "Hello," she said, "is someone there?"

"Yes, Mrs. Stannard, it's me…Tom Gannon."

"How did you get through?"

"Mrs. Stannard…I only wanted to know how April is…"

"Not well."

"Is there anything I can do?"

"You can leave us alone…didn't my husband make that clear enough?" Then, I heard her speak to someone else. "Nothing," she said in an angry whisper. "It's no one." When she spoke into the phone again, her voice was cold as stone. "I'm going to hang up, now."

"I'm sorry…I didn't mean to be a bother…just tell April I asked…"

Mrs. Stannard hung up. I replaced the receiver and looked out the windows toward the tops of the distant cliffs, where two red-tailed hawks circled on wind drafts. I walked to the back door and stepped outside onto the upper platform of the stairs. I closed the door behind me and leaned against the wooden side rail, as another explosion echoed in the valley. An old-fashioned sloop, its bright sails puffed with wind, glided south like a swan on the sun-drenched river. A lone figure stood at the helm working a brass-plated wheel, reflecting sunlight as it turned, and a small American flag fluttered at the stern.

Suddenly, the kitchen door opened and Mother stepped out. She closed the door and stood with her hands crossed at the wrists, clutching her bathrobe lapels tightly against her chest. She looked at me with tired eyes. The almost girlish glow, that had brightened her expression the morning before, was gone. Now, deep lines and hard ridges gave her face the look of shattered glass.

"Well?" she said. I looked away from her and watched the sloop disappear beyond a tree-covered bend. I felt my mother's hand on my shoulder. "Tom…how is she?"

"I don't know," I said, turning abruptly. "Her mother answered the phone and wasn't happy to hear from me."

Her grip tightened on my shoulder. "They're worried, I'm sure."

"She's never liked me, anyway…"

"Who…Mrs. Stannard?"

"Yeah."

"Listen to me, Tom." She pulled me toward her now. "Don't you know who the Stannards are?"

"Of course."

"Do you?"

"*Mother.*"

"Then act like it! I mean…you're a smart boy…a history student, for goodness sake…I'd think you'd know better…"

"Mother, please don't start with the whole Protestant, Catholic thing…"

"You've known this girl for…how long? Since last winter, I think…and we've never met her parents. Why is that?"

"Hank Gannon's litany of Irish resentments," I muttered. "It's a sad, old song Mother…"

"*My* family is *English*, Tom…of course, the Brents *are* Catholics…like the Gannons are…"

"Yes…and *all* of those prejudices are *mutual.*"

"It's a *bit* more complicated than that. But, the point is, the past isn't just something you read about in a book. It *lives*, unfortunately…it doesn't change overnight. So, don't expect it to…not *even for you.*"

"Have you and Dad gone out of your way to meet *them*?"

"That's not fair," she said. Then, tears seemed to be welling in her eyes.

"Mother, I'm sorry," I said. "I'm sorry. This is all *my* fault anyway…nobody else's. I just think…we could discuss it some other day."

She frowned and shook her head. "Your father and I think April's a *fine* girl, Tom…intelligent, forthright. It's just unfortunate that…her parents…"

"Mother…I've *seen* what you mean…I *know* what you're saying about them."

She released her grip on me, and I glanced toward the river, as another cannon shot rolled up the valley. I looked at my watch; it was nine-thirty.

"Son. We need to be *careful*…dealing with these people." I looked at her and shook my head in confusion, as she continued. "It *is* strange the way they're distancing you from that girl all of a sudden…even good old-fashioned snobbery doesn't explain it. I've had this odd feeling, since yesterday…since Charles Stannard's call…out of the blue…"

"Whadya' mean…offering Dad a job? He said the same to me, the day before…I just hadn't mentioned it, yet…"

She stared at me grimly. "I just don't believe him. I don't even think that's the reason he called. It was an excuse, to get me on the phone."

"Excuse? For what?"

"I've never spoken to this man before…and my son's been seeing his daughter for months. He gets on and introduces himself in the most…offhand…*inappropriate* manner."

"That's the way he is, Mother."

She frowned. "Please. He *mentioned* the job with his family's foundation, but…it…it wasn't sincere. But that's not the important thing. It was the *way* he asked about your father that struck me. 'Do you know where your husband is?' That's what he said. Not 'may I speak with your husband?' or 'how can I reach your husband?' or fifty other things he might have said. No. 'Do you know where your husband is?'"

"I don't get it."

"I find it an odd choice of words, Tom. Unless…he already knew, or suspected…something…and was trying to find out what *I* knew." Another cannon shot rumbled in the valley, but it was the sound of our telephone ringing inside the kitchen door that shocked my mother. Her grip tightened at the lapels of her robe, and now she stared past me, toward the river. "Your family needs you," she whispered. "*I* need you."

We heard footsteps in the kitchen, and then Liz's voice, muffled, beyond the door. "Hello? Oh…hi. Yes…we're…yes…yes, she is…"

Mother turned and pushed the door open. I followed her into the kitchen and saw Liz standing near the sink, holding one hand over the speaker. "It's just Laureen Spencer," she said.

"Don't stay on long, Dear," said Mother, touching Liz's shoulder and walking toward the dark hallway.

We were together in the living room when the phone rang again, at eleven o'clock. It occurred to me, now, that the cannons had stopped, and when I looked at Mother and Liz I saw the same realization in their eyes. I jumped up from the couch and started toward the telephone next to the front door.

"Take it in the kitchen," Mother said, barely glancing at David and Mary sitting on the floor near the television.

As the phone continued ringing, I hurried to the kitchen. This time, I closed the door at the end of the hallway and then bounded to the phone. "*Yes*?"

I heard Arthur Spencer's grim voice. "They've found a body in Lents Cove."

"Is it…"

"I don't know, Tom. The State Police are bringing it to the coroner's office in Peekskill, but they've made no statements. We'll have to go to Peekskill to see for ourselves. Can you join me there?"

"I'll check the bus and train schedules right away," I said.

"I'm leaving Manhattan now. I'll be there in forty minutes or so. Meet me at the police station on Main Street. That's where the coroner's office is."

"Arthur...is this everything you know?"

"Son, my information comes from Jim Hardin, the State Police Commander. He's an old friend...and all he would say is that his boats were on Lents Cove this morning..."

"We heard the cannons," I interjected.

"...And they stopped...about ten-thirty...because the tide was changing. As they sat there in a circle...a half-dozen boats, he said, waiting for the current...a body came to the surface."

"Christ..."

"How is your mother, Tom...the children?"

"Well enough...I guess."

We hung up. As I turned, I saw that Mother and Liz had already entered the kitchen. They stood together with their backs to the closed hallway door. Liz gripped Mother's hand and Mother whispered. "Well?"

"Arthur says the State Police found a body in Lents Cove, and they're taking it to Peekskill. They won't tell him *anything*...for Christ sake."

Liz now gave me a pleading look. "Should *we* call the State Police?"

"I doubt it'll do any good," I said. "Arthur knows the top commander, and *he* won't say anything." Then, looking at my mother, I said, "Arthur's going to Peekskill right now, to find out for himself. He asked me to meet him."

"Call a taxicab," said Mother, turning abruptly on her heels and pushing through the hallway door, hurrying to her bedroom to get dressed.

Twenty minutes later, when the driver from Highland Cab Co. pulled up and stopped near the house, the five of us were waiting on the porch. As we filed down the steps toward the taxi, I noticed the driver remove his cap and scratch his head with its stiff, black brim. Clearly, he hadn't anticipated carrying a crowd. I got in beside him, while Mother and Liz got in back with David between them and Mary on Liz's lap.

As the driver fitted his cap back on his head, and threw the gearshift into first, he gave me a sarcastic smirk. "Family excursion?"

"Just take us to Peekskill," I said in a cold flat voice.

The driver scowled, incensed that a young person had addressed an adult in this manner. I felt my mother's hand on my shoulder, suddenly, gripping me tightly. The driver stared indignantly into my eyes, and then stepped abruptly on the gas.

The ride down the mountain road to Peekskill was silent, but as we neared the city limits, the driver ventured another question. "So…what's in Peekskill?"

I turned toward him without a ready answer, but heard my little brother's voice.

"We're going to meet our Dad!" he said from behind us.

"We need to go to the police station," I said blankly. "On Main Street."

"I know where it is, son," the driver said.

I heard Mother whisper to David. "Shush."

"Well *aren't* we?" he insisted.

CHAPTER 13

It was just past noon when we walked into the small, drab police station lobby. Arthur tossed a lit cigarette into a sand canister and turned to face us. "The body they've found is *not*..."

"Joe," my mother said, grimly.

He breathed out heavily and shook his head. Then, he pointed to a set of tan, metal doors with *Police Headquarters* and *City Coroner* stenciled on in white paint. "Mary...I saw the State Police Captain...Blanchard...a few minutes ago. He tried to call you at home, but you'd already left. He wants to meet you, right away."

"Are the boats still out?" I asked.

"They came to shore with the body," Arthur said. "Blanchard ordered them to wait."

Mother nodded at Arthur. "We need to see this Captain Blanchard, then."

Arthur pointed to the doors again. "They'll send for us, soon; he's been given a temporary office, here." Then, he leaned toward Mother and whispered. "There's something odd going on. They seem...too nervous...Blanchard's biggest worry is the *newspapers*...the mayor called him twice in the ten minutes I was with him. The local police chief keeps walking in and out...demanding information. Those two FBI men...watching everything..."

"Why is the FBI here?" Liz blurted.

Just then, a young patrolman from the Peekskill Police pushed through the metal doors and held them open. "Mr. Spencer, sir; they're ready for you, now."

Mother spoke tersely. "Tom, come with us. Liz, stay here with the children."

The young patrolman led us down a long hallway of busy squad rooms and large offices to the doorway of a smaller, windowless office. Inside, Captain Blanchard of the State Police waited behind a gray metal desk. I could see that he was about forty years old, a much younger and fitter man than he'd seemed in the rain and glare of the cove the night before.

Sitting to his left were the two FBI agents, all-American guys with square faces, close-cropped hair and conservative suits. Two State Police troopers stood impassively against the wall to Blanchard's right. And a policeman from the Peekskill force sat in the corner behind Blanchard. This man was at least fifteen years older than the other men, and his nose had the purple blotches of a veteran drinker. His jacket was covered with ribbons and brass.

Blanchard stood up and greeted us with a businesslike smile. "Mrs. Gannon...Mr. Spencer." He pointed to two wooden chairs in front of his desk. Then, he glanced across the room at the young patrolman. "We need one more."

I waved him off. "Don't bother...I'm fine." Blanchard nodded appreciatively.

Arthur helped Mother to one of the chairs, and then sat next to her, as I stood closely behind them. Once the young patrolman had left the tiny room and closed the door, Blanchard sat down again and stared briefly at Mother. He introduced the FBI men as Agents Valeriani and Boone. He said the officer sitting behind him was Chief Walton of the Peekskill Police. He made no reference to the troopers.

Then, he got to the point. "Mrs. Gannon, my men found a body in Lents Cove this morning. It is *not* your husband." Mother sighed. Arthur leaned against her but kept his eyes on Blanchard. "It's the body of a Negro male. Now...since I've got nothing to report about Mr. Gannon...this discovery only complicates my job. I hope to have something to tell you soon. Meanwhile...may I ask for your help, as we sort out these unfortunate circumstances?"

She nodded. "How can we help, Captain?"

"Mrs. Gannon...there's a bunch of newspaper and radio reporters waiting for me, up the street at City Hall...the Mayor's urged me to get up there, and tell them something...but I've delayed that...I wanted to speak with *you*, first."

"I don't understand," she said.

Blanchard smiled wearily. "The reporters know we found your husband's car last evening at the cove...where this body turned up. The rumor's already out that it's not Mr. Gannon. Of course, I'll have to go confirm that. What my problem is, d'ya' see…the press may be inclined to make something out of a coincidence…report your husband's disappearance…and this body…as if they're one story. D'ya' see what I mean? Now…nothing's served by speculation like that in the papers…I'd like to avoid it…"

"Reporters are like dogs, Mrs. Gannon," said Chief Walton, suddenly. Blanchard's face betrayed impatience over his host's blunt interruption. "Believe me…they're stupid and they run in packs. And they get a whiff of somethin' in their snouts…these reporters…they'll be busy chasin' it down for a week…won't pay attention to nothin' else."

Blanchard sighed, wearily. "Anyway, Mrs. Gannon…we'd like to see the press stick to the facts…"

"You're sure there *is* no connection?" Arthur interjected.

"None that we can tell," said Blanchard.

"Then, what do you want from Mrs. Gannon?"

"After I give my statement to the press," Blanchard explained, "they're gonna want one from the family. I'd like to have the family's agreement…that we'll stay on the same page together…publicly, I mean. Promise to speak with *me*, first, before speaking to the press…give me a chance to find your husband, Mrs. Gannon, or tell you what's happened to him…and keep this thing free of needless speculation. That way…we'll have the least chance of embarrassment…for everyone."

Mother and Arthur glanced at each other. Finally, Mother turned toward Blanchard again and spoke in a strong voice. "We'll do nothing to impede your search."

"Thank you, Mrs. Gannon," he replied, with grateful deference. "May I ask if you've *heard* from your husband?"

"*No!* What are you suggesting?"

Blanchard smiled, politely. "I'm not ready to suggest *anything*, Mrs. Gannon. I'm just pursuing leads…scenarios…still at the question stage. Like why does a man drive to the river and leave his briefcase, his travel bag and his jacket in a locked automobile? Has he gone for a walk and had some unfortunate accident? Does he plan to…drown himself…or just disappear for some reason?"

"Captain," Arthur said, glancing briefly at Mother. "You said you hadn't ruled out homicide, last night. Has that changed?"

"No, sir. We look at every possibility. But we've found no evidence of foul play, so far."

Chief Walton interrupted again, addressing us in the pointless boilerplate of a sympathy card. "These situations are difficult for family and friends. We appreciate what you must be going through."

Arthur ignored Walton and pressed Blanchard. "If he *had* done something to himself, would you be…I'm sorry Mary…having such trouble finding his body?"

"Bodies *do* float away in that river," Blanchard replied, before looking at Mother. "I'm sorry about this rough talk, Ma'am." She gave no response. "Do you know of anyone who would have reason to harm your husband?"

"Not really, Captain, no," she said.

"How about *you*, Mr. Spencer? Any enemies he might've had?"

"*Everyone* has enemies, Captain," Arthur said. "Whether they know it or not."

Blanchard smiled. "Well. You need a definite suspect and clear motive for murder…and a body that tells you it's been murdered. You can't claim homicide by default."

"All right," said Arthur. "What if he *did* decide to 'disappear' as you put it…where would he go…without his car and his things?" Blanchard nodded in silent assent to Arthur's logic. "And what about the suit jacket?" Arthur added. "Last night, the boy told you his father never puts a jacket on the back seat, the way you found it."

Again, Blanchard only nodded, as Mother reached into her purse and found a small handkerchief. She raised it to her face and pressed it against one eye and then the other and Blanchard frowned sympathetically. "We can come back to this, Ma'am," he said. Then, he looked at Arthur. "Mr. Spencer…I believe you're making my point. Speculation only upsets everyone."

"All right, Captain," said Arthur. "Then what about this body?"

"Well…that's a whole other kettle of fish…most unfortunate." Blanchard's demeanor suddenly changed. Hardness emerged on his face; he seemed again to be the arrogant officer we'd encountered the night before. The more I saw of this man, the less I liked. "We found no driver's license…Social Security card…ID of any kind on the body," he said.

"Isn't that odd?" said Arthur.

"Depends," said Blanchard.

"Do you know how he got in the river…or when?"

"Coroner's running tests. We may never know everything we want to. There's some decomposition starting…coroner thinks the body was in the water twelve hours…maybe fifteen tops."

"So, he drowned?"

"Not clear," Blanchard shrugged. "Some water was found in his lungs…not as much as you generally see in drowning cases. But it *could've* been enough. Coroner's also looking at a possible heart attack…appears to be some evidence o' that."

"So, what will you tell the press?"

"I'm gonna rely on what the *coroner* tells me, Mr. Spencer." Distinct annoyance had risen in Blanchard's voice.

Arthur looked at his watch. "Captain," he said, "how does someone get into that cove unnoticed…with all your people out there, since before dark, yesterday?"

"More speculation, Mr. Spencer. You saw what things were like out there, last night…heavy rain and fog. How far up and down river could *you* see? Anyway, this poor fella could've been in there before we arrived…aside from which, there's no way to know where he went in…might've been upriver…could've been carried downstream."

"It *does* seem an odd coincidence, though," Arthur said. "Even if you don't want to say so publicly, don't you think it might be prudent to investigate whether there *was* a connection between this, and…Joe's disappearance?"

Blanchard stared back at Arthur, before answering in a carefully measured way. "*Sounds* dramatic…I imagine it's the way the press'll want to play it…but we think these are unconnected events."

Mother and Arthur stared at each other again.

"Captain," I said, interrupting. "Was it an *older* man you found? Old enough to be someone's grandfather…in his sixties or seventies?"

Blanchard seemed surprised by my question. The FBI men were erect in their seats, staring intensely at me. In the corner, Chief Walton sat immobile as stone. Blanchard stared at me and finally spoke, in a voice that seemed artificially calm. "That's a reasonable description. Why, son?"

"Speak up, Tom." Mother's voice was insistent, as she turned in her seat, and glanced back at me. Arthur turned to look at me as well.

"A wild guess," I said. "I saw a man like that at the bus terminal, yesterday."

"Of course!" Blanchard smiled politely again. "You told us last night, didn't you, that you'd been to the bus terminal…your father dropped you there after your morning chat at the cove. What time did you observe this man?"

I answered carefully. "Between nine-thirty and ten."

Agent Valeriani jumped in. "Did you speak with him?"

"No. I noticed him sitting across from me in the waiting area. That's all."

Chief Walton sounded confused. "Why were you in the bus terminal?"

"I was waiting for a bus to school…"

"What school?"

"St. Paul's. In Highland Falls."

Walton nodded. "I'm familiar with it."

"Sorry, Chief," said Blanchard, giving him a sheepish look. "The boy told us he'd been dropped by his father at the terminal, yesterday. I should've mentioned it."

Agent Valeriani spoke up again, and his eyes seemed to be searching me. "What made you notice this man?"

"I just noticed him. That's all."

"I see," said Valeriani, sounding unsatisfied with my answer. He sat back in his chair and glanced at his partner.

Walton spoke abruptly. "Did you see this Negro man get on a bus?" His expression was fierce.

I felt my dislike for these cold men growing into a suspicion—for some reason, they weren't telling us everything they knew. "No," I said, as calmly as I could.

"Well, here's my problem," said Blanchard, glancing at Walton. "There was an incident, here in town, yesterday…seems a man of this general description, an elderly Negro man, caused some trouble on a bus scheduled for Newburgh and Albany."

Arthur leaned forward. "Trouble?"

"He became belligerent," Blanchard said, with a long sigh. "We think he was drunk, maybe, or not right in the head. The driver had to put him off the bus outside the terminal."

It was strange hearing Blanchard's reluctant disclosure of what I'd seen in the terminal alley, and to hear him describe the old gentleman as crazy or drunk. But it was chilling to realize that no one was volunteering a thing about the little girl. As I looked around the room, I was struck by the poker-faced stares of the FBI men. I looked at Blanchard. "Was the man arrested?" I said.

Chief Walton answered. "He was."

"By *your* men?" I said.

The Chief stared at me and nodded. "He was charged with breach of the peace, but…we couldn't hold him."

Mother looked at Blanchard and spoke up. "Do I understand you…Captain…*this* is the man who was found in the river?"

"We're still trying to establish that," he said.

Arthur pressed him. "What's the *problem*? Hasn't the bus driver seen the body, yet?"

"No…sir." Blanchard's voice sounded heavy and frustrated. "The driver gave us a brief statement, yesterday, right after the incident…then he told us…if we had any more questions…we'd need to speak to his attorney."

"Why would he hire an attorney?" Arthur said, shaking his head in disbelief. There was silence all around. "Is he planning to press charges? Is the bus company?" More silence. "Oh, I see…they thought *they'd* get sued."

Walton waved his hand rapidly. "The bus company wants to forget this ever happened. It doesn't do their business or public relations any good. The driver was questioned…like the captain said. There wasn't much he could add to the basic facts of what happened."

"Except, he hasn't seen this body," Arthur countered. "And now, he's got an attorney!"

Again no one responded, so I asked another question. "What about the other passengers?"

"None of them wished to be interviewed," said Walton, in a cold voice.

Then, I gave them one last chance to prove to me that they weren't hiding something. "Was the old man travelling with anyone?" I asked.

Walton snapped at me. "No, he wasn't!" My hands began to tremble. I shoved them into my pockets.

Blanchard spoke more diplomatically. "Uh…not to our knowledge, he wasn't. Did *you* see him with anyone?" The room grew silent again and my head began spinning, but I fought against it. Mother and Arthur turned again to look at me, and as I stared into their faces, the spinning stopped. "Try to remember what you saw," said Blanchard. "Maybe there's another witness we should…find…and question."

"No, Captain," I said. "I didn't notice anybody with the man I saw."

Walton frowned. "You're sure?"

"Positive," I said with finality, wondering if they believed me.

Mother looked at Blanchard again. "I can see why the bus company doesn't want to pursue it," she said. "But if this man has family somewhere, *they'll* demand a full investigation."

Arthur interjected. "Captain, the chief just said the man on the bus was arrested for disturbing the peace. What ID did *he* provide? He was fingerprinted, I assume? Photographed?"

Walton frowned and answered for the captain. "The man refused to cooperate with the arresting officer."

"But you released him," Arthur said. "You wouldn't do that before making an ID."

Walton glared at Arthur. Then, Blanchard stared at his desktop and rubbed the back of his neck with both hands. "Might as well tell him, Chief."

After a long pause, Walton finally spoke. "The man wasn't...*per se* released. He...walked out. He was left alone in an interview room by my officer...who'd gone to set up for prints and pictures. While he was out of the room, the man walked..."

Blanchard sighed, still rubbing his neck. "Tell 'em the rest."

"He must've taken the arrest file with him...all the paper work, which was left on the desk by my officer...it was gone when he returned."

"Only a thief or...crazy person...would even *think* of doing that," Blanchard grumbled.

"The officer's on suspension," added Walton. "He's been told...take a *long* vacation."

"But you'll call him back, now," said Mother, "to view the body...so he can tell you if it's the man he arrested."

"Well you see, that's just it, Mrs. Gannon," said Blanchard. "What if it *is* the same man? What do I do...announce it...embarrass everybody? How does that help me find your husband?"

"This entire matter *is* an embarrassment...to my department, Ma'am." Walton seemed to be pleading, now. "It's embarrassin' enough to admit it here, but...like the captain said...we're tryin' to work with you. I'm not callin' that officer back, though. I don't wanna see his face. I sure don't want the press talkin' to him and blowin' this outta perporshin'. We're closin' the books on it. We need to move on...find your husband."

"And after all," Arthur added, with sarcasm, "we're only talking about a dead Negro."

"Now *that's* just unnecessary!" Blanchard sputtered. "I don't think I've been disrespectful to you...have I?"

"No, Captain, you haven't," Arthur conceded with a nod. "I apologize...but...you don't really think you'll keep this out of the papers..."

Walton's eyes bulged and his faced grew livid. "Captain Blanchard's men found a body with no ID on it. Now...there's nothin' I can do about that. The press'll write what they write, but I don't have to help 'em. We've checked statewide missing-persons reports...checked mental asylums, and nursin' homes, for reports of residents walkin' off...we found nothin'. Now, if this body *is* the same man who caused trouble on the bus yesterday...so what? We didn't ask for this here, in our town. In my opinion the bus company's actin' in the most reasonable way…which, we could all take a lesson from. *They're* the aggrieved party. It was *their* bus disrupted, *their* driver and passengers inconvenienced. Now, *you're* tryin' to make this seem like the important person is the one who caused all the trouble…well, that's not right. I'm sorry he's a Negro, but it's just not right."

"I must say, gentlemen," Arthur sighed, "you're the least curious policemen I've ever met."

Captain Blanchard frowned and shook his head. The federal agents' wing-tipped shoes shuffled beneath their chairs. Chief Walton pressed his lips so tightly together that the lower half of his face seemed to collapse around his mouth. He leaned back in his chair in the corner and glowered at Arthur. "Are you tellin' me my job? Who are you…to come in here…and…"

"Gentlemen, please!" Blanchard interjected. "There's a lady present, and she's upset enough. This is just what I'd hoped to avoid. Now, Mr. Spencer…we'll take prints off the body and do a trace job, but frankly, I don't think we'll come up with anything. I suspect that this was some unfortunate person, wand'rin' around, probably touched in the head. I'm awfully sorry about it. But I don't want this monopolizing my time, while I'm trying to find Mrs. Gannon's husband. And yes, if I can avoid embarrassing Chief Walton and the local police, needlessly, what's the problem in that?"

I raised my hand tentatively. "Can *I* see the body?" There was stony silence. "At least that'll tell you if the body you've got is the person I saw at the terminal." More silence. "Then…*you* can decide what you want to do about it."

Agent Valeriani looked over at Chief Walton, suddenly, and said, "it's an excellent idea." Walton stared back at him, angrily, and Blanchard was surprised by the agent's intervention. But Valeriani pressed Blanchard. "Don't you agree…Captain?"

"Uh, yes…sure." Blanchard turned and glanced at Walton, and then looked at Mother. "As long as the boy's mother doesn't object…"

She quickly responded. "Why would I?"

"All right, Mrs. Gannon," he said, glancing at his watch. "I just need to ask a few more questions, first…"

"Go ahead," she said.

CHAPTER 14

"Mrs. Gannon," said Blanchard, "was your husband distressed about testifying to the McCarthy Committee?"

"That testimony was *Joe's* idea," Arthur interjected. "I told you that, last night."

"Yeah. But we've all seen people facing those committees on TV. There's *got* to be a lot of anxiety involved with that level of scrutiny…even when you *are* a good American, with nothing to hide."

Mother shook her head. "I don't think *this* is the answer, Captain. My husband's a strong person…he endured terrible conditions as a Marine…business setbacks…the loss of some clients…"

"*And* questions about his loyalty," prompted Blanchard. "Isn't that right, Mrs. Gannon? I assume this bothered him?"

"It confused him," she conceded.

"So, you'd describe his state of mind as confused," Blanchard said, with a glance at the FBI agents. "Now, I'll tell you what confuses *me*. Here's a Marine veteran in good standing…awarded the Silver Star, I believe?"

"Yes."

"So…a war hero…an attorney with apparently good prospects…church-going man…family man…no ties to the Communist Party or subversive organizations, that *we've* found." Blanchard glanced again at the agents. "Maybe a friend or two over the years that might be a problem, but that's about it. Yet…he feels compelled to go clear his name with the McCarthy Committee. Clear his name of *what*, Mrs. Gannon?"

"I don't know what you mean," she muttered.

"I mean, is it possible we don't know everything there is to know about him...that he's been hiding something...even from *you*?"

"Captain," she said, "I haven't always understood everything my husband's done. I imagine most wives would say the same. But I *assure* you, it's not in his nature to hide something, or lie to me...*or* give up his beliefs. And *that's* why I doubt he was even *going* to Washington. I believe he was already starting to reconsider the whole thing."

"My mother's right, Captain," I interjected.

"What's that?" Blanchard said, looking up at me sourly.

"My father and I talked about it, yesterday," I said. "He seemed to be...thinking it over...hard."

"Interesting." Blanchard frowned and looked at Mother again. "He discussed it with *you too*, Ma'am?"

She nodded. "He asked me what I thought. I told him I didn't like the idea."

Agent Boone leaned forward suddenly. "Why not?"

"Because I thought it was unnecessary, Agent Boone. He's blamed himself for things that aren't his fault...false accusations. Yes, for a moment I think, he *may* have believed he had to go clear his name in this...absurd ritual..."

"*Absurd ritual*...Mrs. Gannon?" Agent Boone's voice was deeply sarcastic.

She nodded. "When someone can point to you and lie about you, with no basis or facts, and be protected...and when the *victim* of the lies has to go before a committee and prove the lies are false...something's wrong..."

Blanchard started in again. "Tell me this, Mrs. Gannon. Would you say your husband is a vindictive man?"

"No," she whispered. "Why would you say that?"

"He had *debts*...isn't that so?"

"We had debts, two years ago, but paid them off." I could hear her voice rising toward anger.

"What have you *lived* on?" said Blanchard, looking quickly toward the FBI agents. "I understand your husband's law practice suffered...because of the accusations..."

"My husband has been working...for Mr. Spencer. And we've been living more or less free in Garrison...in my father-in-law's house. My parents have helped...people have helped." Mother reached for Arthur's hand.

"So, there *has* been pressure...of a financial nature." Blanchard sounded as if he were scoring debating points.

"Undoubtedly," she said.

"But he's dealt with it," interjected Arthur. "Joe and I have been working on several projects."

Agent Boone leaned forward again. "Like this St. Nicholas Avenue deal?"

"That's right," Arthur said.

"Well, from the stories in the paper today, it looks like your bid was overtaken," said Boone, smugly. "That's *got* to be disappointing."

Arthur was angry. "Where are these questions leading, sir?"

Boone ignored Arthur and pressed Mother. "Your husband *is* a liberal, Mrs. Gannon, wouldn't you say so? I gather this from the business projects and causes he supports. He seems to like *questioning* things..."

"That's not a *crime* yet...is it?"

"Not necessarily Ma'am, but it causes misunderstanding...and trouble," Boone countered. "Like that controversy in New York, two years ago. Your husband and Mr. Spencer wanted to open a theater...in a neighborhood that didn't *want* one."

Arthur blurted. "As many were *for* it as *against* it!"

"Now, I'm no real estate expert," said Boone, "but I *do* know people. A group of folks in a neighborhood get together and say they don't want a particular thing...they should be allowed to say so, shouldn't they?"

"Certainly," Arthur nodded. "And they *did*. We disagreed, and so did some of their neighbors. We happened to win that argument. They didn't like it."

"I should say not," Chief Walton interjected.

Boone turned to Mother again. "Mrs. Gannon...why is your husband so sympathetic to causes that stir up trouble? Is there just something about this country he doesn't like?"

"My husband *loves* this country, and works hard to serve it," she replied, her voice shaking with anger. "You know that as well as I do, Agent Boone...it's in your files. My husband and I have been to your office in Manhattan more than once to be questioned. You have everything there is to know about us at your disposal...including the fact that we refused to *spy* for your superiors...on my husband's friends and clients."

Boone smirked. "It wasn't the FBI that questioned your husband's loyalty, Ma'am. It's not the Bureau's fault he's had trouble clearing his name."

Blanchard continued. "Did your husband try to sue his accusers for defamation, Mrs. Gannon?"

"Yes."

"And?"

"No court would hear the case...for *two* years. But my husband recently reached a settlement...the person who made the accusations has retracted them."

"Right," Boone nodded. "But this man who agreed to an honorable settlement is the very same man your husband was intending to testify about, in Washington. Isn't that correct?" Mother made no reply. "We found your husband's paper work in the car, Mrs. Gannon. We *have* the name."

"Well, then," she said. "You don't need it from me."

"And *you* deny your husband is vindictive," Boone said, sarcastically. "I've had enough of this Communist rhetoric...and lies about the Bureau." He waved his hand in disgust and sat back in his chair. Then, he looked toward his partner, but his partner refused to return his glance.

"Now d'ya' see?" said Captain Blanchard, frowning, shaking his head. "This is just what I'd hoped to avoid...this kind of embarrassment."

Chief Walton led us down the hall to the coroner's wing and into a small viewing room with a three-by-five-foot proscenium window in its back wall. Thick, gray curtains blocked the view from the other side of the glass.

Blanchard's troopers remained in the hall, as Walton took us inside and closed the door, shutting out the hallway light. Then, as we waited in the cramped darkness, the Chief rapped on the window.

The gray curtains parted with two quick jerks of an unseen cord, and we were enveloped suddenly in white light. As my eyes adjusted, I began to see beyond the glass. There, on a pallet encircled by white hospital drapes, lay the body of a black man with his feet toward the window. Everything but the man's face was covered beneath layers and folds of white sheeting that glowed under intense medical lamps.

"Get as close as you want," Captain Blanchard said.

I took two steps forward and leaned against the window, feeling its coldness on the tip of my nose. I studied the dead man's face. The eyes were closed and the head had been elevated slightly, which distorted the face in a lifeless frown.

"Can I see more of him?" I said, turning toward the police and FBI men. "Can the sheets be pulled down a little off his head?"

"This is the way we do it," muttered Walton.

Blanchard sighed. "What d'ya' think, son? Is he the man you saw at the bus terminal?"

"The man I saw wore glasses...steel-rim."

"This man wasn't wearing glasses, when he was found," Blanchard said.

Agent Valeriani spoke up. "What about the man you arrested, Chief?"

"I'm…not sure," Walton stammered. "I never did see that person, myself."

I looked through the glass again. "Is there an old pair around that you could put on him?" I suggested.

"Well, I don't know," muttered Walton.

"That's a good idea," said Valeriani.

"But I don't think we *have* anything like that," Walton grumbled.

"I bet we can get a pair in the five-and-dime up the street, Chief," Valeriani countered.

"Oh…let me check," Walton said, staring at Valeriani before turning on his heels and leaving the room.

I looked into my mother's face, which seemed oddly serene in the white light reflected through the window. She nodded, but said nothing. I reached for her hands and gripped them tightly.

"You're doing fine, son," said Arthur.

There was silence in the crowded little room until Walton returned. "All right…we found something," he said, closing the door again.

I turned to the window. A morgue technician in a white cap, gown and sanitary mask stepped through a seam in the drapery that encircled the body. He held a pair of cheap wire glasses in his blue, rubber-gloved hands. And though they looked nothing like the glasses I remembered, when they were placed over the dead man's closed eyes, his frowning face seemed to soften in the illusion of life.

"That's him," I said.

"You're certain?" said Blanchard.

"Yes."

"Had you ever seen this man before yesterday?"

"No."

"Mrs. Gannon…Mr. Spencer," Blanchard said. "Step forward please, and observe the face of this man." I made room for Mother and Arthur at the window. Blanchard gave them time to look. Finally, he asked them. "Have you ever seen this man before?"

"No, Captain," said Arthur. Mother turned toward Blanchard and shook her head.

"That's all," said Blanchard.

Back in his temporary office, Blanchard got our signatures on formal statements. Then, he came out from behind his desk and walked toward the door, where he briefly paused. "Thank you for coming down," he said, with a per-functory smile. "For your patience. Someone will be with you shortly…to see about your vehicle."

He left the room with the other men, and I stood near Mother and Arthur in the silent office. They stared at me. They seemed frustrated. I needed to tell them about the little girl.

Suddenly, Agent Valeriani appeared in the open doorway and came back into the room. He walked toward me, and held out a small white card, with the blue FBI insignia and his phone number on it. "Please take this," he said. "Call me if anything occurs to you…that may have slipped your mind. Or just call me, for any reason…any time." I took his card. Then, he faced Mother and Arthur. "Ma'am…Sir…I'm sorry…very sorry." He turned away abruptly and left.

Soon the young patrolman appeared and we followed him down the hall and out through the double, metal doors into the lobby again, where Liz, David and Mary were waiting on a small wooden bench. They stood up when they saw us. Liz grabbed David and Mary by the hands and her face was urgent with curiosity as she stared at Mother. But Mother shook her head, signaling that this was not the time to speak.

"Where are we going *nowww*?" David whined. He stamped his feet on the tiled floor, and violently swung Liz's right hand back and forth, until she suddenly jerked his arm straight. He froze. Mary raised one finger to her lips and whispered, "shush."

We followed the patrolman out into the glare of Main Street. It was two o'clock now, and it was hot and windless. I could smell the brackish water of the nearby marshes at low ebb, baking in the sun. The patrolman led us to the police garage in back of the stationhouse, and we entered a large, dark mechanic's bay, where several police lab investigators and plain-clothes detectives seemed to be idling. The patrolman walked over to one of the detectives and they conferred briefly, in whispers.

The patrolman then turned to look at Mother. "There's no problem letting you have your car," he said, "but they have no keys for it." Mother reached into her purse and retrieved her own set of keys, which she held up for the patrol-man to see. He nodded. "Oh…okay."

Arthur spoke up. "Could we speak to the detective or the patrolman who first discovered the car?"

"He's not here," said the detective, who stood near the patrolman.

"But, who *is* he…can we get his name?" said Arthur.

"He's *not here*," the detective repeated, with annoyance. "Car's in the lot," he muttered to the young patrolman, before turning and walking away.

The patrolman led us through the auto bay and out a rear door into a parking area, where the bright sun reflected off hot blacktop. He pointed toward a dozen vehicles parked in a row against the high, chain-link fence that enclosed the police lot. "It's one of these." Then, after smiling politely, he went back inside the garage.

We walked along the line of cars until we found ours, caked with dark, cinder mud below the doors and on the tires. It looked both familiar and strange jammed into the row of abandoned and confiscated vehicles.

I whispered to Mother and Arthur. "They're lying."

Liz stood a few feet behind them, and I stared into her eyes to make sure that she'd heard me. She looked at David and Mary, and said, "go ahead and get in." They instantly obeyed her and ran toward the car.

Arthur, Mother, and Liz drew closer to me, as David and Mary squeezed into the rear seat and closed the door behind them. David's face popped up in the rear window and he watched us with grave suspicion.

Mother whispered. "Lying about what?"

"Everything." And then, I told them what I knew about the old man and the little girl being thrown off the bus as the police arrived, and how I'd forgotten it in the distractions about Father and April. I told them that the old man had been neither drunk nor crazy. I said I feared the police were using the wrong dredging method in the river. And then, I said I believed they knew more about Father's disappearance than they were saying.

"A conspiracy?" Mother said. "Between the State Police *and* federal agents…why?"

"I don't know, Mother."

"Why didn't you mention this little girl, inside?" she said, scolding me.

"Why didn't *they*?" I countered.

She stared at me. "It's too fantastic," she said. "Who would believe it?"

"No one," Arthur whispered, ruefully.

I nodded. "Mother…it seems like they're making Dad responsible for his own disappearance. That was Blanchard's attitude from the beginning…last night."

"Is that true, Arthur?" said Mother, turning to look at him.

He frowned and nodded gravely. "I can't say it isn't."

"And that interview," I pressed. "That was Alice in Wonderland…lies, half-truths and nonsense. Every time Arthur tried to get real information from them…or even suggested a connection between this body and…Dad…they changed the subject. Did you see their faces, when I asked them if it was an old man they found? And they wouldn't mention the girl…even when I gave them a chance to. *Why*, Mother? They didn't really want me to see the body…only that one agent seemed to. And when Blanchard's 'we're all in this together' routine didn't get the reaction from us they expected…they moved on to intimidation…cross-examining you about Dad…his patriotism, for God sake. *That* was the message. 'Stop asking questions and shut up.'"

"They *do* seem determined to tie Joe's disappearance to this damn testimony, Mary," said Arthur.

"What can we do?" she asked.

"Stay calm," he said. "We don't know why they're acting this way…holding back information. I'll go to the press conference and see what Blanchard says. Then, we'll talk about what to do. Maybe we can hire detectives of our own, if necessary…get some legal advice about taking this over the heads of the police, if we have to. Let's just pray something turns up…about Joe."

"And this poor young girl," Mother sighed, in disbelief.

Tears welled in Arthur's eyes suddenly, and he had to look away. A moment later, Mother handed me her keys and walked toward the passenger side of the car. Liz kissed Arthur on the cheek and followed Mother.

For a moment longer, Arthur and I stood together in the black and white heat of the police lot. "Do you think…there's any hope my father's alive?" I said.

"*Hope*?" His voice was filled with anger. "Better get your family home, son." He put his arm on my shoulder briefly, before heading back toward the police station.

CHAPTER 15

The cannons started again after we'd returned from the police station. They'd kept up until dusk, when an even more unsettling silence had descended on the river. And now, after a sleepless night, I stood at the kitchen sink sipping orange juice and welcoming its reviving bitterness on my tongue. Liz opened the back door and stepped inside wearing soggy sweat socks and her blue jeans rolled to mid-calf. The sleeves of her red flannel shirt were rolled to the elbows, and her hair was tied in a knot on the back of her head. She looked damp and breathless, as if she'd been hiking in the woods.

"Where'd *you* go?" I said.

"Nowhere," she grunted, bending down to peel off her socks. I glanced through the open door to the top landing of the stairs, and saw her muddy sneakers lying in their own small puddle. "I washed the car," she sighed.

"No cannons this morning," I said, blankly, as she nodded. "Have you seen Mom?" I asked.

"Giving Mary a bath…I think. David went to school." Finally, she looked up at me and said, "did you hear the phone ring last night?"

I nodded.

We heard footsteps in the hallway, and then Mother came into the kitchen, still in her bathrobe. "Why aren't you two dressed for school?" she demanded.

Liz sighed in frustration, as she turned away and closed the back door. I answered for us. "Mom, we're not going to school." She stared at me, as I quickly changed the subject. "Who called last night?"

"Arthur," she said, walking to the sink and standing next me, gazing out the windows. "He said to be sure we got the morning papers…I was going to do that next…"

Liz came back into the kitchen. "*We'll* do it," she said.

"Did he mention the press conference?" I asked.

Mother moved her head slowly back and forth as she stared out the windows and then she answered me in a distracted voice. "There was nothing new, he said…about your father…nothing about that poor girl you saw. We weren't on long…he said he'd give us the details when he got here, today."

"He didn't want to talk about it on the phone, did he?" I said.

But she ignored my question and finished her own thought. "Arthur said to make sure we got the *New York Post*." I glanced at Liz, as Mother walked to the stove and lifted the coffeepot off its low flame. She poured coffee into a cup and held it to her lips with both hands. "You're going to school *tomorrow*," she muttered.

"Let's get the papers," said Liz, pulling the keys from the back pocket of her jeans and tossing them to me, as she walked toward the hallway. "I'll get some dry socks and shoes."

By nine-fifteen, we were heading north on 9D. I reached for the radio knob, but Liz quickly grabbed my hand.

"There might be some *news*," I protested.

But she sighed and squeezed my hand. "Can't we just wait?"

"Sure," I sighed.

A few minutes later, I turned off the highway and started down the steep hillside on which Main Street descended through the little village of Cold Spring, ending at the riverfront. About halfway down, just before we crossed High Street, Liz whispered, "Tom…wait!" And I stopped short at the intersection so Liz could get a look at her favorite block.

High Street was lined with antique houses—grand old structures, four stories high, with lofty views of the river, built in the 1880s by prosperous river captains and merchants. Every house was painted brilliant white, and the front windows were shaded with green and white striped canvas awnings. I knew why Liz loved them, because I did, too. There was something comforting about the way they sat back on their quiet lawns, shaded by ancient oaks and elms, bursting with lush shrubbery and dazzling flowerbeds. A few had swimming pools, now, in their backyards behind arbor gates and hedgerows, and most had TV antennas on their high rooftops. But none of these concessions to modern leisure changed the impression the street gave, of time having stopped at an innocent moment long ago.

Another car rushed down upon us, suddenly, from behind. Its tires screeched and its horn blasted as it swerved to avoid us. The angry driver shook his fist from his window, as he passed through the intersection on Liz's side and sped down Main Street.

"*Jesus*, that was close," I said.

Liz glanced at me. "I'm sorry. It was *my* fault."

"No," I said, shifting into gear. "It wasn't."

Once past the intersection, we could see to the bottom of the hill, where Main Street disappeared into a little tunnel beneath the New York Central tracks. A few boaters, who didn't belong to the Highland Yacht Club, were launching from the public marina just beyond the tracks, and the silent cliffs on the western shore towered against the brilliant morning sunlight.

Wilson's cigar and newspaper store was on lower Main Street, in the center of Cold Spring's modest business district. The owner, Jack Wilson, was a burly man with broad shoulders and a wide, square face. He'd been a Navy seaman stationed near Manila in 1941, when the Japanese invaded the Philippines, soon after Pearl Harbor. He was captured with other holdouts four months later on the Bataan Peninsula, and forced into one of the infamous "death marches" to a work camp. The ordeal had left him with a scar of resignation, it seemed—a proud allegiance to certain fixed ideas about the world. He was a good man; and he and his wife Elaine, a secretary for IBM, and their nine-year-old son, Johnny, were steadfast neighbors.

Mr. Wilson waved when he saw us coming into his store. An electric fan at one end of his counter swept back and forth, pushing the sweet, pungent aromas of pipe tobaccos, cigars and candies around in a dizzying swirl. There was a man examining the cigar box display in one corner, and another man leafing casually through a sports magazine near the door.

I walked with Liz to the newspaper rack and we began pulling out copies of all the main morning papers from New York, checking to make sure of the date—Thursday, June 3, 1954. We picked up a few of the local Highland papers, too.

"Morning, you kids," said Mr. Wilson, with a subdued smile, as we laid the papers on his grainy, wooden counter.

I put two dollars down on the stack of papers and tried to be blasé. "What's new?"

But it sounded like sarcasm. And he frowned, as he picked up the money and looked around, making sure that the other customers weren't listening. Then he leaned toward Liz and me, and whispered, "is your dad really missing?" We nodded. "Says he was to testify, for McCarthy's Committee," he added confidentially, pointing to our papers. "You think the Communists found out...and did something?"

"To my father?" I said. He nodded gravely.

Liz was skeptical. "*Communists*?"

"That's right," he said, as he fished for coins in the well-worn drawer of his old wooden cash register. "To keep him from testifying." Suddenly, there was a loud crash in the storage room behind the counter. He turned and shouted. "What are you doin' back there?"

After a pause, we heard Johnny Wilson's high-pitched voice. "Gettin' more papers out, Pop!"

Mr. Wilson turned a grave face toward Liz and me. "You've seen that new TV show...where the FBI man investigates the secret Commie cells?" He placed our change on top of the papers. "Oh, what's the name o' that show?" he muttered.

I picked up the loose coins and said, "*I Led Three Lives*?"

"That's it!" he said, with satisfaction. "See...the Feds haven't *found* all the cells. Oh, they got the Rosenbergs, and that Hiss...and a few *other* Ivy League Reds in the State Department. But there's plenty more. Now...if *I* was in charge...I'd start lookin' at some o' these phony intellectuals at the colleges...the ones who encourage the young kids to criticize the government...teachin' all kinds o' anti-American ideas. That's why my Johnny isn't *going* to college...until all this business is cleared up. I'm gonna give him to Uncle Sam first...for his *real* education." I nodded politely. In the corner of my eye, I could see Liz staring down at the newspapers on the counter. "Oh, yeah," he said, "there's plenty more cells...and some of 'em, I'm afraid, would stop at nothing...even...hurting Joe."

"I don't think that's what's happened, Mr. Wilson," I said, smiling politely.

But he was determined. "They've bored in like termites...waiting for orders from Moscow. Problem is, McCarthy won't find 'em. He's a drunken fool...got some pretty odd characters workin' for him, too...embarrassing the Army like they're doin' now. We just need a *better man* than McCarthy...a man like your dad. You know...I always thought your dad might run for office one day. He'd get *my* vote...we have a lot o' respect for 'im. And my Johnny...he wants to be a *Marine* like your dad was...doesn't want to *go* Navy, like his old man..."

Liz tried to close the conversation. "Well thanks, Mr. Wilson."

"I've known your dad since we were kids...up here...in the 'Thirties. He's a good man...good as they come...and if *he* thinks there's somethin' fishy the people in Washington should know about…I'm with him all the way. You tell your mother."

"We will," Liz assured him.

"Tell her we're prayin'…Mrs. Wilson and me," he said. "An' I just hope you're right…about him not bein' hurt an' all." Just then, Johnny stumbled out from behind the counter, balancing a large stack of newspapers against his chest. His legs buckled beneath the weight, and only his eyes and the top of his head were visible over the newspapers in his arms. His father chuckled mordantly. "You okay there, high-pockets?"

"Yes, sir." Johnny struggled unsteadily toward the racks.

"Wait for me, Liz," I said. "I'm gonna give him a hand."

"All right," she said, gathering up our papers. "I'll be in the car."

I caught up to Johnny and removed half the papers from his stack. "Thanks a lot, Tom," he said, his broad smile visible now, and his short-cropped hair glistening with perspiration.

I walked with him toward the racks. "John…why aren't you in school?"

"We start late, today," he said, "'cause of our Spring assembly…I'm helpin' out Pop, before I head over." Then he spoke in a low, serious voice. "Jeez, Tom…I heard about your dad an' all."

"Yeah." I nodded, as we dropped the newspapers on the floor below the racks and he started arranging them by title, just the way his father wanted them.

"Is there somethin' I can do to help, Tom? Anything…wash your car…mow your lawn…you know…whatever you need."

"Thanks, Johnny, that's awfully nice. Can I let you know?"

"Sure." He finished arranging the papers and turned toward me with an open smile. We stared at each other for a moment. Finally, he nodded, and said, "well…I better go." Then he walked back behind his father's counter, and disappeared into the storage room.

Liz stood near the front of our car talking with Edith Neumann, who owned the dress shop a few doors up from Wilson's.

Edith was about forty-five years old, but looked ten years younger. She had straight, black hair that curled just above her shoulders and was cut across her forehead in bangs. She almost never wore the kinds of dresses that she sold to her customers, instead favoring tailored, cuffed slacks and men's shirts. She'd worked in Hollywood for years as a costume designer, but quit and moved east in 1949 when the head of her studio demanded she sign a "loyalty oath," which was mainly a ploy to abolish her union, she said. After a brief time in New York, where she worked on one Broadway show, and then found she couldn't get another job, she settled into one of the nice old houses up on High Street and opened her shop. It was very popular among women in the area, including Mother and Liz.

As I approached, Edith turned and greeted me with a grave frown. "Hello, Tom."

"Hi, Edith," I said, smiling politely, and glancing at Liz, who had an odd expression on her face.

"Liz told me about your father," said Edith. "I saw the papers this morning…I just don't know what to say…I'm shocked." I nodded, and she extended her right hand to me.

Liz picked up their conversation again. "So, maybe I *will* stop by one day next week."

"That would be fine," Edith smiled, warmly. "I'll make some iced tea, and we can relax in my yard…swim in the pool. Tom…you come, too."

"All right." I nodded politely, and let go of her hand. I glanced again at my sister.

Edith suddenly seemed uncomfortable. "Well. I should be running along. Please tell your mother I asked for her." Then, after kissing Liz on both cheeks, she smiled once more at me and started up the street.

I glanced at Liz, and muttered, "did I interrupt something?"

"What?" She laughed nervously. "Don't be silly."

We got in the car and sat for a moment, with newspapers piled on the seat between us. "Ready?" I asked.

She sighed. "Yes." And we began to riffle through the papers. A moment later, Liz stopped paging. "Listen to this," she said, reading from the *Daily News*.

PEEKSKILL—State and local police continued searching, yesterday, for Garrison attorney Joseph P. Gannon, who has been missing since Tuesday. As his officers dredged the Hudson River between Lents and Tomkins Coves, and scoured the nearby woods, State Police Captain Roy Blanchard told reporters that the missing man might have drowned.

Police found Mr. Gannon's locked automobile late Tuesday afternoon at Lents Cove, and obtained a court order to pry it open. They then met with the missing man's family who are 'understandably distraught and confused,' Blanchard said, at a press conference here.

Mr. Gannon had been scheduled to testify in Washington before the Investiga-tions Sub-Committee, chaired by Senator Joseph McCarthy. Police found docu-ments relating to this in Mr. Gannon's vehicle, but have revealed nothing more of their contents.

An Investigations Committee spokesman would say only that preliminary dis-cussions had taken place with the witness. 'He was on the schedule for a private interview, and perhaps, full testimony. We gather he won't be coming now,' the spokesman said.

Police think recent business reversals, debts, and the Senate appearance may provide a key to Mr. Gannon's state of mind and possibly his disappearance. 'We can't say for sure until we get more facts,' Blanchard said, yesterday, 'but this man did appear to be under considerable pressures.'

In a separate development while dredging the river, yesterday, police found the unidentified body of a Negro man, aged 65 to 70, probably homeless. Police said inquiries with nursing homes and psychiatric facilities across the state turned up no reports of missing patients. An autopsy showed the man had suffered a recent heart attack. It is unclear whether this was a factor in his death, which police have listed as a drowning.

At the press conference, Captain Blanchard said he had talked with people who apparently noticed a colored man 'hanging around' the Peekskill bus terminal, earlier this week. Witnesses, who have seen the body, are 'reasonably certain' it is the same man they observed near the terminal, Blanchard said. Unless the remains can be identified, 'which seems unlikely,' City Coroner Frank Cheswick said, yesterday, 'they'll be cremated and interred at potter's field.'

When she'd finished reading, Liz paged silently through several other news-papers, while I stared absently at the windshield.

"'Radical Catholic attorney finally gets religion, maybe too late,'" Liz sud-denly said.

"What the hell is that?"

"The *Journal-American* headline," she said, bitterly.

"Screw them."

"Wait," she whispered. "What about the *Post*? That's the one Arthur told Mom to get."

"Right." I pulled the *New York Post* out of the pile on the seat and leafed through many pages, finding nothing, until I reached the Op/Ed section in the centerfold. "Here's something," I said. "It's a commentary, by the columnist George Stepanski."

"*Well?*" she said, impatiently.

I read her the column.

Fellow skeptics: news reports imply that missing Garrison attorney, Joe Gannon, ended his life distraught over testimony he planned to give to the McCarthy Committee. That was the basic message from police at a news conference in Peekskill, yesterday, but I'm not so sure.

Joe Gannon's brand of legal work with a social conscience has earned him an interesting reputation. For many in New York's Negro and Puerto Rican communities, he's a hero. And he's been praised before on these pages. But his work has also earned him powerful enemies, and accusations of supporting 'un-American' causes.

Well, he's no Red. Never has been. Check his war record. His only affiliation is the Democratic Party—last I heard, that was still considered legit. But his ideas about fairness in jobs and housing have angered this town's Red-baiting columnists, and self-serving businessmen…and all their political hacks…and the bigots who wrap their repulsive ideas about Catholics, Jews and colored people in the American flag.

Police say they found Mr. Gannon's car parked up the river near Peekskill, two days ago. There were some papers in the car, apparently, outlining testimony he was considering giving to Joe McCarthy's staff. What would he need to confess about himself? Nothing, from what I've learned, which means he was planning to testify about someone else, though police won't confirm it. Neither will spokesmen for McCarthy.

My sources say he finally got tired of being kicked around by people whose own backgrounds are vulnerable to scrutiny. He came across some incriminating evidence, and decided to use it, to pay them back in kind. It must have seemed ironic to have the chance to turn his accusers in, using their own dishonest tactics on them. But then, he remembered something—he's got a moral conscience. And that's what makes him different from the creeps who spread lies about him…and others like him.

No, Joe Gannon wasn't going to Washington when he disappeared. He wasn't going to testify. How do I know? Trust me on this one, fellow skeptics. He just wasn't. The only question is: Did a change of heart cost him his life?

"Jesus, that's pretty strong," Liz said.

I nodded. "I bet Arthur talked to him." I turned the ignition key, pulled back quickly onto Main Street and headed up the hill.

Edith Neumann waved to us from the doorway of her shop as we passed. And for the ten minutes it took me to get us home, I couldn't keep her out of my mind. It was fairly well-known that she designed all the costumes for the annual senior play at Highland Falls High School every spring, and charged the school district nothing. And it was almost as widely rumored, though never openly discussed, that she and Doris Dickinson, the drama coach at the high school, were lovers.

I pulled into the garage and turned off the engine. Then, I turned and looked at Liz. "How well do you actually know Edith?" I said.

"What?" Liz replied, surprised by the question.

"*Edith*," I repeated. "How well do you *know* her?"

"I know…what everyone else seems to know," she said.

"That's *not* what I mean."

"I *know* what you mean." Then, she turned away and stared out her window at mother's tractor. Finally, she looked back at me. "Tom…don't be angry…not now…I couldn't bear it…"

I stared at the dashboard and shook my head. "Liz…for Chrissake. I'm *not*."

When I finally raised my head and looked at her, she smiled weakly, her eyes examining me closely. Suddenly, she leaned across the seat and we put our arms around each other. "I've been trying to figure some things out, Tom," she muttered, as she pulled away again. "I just…talk with her…about things."

"*Things?*"

"That I don't understand," she sighed.

"And *she does?*"

"That's right," said Liz, emphatically.

"Why don't you talk to Mom about it?"

Liz frowned and looked away again. "She started to ask *me*…once…she stopped."

"What about Dad?"

Instantly, she began to cry. I leaned over and tried to hold onto her again, but she pulled away with a jerk of her arm, and wiped her eyes with her red flannel sleeve. She took deep breaths and sniffled loudly through her nose. "I'm just worried. All right?"

"I *know*," I sighed. "Me too."

We sat for a while longer, silently, each of us staring straight ahead, through the Buick's windshield. "Edith invited me to come stay with her and Doris this summer," Liz finally said. "In Maine…they rent a house…"

"You're not going," I said emphatically. "*Are you?*"

"I'm *eighteen*, Tom…I'm graduating from school in a few weeks…and I *have* to get away, for a while…"

"Why?"

"*Why*?" She laughed sarcastically. "You're the one who said I should get out more!"

"Oh, Liz…I was an asshole to say that…"

"I know," she said. Then, we both laughed. We sat quietly for another moment. "Anyway, I told her 'no,' because…I'm spending the summer with Laureen, in Georgia, maybe Alabama. We're going down with a church group to work with local ministers…see how public schools are doing, registering colored kids. I already mentioned it to Dad. He said he'd think about it. Now…I feel…*obligated* to go…no matter what."

"Are you *serious*? Do you know how *dangerous* that could be?"

"It's a big group," she smiled. "We'll be all together."

"Liz. You can't…you gotta help me find out…what happened…"

She looked down at the newspapers on the seat between us. "What do you *think* happened?" she muttered.

"I wish I knew, Liz. I stayed awake all night trying to figure out why he'd leave his car there, with all his things. There's no good answer for it." She looked away and stared through the windshield again. I could tell she was looking at the old golf clubs in the corner. "You have to help me," I repeated. "Mom can't do it…she's trying to keep herself from just going nuts."

"What can *we* do, that Arthur isn't doing?" Liz said.

"Maybe nothing. But now, *I* feel obligated *too*…to try for Mom *and* Dad…and that little girl I saw at the terminal. I can't get her face out of my mind."

Liz called out to Mother as we came in the back door and dropped the papers on the kitchen table. There was no answer, but a moment later, our sister Mary appeared in the dark hallway beyond the kitchen. "She's in a livin' woom," she said, in a flat voice. She looked fresh and bright in one of the new spring dresses Mother had recently bought for her at Edith's, and her brown hair was still wet, smartly combed. "She's ty-udd." Liz grabbed her hand and we all went to the living room.

Mother was resting on the couch. When she heard us come in, she opened her eyes and smiled wearily. "I'm afraid I didn't get much sleep last night. What *kept* you?"

"We were reading through the papers," said Liz. "You wanna see them?"

"Maybe later," Mother replied, sitting up against one corner of the couch. While we were gone she'd rallied herself, enough to dress in a blouse and slacks, but her slow movements and tired voice gave the impression of a person depleted by chronic illness. "Just tell me what they say…in general."

"It's all predictable," I said. "The police are following the same line they gave *us*. They fed that to the press…"

"Oh, dear," Mother sighed.

"Mr. Wilson says 'hello', by the way," I added.

"I'll have to call Elaine," said Mother. "What about the *Post*…did you get a copy?"

"Yes. There's a good column by George Stepanski…*skeptical* of the official line."

"Oh!" Mother's voice lifted, slightly.

"Arthur must have spoken with him," I said.

She nodded. Then her tired expression hardened, and she seemed determined to say something. But she looked across the room at Mary, who leaned against an armchair listening intently. "Mary…Dear…I need your help. Would you go outside and watch for the Spencers? They'll be coming soon…and I need you to watch for them."

"Aw-wight Mama."

"Don't get your pretty dress dirty," Mother said.

I woon't." Mary walked to the front door and stepped out onto the porch. The screen door slammed behind her, and a moment later, she began to hum an unknown tune as she sat in one of the wicker porch chairs. Mother turned and stared hard at Liz and me. "You will never guess who called, while you were gone," she whispered. "Gerry Moran."

Liz was shocked. "*What*?"

"He said he'd read the papers, today…and was concerned…about your father."

"Oh, I'm sure," Liz said.

Mother frowned in agreement, and then looked at me. "Did *you* know your father was planning to meet this man, Tom?"

"No!" I said. "When?"

"He said your father planned to meet him on Tuesday morning in New York…and never arrived…"

Liz blurted. "Meet? For what?"

"I don't know," said Mother. "He wouldn't say over the phone…he wants to meet and tell us…in person."

I shook my head in disbelief. "When?"

"This morning. Under the clock at Grand Central Station."

"A public place," I said.

Mother frowned. "He'll wait by the clock until noon, he said. I think we should find out whatever we can…"

"*I'll go*, with Liz."

Mother shook her head. "*You* can't go. I want Arthur to do it."

"We have to leave *now*, if we're going to make it by noon," I said urgently, sitting at the edge of the couch. "Listen, Mother…let *us* go and hear what he has to say. How hard can that be? There's nothing to fear in a public place. Wait for the Spencers, and…if you hear from Dad…or anything…Arthur can help you." Mother stared at me with an odd smile, and I smiled back, as if we were agreeing that there was still hope. "Your parents, and Dad's…they'll be calling…*you* should be here," I added.

She nodded, gravely. "Call me…if there's the slightest trouble…and don't tell this man anything."

"Of course not," I said. Then she sighed and shook her head with a weary expression, not quite a smile.

CHAPTER 16

After parking on a tree-lined street in the Upper 30s, we hurried north to Grand Central Station, entering at 42nd Street. We pushed through the waiting room and down the Romanesque archway, out onto the great lobby concourse, where somber shafts of light streamed in from the station's massive east windows. And in the center of the busy lobby, above the information booth, the moonfaced clock glowed in the angular light.

We walked to the booth and waited; it was exactly eleven-thirty. I glanced up for a moment into the vast, elliptical ceiling—where mythic zodiac figures were drawn in gold paint against pale green, and outlined by electric-light stars in precise renderings of constellations. Suddenly, I remembered the winter night when I first met April.

Liz tapped my arm and pointed to a man in a dark raincoat and hat, standing fifteen feet away. His hands were thrust into the pockets of his coat, and he bounced nervously on the balls of his feet, as he surveyed the gates on the lobby's north side. We drew closer, noticing the black leather travel bag at his feet. I called out. "*Gerry Moran?*"

He spun around. His pallid face was drawn tight with nervous concentration, and his dark, unblinking eyes focused like camera lenses. "Who are *you?*" he demanded.

"Joe Gannon's children," I said.

"*Where's* your mother?" he groused, as he looked around the flowing crowd.

"Home," I said. "She sent *us*."

"Really," he scowled, leaning down for his bag. "Don't have much time. There's a coffee shop in the gallery." He nodded toward the retail arcade below the Vanderbilt Avenue staircase, and started walking. We followed him off the concourse and under the staircase promenade.

Inside the windowless café we waited in awkward silence, as the hostess looked for the "booth all the way in back," that Moran had requested. I watched him in the dull light; he looked like a man of about forty who was suddenly aging. Then I looked away, noticing the café's low ceiling, supported by gothic arches. The place seemed modeled on a Dutch beer hall—every surface, except the old wooden flooring, was covered in yellow subway tiles. The hostess returned, and we followed her through a maze of tables to a booth in a corner arch that was sealed, like a catacomb. She placed three lunch menus on the table, and Moran tried to give her a fifty-cent piece, as Liz and I sat down together facing the corner. The hostess refused the tip, but thanked him with a polite smile and walked away. Then, he slid his bag along the bench on his side of the table and sat down with his back to the wall. And as he pushed his hat-brim off his forehead, and loosened a few buttons on his raincoat, it occurred to me that he wasn't dressed for a sunny June day in Manhattan.

"How old are you two?" he said, sliding a hand inside his coat and retrieving a pack of Lucky Strike cigarettes.

"I'm eighteen," said Liz. "My brother's seventeen."

Moran nodded and mumbled something, while striking a wooden match and lighting the cigarette that now dangled from his lips.

Liz shook her head. "I'm sorry?"

"*Names*," he said, more distinctly, removing the cigarette and exhaling pale blue smoke. He shook out his wooden match. "What are your *names*?"

"I'm Liz," she said.

He nodded at her and then glanced at me.

"Tom."

"Good." He snapped off the burnt end of his match in the ashtray and put the part that was left in his raincoat pocket. This odd gesture seemed involuntary. "I didn't expect a couple of teenagers, but you're certainly old enough to know what's going on in the world."

"You had something to tell us?" I said, bluntly. He smiled.

A waitress suddenly appeared with her pad and pencil poised. "What'll it be?"

Moran leaned back and drew another puff on his cigarette. "I'll just have coffee," he replied, keeping his gaze fixed on us. "What would *you* like?"

"Same," I said to the waitress. Liz nodded to her.

"Three coffees," the waitress said, making some quick marks on her pad. Then she retrieved the menus, turned on her rubber soles, and walked away.

Moran stubbed out a half-smoked cigarette, and took another from the red and white packet on the table. "You know, I never meant to hurt your father...or your family," he muttered, as he lit the new cigarette. "I mean...not the way things worked out."

"Really," Liz replied, with cold sarcasm.

He stared at her, shaking out the second match, breaking it off and shoving the unburned part in the same pocket where he'd put the first one. Then, he whispered from behind another cloud of blue smoke. "I just never thought it would go this far."

Liz turned to me and rolled her eyes as the waitress reappeared. She placed her tray down at the edge of the table, and deftly distributed three white crockery cups of coffee on thick saucers, and a small, fat-bottomed glass of cream. Then, holding the empty tray against one hip, she looked down at Moran. "That be all?"

"For now...thanks," he said, glancing up briefly. He waited for her to leave and then started again. "Anyway...like I told your mother, I was supposed to meet your father...Tuesday...here, in this café. He never showed up. It was odd, because the meeting was *his* idea. He'd called me the day before, and..."

"Memorial Day?" I interrupted.

"That's right," he nodded, puffing his cigarette. "You were having some kind of a party, I gather...he didn't wanna stay on long, or get into details. He said he had information that I should know about...because it was damaging to me...he wanted to meet and discuss it. He said he wanted me to think about making another press statement."

"*About what?*" Liz said.

"I don't know...maybe this information he had...or where it came from? But when he didn't show up, and I didn't hear from him again, I just assumed he'd changed his mind...decided to forget it...put it all to rest. Then, I saw the papers this morning and got concerned. I gather...there's still no word?"

I shook my head. "No."

Suddenly, he began looking around at all the tables in the café, and at the booths along the wall behind Liz and me. Then, he leaned across the table toward us and whispered. "So...whadda you kids know about all this?"

"He didn't think you kept your end of the bargain," I said. "Your retraction was barely covered by the papers...*that's* probably why he wanted you to make *another* statement."

Moran sighed and sat up straight again. "The newspapers don't care, believe me," he said. "Most of them care very little about the…*truth*…the so-called *public interest*. They sell a product…that's all. They print what the public will buy." He sighed again, puffed his cigarette, and glanced quickly around the room. "What people are buyin' *now* is stuff about Reds, spies and traitors," he added. "Not retractions."

"The public isn't *one* single thing," I said.

He smiled and nodded in a patronizing way. "I know he was upset over the way it all came out, but I kept the agreement. I admitted I'd raised doubts about him and his associates without hard evidence. I made the statement he asked me to…never mind about *my* reputation. I even called a few editors, and tried to get them to interview me. They weren't interested. What more could I do? It's two years after the fact, now, and it's old news. I told your father there wasn't much more we could do…except move on."

"He *couldn't* move on," said Liz bitterly. "That's the whole point!" As he listened, he seemed more amused than shocked by her anger. "There was too much *damage* done…to his reputation," she said. "*You* did that…not newspaper editors."

"If you really want a reporter to listen to your retraction," I added, "call George Stepanski at the *Post*. Have you read *his* column this morning?"

"Uh…yeah…I read it," said Moran, his eyes darting around. "He tried to reach me yesterday, but…uh…I was out. Has he spoken with your family?"

"Indirectly," I said.

He smiled again and shrugged, before drawing another deep drag off his cigarette. "So tell me, if you know," he said, "what your father *had* on me?"

Liz shook her head in disbelief. "You've got some nerve."

He smiled calmly. "I just wanna know for my own sake, Miss. I'm here to *help* you."

"Yeah," she sneered. "You've been a lotta help so far."

"Answer my *question*, first," he smiled.

"All right," I said.

"*Tom!*" Liz scolded.

"No…it's all right," I assured her. Then, I looked at Moran. "He had something about you belonging to a…socialist group…in college."

He nodded. "You mean the John Reed Club."

Liz was surprised. "Jeez, Tom…was *that* all?"

Moran frowned at her. "It's enough, Miss…in *this* atmosphere. The Reed Clubs were Communist fronts. They answered to Moscow. Of course, I didn't know that at the beginning." He looked at me with his cold eyes. "That's almost twenty years ago, now. I had it expunged from my transcript, right after the war. Did he happen to say where he got that information?"

"No," I said, deciding there was no reason to mention Grandfather Hank.

"Did he say what *proof* he had?"

"Pretty sure he had a transcript…"

"The *original* transcript?" Moran was clearly agitated.

I nodded. "And a college yearbook listing, from Nineteen thirty-six…clippings from the college newspaper, too, I think…"

"Quite the portfolio," he muttered. His face looked drawn and nervous again. "And now, the police have it…the papers said they found documents in your father's car."

"*You're* a lawyer!" said Liz. "Tell us why they haven't released anything about that…your name…if they have it."

"I'm sure they *have* it, Miss," he replied. "They're just being careful…checking with the McCarthy Committee first." His eyes darted back and forth. "So, you have no idea where your father got this material?"

"Does it matter?" I sighed with exasperation.

"To *you*, it does," he said.

"Why's that?"

"Because it came from the people responsible for your family's troubles…but through an *intermediary*…probably a friend…a family member."

"This is what you called to tell us?" I said.

Moran lit another cigarette, and disposed of the match in the same way as the others. He took a deep drag and exhaled, staring at me. "Listen, kid…what I came here to tell you is…I'm *not* your father's enemy. I was *just* a messenger…another intermediary. That's the way this whole thing works…everything's done through intermediaries. Your father was beginning to understand…and *that's* why he called me…and wanted to meet."

Liz snorted. "He called you because he's a gentleman. It's not his style to accuse someone without evidence, or fair warning. I'm sure that seems odd to *you*…"

"You really don't get it, do you?" Moran said, in frustration. "Your father wasn't gonna testify against me…"

"We *know* that," I said, with an angry wave.

"He *toyed* with the idea for a minute," Moran said, "and told *you* and his friends that he was gonna…because he didn't want the person who brought him the information to know he *wasn't* gonna use it." Liz and I stared at each other. "Your father called me to *warn* me...*help* me for Chrissake. He was gonna *give* me the evidence, not *use* it against me."

Liz and I were stunned. Moran dragged on his cigarette, and his expression was suddenly calm again. "Your father wanted to know where the information *came* from...how it *got* to the intermediary. That was his *main* concern...and he thought I might have some idea about that. He was offering me a bargain...my help identifying the people behind all this, in return for the information he had about me. I'm pretty sure he already knew who they were...he just didn't seem to know how they got to someone so close to him...what the relationship was...*that* worried him, I think. So, he wanted to make sure the person who gave him the stuff would be safe, before asking me to blow the whistle on...these *other* people."

I glanced at Liz, and then glared at Moran. "So...who *are they*?" I said.

"Some people I used to worked for," he replied. "They had an interest in the same property your father and Spencer wanted to put the theater on...they weren't happy when they lost out...so...they had me go to the papers with the...*subversion* stuff..."

"The neighborhood group that opposed the theater?" I said.

"No, no," he frowned, shaking his head. "I wasn't really working for *them*. I worked for an investment group that thought they could come in and snap up the site from the City, while your father and his clients were busy fighting it out in court as some great...civic cause. *Those investors* were my *real* clients. They paid me, so I could represent the neighborhood group *pro bono*. The deal was...*they'd* come in and acquire the property, and the local citizen's group I technically represented agreed not to oppose. But nobody counted on your father winning in court so easily."

"So...you were ordered to punish him," Liz said, bitterly.

He frowned and nodded. "Power doesn't exist if it isn't used, Miss. These people couldn't let themselves be stiffed by some Brooklyn attorney, operating on his own say-so, outside their thing...I mean, come on...with his little list of mid-sized brokerage clients...a few company presidents...and those *Negroes* for heaven's sake? God almighty, these people hate the coloreds! No. They did not like the idea of your father getting that prime real estate for a group of colored businessmen from Harlem."

Liz sighed in frustration. "So what were *they* gonna do with the site?"

He shrugged. "They told the Mayor that they'd construct offices." Then, he smiled sarcastically. "Actually...they were gonna turn it over to the Bridge and

Tunnel Authority for next to nothing in return for…*considerations*. Of course, the Authority wanted to run an elevated highway right through there." He laughed bitterly. "The local citizens' groups had no idea…"

"You still haven't told us who they *are*," I interjected.

"*That*, I can't do," he said.

"I thought you had no qualms about giving people's names out," Liz sneered.

Moran shook his head. "It's just too dangerous, Miss…for *you*. I don't want to be responsible…anyway, you can figure it out from what I've told you."

"Do you know Charles Stannard?" I said. "Andrew O'Leary?"

"I've got a train to catch," he muttered, stubbing out his last cigarette and looking at his watch. I looked at mine; it was a quarter past noon. Then, he stuffed the empty cigarette packet inside his coat. "You're a lawyer's kids," he said. "You study Latin in school…right? Well…*qui bono…who gains*? Ask yourselves who gained from your father being sent to the junkyard two years ago. Who gains from doing the same to me, now, because I know too much? Your father realized he was being set up to eliminate *me*, the same way they used *me* against *him*. Pretty neat, huh? He realized that, by the time he was finished testifying about *me* in Washington, he'd of finished the job on himself, too…he'd be no further threat to these people, or their interests. Because…he'd have no credibility left with *anybody*…liberal *or* conservative. See how it works?"

"You think he was *murdered*?" I asked bluntly. I heard Liz sigh.

"Well," he said, reaching for his travel bag. "What do *you* think?"

"I think it's odd, the way you're getting out of New York," I replied.

He smiled wearily, slid to his right, and stood up beside the table gripping his bag with his left hand. With his right, he reached inside his raincoat and pulled out a leather billfold. Then, he deftly extracted a five-dollar bill from a thick wad and laid it on the table. "That should cover everything, including a tip," he said, glancing at his watch again. "My train leaves in twenty minutes." We stared at him. "Lemme tell you kids something…*my* opinion…your father's a good man, all right? That's why I settled the case…without consulting my *former* clients. I just thought…enough's enough."

Liz shook her head in disbelief. "How do you sleep at night?"

He looked at his watch. Then he scowled, and sat again at the edge of his seat, gripping his bag. For the first time, he seemed angry. "Listen! *I* was convinced of my own morality once…just like you two, and your old man. *I* thought progressive socialism was the answer to the world's injustices. That was the Depression…people were starving in America. Of course, it was just another market cycle on Wall Street, but the government was powerless to help people who farm or work for wages…the investment bankers wouldn't permit it. I was in with a college crowd that thought socialism could change all that. It *sounded* good to support humane ideals…strong unions, fair pay for work, social and civil rights for immigrants, and colored people. But it was *crap!*" He paused and surveyed the coffee shop. He glanced at his watch. "See…it leaked out that the Soviet economy was failing…Stalin was murdering thousands of Russian and Ukrainian farmers…*and* his former comrades in the Bolshevik revolution. That bothered me…I said so. My friends in the Reed Club, including my girlfriend, tried to talk me through it. They said we had a *different brand* of socialism here…we'd use socialist principles to regulate American capitalism. But when they couldn't stop me raising questions, they began to distance themselves. I thought these people were my friends, and they shunned me…even the girl." He sneered, suddenly. "American socialists didn't want to *know* the truth about Stalin…they kept on raising money for the Loyalists in Spain…listening to Paul Robeson sing about the beauty and tolerance of the Soviet." He glanced again at his watch. "When I joined the Reed Club, I never signed up to be in the Communist Party. But you'd see party members taking over more and more at the club meetings. They'd shout you down, when you tried to bring up Stalin's murders…and the millions of starving Russians. I wasn't the *only* one asking about these things. Finally, Moscow ordered the American Communists to shut the Reed Clubs down, to stop the questions. That's when I saw that we were just college kids being played for suckers by these professors, and deluded trade unionists, who ran the clubs…and all these actors and writers who fancied themselves great political thinkers." He sneered again. "So, I left that nonsense behind me, and went to law school…learned my lesson. But a lot of my friends, who were writers…they felt they *couldn't* leave…they were getting articles and stories published…plays produced…because socialist thought was *just the thing* in the arts, then. Of course, they'd never done a proletarian day's work themselves."

Liz laughed, sarcastically. "So your girlfriend dumps you, and you're disappointed by your friends' literary ambitions. *That's* the basis of *your* political beliefs?"

"These people were *dishonest*…corrupt," he countered. "For them, a worker was a character in a script or a folk song. Some of these so-called friends of mine ended up in Hollywood, writing screenplays about the same crap, but when the blacklist finally caught up with them after the war, they started saving themselves by turning each other in. *Anything* to keep their thousand-dollar-a-week studio jobs…their beach houses and swimming pools and mistresses…they finally renounced what I'd renounced ten years before. Oh sure, a few tried to make a big scene out of resisting HUAC. A few even called *me* for legal advice…after so many years of not speaking to me! You know what my advice was? 'Admit you were wrong, tell them you were a stupid college kid, but you've grown up now. And when they ask you for the names of others you saw at those discussion meetings, give them the names.'"

"You weren't afraid they'd give *your* name?" said Liz.

"Wouldn't have mattered, Miss. I'd already gone in to HUAC, and testified…about myself…*and* about *them*…in closed session. I told the House Committee I'd gone to a few meetings in college, and saw other people who were far more serious about it than I was. When they asked me for their names, I gave the names…people they were already investigating from the movie world…and a few college professors. The Committee *mainly* wanted to nail Hollywood types, for the publicity…so they were willing to work a deal with me. I was lucky. I could give them some pretty famous names. You'd be surprised. HUAC agreed not to disclose *my* past affiliations if anyone else raised it, in return for my testimony."

As Moran started to get up again, Liz reached across the table at him. "*Wait a minute,*" she said. "You have a *deal* with HUAC. *That's* why your name hasn't been released by the police, or published in the newspapers."

"Who knows?" he shrugged. "My testimony was in 'Forty-seven. That's a lifetime ago. These House and Senate Committees make *a lotta* deals…it's *all* deals down there, and sometimes deals conflict. Then…they have to choose which one to keep. I can't help them anymore, so…they may decide to write me off. Anyway, I gotta go…much fun as this little civics lesson's been. Get wise to yourselves. There's a Communist conspiracy in this country, and not just in publishing and movies. They were in the State Department for years, the White House, schools, labor unions…even Los Alamos. You don't think Stalin's scientists cooked up that atom bomb all by themselves, do ya'? American traitors gave them the plans. The Rosenbergs were *not* innocent. Alger Hiss *is* guilty. Oppenheimer *is* disloyal. And most of those Hollywood Ten jokers…they *were* Communists but didn't have the guts to say so. They deserve what they got."

"So," Liz said, "*some* types of purges don't bother you."

"Miss Gannon…Communism is *not* valid, and doesn't *deserve* protection. Now, I'm very sorry about your father. I've done everything I can…for *his* sake." He got up and stood over us for a moment, before leaning down to whisper. "Just remember…be careful who you talk to about this…the person who brought the information about me to your father prob'ly can't be trusted. Find out where *that* person really stands…whether he was just another dupe, or knew what he was doing. That's what your father was trying to find out and…well…look what happened."

Liz and I waited at the table until we were sure that Moran was gone. Then, we quickly left the café, proceeded up the marble staircase, and out into the bright sunlight of Vanderbilt Avenue. As we turned south, heading toward 42nd Street, Liz glanced at me. "Do you believe him?" she asked.

"About Dad offering him the information? Yeah. It's just *like* Dad."

"I mean about…Grandpa Gannon," she said. "*He brought* the information to Dad, and encouraged him to use it. How much of this do you think *he* knows?"

"He's a resentful man, Liz…and a drunk. I think *anything's* possible, but I intend to find out for sure." We reached the corner of Vanderbilt Avenue and 42nd Street and waited for the light to change, so we could cross over and head back to the car. "Liz," I said. "Can we do something…before we go home?"

"*What?*"

"Stop at the hospital, so I can try to see April again." Liz looked at me with a strange expression. "She *needs* me," I said. "Needs my *help*, I mean."

"Your help? For what?"

"I'm not sure, but I know she *does*."

And as Liz shook her head in confusion, we started hearing the wails of sirens above the noisy midtown streets. The sirens grew louder and closer. Two police cruisers, racing east on 42nd Street, suddenly turned on screeching tires and passed us. We watched them heading north on Vanderbilt, as more sirens came along 42nd Street. Suddenly, an ambulance careened around the corner onto Vanderbilt, followed by a third police car. The vehicles all stopped abruptly at the station's Vanderbilt entrance, and four policemen leapt from the first two cruisers and ran inside. Two ambulance attendants followed them in, carrying a stretcher and medical bags. Officers from the third cruiser got out and directed traffic around the double-parked vehicles.

CHAPTER 17

Liz stayed with the Buick; I walked into the hospital with calm determination and found the lobby jammed with midday visitors. But I saw no security guards. So, I slipped through the crowd, past the wall of benefactors and into the elevator bank, where about twenty people were waiting. Several turned and glanced at me, and I nodded politely. When I saw their blue visitor's passes, I slid my hands into my pockets, but quickly realized that I was an object of distraction, not interest. As they turned away to stare at the elevator doors, I looked up and noticed that all of the dials were frozen.

Suddenly, a very tall woman, whose wide-brimmed hat seemed to hover above the crowd, turned toward me and raised a gloved hand. "Sir...excuse me...sir!" With relief, I realized she was waving past me to an elderly guard just coming out of the nearby men's room.

The old guard looked at her. "Yes, Madam?"

"I've been waiting for almost *fifteen minutes*," she insisted.

Other frustrated faces turned, as the elderly guard gazed up at the dials, two of which were stuck at the very top, on "P", the Private Floor. The fit of his uniform suggested he wasn't even a regular guard—someone's grandfather, probably, earning some part-time cash. But this woman's complaint had dissolved all patience in the crowd, and the poor old man knew he had to deal with her. "Looks like there's a *jam* upstairs," he said.

"We know that!" the woman hissed.

"Isn't there something you can *do*?" said a man in a business suit.

"I don't know *what*," the guard said, as he squeezed through the restive crowd, and gave the Up and Down buttons a few perfunctory pushes. "I'll tell

Maintenance," he muttered. Then, he squeezed back out and walked quickly toward the lobby.

"We'll never see *him* again," someone said.

Just then, a loud rumbling silenced everyone. Behind us, a thick, metal door was opening between two faux columns built into the wall, opposite the public elevators. The door moved spasmodically, revealing the wide, deep interior of a service elevator. There were six black hospital orderlies inside—four men and two women—dressed like Pullman porters in starched white linen jackets with high collars. The flat aroma of hospital food seeped from the big aluminum boxes on their push trolleys.

A stocky orderly at the front of the group muttered, "how'd that hap'm?" as he reached up and pressed repeatedly against a button inside the elevator.

Someone called out. "*We're* having problems with *our* elevators, too!"

When this drew laughs from the frustrated crowd, two of the male orderlies frowned and stared down at their feet, but one of the women spoke in a cold voice from the back. "Try it again."

"Come awn, now…come awn," urged the stocky orderly, pushing again and again at the button. At last, a mechanism shuddered in the elevator shaft and the door lurched into a slow, closing motion. Applause kicked up, and the embarrassed orderlies bowed their heads in silence, until they were safely behind the false proscenium again. Then, the crowd turned back to its own sullen business.

"Here's one!" somebody shouted, as an elevator arrived. But its doors parted to reveal a clot of angry riders, and a harried security guard at the controls. The crowd moaned in a single voice.

"Step aside…please!" the guard barked. "Let 'em out!"

The stubborn crowd formed a narrow escape channel.

"What the heck's goin' on up there?" somebody shouted.

"Two cars stopped on the top floor," an escapee growled. "They're shovin' everybody on the other two…it's a big mess."

Another voice called out. "Top floor is the Private Level! Bet some *celebrity's* leaving."

"All right…let's keep 'em moving," the guard barked.

"*You* keep 'em moving, buddy," somebody shouted, angrily.

Suddenly, a woman just in front of me whispered to the woman beside her. "I bet it's Rita Hayworth. I heard she's been here, drying out."

"No," said the other woman with dramatic certainty. "I read in Winchell she left for Monaco. It's probably Gene Tierney…"

"*Really?*"

"Nervous breakdown," the other woman confided, with a grave nod.

"All right!" the guard announced. "I can take twenty people on the first run." The simmering crowd, now easily twice that size, crushed forward and the harried guard shouted again. "Easy now, easy! Just the first twenty…there *is* another elevator coming…please be patient!"

It was almost one-thirty, now, and I couldn't afford to waste time. I blended with the last elevator escapees heading back toward the lobby, where visitors queued up in three long lines at the reception desk. And now, there were two security guards stationed at the entrance, observing the crowd. With one last idea, I lowered my head and pushed forward against the wave of people who were trying for the doors on my left. It felt like the mad opening crush of a cross-country race—angry elbows, shoves and errant feet—but I managed to squeeze through, hurrying to the door in the dark alcove, where Mr. Stannard had refused to let me see his daughter. My heart raced; I expected to be stopped at any moment by the guards. I grabbed the knob, pulled the door open just enough to walk through, and then waited inside the stairwell, leaning out of sight against the cool cinderblock wall until the door closed behind me.

The bright lighting inside the stairwell made a stark contrast with the lobby. I stepped away from the wall and looked up and down the stairs from the first floor landing. Every step and every inch of mocha-colored cinderblock glowed with smooth fluorescence. The air began to move, and I smelled something vaguely like spoiled food. I heard an echoing bang—the sound of a door closing somewhere on the basement level—followed by footsteps in a hallway underneath me. I stepped quietly across the landing to the stairway leading to the second floor.

Suddenly, the footsteps stopped and I listened, as a man whispered harshly from below. "All right, here's the deal. I'll start ya' on Lou's say-so. 'Cause his agency vouches for ya'. But I'm gonna make ya' life miserable, till ya' learn the ropes…same way I treat everybody."

"I understand, sir," said another man, whose voice was an ooze of youthful sincerity.

"Then after a while, maybe, we'll start ta' get along…all depends how hard ya' wanna work."

"I *do* want to work, Mr. Boyd."

"We'll see. Call me Randy, by the way. It's minimum wage…"

"The agency said there was opportunity…for advancement."

"There's always room on the ladder for smart young fellas that know how ta' give their boss what's needed."

"Yes, sir."

"Lou told ya' about the...*special needs* we have in the position...right?"

"Yes, but he said...*you'd* give me the details."

"Shit. We're busy ta'day. We got some trustees and their daughter upstairs...I gotta get back ta' the kitchen...so listen...I'm not gonna explain it again. I start ya' off...minimum wage...till we see what type information ya' bring me..."

"Yes, sir..."

"I got troublemakers organizin' a union...rilin' up my orderlies. I can't have subversion like that. I'm under the gun with management, see? We had happy people workin' here, before this. Now...I got nuthin' but com-plaints...demands...every week. I'm talkin' uneducated Nig-roes. Y'under-stand me? And goddamn Porta Reekins, makin' demands about work conditions, paid overtime, medical coverage...I mean what the hell...they're lucky ta' have a job..."

"Right."

"Goddamn right I'm right. S'what happens when Reds get in a place and start organizin'. Now, we know who *some* o' these agitators are, but we let 'em alone so far b'cause we wanna make sure we get 'em *all*...'specially the ring-leader...that's the sonofabitch I really want. I got a couple other guys on staff, workin' the same angle...couple white guys, like you...couple good colored boys, too...but the way we work it, see, we don't let ya' know who the others are. That way, nobody slips an' accidentally exposes anybody. So watch it...until ya' know who ya' talkin' to."

"All right."

"Don't bring nuthin' up, till somebody approaches *you*...maybe they'll ask what ya' think about unions, or...if ya' wanna go to a union meetin'. That's when ya' say 'sure', ya' might be interested ta' learn more. When they take ya' to a meetin', pay attention...see who's there...who's in charge...then bring the information ta' me. The more ya' bring...the better ya' do. See?"

"What if I need to sign some...document...you know, like a petition...or join the union or something?"

"Sign it. Do whatever ya' haf' to..."

"But...the hospital's gonna know I only signed because...I mean...they're not gonna think I'm any part o' this..."

"Naw…don' worry about that…wait a minute." There was a pause. "Did you hear somethin'?"

"No…what?"

"Like…there's somebody on the stairs…"

"I didn't hear a thing, Randy…"

I held my breath. Suddenly, footsteps started up the stairs from the basement. I moved quietly upstairs to the second-floor. The footsteps stopped.

"Who's up there!" I could feel my lungs tightening in my chest as I held my breath. The footsteps resumed, moving closer to the first floor, and I quickly made it across the second-floor landing to the next staircase. I got ready to climb to the third floor, but the footsteps stopped again.

I heard the younger man whispering up from the basement. "Everything all right, Randy?"

"Yeah. I guess it was nuthin'." Finally, after another long silence, I heard him walking back down to the basement. I stepped away from the wall banister and listened into the stairwell. "Oh…yeah…a'nutha thing. You're a high school grad, right?"

"Yes, sir."

"Management says I gotta have diplomas ta' back me up…othawise…we start replacin' these troublemakers…somebody's liable ta' claim unfair labor. I don't want some bleedin' heart reporter…or goddamn liberal assemblyman comin' in here, fuckin' with me, and my job…do you?"

"No."

"It's *us* against *them*…remember that." There was another silence. "Christ, I don't know why I keep havin' this feelin like somebody's listenen'. Screw it…let's get ta' work."

I heard their footsteps, fading, and the air moving again. Then, a distant door slammed and the air stopped flowing. I glanced at my watch. It was one forty-five.

It took ten minutes to climb the remaining flights of stairs to the Private Floor. I found the stairwell door unlocked and pulled it open a few inches, feeling cool, fresh air against my face.

As I listened for guards and nurses, I heard the distinctly cold voice of Constance Stannard. "Can we discuss the foundation with Richard, later? I want to take my daughter home."

"And *I* want someone to check with Boyd," insisted the voice of Charles Stannard.

"Of course, Charles," she said, with an imperious sigh. "Lanning…take care of it."

"Yes, Ma'am."

"Use the stairs."

"Yes, Ma'am."

A jolt of fear ran through me, as I eased the door closed and quickly climbed the final flight of stairs to the roof door. It was locked. Suddenly, the Private Level door opened below with a shudder of wind that rattled the door at my back. I looked down and waited to be discovered. A young man walked across the Private Level landing and stopped for a moment to consider something, as the door closed behind him. I remembered him from the Stannards' party. He was the young investment banker who'd paid so much attention to Martha Bradley. He stood calmly on the landing, dressed in a dark blue suit, and a crimson-and-white rep tie. His chestnut brown hair was neatly trimmed and brushed, but thinning on top. Gold-wire glasses were perched on his straight nose, in the absolute center of his symmetrical face. Finally, without ever looking up, he descended the stairs.

Minutes later, when the sounds of his echoing footsteps finally faded in the stairwell, I looked at my watch. It was two o'clock. I crept down to the Private Level door again, and inched it open.

"Yes, of course…but I'd be more comfortable if we discussed it in my office." I quickly recognized the voice of Richard Simon, the Stannards' doctor friend, who'd taken charge of April at the party.

"You need to get a grip on this staff situation pronto, Dick," said Mr. Stannard. "We'll support you…with the other trustees. You're clearly the best candidate for chairman…but some may not like what we're doing, so, *I say* we move quickly. It's up to you…"

"All right, Charles," the doctor said. "All right."

"Once Lanning checks with Boyd," said Mr. Stannard, "we'll be able to assess the situation…how close he is to finding the union instigator…"

"Yes, Charles," said the doctor.

"Our foundation will make the pledge to the hospital, now, enough to cover the expansion program…and *you* can take all the credit for that…then the board will *have to* approve you. We're announcing several *other* projects…at City Hall, this afternoon. And I'd just like to know whether we're moving along here."

"I understand, Charles," said the doctor.

"We cannot have a subversive union like this getting a foothold and wasting everyone's time and resources, appealing to the misguided sympathies of trustees…or your staff. I just can't have bad publicity, right now. I'm *depending* on you, Dick…keep things quiet and under control."

"I *will*, Charles. Now please…can we go to my office? I don't want to talk about this out here…"

"Certainly, Dick. But…there's no one else here…only my daughter."

"Dick is *right*, Charles," Mrs. Stannard scolded. "We should go."

"I'm just two floors down," said the doctor. "Security is holding elevators for us, outside. I'll have one of the guards come back in, now, and watch the stairwell."

"I don't think that's necessary," said Mr. Stannard. "Constance is leaving with our daughter as soon as the car arrives…"

I waited, as the Stannards and Dr. Simon opened a door at the other end of the private ward. I could hear them speaking to the guards out near the elevators, as wind rushed up the stairwell from behind me. And then, the voices disappeared beyond the closing distant door.

I walked quickly onto a long, bright hallway covered in thick, forest green carpeting, and lined with potted plants and sofas upholstered in rich floral prints. There were oil paintings of pastoral scenes on the walls, and a series of large windows allowed brilliant sunlight to envelop the hallway, all but obscuring the door at its far end. Tiny glass panels along the tops of the windows were open, taking in air that swirled far enough above the river and the streets to be free of earthly smells. Beyond the windows on one side, I could see the Hudson Valley heading north for miles. There were six doors down the hallway, three on each side. The second door on the left had luggage stacked in front of it. I hurried there and checked the tags. They said STANNARD.

I opened the door and slipped inside, knowing I had just minutes before Mrs. Stannard returned with their driver. The air was cold in the dark vestibule of what seemed to be a large suite of rooms. I smelled the faintly sickening odor of disinfectant coming from a bathroom on my right. Straight across the vestibule, an open door led into the suite. From somewhere beyond the door came an odd snapping sound, like the mainsail of a sloop tacking against the wind. And then, a flat, spiritless voice called out. "Mother?"

I walked to the open door, but stopped, and peered in at a sun-drenched sitting room. I saw a wheelchair near a settee and a writing desk. A long hallway beyond the sitting room led to more rooms, and white linen curtains snapped and swirled in a strong breeze through an open window. Suddenly, I realized that April was standing there, at the window, looking out on the city and the river. The wind blew against her face, and the curtains danced around her, almost hiding her in their folds. Her pale, blue suit blended against the distant sky. Then she turned, and she seemed to gaze through the curtains toward the doorway. I could see her eyes through the thin curtain material, but she didn't seem to see me standing in the darkness of the vestibule.

She looked like a stranger. Her hair had been cut short, and her face was frozen in the Stannard look—passionless, imperious—ageless as a statue. She turned and stared out the windows again, and began to sob. Her body shook convulsively, as she lowered her head, and gripped the windowsill with both hands. I looked away and stepped back from the door, embarrassed, but suddenly, I heard her voice again. "*Don't go!*" she whispered.

I ran into the bright room and she turned to face me, with her back to the open window. "What happened?" I said, urgently. But, she didn't answer. I put my arms around her, and she pressed her face down against my shoulder. She felt brittle, thin, almost lifeless, except that I could feel her warm breath gathering against my shoulder. And now, thoughts and memories crashed together in my head, all at once. "You're pregnant," I guessed.

"*Was,*" she whispered back.

The hallway door opened with a flash of light, and Mrs. Stannard called to her daughter. "Are you ready? Lawrence is downstairs with the…car." Even before she'd finished speaking, her eyes froze on me, as she stood in the inner doorway. "We'll just see about this," she snapped, turning and hurrying back to the outer door, yanking it open. "LANning…come here!" she bellowed down the hallway.

I followed her out and stood in the vestibule to face her, as she turned and waited, holding the hallway door open.

"Tom…leave now," April pleaded, as she came up behind me and put a hand on my shoulder. I turned and looked into her face only inches away. She seemed slightly more alive now, except for the placid, wet chill in her green eyes. Her hand slipped from my shoulder down to my arm. Her grip was soft, and her voice wavered as she spoke to her mother. "Let'm go. He's only a boy…who cares about me…"

But Mrs. Stannard glared. "You social-climbing felon. You're a degenerate! And you're going to jail now. You'd be there already…for what you've done to my daughter…if her own father hadn't refused to listen." And then, she glared at April. "He'll listen, now…"

Suddenly, the young investment banker appeared, and stood with Mrs. Stannard in the doorway. "What is it, Ma'am?"

"Lanning…hold this person here while I have security call the police. He doesn't leave!" She hurried away.

"Let'm by Lanning," said April. "Tom…please go…"

I turned to her. "You should have *told* me…"

She kissed me on the lips, and pleaded. "*Go!*"

"So *this* is the person?" said Lanning, shaking his head in disbelief, as I walked toward him. Abruptly, he stepped inside and let the door close behind him.

"*S'none* of your business, Lanning," said April.

I walked up to him. "Are you going to let me through?"

When he shook his head, I punched his face as hard as I could with my right hand. His glasses flew into the air. He was surprised. He raised his hands and tried to hit me back, but I stepped forward, lowered my head, and drove my right hand straight up from my waist to the underside of his chin. I heard his teeth grinding together, and a soft, animal grunt in his throat. His eyes rolled back, and his arms slumped to his sides. My right hand began to throb, as I grabbed him by the lapels and pulled him away from the door. Then I threw him to the side, and he stumbled into the bathroom, landing in a stunned heap on the floor.

I opened the door and looked left down the hallway. I could hear voices beyond the far door. Looking right, I saw the unguarded stairwell entrance.

"What're you *doing?*" April pleaded. I suddenly realized how slurred her speech was.

I turned and shouted at her. "Stop taking the pills! Call Martha!"

Then, I stepped out into the hallway, letting her door close behind me. Suddenly, the far door burst open and slammed against the inside wall. Mrs. Stannard stormed through with three security guards behind her.

"That's him!" she shouted, and the guards bolted past her like hunt dogs.

I ran for the stairwell, pushed the door open, and sprinted across the landing and then down. I nearly slipped on the smooth steps, but made a lucky grip on the banister and kept going. I covered two flights before the guards exploded into the stairwell above. As I sprinted down, floor after floor, their clomping footsteps and heavy breathing seemed to fade a bit, and by the time I reached the 12th floor, my lead had increased by a third flight. But when I reached the 11th floor landing, I heard shouts and footsteps coming up the stairwell from far below. I paused for a moment to think, and the door to the 11th floor suddenly opened from inside.

"What's all this?" muttered a stocky black orderly, standing in the doorway. Immediately, I recognized him from the stalled service elevator. He seemed to recognize me, too, without knowing why. As he stared into my eyes, I tried to bolt past him, but he moved with surprising agility to block my way, and he held me with powerful hands.

"You don't understand," I whispered, breathing heavily, as footsteps came closer on the stairs above and below.

He shook me violently by the shoulders. "Listen boy…what *is* this?"

"Help me, and *I'll* help *you*," I gasped. "I know about Randy's plan to break the union…he has spies."

"Come here with me," he said, with a sudden smile. And my heart sank, as he pushed me onto the ward and closed the stairwell door. I glanced down the hall and saw a dozen orderlies clearing up used lunch trays, bringing in fresh bedding, and throwing dirty linens into large white canvas caddies on wheels outside each room. One by one, they stopped working and stared at us. "Nuthin' goin' on here!" he barked. And they resumed work without argument or expression. Then, he pointed to an empty laundry caddy. "Get in," he ordered. I hesitated. "Before one of the nurses sees you," he said.

I climbed in and leaned back, while he grabbed piles of freshly laundered sheets and towels from a nearby closet and dumped them in on top of me. Soon, I was completely hidden. With a strong push, he set the laundry caddy in motion, and I could feel myself being rolled along the ward. I heard shouts in the distance, now, and the piercing sound of an alarm bell. The laundry caddy banged gently against a flexible metal obstacle and stopped. I heard clicking, and I knew that the orderly was pushing buttons on the service elevator. I heard the mechanism slam into motion and felt relieved enough to breathe. I smelled detergent and bleach and my own sweat.

"Hey, Jim!" A distant voice was calling out from somewhere on the ward. "You seen a kid…maybe seventeen, eighteen…running on the stairs…or in here?"

The orderly answered back with a flat voice. "No, sir!"

"If ya' *do* see 'im…call the security office!"

"Whud he do?"

"Broke in a patient's room, up top…tried to attack her and her mother…assaulted a man who tried ta' help them…we're checking each floor, from here on down…"

"I'll sure keep an eye out," promised the orderly, as the service elevator rumbled open, while footsteps and voices faded beyond a distant door slam. The laundry caddy wheels bumped beneath me, as the orderly pushed onto the elevator. I heard button clicks again, and a pause, and finally the slow rumbling of the door sliding shut. The alarm grew faint, as the elevator groaned and slowly descended.

"You just sit in there till I tell you," muttered the orderly.

"Okay," I said, from beneath the muffled sheets.

"Name's Jim."

"Tom."

"You didn't hurt no woman, now…did you Tom?"

"No, sir…"

"Musta done somethin'."

"I *did* punch a man…he tried to keep me from leaving…"

"Leavin' where, son?" His voice betrayed annoyance.

"My girlfriend's room…she's been…ill…and her parents won't allow me to see her…speak with her…"

"Who's your girlfriend? What's 'er name?"

"April…April Stannard."

Silence. "I see." More silence. "All right, boy…tell me what you know about Randy."

"I overheard him talking to a guy…about an hour ago…downstairs in the basement. Some guy he just hired…as an orderly…but he's being used to supply information about union organizing. He's supposed to let himself be brought to meetings, learn who the organizers are, and report back."

"That so?"

"Boyd said there are others…informers…already on your staff…"

"Did he say who?"

"No. He said none of them knows the others…he said some are…white…and some…"

"Colored?"

"Yeah…"

"Sum-bitch…"

"This new man is white…I didn't hear a name, though…"

The elevator slammed to a halt. "Quiet down, now," Jim muttered.

The elevator door opened and I heard voices as the caddy was pushed off. Suddenly, a man nearby called out. "Hey, Jim, where you been? You hear 'bout this kid, who snuck upstairs? The Stannard girl's room!"

"Yeah," replied Jim. "I heard somethin'…"

"Where you takin' 'at laundry?" the man said.

"Ta' the god damn laundry room, on the other god damn side o' the building. Now, where else would I be bringin' it, man?"

"I dunno…just askin'. Looks awful clean ta' me."

"Don't you have some work in the kitchen ta' do…Teddy?"

"Lunch break…bunch of us been talkin' 'bout this kid…wondrin' how he got past the guards and made it all the way up there to the Private Floor. Randy's madder n' a rooster with his dick cut off…and they're callin' the police in. Somebody's gonna be in trouble for this…ya' know? They already fired one guard…some old-timer that left his post, I heard…"

"We'll talk about it, later…okay Teddy?"

"Fine. Oh…by the way…Randy hired some new *ofay*…I'll be workin' with him till he learns the ropes…"

Jim pushed me away from Teddy and the other voices. The wheels of the caddy clicked, as they rolled below me on the tiled hallway floors. I heard Jim's breathing as he walked behind it. Finally, I felt him pulling the thing to a stop. Then, I heard his footsteps and a door opening.

"All right…get out, boy," he said. I pushed up from beneath the linen and saw Jim holding a door open. "Come awn," he urged. I looked past him and saw a little hallway where the stairwell ended next to another door with an Exit sign above it. I jumped out and walked quickly through the open door. A moment later, he opened the Exit door and warm air rushed in as he peeked outside. Then he looked up, stepped out, and checked behind the door. Finally, he waved and I followed him out, letting the Exit door quietly close. We stood at one end of a long, narrow alley formed by exterior building walls, twenty stories high, stretching into a distant patch of pale blue sky. Along the walls, on both sides of the quiet alley, there were endless rows of dust-encrusted windows painted black. I heard traffic sounds, and the warm air smelled of city soot and garbage. "Let's go," he muttered. We walked toward an iron gate at the other end of the alley. Beyond the gate was the street, where cars and taxis moved beneath the bright sun. I knew this was Riverside Drive. I could smell the Hudson, and could see through the trees across the street to the brown Jersey palisades. When we reached the gate, he looked at me. "I'll unlock this, here, and let you out," he said. "I was you…I'd go on over't the park there…walk on down a couple blocks…nice n' easy…then come back out an' ketch a cab or somethin'…"

"Oh, shit," I muttered.

"What?" He was getting impatient again.

"My *sister*," I said. "She's waiting for me…in the short term parking lot, out front."

"Sweet Jesus."

"If I go around there, the guards'll see me."

"Shit," he grumbled. "They prob'ly got the police there by now, too. All right. I'll go on up through the lobby…see if I can find her, and send her around here for ya'…"

"She'll be in a 'Fifty-one Buick, black," I explained. "She's eighteen. She's got medium length brown hair, blue eyes. Her name is Liz."

"Liz. 'Fifty-one Buick," he said, with a strange smile. He reached out his hand and I grabbed it, briefly. He unlocked the gate with a long key on a big key roll he had in his pocket. Then, he looked at me. "You seem like a good kid, Tom. Don't get yourself hurt."

"You either," I said. "It's *you* they're after."

He smiled wearily, and shook his head, as he turned and walked back to the building. He used another key to open the basement door, and for a moment, he looked back at me. He raised his hand in a brief wave before stepping in ahead of the closing door.

I waited at the gate and watched cars and people go by. A gust of wind rose from the river and I smelled trees and earth from the embankment across the street. I looked at my watch. It was nearly three o'clock, but the sun was still high, and the black iron gate was warm. At last, I saw Liz driving slowly up Riverside. I carefully opened the gate and looked up and down the street. A New York City Police cruiser sat idling next to the curb, one block north, facing uptown. Liz stopped. I closed the gate and walked across the sidewalk. Stepping quickly into the street between two parked cars, I opened the passenger door and jumped into the Buick.

"Lie down," she ordered, grabbing my head and pushing me down beside her. She gunned the gas, as she reached over my body to pull the door shut.

"Don't go too fast," I urged. "There's cops up the street." She relaxed her foot on the gas pedal and reduced speed. I was beginning to feel safe until she stopped abruptly. "What's wrong?" I whispered.

"Amber light," she muttered under her breath. "Now it's red. Stay down."

"Do you see the cop car?" I said.

"We're right next to it," she smiled, staring straight ahead. When the light changed, she shifted into first, stepped carefully on the gas, and drove smoothly toward the highway. Moments later, she glanced down at me. "Gerry

Moran was killed by a train at Grand Central," she said, as I sat up quickly. "It's on the radio…they say he fell on the tracks."

CHAPTER 18

❀

We drove for several miles in silence. Then, I told her about the confrontation with Mrs. Stannard and Lanning Eliot, and the conversations I'd overheard, and about Jim. Finally, she asked about the one thing I hadn't mentioned. I hesitated, but she glanced at me again and again, waiting for an answer, until I whispered, "they…made her have an abortion."

"*She* didn't want to?"

"I don't know, Liz…did she have a choice?"

"People *always* have choices," Liz said. "The Stannards can do *whatever* they want."

"Well…I guess that's what they did," I said, staring from my window into the dense forest of old pine trees along the east side of the river highway. The sun was still high enough to pierce its green canopy, and disparate rays of gold light glowed in the barren, brown undergrowth.

"Did you ask her about it?" said Liz.

"I said…it would have been nice to be told…"

"And?"

"She didn't answer me. She's not right…they have her on *drugs*, or something."

After a moment, Liz breathed a long sigh. "You know…a couple of girls at my school got pregnant, last year."

"Oh, yeah?"

"They went to this place in Poughkeepsie…it's run by nuns…they stayed for a few months…had their babies, and went home. They're back in school this year. The babies were…adopted, I guess…or went to some orphanage…"

"*Orphanage?*"

"Whadya' *think* happens?" she said, with an odd smile. I had no answer; I'd never actually thought this far along before. But of course, Liz was right. Not only April's life but ours, too, seemed to be little more than lousy choices. And now, I couldn't decide which was worse—the idea of nameless children waiting to be claimed by strangers, or the sheer nothingness of the alternative. "*Girls* get pregnant, Tom…*boys* don't," Liz said, sounding exactly like an older sister.

"What's *that* supposed to mean?" I said.

"It means that I *know* you feel bad…but for *her*, there was more *involved*. Something *had* to be done. What were *you* gonna do about it?"

I lowered my head and brought my hands to my face, and rubbed my palms against my tired eyes. "I don't know."

"I'm proud that my brother wants to take…*responsibility*. You should. But don't take all the *blame* on yourself."

When Liz turned the radio on again, I was relieved. I leaned back in the passenger seat with my eyes closed and we drove on. We didn't have to wait long to hear a news update.

"More now on Gerald Moran, the Manhattan attorney, who died beneath the wheels of the Northern Star as it pulled into Grand Central Station today.

"Witnesses told police at the scene that the victim lost his balance on the crowded platform. But WCBS News has learned that several other witnesses saw the victim arguing with three men, seconds before the incident. According to police sources, *these* witnesses saw the men surround Moran, and push him off the platform, as the train arrived. The men then slipped away in the crowd.

"The Northern Star was scheduled to leave Manhattan at twelve forty-five on its regular run to Canada, through Albany and Burlington, Vermont. Police said the deceased man was carrying a large amount of cash, along with his passport, and a first-class ticket to Montreal.

"Gerald Moran was an attorney in private practice, who frequently represented commercial real estate developers and investment banks, and often lobbied for clients at the New York State Assembly, and in Washington. He was forty-two, and unmarried. His closest surviving relative, a sister who resides in Valley Cottage, New York, identified the body. For the latest updates on this, and other breaking stories…"

I turned off the radio and stared at the highway. "How do you explain somebody like that?" I said.

"I don't know," Liz said. "Explain some of our *own* family." I nodded, and then turned to look at my sister. Suddenly, I felt a hopeless wave of affection for her—this beautiful, loyal girl. I knew that we were held together permanently, now, by everything that was happening. I pulled out my wallet and retrieved Agent Valeriani's card. Liz glanced at me. "What's that?" she said.

"One of the FBI men told me to call, if I thought of anything," I replied. "He seemed, I don't know…sympathetic, maybe."

"*Sympathy*…for *us*? The *FBI*?"

"Maybe it was the way he apologized to Mom, and Arthur…for the crummy treatment they got from his partner…"

"That's a game they play…don't believe it."

"Something's telling me to call him, Liz. Maybe I'm wrong…but I think we should try."

Reluctantly, Liz turned off Route 9 near Tarrytown and found a rest stop with a telephone booth out in front. She waited in the car, as I stepped into the booth and dropped a dime in the slot. I dialed the New York City number on Valeriani's card, and my coin tumbled into the return cup as the connection clicked in.

A brusque female voice answered. "Bureau."

I stared at the card and said, "extension seven, please." I heard another connection and then a man's voice.

"Valeriani."

"This is Tom Gannon."

"Oh. What can I *do* for you, son?"

"You told me I could call."

"Yeah."

"Well I thought we could meet…maybe."

There was a half-beat of silence at the other end. "Where are you calling from?"

"A phone booth. It's near…"

"Doesn't matter. Why do you want to meet?"

"Somebody pushed Gerry Moran in front of a train at Grand Central…"

"That's not confirmed…"

"…Right after he told me an interesting story…"

"*You* met with Moran…today?"

"My sister and I did."

"Why?"

"He *wanted* to meet…he told us some people were trying to use my father, to ruin him…the same people who paid *him* to discredit *my father* two years ago…"

"First of all, there's no proof Moran's been murdered…"

"Come on…they're already saying it on the radio…"

"Did he tell you who these people are…the ones he said paid him, to accuse your father?"

"No. But we have a pretty good idea. Did *you* know my father was supposed to meet with Moran, on Tuesday?" I waited for a response, but heard only silence on the line. "Anyway, he never made it, and now…Moran's dead. Why are the police lying about my father's disappearance?"

"Even if you're right about that," said Valeriani, "what makes you think *I* know anything?"

"Oh, I think you know what happened to my father. Maybe you're just not in a position to do anything about it…"

"Listen son, I'm pretty busy…"

"You want to know about the little girl…don't you?" Again, there was no response. "I saw her…*with* the old man at the bus terminal…Tuesday morning."

"So *you* lied," Valeriani snapped.

"I saw them get thrown off their bus…I saw the police arrive…I saw enough to know that it's the *police* who are *lying*…about *that* anyway…and maybe about a lot more stuff…like how the old colored man got in the river. His body wasn't supposed to turn up, was it? And it's causing problems for the police. I think they're lying to protect somebody. And I think that poor old man they found in the river is connected, somehow, to my father. I don't know how…but he is. There may even be a connection between my father's disappearance and Moran's murder."

"What connection could there be?" said Valeriani.

"I don't know…but…the police seem desperate to keep people from *making* one. Isn't that why you're all pretending you don't know about the girl…pretending she never existed?"

"Go home, son."

"You asked me if I'd lied to you. Well, yes, I did. But I'm telling the truth, now. So what about *you*?"

"Go home."

"What happened to the little girl, Agent Valeriani?"

"If you're wise, you won't repeat this to anyone. Don't call me here, again." He hung up.

I replaced the receiver and stared in frustration at the hewn fieldstone-and-timber rest stop near the phone booth—a fake Revolutionary cottage, built under the Works Progress Administration during the Depression. Now, I noticed the commemorative plaque above the front door.

On September 23, 1780, British spy John Andre was stopped near this spot by three local men—John Paulding, David Williams and Isaac Van Wart—who likely meant to rob him. Major Andre, dressed in civilian clothing, was trying to reach British-held Manhattan with the West Point fortification plans Benedict Arnold had given him. The documents were discovered in Andre's boots, and he was turned over to Continental Army officers. The West Point plot quickly unraveled. Arnold escaped capture, but his accomplice Andre was hanged on October 2, in Tappan, NY.

I walked back to the car and slumped into the passenger seat.

"Well?" Liz said. "Did you get him?"

I nodded. "He told me not to call him again." She smirked. "No," I said. "He's *afraid* of something...like Moran was."

"Has he heard about Moran?"

"Yeah. He was surprised we'd met him...but that wasn't what bothered him...it was when I mentioned the little girl from the bus terminal. He didn't want to talk about *her*,,,and he warned me not to..."

"He threatened you?"

"It wasn't a threat...it was a *warning*...for *my* safety."

At a few minutes after five, Liz turned the Buick off 9D and sped up the gravel drive toward our house. The sun was well beyond the river, turning red above the cliffs. There were lights on inside already, and as we neared the house, I saw Mother's grim face in one of the living room windows beneath the porch. We saw the Spencers' Olds, the Gannons' Ford, and the Brents' Packard, parked at odd angles along the crest of the hill.

Liz guided the Buick down into the garage. She turned off the engine and we sat for a moment as the cooling, contracting engine block ticked. Finally, she turned to me. "What about that man...*Jim*?" she said. "The one who helped you. Shouldn't we try to do something...call one of the newspapers or a congressman...tell them what's happening?"

"Let's tell Arthur," I said. "He'll know what to do."

"All right."

"But let's not mention *this*." I held up Agent Valeriani's card and quickly hid it in my wallet. She nodded, warily.

Moments later, we stepped through the kitchen door. There were dirty dishes soaking in the sink and used glasses and cups on the counter. The newspapers we'd brought home from Wilson's were scattered across the table, and several were opened to the stories about Father and the body discovered in the river. We could hear soft voices in the living room.

Suddenly, Mother came into the kitchen, looking relieved. "Where have you *been*?" she demanded.

Liz grabbed her hands and said, "we met Moran. We *also* went to the hospital...so Tom could see April. Is there anything new?"

Mother shook her head. "Captain Blanchard called to ask if *we'd* heard anything. He said he was going to halt the river search...I guess he has...we've heard none of those...explosions."

"Moran's been killed," I said.

"Why do you think I've been so worried?" Mother said, urgently.

"It happened right after we saw him," said Liz.

"They say it may have been *murder*," whispered Mother. "What did he tell you?"

"That Dad wasn't going to testify about him," Liz whispered. "In fact...he planned to give *Moran* the evidence he had..."

Mother's face hardened. "Why would he do that?"

"A bargain," I said softly. "In return for Moran's help...finding out where the information came from."

"But...why go through the charade of making us all think he *would* testify?" said Mother.

"He suspected he was being used," I said. "That...maybe Grandpa was, too..."

"*Maybe*?" Mother frowned, before turning to look into the hallway that led to the living room. She sighed and turned to us again. "You didn't tell Moran that your grandfather was the one who gave..." We shook our heads. "Did he tell you where *he* thinks it came from?"

"He wouldn't," said Liz. "But Tom thinks it's Andrew O'Leary...and...Charles Stannard."

Mother looked at me and I nodded. "It makes sense," I said. "It explains...almost everything..."

"Moran's been working for them, all along," Liz said. "He was secretly working for them two years ago...during the fight over Arthur's theater..."

"Did he *say* that?" Mother whispered.

"He didn't deny it," I answered, firmly.

Suddenly, Grandfather Hank's voice boomed out from the living room. "Is that my grandchildren?" he shouted. "Tell them to come here to me, Mary!"

"Is he drinking?" I whispered.

Mother rolled her eyes, and then fixed her gaze on me. "You saw April…how is she?"

"She's leaving the hospital," I replied. "Probably already left." Mother stared wordlessly. "She wasn't really…ill, Mom, you know?"

Her eyes narrowed and her lips pressed together. She looked at Liz who was staring away toward the windows. Then she turned, and looked at me again, nodding once. "That's that, then."

"There they are…my grandchildren!" Hank Gannon beamed from his favorite armchair near the front door, and the television. As Mother returned to her chair, just inside the kitchen hallway, Liz and I dropped to the floor and sat, Indian-style, at her feet. Grandmother Libby was sitting with the Brents on the couch. Arthur, Hazel and Laureen sat in kitchen chairs that someone had brought in and placed in a row near the windows. The television was on but the volume was down; no one was paying attention to it. I could see it was the CBS Early Show. For a moment, I watched Katharine Hepburn spar with James Stewart in a library. I looked at my watch. It was almost five-thirty. The first real news reports weren't for another hour. "So!" blurted Grandfather Hank. "You met today with that snake in the grass…Gerry Moran!"

"He wanted to meet," Liz muttered.

"Well, you won't be meetin' him no more," he replied, with a wicked laugh, as he reached for a glass of whisky on the nearby lamp table. He took a good, long swallow.

"You watch your tongue, Henry Gannon," muttered his wife, in a voice edged with anger. "These are your son's children."

"It's a man who went to some lengths to hurt my son, with dirty lies," he scoffed. "Now, he's dead, and can't hurt us no more. He got what he earned…that's all I'm sayin." He sipped at his whisky glass and stared around the room.

The Spencers seemed uncomfortable. The Brents watched their daughter with obvious frustration.

Liz turned and looked up at Mother. "Where are the children?"

"I told David to take his sister for a walk," Mother said. "They'll be back."

"*And so?*" said Grandfather Hank, suddenly scowling at Liz and me. "What did this Moran have to say for himself?"

I sighed angrily and hung my head. But Liz answered. "He said…Dad wasn't going to testify, at the McCarthy Committee."

There was a sudden intake of breath around the room. Arthur closed his eyes and began to smile. The troubled faces of Alice and Phillip Brent softened. Even the stern Libby Gannon seemed stunned by emotion. Her head sank forward in a sigh of grief, as she wept for her son. Grandmother Alice reached for her hand and held it.

"*Not testifying*," said Grandfather Hank. "How would *he* know such a thing?"

Phillip Brent's voice rose. "Doesn't *matter*, Hank."

"Ah!" Hank Gannon waved his hand in disgust.

I interrupted them. "Moran said that Dad called him this week…and arranged a meeting to discuss the testimony. He said Dad wasn't gonna use the information against him…he was going to *give* it to him."

"*What*?" Hank Gannon gripped the sides of his armchair.

"But Dad wanted a favor," Liz added.

"What sort of a favor would *he* have for my son?"

I glanced at Arthur. His smile had hardened into a grim scowl. Then, I looked into the sneering face of Hank Gannon. "My father wanted his help," I said, "finding where the information came from…because…he didn't trust it."

"It makes no sense a'tall," said Grandfather Hank. "It come from *me*. I got it…to *help* your father. If Moran told you this…it's another lie of his…"

"Are you saying *you* gave the information to Joe?" said Grandfather Phil, shocked.

"I did…yes. It's no secret…I make no apologies for helping my son…"

"So, where *did you* get it?"

"Never you mind where I got it from…Mr. *Brent*."

Grandfather Phil turned and stared angrily, helplessly at Mother. Then, abruptly, he stood and faced his wife. "We're leaving, Alice." He looked at Mother again. "Mary, we'll spend tonight and the next few days in the city. Please call us if you hear…anything…or need anything. We can be here in less than an hour." Then, he looked across the room. "Arthur…Hazel," he said, "it was good of you to come and be with us. Laureen, dear…take care."

Alice Brent stood with her husband, as the Spencers rose together and shook hands with them. There was an odd, silent pause, and then they all kissed each other's cheeks.

"We'll be going, too, Mary," said Arthur, as Hazel turned to embrace Mother. Liz and I jumped to our feet. Grandmother Libby stood. Grandmother Alice faced her and they gripped each other's hands. Suddenly, Laureen kissed me firmly on the cheek. She smiled fleetingly, and then turned to speak with Liz. Arthur and Hazel glanced at me. Then, Liz began speaking quietly to them as Laureen stood by and listened.

Moments later, the Brents and the Spencers rushed out the front door without a word to Hank Gannon, who gripped his whisky glass and stared straight ahead, transfixed by the nearly silent television screen, where Cary Grant was saying something that troubled Katharine Hepburn.

Grandmother Libby looked sternly at Mother. "Mary," she said, "we'll be leaving, too." My mother nodded, and made no attempt to dissuade her. Automobile engines started up, and I heard crunching gravel, and saw the flash of lights across the porch windows, as the Brents and Spencers drove out toward the highway. Hank Gannon mumbled bitterly at the black and white figures on the television screen. "On your feet, then," Grandmother sighed. At first he ignored her, but she finally got him up, reached deftly into the pocket of his trousers, and pulled out the car keys.

His knees wobbled as he growled, "what's 'at…eh?"

"It's me drivin'…that's what." I'd never seen Grandmother this angry. "Come on now, if you're comin'," she said, starting toward the door without him.

Liz and I walked him out, across the porch, and slowly down the steps. We guided him to the passenger side of his Ford, as Grandmother went to the driver's side. Liz and I put him in and closed the door firmly. He was already asleep. David and Mary appeared and stood next to Mother on the porch, as Liz and I kissed Grandmother.

"I'll be in touch, Mary," she called out, as she got behind the wheel. Mother nodded and waved to her.

Liz and I waited, and watched the car move toward the highway in the growing shadows. Finally, when it turned south, we looked back at the house. The porch was deserted. We hurried inside and found Mother sitting pensively in her armchair. David and Mary stood next to her and stared at us.

"Liz," said Mother. "Take the children to the kitchen…give them some dinner…be sure you're ready for school in the morning." Liz nodded, and pulled David and Mary into the hallway toward the kitchen. But they resisted. "Stop that nonsense!" Mother shouted, and immediately they did. A moment later, Liz closed the kitchen door, and Mother looked at me sternly. "Sit down," she said.

"All right." I sat, with some confusion, in Hank Gannon's chair.

Mother reached into the front pocket of her dress, and pulled out a folded blue envelope. She held it up, so I could see Father's name typed across its face. "What's *this* about?" she said, coldly.

"Something happened in history class." She stared, silently, waiting for more. "I gave Father McHenry an answer he didn't like."

"Didn't like it *why*?" she said.

"He thought it was disrespectful."

"Was it?"

"I hope so."

She sighed, angrily. "Then…we'd better see him about it."

"You found that on my dresser…"

"I did…after he called, asking about us…about *you*."

"*Me*?"

"*Yes*," she said. "He was concerned. He'd seen the stories about your father in today's papers. And…you hadn't been to class for two days…"

"Well…I'll go back tomorrow."

"I'm afraid it's not that simple," Mother sighed. "We're to meet him tomorrow in the school chapel…following the eight o'clock student mass. And then, you're to meet with Father Stevens, in *his* office. It's to be *decided* whether you'll continue at St. Paul's, or not."

"Did Father Stevens call, *too*?" I said.

"When he saw the newspapers," she replied, abruptly standing. She held the envelope out and waited for me to take it. "Be ready to leave at seven-fifteen," she said. "We'll attend mass before we speak to Father McHenry. You can say a prayer for your father…and…your girlfriend."

"Mother, listen," I said, standing up quickly, taking the envelope. But she raised her hand in a clear signal that meant she'd finished talking for now. She leaned forward and kissed me on the cheek. She looked at me, shook her head, and then walked down the hall into her bedroom and closed the door.

I collapsed into Grandfather's chair, and stared briefly at the crumpled blue envelope with my father's name on it. I heard faint voices from the television and smelled whisky from the unfinished glass on the nearby table. Then, I breathed in deeply and turned the TV volume up a little. I watched the very end of the movie and then the CBS Evening News. Toward the end of the newscast, the announcer referred to a major city development. I reached forward and put the volume up higher.

"Finally…investment banker and philanthropist, Charles L. Stannard, appeared this afternoon at a City Hall press conference with the Mayor's Development Commission."

A film clip of Charles Stannard and several other men, including Lanning Eliot, appeared. They stood together behind a podium. Looking closely, I noticed, with embarrassed satisfaction, that Lanning's cheek was puffed out.

"Mr. Stannard introduced a team of investors, and architects, who outlined a master plan to develop three sites in Manhattan," said the announcer over the news clip. "The old railroad yards near the waterfront in the west 'Thirties…a parcel in Greenwich Village just south of Washington Square…and a dilapidated stretch of tenements along Broadway in the west 'Sixties. All three sites are to be anchored by new office skyscrapers and high-rise apartments, and will feature extensive new superhighway access."

A different clip suddenly appeared on the screen. It showed Charles Stannard and Robert Moses shaking hands and smiling at the podium, as the announcer continued. "New York State Bridge and Tunnel Authority Commissioner, Robert Moses, endorsed the ambitious plan. Stannard also announced formation of the Stannard Trust, which his family has endowed with fifty million dollars, earmarked for low income housing in blighted areas of the city and state. Mr. Stannard said he hoped the foundation's public housing projects would qualify for Title I federal funding, overseen by Mr. Moses. Neither Stannard nor Moses would confirm if the three *commercial* developments announced today would also qualify for government assistance."

Finally, standing with Moses at the podium, Charles Stannard spoke.

"I am honored to announce my family's initial investment of fifty million dollars to create a fund that takes advantage of state and federal renewal money and tax abatements, enabling development of low-income housing, mainly for underprivileged Negro and Puerto Rican people in troubled neighborhoods. A creative combination of private and public funding is, in our opinion, a reasonable, effective solution to the slum clearance problem across our city and state. We are gratified that Commissioner Moses stands with us, today, as we announce our group's commitment to the concept of urban renewal. Over the coming months, we'll make detailed announcements of affordable housing projects in upper Manhattan, the Bronx, Brooklyn, and other blighted areas…such as the City of Newburgh, about seventy miles from here, in the Hudson Highlands."

Then, he shook hands with Moses and smiled, accepting applause from the press conference audience.

"Charles Stannard is one of several major Wall Street figures backing development of a TV studio complex, at the old horse and carriage stable on St. Nicholas Avenue," said the announcer. "Bids for that project are now under consideration by the Mayor and his development task force…"

I reached forward and turned off the television.

"So *that's* the foundation Charles Stannard wanted Dad to run?" said Liz. I turned and saw her standing in the hallway between the living room and the kitchen. She'd been listening to the news report.

"Supposedly," I nodded.

She turned and started back through the kitchen door, but then paused. "Oh, by the way," she said. "I told Arthur about the union busting at Grace-Episcopal…another fine community project of the Stannard Organization." She shook her head in disgust and disappeared into the kitchen.

CHAPTER 19

Mother started the engine and let it run. She pressed her fists against her lap and shuddered, and I wondered if she could smell Father fading in the damp Buick.

"I hope you haven't ruined things for yourself," she said, abruptly shifting into reverse and backing out of the garage. We crunched past the sleepy house and moved slowly in dense, white fog to the end of our driveway. She paused—looked left and right—as the muffled headlights of a southbound car appeared in the fog twenty yards away and sped by. She stepped on the high-beam button and turned on the wipers. "I want to pick up the *Times* and *Post*," she said, straining to see. Then, she floored the gas pedal and turned north.

Instantly, we were enveloped in the bright glare of headlights coming up rapidly from behind. Mother glanced into her rear-view mirror, and I turned to look at the car, which was right up to us now. It seemed to be a black or dark blue Chrysler, or Cadillac, judging by its shape in the dense mist and glare. The driver was a man. He wore a hat. I couldn't see his face.

"He's awfully close, Tom, doesn't he see us?" said Mother, looking back and forth from the mirror to the fog-shrouded road ahead.

"He sees us." I rolled down my window and stuck my head out. "Hey mister! You're too close…back off, will you?"

Instantly, the driver responded, slowing noticeably and allowing distance to gather between our vehicles. I rolled my window up and glanced back several times, as his headlights grew dimmer until, finally, they were gone.

"That was odd," said Mother.

"Yeah." I tried to sound calm. "People act funny when they can't see…he prob'ly wanted to follow your taillights."

Mother said nothing more about it, as we drove on into the dense swirls of mist. Finally, with difficulty, we found the turnoff for Cold Spring and descended into the village, as a bit of sunlight pierced the low-lying clouds. Mother parked directly in front of Wilson's. I ran inside for the papers, as she waited in the car with the headlights on, and the radio tuned to a classical music station.

"Morning, Tom!" Mr. Wilson called out from his counter. "Mind that door shuts tight, now…"

"I will." I firmly closed the glass and wood-frame door and glanced out at Mother, who sat pensively, with her hands on the wheel. Then, I walked to the newspaper rack for the *New York Times* and *New York Post*, and took them to the counter. I smelled the fresh coffee that Mr. Wilson always brewed for commuters, who caught the early train to Manhattan. A radio in the back room was faintly playing the old Glenn Miller tune, *Moonlight Serenade.*

"How's your mom?" he asked.

"Fair…I guess." I heard more customers coming in the front door, as I paid for the papers.

"I know she spoke to Mrs. Wilson, yesterday," he said, nodding gravely. "Anything new, yet?"

I shook my head as two men in business suits squeezed past me with their papers and stepped to the counter. I waved to Mr. Wilson and headed for the door as another customer appeared outside. He pushed the door open and stepped in with his head down. I moved aside to let him pass and I glanced again at Mother, who still seemed distracted, waiting in the car. Then, the man closed the door, blocking my exit. As I shot him an unfriendly look, he raised his head, and let me see his face beneath the brim of his dark hat. It was Agent Valeriani, and he seemed nervous.

His eyes narrowed and he shook his head in an almost imperceptible signal for me to say nothing. Then, with practiced agility, he turned his back to Mr. Wilson's counter, removed a small white envelope from inside his dark, gray raincoat, dropped it on the face of my *New York Post*, and put the palms of his hands together as if praying. When I responded, by folding the newspapers over to hide the envelope, he relaxed his hands and walked quickly toward the newspaper rack. I tucked the papers under my arm and left the store without looking back.

When I got to the car, it was clear that Mother had observed none of this odd transaction. Without a word, she put the car in gear and backed away from the sidewalk, heading us up Main Street to 9D, and then south toward Bear

Mountain Bridge. Fog was rising off the highway, now, in a yellow haze of mist and deflected sunlight. We sped by our house again, and I glanced up the driveway, seeing lights on inside. It was seven thirty-five. Liz would be up by now, getting David ready for his bus, and having Mary ready to be picked up for the morning by Mrs. Wilson. A few minutes later, Mother turned west onto the bridge. Halfway across, the sun finally broke through the yellow haze, and the spires of the bridge seemed to vibrate in the brilliant, mountain light, as the wet road surface sparkled.

Traffic was heavy beyond the tollbooths on the western side. We worked through the rotary, and then headed toward the main entrance of St. Paul's. As Mother listened to her music, I glanced at the newspapers folded over on the seat between us. Carefully pulling the *Times* out from beneath the *Post*, I scanned the busy front page and saw a shocking headline.

Suicide Is Possible
In GCS Lawyer Death
Police Say Conflicting Witness Accounts
Led To Premature Reports of Homicide

On the same page, another headline:

Banker Charles Stannard Unveils Urban Development Plan
And Pledges $50 Million for Public-Private Renewal Effort
City & State Officials Praise Solution for Blighted Neighborhoods

Moments later, as we reached the front gates and entered the school grounds, I noticed the stark headline in the national news column.

McCarthy's Enemies Gather
Ike 'Furious' Over US Army Assertions

McCarthy Harangues Fizzle on Television
Senate Leaders Ready a Challenge to His Power
As Dissension Roils His Staff;
Cohn Bridles Under Scrutiny of His Associates

After parking near the chapel at the south end of the quad, Mother got out abruptly and slammed the door. She started toward the sidewalk, and I quickly removed the envelope from inside the *Post* and stuffed it into my blazer pocket. Then, I jumped out and caught up with her.

The ancient oak pews of the chapel were nearly filled for the eight o'clock student mass, as we entered and found a place to sit near the front on the right. I noticed many familiar faces—students, parents and teachers—but no sign of Father McHenry. I took my mother's advice and said a prayer for my father, and April. Then, when the service ended forty minutes later, and worshippers started filing out, I saw McHenry standing just inside the open door at the rear of the chapel, dressed in a black suit and cleric's collar. I pointed him out to Mother, and she nodded, as we followed the slowly exiting crowd back down the center aisle.

The Kellers were on line ahead of us. Georgie jerked his body around and smiled, and then waved, but neither of us responded. He lowered his arm and faced forward again, just as his parents were greeting McHenry with a great show of friendliness, while hurrying past him out the door. Their deft exit caught Georgie by surprise, and suddenly he found himself alone with McHenry. The priest said "hello," but Georgie could only nod sheepishly and bolt through the door after his parents.

My teammate, Jimmy Pauling, was leaving from a small side door with his mother—a secretary in the school library. Jimmy waved briefly, and looked away, before I could wave back.

When we finally reached McHenry, there was no one else left inside. And after an awkward moment, the priest spoke directly to Mother. "I'm pleased to meet you, at last, Mrs. Gannon."

"Likewise, Father."

"When I sent my note home...to your husband...I really had no idea..."

"It's quite all right," she said. "How would you?"

"Nevertheless..."

Mother stared at him. "You agreed that we would talk about my *son*."

"Yes. All right. Then...I'll start. Mrs. Gannon...last autumn, during the first part of the term, I came to realize that Thomas is among the best students I've *ever* taught. His grasp of history, of its sweep and meaning, is...rare. But...for some reason...when we returned from the Christmas and New Year's recess, he was *not* the same boy..."

"How do you mean?" she said, urgently.

"Well. He'd changed," said the priest. "So completely...it shocked me, at first. He was diffident and uninvolved...no longer contributed to class discussion, and...more than anything else...he seemed troubled, even depressed. Things didn't improve. In fact, they went from bad to worse during the spring term. And now, I blame myself for not having contacted you. I should have addressed the whole term paper issue sooner, and…"

"*Term paper*?" Mother gave me a hard look.

"Why, yes…you *were* aware that Thomas hasn't turned it in?"

Mother stared at me. "No…I was *not.*"

"Mrs. Gannon…I raise that issue mainly to admit my *own* shortcomings. Frankly, Thomas has done a lot of preliminary reading and thinking about his project…no doubt far more than many students have done to produce entire papers. But…your son is…in conflict with himself, Mrs. Gannon. The term paper is…merely a symptom."

"*Symptom*?" Mother murmured in a despondent tone, looking nowhere. "Of *what*?"

"Mrs. Gannon…I'm neither a psychiatrist, nor guidance counselor, but I'm always concerned for the healthy self-esteem of my students. I look for what makes each of them individuals, and I encourage *that*. One could say I *demand* it, I suppose…intellectual independence…though my students often resist." Mother looked at me gravely as McHenry continued. "Now, *this week*, for the first time since I'd noticed the troubling changes in Thomas…this loss of individuality…I suddenly witnessed its reappearance…I saw his *character*…a more compassionate nature. However awkwardly it may have been expressed, he was in touch with himself again." He paused and looked directly at me. "Have you told your mother about…what happened…in class this week?"

Mother interjected. "He's told me he was disrespectful."

They stared at me, anticipating some response.

"No," the priest finally said. "I wouldn't say *that* was the issue. Thomas…tell your Mother about your concerns, for Mr. O'Leary."

"What about him?" said Mother, sharply.

"He's one of Tom's mates," said the priest. "They're in the same section of my history class. He's a troubled boy…"

"What would *you* know about it?" I interjected. "Or care?"

The priest frowned. "Mrs. Gannon, I wonder if you would speak with me…alone…for a moment?"

"Great," I snapped. "I'll wait outside."

Mother stared in helpless embarrassment, as I walked away from them, and out the door. Then, as I waited on the chapel steps, I heard their voices in the echoing emptiness inside.

"I'm very sorry, Father…"

"Please don't be alarmed, Mrs. Gannon...I'm not. Frankly, I welcome this sort of passion...believe it or not." He paused. "I can see that I've confused you, Mrs. Gannon. Speak your mind, please...it's why we're here."

"Father...how does a man of your professional achievements come...at this stage in his career...to teach adolescent boys, at St. Paul's?"

There was a long pause in the conversation, as a warm gust of wind blew across the steps, and suddenly, the chapel door slammed shut. Jolted, I walked out beyond the shadow of the bell tower to the edge of the top step, which glowed in morning sunlight. I pulled the envelope from my pocket, opened it, and quickly read a brief, unsigned message.

"St. Mary's Roman Catholic Church in Beacon, tonight (Friday). Arrive 9PM. Park in back. Enter church from side door. It will be open. Go to confessional on left side of church. Wait in box closest to altar. Come alone."

The chapel bell began to ring for nine o'clock, as I slipped the note back into my pocket,and looked out over the deserted quad. Dark vines of green ivy thickened on the gray, fieldstone dormitory buildings to the right and left. Straight across the quad, the brick façade of the old main building was awash in golden sunlight. The chapel bell's last bong echoed away, and I heard the faint, tinkling of the first-period bell. And then, silence. I sat down on the warm, stone steps to wait for my mother. The breeze grew stronger, drying the grass on the sun-dappled quad, and rustling the limbs of ancient oaks and elms. For a moment, I imagined I could hear my father's voice in the silence beneath the whispering trees. And then, as suddenly as it had arisen, the breeze subsided, and faded in the warming sunlight.

A black, 1954 Cadillac moved slowly by on the street below the chapel steps. I looked down into the passenger window and saw Andy O'Leary Jr. staring back at me. He neither smiled nor waved, as his father drove along the edge of the quad, toward the headmaster's residence, a quarter-mile away on the crest of the hill overlooking the athletic complex.

A moment later, the chapel door opened and Mother emerged. "Let's go," she said, brusquely. We walked down the steps and then quickly along the tree-lined street to the car. We got in without a word to each other, and Mother drove around toward the visitors' parking area behind the main administration building. Finally, she turned to me with a serious expression. "How well do you know your friend...Andrew O'Leary?"

"Since freshman year, I guess…"

"Does his father abuse him?" I hesitated to answer. "*Does* he?"

"He's never said anything…but…yes…"

"Then why have *you* never said anything, Tom?"

"I thought…everybody knew…"

"That's *not* an answer," she sighed. "Did you know that Father McHenry has been meeting with him, privately…in his office, several days a week…trying to break down his unwillingness to admit his father's abuse?"

"McHenry told you that?" I scoffed.

"*That's* what the incident in class was about…Father McHenry trying to draw Andrew out…to force him out…"

"But, Mother…that's…"

"No!" she asserted, sternly. "You're wrong…you misunderstood *then*, and you're wrong *now*." I didn't know how to answer her, so I stared straight ahead through the windshield, and let her have her say. "This priest is a good man, Tom. He likes and respects you. But he's right about your attitude, lately. I think you should stop listening to that voice inside your own head…try listening to someone else…*for a change*. People are concerned about you…this teacher is one of them. He was *glad* you stood up for Andy in class this week…glad that *someone* finally stood up. But you misunderstood his intentions. Yes…he admitted he'd been rough with Andrew. He said the boy is very stubborn…that he simply will not admit anything about his father…"

"I just saw them," I muttered.

"Who?"

"*Andy*…with his father. They drove past, while I was waiting…"

"Listen to me," she said, when we'd reached the visitors' lot behind the administration building. "Are you listening?"

"Yes…I'm listening."

"I want you to speak with your friend." She turned off the engine. "If there *is* trouble about his father, we must help."

"All right…"

"We do not allow things like this to go on…we try to do something…*about them*." She hammered at each word, as if speaking to a spaced-out child. Then, she paused. "And…you owe Father McHenry an apology…"

"He's allowing me back in class?"

"He said he'd recommend it to the headmaster," she said, in an uncertain voice that trailed off. "You need…to complete a term paper…of course." She stopped talking entirely now, and seemed lost again, distracted. I could tell she was thinking about Father. The thought had surprised her; overtaken her.

We climbed the rear steps and entered the main building through heavy steel doors, and proceeded along the dark hallway to Father Stevens' office, where Miss Drummond greeted us. The big wall clock behind her counter said nine-twenty. The door to Father Stevens' private office was ajar, and Miss Drummond saw me stare at it.

"They're waiting in the boardroom," she said to Mother. "Will you be joining us, Mrs. Gannon?"

"They?" said Mother, still a bit distracted. Now, Miss Drummond seemed confused. "You said '*they* are waiting,' Miss Drummond. Do you mean Father Stevens and Father McHenry?"

"*Not* Father McHenry," she said. "After all, *he* is the subject of the inquiry."

"Inquiry," said Mother, in a flat voice.

"Why, yes…wasn't that clear?" Miss Drummond glanced nervously at the clock.

"I see," said Mother, her voice stronger, coming to a realization. She stared at me and said, "no…I think my son can handle this. Do you mind if I wait here, Tom?"

"No," I said.

Miss Drummond extended her hand to Mother. "Mrs. Gannon, why don't you wait in the headmaster's private office. I'll pour some fresh coffee." Mother nodded and followed her in. A minute later, Miss Drummond reappeared and closed the headmaster's door. "All right, Thomas," she said, and we left the office.

Her high-heeled shoes clicked on the ancient wooden flooring, as we walked along the hallway together. Two freshmen giggled as they passed us. When we reached the brown oak door with the word BOARD painted on in gold letters, she knocked twice. A muffled voice answered. "Yes?" She turned the doorknob and we went in.

"Ah…Mr. Gannon," said Father Stevens, from his seat at the far end of a long, oak table. "Please." He pointed toward the empty chair at my end. To his left sat Andrew O'Leary Sr., who had not looked up as we'd entered. Closer to me, on my left, sat his son, staring into space.

"Hi, Andy," I said. He turned and smiled, briefly, before looking down at the tabletop.

I sat down as Miss Drummond walked to her seat, beside Father Stevens, just off the table. As she sat in her chair, she crossed her long legs and rested her stenographer's pad on her knee. Mr. O'Leary still hadn't looked up. He pretended to read from the thick stack of documents on the table in front of him, but I could tell that he was eyeballing her legs.

"Mr. Gannon," said Father Stevens, smiling formally. "I told your mother, yesterday, that…we are deeply concerned for your family. The entire St. Paul's family…has you in its prayers."

"Thank you, Father." I said.

"A Novena of Masses is being offered in your father's name," he added. "We pray an answer is given to you, soon. I'm sure everyone in this room feels great sympathy…your father is well respected at St. Paul's School."

I watched Mr. O'Leary nodding silently at the tabletop, as Father Stevens spoke. Finally, he looked up and our eyes locked. "We're all very sorry," he said. Then, he quickly turned away and looked at Father Stevens.

"Right," said the headmaster, riffling through his own stack of documents. When he found one piece of paper in particular, he pulled it out and laid it on top. Then, he looked up at me again. "Mr. Gannon, we wish to commend you…for your loyalty." He paused, nodded toward Andy Jr., and continued. "Your courage…standing up for this young man, against the capricious bullying of your history teacher…Walter McHenry."

"Father Stevens, I think you have the wrong idea about that…"

"Unfortunately, this isn't the first complaint I've had about Father McHenry," he said, ignoring my reply, and staring intently at the sheet of paper. "I have a list…the names of twenty-three students, who've made sworn complaints…"

"Sworn complaints, Father?" I knew how unorthodox McHenry was, but it seemed odd that a group of St. Paul's students would have complained so formally about anything.

"I'm afraid so," he said, frowning gravely.

"What are the complaints?" I asked.

Referring to several different sheets of paper in his stack, he enumerated them. "Habitual tardiness to class, lack of lesson preparation, inattention to students while in class, inconsistent grading, poor personal hygiene, inappropriate emotional outbursts…"

"Failure to teach from the official text, approved for the course," interjected a grave Mr. O'Leary.

"Yes." Father Stevens nodded in agreement. "Yes...the failure to cover syllabus material, and teach from the approved text...a serious professional charge..."

I searched the headmaster's face for some sign of the meaning of this. "What does Father McHenry say about it?" I asked.

"He denies it," the headmaster replied.

O'Leary jumped in again. "Other issues have come to light, concerning his *political* background. His support for subversive groups...socialist ideology...beliefs that are inconsistent with American values, which he *can't* deny...it's all published in black and white in books..."

I frowned skeptically. "*Books?*"

"He wrote a book that defends the Marshall Plan," O'Leary said.

"That was a government project," I replied. "The State Department's postwar strategy to keep Germany free of Communism...create a buffer against Stalin's expansion west."

"That approach has been discredited, Mr. Gannon," interjected the headmaster.

"By *whom?*" I said.

O'Leary stared at me, angrily. "The Marshall Plan was a dangerous, subversive idea," he said. "Hatched by Roosevelt's Communist cronies...who were still in the Truman State Department. The taxpayers of this country should *not* pay to rebuild former enemies...and we do *not* negotiate with godless nations...appease men like Stalin...or this *new* gang in the Kremlin now."

"How does a strong West Germany appease Russia?" I said, with great skepticism. O'Leary frowned angrily, and looked at Father Stevens.

The headmaster now reasserted himself. "Mr. Gannon, this latest classroom incident is the *final* straw. I appreciate your modesty...and respect for a teacher...misplaced though it may be in this case." I looked over at Andy Jr., who furtively returned my gaze, and then looked away in great embarrassment, as the headmaster continued. "We have testimony from your classmates...corroborated by young Mr. O'Leary, here...which details how you faced down this bullying teacher."

"Father Stevens," I said, shaking my head.

He pressed on. "It rests with *you*, now, to provide *your* account of what happened in history class three days ago. We'll need you to sign an affidavit to your account. When included with all the other sworn statements, your testimony will help us remove this man from our teaching staff. To assist you, we've prepared a general description of the incident...including your brave statements in defense of Andrew…and this teacher's threats to you." Miss Drummond stood up, then, took a sheet of paper from Father Stevens, and walked toward my end of the table. She placed the paper in front of me and walked back to her seat. "We also have listed the complaints of the other twenty-three witnesses," said the headmaster. "Please read the document…tell us if it doesn't reflect your knowledge of the circumstances. If any statement attributed to you…or to Father McHenry…is inconsistent with your own recollection, we'll make the necessary corrections…including…anything you may wish to add." He paused, and I stared into his eyes. "Go on, Mr. Gannon. Please take a moment to read the document."

I looked down at the sheet of paper in front of me. There were two long paragraphs. The first recounted the classroom incident between McHenry and me, but in the most melodramatic language, suggesting McHenry was unhinged. The second paragraph included assertions by other students, that McHenry had frequently wasted time in the classroom, ignored the official textbook, and often voiced anti-American opinions. The names of 23 students, including Andy's, were listed. At the very bottom, was the phrase: "I do so attest and declare," and below that was my name, typed next to a long black line awaiting my signature.

As I stared at the affidavit, I couldn't help noticing it had been produced on the same typewriter Miss Drummond used to type McHenry's note to my father. I looked up and stared at her hopelessly beautiful face, and felt tremendous sorrow. Suddenly, she stared down at her steno pad and fiddled with her pencil. I looked at Father Stevens, and said, "I need to use the bathroom…"

"What?" Mr. O'Leary muttered angrily.

The headmaster extended his left hand to calm him. "It's all right, Mr. Gannon," he said. "This is a grave matter…we're all on edge…by all means, take a moment."

I left the boardroom and walked rapidly up the hall to the bathroom near the front of the building. I went inside, and stood in the middle of the large lavatory, relieved to be alone. The strong odor of disinfectant almost covered the stale aroma of furtive, student cigarette smoking. The sashes of four massive frame windows facing the quad had been pushed up. Warm breezes and bright sunlight washed in. The door opened behind me. Andy Jr. walked in.

"Did they send you in after me?" I said sarcastically.

"No," he said. "I told them I had to go, too."

"Why are you letting them do this? The stuff they're peddling about McHenry isn't true. I heard he's been trying to *help* you…"

"You don't know what my father's like…when he wants something…"

"No? I've *seen* the bruises on your back, Andy." He lowered his head in deep embarrassment. "Don't you know it's not your fault?"

"You don't understand," he replied, looking up with desperation in his face. "It's not me I'm worried about…it's my mother…"

"He does it to her, too?" I spit the words. He lowered his head again and began to sob. I grabbed him by the shoulders and shook him. "You can't protect her like this. You've gotta stand up to him…I'll stand with you…I bet McHenry will, too. So will my mom."

"Just sign it…*please*." He pulled away from me and wiped his reddened eyes. Then, he turned and left.

I began to pace the room like a prisoner in a cell, first toward the sinks on my right, then to the row of old porcelain urinals along the opposite wall. Finally, I walked to the open windows, and looked out on the quiet campus. For a moment, I inhaled the warm, sweet air. But suddenly, I spun around and walked back to look at something I'd unconsciously noted on the tan plaster above the urinals. It was a nasty bit of graffiti, scrawled in bright, blue ink: *Miss Drummond suck's Father Stevens cock.*

Sad and embarrassed, I looked away, as if the errant scrawl were the act itself. I left the bathroom and walked back down the hall. I entered the boardroom without knocking, and went to my chair and sat down. Miss Drummond seemed unnerved by the look on my face.

"I've been reviewing your record, Tom," said the headmaster, in a suddenly familiar tone. "Your grades confirm that you're currently our top history student. The St. Paul's community wants to demonstrate its respect for that record…the St. Paul's *family* wishes to stand by you…"

"Father?" I said.

"I intend to submit your name to the school trustees, for their immediate approval of you…as the first recipient of our new St. Paul's Award…the seminar at Yale University, Tom. You'll represent us, there…in the Spring semester…next year." I stared into his eyes as he smiled warmly. "Normally," he said, "we would hold a competition…but not this year, for I can think of no finer candidate. The board will have to approve formally, of course, but I believe they will, since your nomination has the strongest support of Congressman O'Leary and myself."

"*Congressman O'Leary?*" I said.

"We haven't announced it yet, but he'll soon join the Board of St. Paul's School." The headmaster turned briefly and smiled at him before continuing.

"He has graciously endowed the entire Award Program, in perpetuity. St. Paul's will *never* have to be concerned for its ability to participate in the Yale program...quite a generous gift, I must say, and a tremendous boost to our school's academic reputation."

I stood up, and looked across the table at the headmaster and O'Leary. I could see from the corner of my eye that Andy Jr. was peering up at me with great concern. Miss Drummond's big round eyes were wide open.

"I can't sign this," I said, pointing to the document on the table.

"Well, certainly, we can make whatever changes are necessary..."

"I can't sign it in *any* form, Father..."

"I'm sorry to hear it," replied Father Stevens, frowning, as Mr. O'Leary stared at him in a way that implied vindication of some prior disagreement. The headmaster persisted. "Perhaps you should take a little time to think about it." I shook my head. "Do you have any idea of what you're throwing away at this moment?"

"Yes...I do, now."

Father Stevens nodded, and smiled in a suddenly distant way. "I'll have a word with Mom about this."

"Do what you like," I said. "I've made up my mind. Anyway...I'm pretty sure I don't even want to continue here...as a student."

"*Oh?*" he said, surprised, and with a hint of insult.

"I despise this sort of thing, Father." I pointed again to the affidavit. "It's dishonest and frankly immoral...and I think it's time it all stopped. The founders of this school were English Catholics...dissenters...in an unfriendly Protestant society, Father Stevens...and they'd be *shocked* by what you're doing in their name." He frowned at me and sat back in his chair. "Father, this is *over*," I said. "This mad compulsion to confess...to force confessions from others...intimidate anyone who refuses or disagrees. Read the papers!" The headmaster slowly shook his head, as I pointed to O'Leary. "*His* day is over. And if *you* don't wise up...this whole fuckin' school's gonna go up in flames. Your own students'll set the fire." I turned and walked out of the silent boardroom, and saw my mother waiting for me up the hall, outside the headmaster's office. I called out to her. "It's over, Mother. Let's go home." She hurried toward me with a concerned expression. "They're trying to railroad Father McHenry," I said.

She smiled gravely. "He told me."

"They wanted me to help them," I added. "I won't do it."

"Good," she said.

We quickly left the building, and hurried down the back steps, just as Coach Bunning was approaching from the opposite end of the walkway. We met halfway between the building and the parking lot.

"How are you, Mr. Gannon?" he said.

"Things have been better," I replied.

He nodded pensively. "I was sorry to hear of your father's…situation," he said. Glancing at Mother, he bowed his head. "Mrs. Gannon." She acknowledged his sympathy with a silent nod.

"I know I haven't been to practice lately, Coach." He shook his head and waved me off. "I've been…helping my family," I added.

"I understand," he said.

"Sir…the fact is…I'm quitting the team…"

"I see."

"I'm withdrawing from St. Paul's." Mother's head snapped in surprise.

"That's a pity, son…not only for you but for your teammates." Then, glancing up at the administration building, he smiled wistfully. "However…soon, it will be someone else's problem," he muttered.

"Sir?"

"I'm withdrawing, too," he replied with a wan smile. "Resigning…effective at the end of the term. That's why I'm here."

"But why?" I said.

"Too much interference." He paused, and looked up toward the steps. I turned to follow his gaze and saw the O'Learys coming out and starting down the steps together. Mr. O'Leary leaned over with one hand on his son's shoulder and limped down to the walkway. He and the coach stared at each other, briefly. Then, the O'Learys continued across the grass toward their Cadillac. The coach turned to me again. "Interference from…donors. It's all for the best. It's what the administration wants…and I'm too old to worry about these sorts of political shenanigans any more."

I shook my head. "I'm sorry…"

"Not to worry, Mr. Gannon." He extended his aged right hand. I grabbed it and felt its still powerful grip. He squeezed tighter and tighter, until suddenly, he stopped with a jerk and released me. "Good luck to you, son. Cultivate your talent and conquer your ego. Remember…you've plenty of both. I wish you well." Then, looking at Mother, he smiled and nodded his head respectfully. "Mrs. Gannon." And he walked on toward the administration building.

CHAPTER 20

The Wilsons' solid masonry house had been converted from an old Presbyterian church. It was set back from the road on seven acres, encompassing a fallow barley field that once sustained the minister and his family. Mr. Wilson said there'd also been a wood-frame parsonage across the field from the church, but it was dismantled and sent up the highway in a train of wagons, when the congregation sold the Garrison property and moved north in 1901. You could still see a bit of its crumbled foundation beneath the wild flowers and mountain grass that grew thick with once-tame barley.

I drove past the field, along the rough, dirt driveway, and up to the house on a ridge several hundred feet above the river. And it was reassuring to see the familiar gray stone facing of our neighbors' home, its narrow windows framed in black iron, and its angular roof of purple slate shingles that turned iridescent blue in the sunshine.

Mrs. Wilson was sitting in the sun just outside her arched front door in a white Adirondack chair. Mary sat in the lush grass nearby, with a picnic blanket spread out, and Raggedy Ann sitting upright against a smooth stone in the grass. Mary poured imaginary tea from a battered kettle into an old cup for Mrs. Wilson, and when she recognized our Buick, she smiled.

"Hi, Tom," said Mrs. Wilson, as I stopped near the house and turned off the engine. She got up and walked toward me in loose khakis with cuffs over gardening boots and a dark blue, cotton blouse, with the sleeves rolled up. Her graying, black hair was pulled casually back and held with a simple, wooden clip. Several gray strands had broken loose and were floating on each side of her handsome, weathered face.

I got out of the car and smiled. "My mother said to say 'thanks' for taking Mary."

"Nonsense," she said as we embraced beside the Buick. She seemed about to ask me something, but instead put her hands on her hips, and turned to look south over the valley. "Sure has turned into a nice day," she said.

"It's so quiet up here," I replied. She nodded, agreeing, as she gazed down river. "My mother would love to know how you got this grass to grow so thick on bedrock," I said.

"Minerals in the soil," she answered, with authority. "Grass thrives on it." She turned and looked down at her healthy front lawn. "Needs cutting," she added.

I looked at the grass, which seemed neat enough to me. Then, I glanced over at Mary and said, "you ready to come home, little one?"

She shrugged and whispered something to her doll. She waited for a moment, as if listening to a reply, and then nodded. "Annie sez we can go," she said. Then, she got up, gathered the doll in her arms, and started toward the car.

"Did you stop by the store today, Tom?" said Mrs. Wilson.

"We did…Mom and I…first thing…"

"Johnny talk to you?"

"Didn't see him…I was in and out…to pick up the papers…"

"Well, tomorrow's Saturday," she said sternly. "I'm sending him by your place to mow the lawn…I *told* that boy to watch for you…"

"He *did*, Mrs. Wilson…*yesterday*. You know, it isn't necessary…"

"No arguments, now. You and Lizzie need to help your mom handle…everything. And if other folks can do for *you*…you need to let 'em."

"Yes, Ma'am…"

She grabbed Mary's hand and brought her around to the passenger side. I got back in behind the wheel as Mrs. Wilson helped Mary climb up into the front seat. Then, she closed the passenger door, as I started the engine.

"Take care, now," she smiled, as she stood away from the car and waved.

"Thanks again," I said from my open window.

I backed around and headed out toward the highway. Several hundred yards down from the house, I glanced into the rearview mirror. Mrs. Wilson was still standing by her front door, watching us.

Mother made tuna sandwiches for lunch. I wasn't hungry, but sat down at the kitchen table anyway. After several minutes of silence, Mother looked up from her barely eaten sandwich with a troubled expression, and it was easy to read her thoughts.

"There are plenty of *other* schools," I insisted.

"Like St. Paul's?" she replied.

I laughed sarcastically. "I *hope* not."

"Tom…be serious. I want you to finish the last few weeks of this term."

"But I've already…"

"Tom…it's been paid for…don't waste good money and your own valuable time…does it make sense to lose a whole semester, when you're so close to the end? If you don't want to go back next year…"

"How can I, *Mom*?"

"…I'm not *asking* you to," she said sternly. "Just finish the term you started…we'll find something else for next year."

"What's the point?" I said. "I'll just finish out at Highland Falls…"

Now, she leaned across the table and stared at me. "Son…listen to me. You mustn't give up. Accept that the world is *guaranteed* to disappoint us. We can't change that. But, we can't allow ourselves the…*vanity*…of believing *our* disappointments are unique."

"I know."

"I *hope* so," she said. "Now, I want you to find out what happens to Father McHenry." I nodded. "And remember what we agreed," she added, "about Andy."

Mother put Mary to bed for a nap after lunch, and then busied herself cleaning the house. I went for a run, south along the river past the trestle at Manitou Falls, and down to a spot where I could cross the tracks, and walk out on a small sandbar in the deep gorge below the bridge. I stood at the river's edge and looked beyond the bridge span, across the valley. On the high summit of the western cliffs shining in the sun, I could see the green hedgerows lining the Stannards' property. I felt small and empty. But I had my senses back enough to know that my family's love was never an obstacle to what I'd imagined existed in the world. I felt my feet sinking into the wet sand, and my socks turning damp and cold inside my running shoes. I turned away from the river, climbed up over the tracks again, and headed home.

Later in the afternoon, I gathered the history books in my bedroom and got them ready to be taken back to the library at St. Paul's on Monday. I tried writing a letter to April, but found myself stumbling over and over in the opening sentences. Words seemed futile on the page. Finally, my wastebasket half-filled with crumpled paper balls, I put down my pen and briefly thought of calling her, imagining that if I could just hear her voice—but I didn't call.

Liz got home from school at about four-thirty. I went to her room, closed the door and sat down at the edge of her bed. She stood near her desk in silence, kicking off her brown loafers, still dressed in her red school blazer and her pleated blue skirt.

"What now?" she muttered. I handed her the note from Agent Valeriani, and as she read it I told her how he'd passed it to me that morning. "Nine PM," she said, handing it back. "That means after dark."

"You'll come?" I said.

"Why all the mystery…what's with the confession box?"

"He's afraid."

"*Right*," she sighed, as she hung her blazer on the back of her chair.

"He's gonna help us, Liz…that's all I know…"

"You're sure about that?"

"Yes. The *rest* of it…meeting in a church…the confessional box…who knows? He's doing something he's not supposed to be doing. Maybe he wants god's forgiveness…I don't know…I don't *care* if it's odd."

"Maybe he just doesn't want to look you in the eye," she said, and I shrugged. "You still don't want to tell Mom?"

"And send *her* up there?" I replied. "Waste time trying to get Arthur to go? He could have approached *Mom* himself Liz, but he didn't. He *wants* to talk to me…he knows what I saw, and that it proves the police are lying. He probably feels safe with me, and I don't want to scare him off…or give him time to change his mind."

She stared hard at me. "That's *not* the real reason," she said. "You better tell me why you're acting so responsible for all this, suddenly." She stared at me, waiting for a reply.

"Liz…you've been right about me," I said. "I've been a shit…*especially* to Dad." I told her about Tuesday morning—how I'd let Father go with telling him about Charles Stannard's offer. "I didn't know it was bullshit then, Liz. I thought it might help him, but for god sake I let him go without telling him. And now…"

She frowned at me in an odd, sisterly way. "How do we get the car?" she sighed.

"Well," I replied. "I'll say we're going to the movies." She frowned again.

I told Mother we wanted to see a double-feature revival at the Post Office Theater in Cold Spring. "*A Place in the Sun* and *I Confess*," I said.

"*Two* Montgomery Clifts!" she said, her tired face softening in a brief, innocent smile.

I nodded. "We just thought it might be something…you know…to take our minds off…"

"You can have the car," she sighed. "Don't stay out late."

"We won't," I assured her, as Liz listened in discomfort.

We headed off after dinner, pretending to be hurrying to the first feature at seven-thirty, which left us time to kill, since the church in Beacon was only a half-hour's drive north of Cold Spring. We parked down near the river at the public boat basin and walked slowly back up Main Street in the fading light of dusk. Ahead of us, the Post Office Theater marquee glowed above the sidewalk in pink and purple neon.

"We *could* go in for an hour," I suggested.

"Sure," Liz snapped. "That way, we'll even have ticket stubs to show her."

We stopped at the theater and examined the movie posters in silence. Suddenly, I heard someone calling Liz's name. I turned and saw Edith Neumann and Doris Dickinson coming across the street.

"Are you going in?" Edith asked, with a warm smile, when they reached us.

"No," said Liz, in a subdued voice. "We're just killing time…it's a nice evening."

"*Join us*," said Doris.

"Yes," Edith said. "We'll all waste time *together*."

"We'd…like to," I stammered. "But…uh…"

The two women stared quizzically. Finally, Doris grabbed her friend's arm. "Come on, Edith."

"No…wait, wait," said Edith, staring hard at Liz, then me. "What's wrong?" she said.

"*Nothing*," I replied.

"Have you heard something?" she pressed. "About your father?" We shook our heads.

"Edith…come *on*," Doris insisted. "They don't *want* to."

The women went to the window for their tickets and proceeded to the lobby, waiting as the usher tore off their stubs. Then, Doris walked toward the candy counter, as Edith turned and looked back at us through the glass doors.

"Now they think we're snubbing them," Liz sighed, angrily.

"Let's just go wait in the car," I said.

At a few minutes before nine, I started up the long, dark driveway to St. Mary's Church, which sat on a wooded hill, a quarter-mile above 9D. I dimmed our lights, as we glided slowly past the church and into the parking lot—a field of tufted crabgrass thinly overlaid with pulverized tap rock, bordered on three sides by half-buried railroad ties. There were no other cars in the lot.

I brought the Buick to a stop against a railroad tie near the back of the church, and turned off the low beams and the engine. Without the headlights' dim glow, the white clapboard building was a dark pyramid beneath the moonless sky. It was our family's church, where Father had come as a boy during the summers. Its familiarity should have calmed me.

I turned to my sister. "I guess...I should go in."

She nodded. "I'll watch from here."

"Keep the lights off, and the engine."

"Okay," she replied, "but let's have a signal...in case I see something."

"Sure. Like what?"

"Two long beeps on the horn," she said. "If you hear *that*...it means get the heck outta there."

I nodded and got out of the car. I heard Liz locking the doors after me, as I started toward the church. I followed the narrow cement walkway along the south side of the building and quickly reached the door, which was open.

Inside, everything was black. There were no votive candles lit near the altar. I waited near the door for my eyes to adjust, and slowly, the interior emerged like a photograph resolving in a darkroom. I began to see the outlines of walls, and window shapes, and rows of pews leading to the altar. And then, noticing the odor of burnt wax and sulfur, mixed with the smell of incense, I realized I wasn't alone—someone had put the candles out, moments before.

I walked nervously across the back of the church to the confession box. My arm shook as I grabbed the heavy, velvet curtain on the right side of the box and pulled it open. I stepped in and knelt down, and let the heavy curtain fall back. My knees sank into the cushioned padding of the kneeler, and I leaned forward, gripping the wooden ledge at the base of the window-screen inches from my face.

Suddenly, I heard soft footsteps outside the box, and then the confessor's door opening and closing. A moment later, the wooden shutter behind the screen opened with the sound of stone grating on stone. I looked through the screen at a dark, almost invisible profile.

"Are you alone?" he whispered.

"My sister…she's waiting outside. I'm sorry…"

"It's all right," he said. "Does anyone *else* know about this?"

"No," I said.

"Do you have any idea how dangerous this is?" he asked.

"Yes, sir. I do."

"You're going to need to tell your mother…but keep my name out of it. Are we agreed?"

"Yes."

He paused. "Tell me what you think this is all about," he said.

"Two colored people were kicked off a bus in Peekskill…Moran was murdered…and somehow, my father's disappearance is connected…right?"

"Do you know *why* those people were thrown off the bus?" He waited only briefly before answering the question himself. "They wouldn't give up their seats…to a congressman's parents," he whispered, with anger and disgust.

"Congressman," I said. "You mean *O'Leary*."

"That's right," he said. "The bus driver thought it would be a great idea to have the old man and the girl get up and give their seats to a local celebrity's mother and father. So, he told them to go find seats in back. The old man started to move, but for some reason, he changed his mind…sat down again. That started an argument, and the driver stopped outside the terminal and threw them off."

"*That's* what I saw…"

"What else?"

"A town police cruiser pulled up…and then, *my* bus left."

"Well…it must have been shortly *after* that point…*another* person arrived. And got involved." He stopped, and sat silently in the confessor's chair.

"*Please*…tell me what happened."

He turned to look at me through the screened window in the darkness, which hid the features of his face. "Your father…he tried to help the old man and the girl. And…I don't know *all* the circumstances, but…he was murdered…at the police station."

"By the *police*?"

"*No*," he said, emphatically. "*They* just looked the other way…"

"O'Leary?"

"*And* some thugs…he pays…to do things. They did Moran, too." As Valeriani paused, I could hear the inside of my head banging. "Only a few people *know* about this," he added. "People who do business with O'Leary…and are protecting him, because their political and financial interests are threatened. None of this can be proved, you understand, unless someone confesses...that's unlikely." He turned away from the window, and leaned back in the confessor's chair. I heard him exhale. Even in the darkness, I could feel how difficult this was for him.

"When you say...people are protecting O'Leary, does that mean...Charles Stannard?"

"He's got massive deals pending with the City and State...and a lot of money invested. But City and State officials would drop him in a second, if they knew about this. Stannard *has* to keep it quiet. So much of his money is tied up in these projects, but even more...it's his *reputation* that's at risk...his ties to O'Leary which, I bet, he'd cut now if he could...but he can't. This all happened because O'Leary and his thugs couldn't control themselves...went over the line. Then, this colored man's body turned up. You were right; it wasn't supposed to. Someone screwed up and didn't dispose of it properly. But as long as your *father* stays missing, the lid can be kept on...barely...they think. They can manage the investigation...get the papers to say it's an odd coincidence...a drifter who drowned...another man with well-known political and financial difficulties...and good reasons to run off...or kill himself."

"So...how do *you* know all this?"

"There are *some* policemen who aren't happy...shutting up. They're just too frightened to say anything...publicly."

"But *why*..." I stopped, feeling my throat tighten around a wave of angry tears.

"Take it easy, son." For a moment, I struggled to control myself, breathing deeply, forcing air into my lungs. "You all right?" he whispered.

I sighed. "*Why* was my father murdered?"

"He was gonna raise hell about the way these two colored people were treated, even *before* the old man died. Think what the papers would have made of it...especially in *that* town. You're old enough to remember the riots in Peekskill...when they nearly lynched the radical Negro singer...Paul Robeson...at that concert a few years ago? People threw rocks and bottles and turned over cars and almost killed audience members. And the police...did nothing...just like now. They let it happen."

"You're saying the old colored man was *murdered*...for refusing to give up a seat?"

"No" he said. "*That* happened accidentally...I've seen the body close-up...looks like he had a heart attack...probably during all the ruckus with the bus driver. But once your father showed up, things just…like I said…got outta hand. And now, there's too much riding on keeping the truth from coming out. People have been reached…people I would have trusted with my life. A deal's been made because…the powers that be see a greater good in keeping it quiet. I hope you understand…I'm no rebel, or subversive. But *this*…this is wrong…it offends me." He paused. "There's something else."

"You mean the girl," I said.

"The whole damn lie could be brought down, because…*she* knows every-thing. She saw it all…like your father did."

"She's alive?" I said.

"These are men who see themselves as moral…if you can imagine that," he sighed, with angry sarcasm. "They haven't gone *that* far, yet. But…if it came down to it, they wouldn't hesitate. If someone got to her, and she started answering questions about this, some pretty influential people would be…ruined. She needs protection…and I can't guarantee that. Is your family prepared to?"

"Yes," I said. "Where is she?"

"She's being kept in a home for…you know…girls in trouble…it's the one up in Poughkeepsie…the Catholic sisters run it…St. Raphael's Home."

"Why there?"

"Who's gonna think about a place like that? The congressman's sent a few young girls up there before, apparently…and has donated money…there's a prior relationship…let's say." He paused. "I'm not criticizing the nuns. They don't like this one bit…but they're minding their own business, and thinking of the girl's immediate safety. That's not important, right now. We need to do what's right for this girl. I need to know if you're going forward with this…that you'll see it's done right. I need *you* to do it…because *I'm* in a tough spot. I don't care about myself…but I've got family too…daughters of my own…I *need* my job…"

"You don't owe explanations…*to anyone*," I said.

"The girl is only with the sisters temporarily. Arrangements are being made to get her to Canada, I think, within days…maybe sooner. There's no time to waste. Have your mother go up there with some responsible people. No police…and make sure *you* go along…*you've* seen the girl and know what she looks like. You ask for the Mother Superior. You come right out and tell her you want the girl. Whatever you do…do *not* leave without her, once you've gone up there."

"And *then* what?" I said.

"Get the hell away from the place…and be careful. When these people find out you've got the girl…they'll be twice as dangerous."

"Once we do this, how do I let you know?" I said. "How do we contact you?"

"You don't. I'll know you've got her. It'll be in your hands, then, to seek whatever justice you want. You won't hear from me again…unless you can't get her. Then, some other action may be needed."

"We'll get her," I said. "Is that all?"

"There's one part o' this *I* don't understand," he said. "Why was your father even there, that morning? He had the meeting with Moran. Didn't you see him leave for New York?"

"Yes," I said, feeling my throat tighten.

"So, why was he there an hour later again?"

"I *think*, maybe, he never left for New York. He drove around for a while…or went back down to Lents Cove, to think some more. I think he tried to tell me what was really going on that morning…about this testimony, I mean…and even Moran, maybe. He just couldn't figure out a way to do it, without telling me some pretty horrible things about my girlfriend's father…let alone that someone in our own family had…well, betrayed him."

"Who?"

"His father…my grandfather. *That's* what he was going to meet Moran about…to get the proof. But what I think now is, he already knew…after he left me off at the terminal, and thought about things, maybe he decided to go back to Peekskill…confront O'Leary about it."

"Cut to the chase, you mean."

"I guess so."

"I'm sorry, son."

"Well…it's *my* responsibility, now."

"Listen to me…don't get cute with this. This is dangerous stuff. You stay away from O'Leary. Go tell your mother about the girl, and take care o' that. That's our deal…isn't it?"

"Yes."

"All right, now. I'm gonna close this thing over again, and I want you to give me a full minute to leave before you move. Your sister is…out in back?"

"Yes."

"All right. That's it." He closed the window slide. I heard him open the confessor's door, and then his soft footsteps, moving away quickly in the empty church. Then, silence.

I began counting out sixty seconds in my head and reached 'thirty' when I heard a noise, and felt the heavy black curtains move near my left shoulder. Carefully, I pulled the curtain aside a few inches and looked out. There was a figure silhouetted in the open door at the far side of the church, looking in. I began to shake with anger, knowing I'd have to do something now. I wondered why Liz hadn't hit the horn.

"Tom! Tom, where *are* you?" said Liz.

I sighed and stood up, relieved that she was safe. I stepped out of the box and walked quickly to the open door. "You scared the shit out of me," I said.

"You've been in here almost an hour," she answered.

"You were supposed to signal…didn't you see him leave?"

"There's been nothing…not one thing," she said urgently. "Why do think I was worried? I've been standing outside here for five minutes. Finally, I opened the door and called you."

"You didn't see him leave this way?" I said, surprised.

"No," she said. "Nothing. So…what did he say?"

"It isn't good, Liz." Though it was dark, I could see her eyes glimmering as she waited. "Dad…Dad's dead," I said.

She lowered her head. "I knew it," she whispered. Then, with a sigh, "how are we ever gonna tell Mom…that we lied to her?"

CHAPTER 21

At eleven o'clock the next morning, Mother slowed the Buick on Route 9 in the Poughkeepsie foothills and pointed to a flagstone column in the pine forest just off the road. It was six feet high and crumbling at its base, the surviving twin of an ancient gateway. And beyond it, a broken asphalt road disappeared into the woodland shadows.

"This is it," said Liz, when she saw the weathered bronze nameplate—*St. Raphael's Home*—embedded in the stone.

Mother turned in and followed the roadway through forests and open fields, slowly climbing the mountain. Liz and I were in back with Laureen Spencer between us, and Arthur sat in front with Mother. It had been a tense, 30-mile journey from home, and there seemed to be a wordless understanding—we would not speak of Father until we'd seen to the girl. But silence had suspended us in hopeless anger.

"This place…it's huge," Laureen marveled.

"It was a private estate, once," Liz said, in a blank voice.

"Looks old," Laureen muttered.

"Built before World War One," Liz said. Laureen nodded silently as she stared at the forests on both sides of the broken down roadway. "The owner was a man who made millions manufacturing buttons," Liz added. "Max DuFresne…'the button king' he was called. I've seen the house. It's like an old, French chateau…built it for his wife, but she died on their honeymoon…"

"How do *you* know so much about it?" said Laureen.

Liz shrugged. "Some girls at school."

Laureen nodded. "So…what happened to the button man…he get another wife?"

"No. Never even lived here," said Liz. "He signed the property over to the Catholic Church and sold his business. Then, he went home to his apartment in Manhattan and shot himself."

"*Liz,*" Mother sighed.

After crossing a stone bridge above a rocky creek bed, we saw the light gray masonry face of the chateau at the crest of the mountain. We began seeing young women walking or lying in the sun along the face of the green knoll below the house, and on the great lawn that flowed down from the knoll. Some of the young women kept to themselves; others walked in pairs or sat in small groups. Many were obviously pregnant. A few held infants in their arms and sat on blankets in the sun.

Walking and sitting among them were nuns in black silk veils that flowed from starched, white crowns. And a cadre of workmen, most of them quite old, trimmed bushes and pruned flowers or pushed small lawn mowers around the base of the house.

Mother parked in the visitors' lot, and we all got out and climbed a grassy slope to the front door; we trooped into a vast entrance hall with a polished, blue marble floor. Beyond the large windows on the right, lush green fields rolled out to a distant lake. Smaller windows on the left were stained-glass portraits of medieval bishops and prioresses. And in the center of the hall, there was a medieval banquet table serving as a reception desk, with a young nun sitting behind it.

She looked up and smiled, and her eyes focused on Liz and Laureen. "Good day," she said, brightly.

"Good day, Sister," replied Mother. "We've come about a girl who's staying with you."

"The name?" said the nun, as she surveyed a directory next to an old-fashioned cradle telephone. But Mother didn't respond immediately, and the nun glanced up again.

"May we speak to the Superior about it?" Mother finally asked.

"Sister Paul is busy with morning rounds," the nun said, gravely.

"It's a serious matter," Mother replied. "We really must see her."

The nun's smile faded, and she seemed to struggle against her own inexperience to regain a presumptive authority. "*Your* name, please?"

"Mary Gannon. This girl is…about nine or ten years old, I think."

The nun's eyes widened in a cold stare. She stood up and said, "wait here." Then, she turned and walked swiftly out of the reception hall, into a long passageway deep inside the house.

We waited at the desk for several minutes. Once or twice, the silent hall echoed with the insistent ringing of the telephone. Finally, the young receptionist and an older nun appeared at the far end of the long passageway. The receptionist whispered something as they stared at us. Suddenly, the older nun raised her hand to the receptionist, who bowed her head. Then, they walked toward us. When the old nun reached the desk with the younger one behind her, she announced herself in a regal voice. "I am Sister Paul Joseph. What is your business, please?"

"I'm Mary Gannon, Sister. This gentleman is Arthur Spencer...and these are our children."

"Yes?" Sister Paul's expression was skeptical, and the edge in her voice was sharpening.

"We've come for the young girl you're sheltering," said Mother.

Sister Paul frowned, staring at Arthur and Laureen. "You're *not* relatives, are you?"

"No...Mother," said Arthur, politely.

"Then, she's still here?" Mother said. Sister Paul glared without answering. Mother pressed her. "This girl is a crime witness, serious crimes, which the authorities have chosen not to investigate, for reasons best known to themselves. The girl is in danger...but I think you *know* that." Mother paused and Sister Paul continued staring. "So, we've come to take her with us. We intend no insult, but you have no legitimate authority to hold her. We have no way of knowing why you've agreed to keep her thus far, but we assume it's for her safety. And *that* is our only concern, Sister. Whatever your intentions, she is *not safe* here...nor would she be safe in an orphanage or any other facility you may have been told she'll be taken to next. In fact, *we've* been informed that she's to be sent out of the *country*..."

"That's all very interesting, Mrs. Gannon," said the nun, sourly. "Now, I wonder if *you* would show *me* some identification." Mother glanced at Arthur and he nodded. Quickly, she opened her purse and found her driver's license, which she held out for the nun. Sister Paul examined it closely, and glowered, as she handed it back. I thought we were in for a struggle until the old nun's face softened, suddenly, as if in relief. "Mrs. *Joseph* Gannon?" she said.

"Yes. You know my husband?"

Sister Paul grabbed Mother's hand, took a deep breath and said, "I've been expecting you." Then, glancing at the younger nun, she said, "take our guests to the rosary garden, Sister Gertrude." She looked at Mother again. "Forgive me, Mrs. Gannon...I had to be sure...I'll bring the girl."

We followed Sister Gertrude out into a garden surrounded by hedgerows, high and thick enough to block the view of everything in the world but the pale blue morning sky.

"The sisters in our house come here to say their rosaries," the young nun explained, as she led us along a quiet maze of gravel paths, flowerbeds and blooming trees.

"I see," Arthur nodded.

We arrived at a large gazebo of stone and painted wood and Sister Gertrude invited us to sit; then, she hurried back to the house.

As we waited, Mother leaned against Arthur. "I'm surprised she's turning the girl over so readily," she whispered, softly.

"She seems to know who you are," Arthur whispered back, with a shrug. "Seems to know Joe...I suspect she knows this man...the one Tom met, last night."

At that, Mother sighed, leaned back and closed her eyes.

Sister Paul emerged from the garden maze holding the hand of the quiet girl from the bus terminal. She wore a plain brown frock instead of the fluffy blue dress I remembered, and her eyes seemed older, and hard. She clung tightly to Sister Paul's hand and surveyed our group. But when she saw me, her eyes locked in mine.

"This is Isabel," said Sister Paul.

"Isabel," Arthur said, softly, and the girl glanced down.

Mother roused herself and quickly introduced everyone, but the girl slowly raised her head again and stared only at me.

"What happened to that pretty blue dress?" I asked, as a thin smile appeared on her face and quickly vanished. Then, she whispered something to Sister Paul.

"They've come to *help* you," the old nun replied.

"Why can't I stay with you?" said Isabel.

"This is no place for a young girl. These people know what happened...and can protect you...better than I." Then, the nun turned to look at Mother and said, "they've promised...to treat you as one of their own family...isn't that so, Mrs. Gannon?"

"Yes, Sister," said Mother.

"Why don't you get acquainted," the nun said, as she led Isabel under the gazebo. Liz and Laureen made space between them for the girl to sit. "Her things are being packed…including that blue dress she loves," the nun added, smiling at the girl. Then, she walked quickly back to the house.

"I know you remember me," I said.

The girl was quiet for a moment. Finally, she muttered, "yeah."

Mother leaned toward her and whispered, "where's your mother?"

"She…passed," Isabel said, in a voice devoid of emotion.

"Then who takes care of you, child?" asked Arthur.

"My granddad. We been livin' in Jersey…you know Trenton?" We all nodded. "Mama's from there, too. But…she's in Newburgh, now."

"What do you mean?" Mother said.

"That's where she chased after my daddy…an' died," she replied. Mother looked at Arthur with alarm, as the girl continued. "Daddy got mad'n slugged her, an' she died…an' then…"

"How do you know all this?" Arthur said, interrupting her.

"My daddy called my granddad on the phone an' told'm," she said, without emotion. "'Said he was waitin' in Newburgh for my mama to bring money to'm…so he could go buy his medicine 'cause he's so sick without it…needs it every day. But Mama didn't come with no money. So he hit 'er. He tole Granddad he didn't mean to…didn't know what he wuz doin'…'cause a bein' so sick an' all…*crazy* sick."

"We understand," Arthur said. "Don't trouble yourself about this."

But Isabel couldn't stop. "I heard my granddad on the phone say 'you better bury my daughter or I'll kill you, too.' Daddy begged Granddad for money, so he wired him some…enough for his medicine and ta' get Mama buried. Granddad and me took a bus up there next day…t'Newburgh…found Mama at the funeral parlor where Daddy said she'd be, but Daddy was gone…with all the money…jus' lef' my mama there. So, Granddad talked with the funeral man an' give'm some more money to buy Mama a box. Then the man helped us bury her in town, there…with the other colored folks. Granddad said it was a good place…better'n Trenton any ways."

"So, you were going to visit her grave," I said, "when I saw you at the bus terminal."

Isabel looked at me in silence.

Sister Paul reappeared suddenly, with Sister Gertrude lugging a faded wicker suitcase.

"You must *hurry*, Mrs. Gannon," the old nun urged. We all stood abruptly, and the urgent sound of Sister Paul's voice dissolved Isabel's eerie self-possession. As she began to sob, Arthur put one hand on her shoulder. Mother glanced at me and pointed to the suitcase. "There isn't much time," said Sister Paul. "You *must* leave…*now.*"

We filed out of the gazebo and I took hold of the suitcase. Arthur lifted Isabel in his arms, and she shrieked in fear.

"How do you know my husband?" Mother asked the old nun.

"I know…*of* him," she said.

"But *how?*"

"We *read* the papers, Mrs. Gannon. And our work acquaints us with the world. We learn *much* here about the character of men." Sister Paul then turned to Arthur, who held Isabel tightly in his arms. "Please take care of that child, Mr. Spencer."

"We will, Mother," he promised.

"Now please hurry," the old nun urged again. "God has brought you here…but He will be relieved to see you go!"

The nuns led us out of the garden, back through the entrance hall and out the front door. The sun was bright and warm as we moved quickly down the grassy slope to the car. We got in and resumed our places—with Isabel in front, between Mother and Arthur. Mother started the engine and hit the gas pedal. We spun around the parking area in a wide semi-circle, kicking up gravel. The nuns watched with mournful expressions, and several of the young women who'd seen Isabel coming out with us stood nearby and waved as our car started down the mountain.

In minutes, we reached the end of the winding, asphalt road and the old gate column at the edge of Route 9. Mother paused briefly to look up and down the highway, and then she hit the gas hard, turning south with a screech of tires, pushing the Buick as fast as it would go. Moments later, two black Ford sedans sped by us heading north, shaking our car as they passed.

I turned to look out the rear window and saw the red taillights of the black sedans flicker as their drivers hit the brakes, swerving into the half-hidden driveway of St. Raphael's. When I faced forward again, I saw Mother's eyes in the rearview mirror, staring at me.

We drove on, following the river road south to Garrison. Every few minutes, Mother checked the mirror to see if we were being followed. And as the miles ticked by, Isabel seemed to grow calm again. When we were nearly home, she turned to Mother and asked an earnest question. "The man who tried to help my granddad…he's your husban', Ma'am?"

"Who told you that?" Mother asked.

"Sister Paul."

Mother glanced briefly at Isabel. "You do know…your grandfather…is…"

"He's in heaven, Ma'am."

"That's right," Mother said.

"Sister Paul says I should pray every day…and think of'm in my prayers…"

"It's good to pray," Mother agreed, with a falling voice.

"An' Sister Paul says I should try'n help you, too, Ma'am."

"Help *us*?"

"By tellin' you…how your man tried helpin' Granddad and me."

"Sister Paul told you that?"

"Yes, Ma'am. When I was brought there, I told *her* about it, an' she told me never ta' tell a soul…ever. But, this mornin'…she said…I could tell *you*."

Arthur turned to look at Isabel, and I could see the apprehension in his sad profile. Mother was looking forward, holding the steering wheel in both hands. Liz and Laureen waited beside me in silence. Finally, in her odd, emotionless way, Isabel told us how Father had died.

"My granddad and me were takin' the bus ta' visit Mama's grave, like your boy said, Ma'am. An' the driver all o' sudden stops outside the bus station…tells us we haf' ta' get off, 'cause Granddad wouldn't let'm take our seats and give'm to a couple old white folks. Granddad told the driver, 'why don't these *white folks* go sit in back?' So, he called Granddad a bad name and punched his stomach real hard. That hurt Granddad…I told'm we should get off…so he wouldn't get hit no more. But the driver got off, too, an' just kep' on hollerin.' 'How dare you talk t'me like that,' he says. '*I'm* the boss o' this bus.' Then, a policeman come by, an' the bus driver tells him what happen. Cop says he'll take care of it, an' tells the driver, 'get back in the bus.' But the driver's so mad he starts screamin' at the cop, too…the cop tells my granddad and me ta' get'n his car. So we do, 'cause Granddad thought the bus driver might hit him again. That's when the other man comes up in a car like this one here…your husban' I guess, Ma'am…he goes over to the cop and I hear'm say he's a lawyer…says his name…Joe. The bus driver starts up the bus'n heads off, but the lawyer keeps askin' the cop, 'what's goin' on?' The cop says he's takin' us ta' jail. The lawyer says, 'for what?' Cop says, 'public nuisance'n disorder.' So, the lawyer says, 'what'd that old man an' little girl do?' Cop says it's none of his business. So the lawyer he comes on over'n asks Granddad what happen. Granddad told'm…then the lawyer says he'd be *our* lawyer for free…if we wanted…an' Granddad says, 'okay.' So, the lawyer gets in his car'n follows us down the police station. All o' sudden, Granddad starts holdin' his hands on his chest an' starts breathin' real heavy. The cop turns around and sees Granddad's sick…he says a real bad word then, an' makes a call on his phone…says he's gonna need help. He parks b'hind the police station, and your husban' comes right on b'hind us, and parks, an' gets out'n tells the cop, 'you better get this man to a hospital.' A lot more cops come outta the station then…must o' been ten of'm. They crowd 'round the car, an' keep tellin' your husban' he's a troublemaker and should mind his business. He says he's our lawyer'n Granddad should go ta' hospital, but the cops lift Granddad out of the police car'n take him in back o' the station house. An' they take me in, too…so your husban' follows us. They take us in this room with a bunch o' tables with white sheets…like a doctor's office…an' they lay Granddad down on a table. He looks like he ain't breathin'. Your husban' says he's gonna take 'em all before a judge and charge 'em with false arrest, an' the bus driver with assault…'*murder* if that man dies,' he says. So the three biggest cops grab'm…say *they arrestin' him* for public disturbance now…an' they pull'm in another room and shut the door. Then, a man comes in…says he's a doctor, an' looks at Granddad…listens to his chest. He looks real mad, an' whispers somethin' to the cop that picked us up. Then, another cop comes in with a mess o' ribbons on his jacket. All the other cops and the doctor gather 'round'm and talk real quiet. The doctor listens to Granddad's chest again, an' then looks real sad at me an' leaves. Then, these other men come in…with regular clothes on…not cops. They see Granddad lyin' on the table'n start laughin'. One of 'em, he had a bum leg. So, now, the cop with the ribbons takes the man with the bum leg on over to a corner an' they start arguin'…but then they settle down…start whisperin'…but I can still hear 'em. The man with the bum leg says, 'don't you remember what happened when that nigger come here to sing? You want those kinda stories in the papers again?' He says, 'either *you* take care o' this, or *I* will.' That's when the cop with all the ribbons told all the other cops, 'get out.' Then, the man with the bum leg…an' those men he come in with…they go in the room where your husban' is. The three big cops who was in there come out, an' shut the door…an' take me down the hall t'another room, an' leave me in there. I don't know where the cops went off to, then. But after a while, I hear men's voices hollerin' through the walls…an' rumblin' in the floor…and furniture movin' around, an' breakin'…went on for a while…then, it got quiet again. I open the door'n look out the hallway, but couldn't see nothin'. I snuck a bit down the hall'n stood outside that room with the tables, an' I peek in b'hind the crack in the door, an' see Granddad ain't there no more. All o' sudden, I see some o' those men…they got blood on 'em, an' cuts on their faces…black eyes…noses bleedin'. I could see one man's arm looked broken bad. One o' the others had to hold it up for'm. Guess they didn't notice me standin' outside the door, peekin' in at 'em. A couple more of 'em come outta that room then, an'...well Ma'am...they had your husban' with 'em. He was hurt just awful...both his hands blown up like big balloons...all black'n blue. Then, the man with the bum leg come out and says, 'get that sonofabitch outta here. Take care of it,' he says. Wasn't a cop around, nowhere. I snuck on back to that other room an' cried. After while, these two white ladies come in, an' say they gonna help me. I ask 'em how my granddad is, and they say he got sick'n died before he could get ta' hospital...so, they just gonna take care o' buryin'm. I ask 'em, 'what about that *other* poor man...that lawyer?' That's when they look at me funny, an' one of 'em says, '*what* other man? There's no other man.' So, I shut up...an' they took me out to some car back o' the police station, an' drove me on up to Sister Paul."

"She's asleep," Mother said, closing the door and easing into the armchair in Father's den. She'd put Isabel in Mary's bedroom to rest when we got home, and then went to her own room to be alone. She'd been there for an hour, crying. Liz and I sat with Arthur and Laureen on a couch, near Father's desk. We watched her ravaged face, waiting for her to say something more. The room's only window was open, and we could hear the distant mumble of Johnny Wilson's engine as he cut the last part of our lawn near the river. David had wandered down to watch him, and Hazel was sitting on the porch with Mary, reading a story. It was two o'clock, and the air was humid and still.

"We're *not* letting them get away with this," Liz said, bitterly, as Mother sighed and pressed her handkerchief against her swollen eyes.

"Mary...tell me what to do," Arthur said, nervously.

"What *can* we do?" Mother sighed, her voice shaking.

"Make them pay for *what they did*!" Liz interjected, with a raw voice.

But Mother frowned and shook her head. "Our only real proof is this girl, and I'm...afraid...exposing her to the authorities is risky," she said. "We've made a *promise*." Liz sighed and slumped back on the couch, shaking her head and starting to weep in frustration. Mother looked at Arthur. "Do *you* think we can trust the police?" she asked.

"I don't know, Mary," he said. "I think...I agree...that, it's risky. This girl has pretty much confirmed what the agent told Tom, and so...we'd be taking a big chance trusting them...now. Part of me says we could find someone in the *state* police to help us, but I'm afraid to play things straight, Mary…by *their* rules, I mean…we'll just be handing *them* all the cards."

Mother kept pressing her handkerchief against her eyes. I turned to my sister and said, "we *can't* go to the authorities. It's not safe…*for Isabel.*" Liz frowned, but she knew I was right.

"They'll pretend to be concerned for the girl," Arthur added, "and they'll get the child welfare agencies involved. Then…they'll have her, Liz. We'll *never* get her back." He paused and looked at Mother. "*No one*…is taking that child," he said with grave determination.

Mother nodded. "Tom," she said, "what about your friend…won't he come forward and help us, now, with what *he* knows?"

"I don't think so," I said.

"So we just do nothing," Liz sighed.

"I didn't say *that,*" Mother snapped. "We just have to think a little harder…"

"Mary…I have some ideas, that *might* work," Arthur said. "Will you let me think about this…and get back to you?" She nodded, and then gazed around the room where Father had spent so much time in the past year and a half. This was his room—still so imprinted with his presence, that it might never have another purpose. "I'd like to have someone come and stay with you and the kids, too," Arthur added.

"What do you mean," Mother sighed. "A bodyguard?"

"Yes," Arthur said, firmly.

She stared at him for a moment. "I suppose," she muttered, with a deep sigh, holding the handkerchief to her eyes again, and then lowering her face as her body shook in deep sobs. Immediately, Arthur reached for the phone on Father's desk and called a man who worked for him in New York; he told the man to drive up to Garrison right away. Mother struggled from the armchair and gave the room another quick scan. "Excuse me," she said. "I need to lie down."

"Of course," Arthur said, standing up quickly.

Now, everyone was up. Liz stepped across the room and put her arm behind Mother's back as they went toward the door. Suddenly, Mother turned and gave me a hard look. "Tom…I want you to drive Johnny Wilson home, when he's finished the lawn."

"All right," I promised.

"I don't want him walking home…do you hear me?"

"Yes," I said. Then, she sighed, and left the den with Liz.

It was about four o'clock when I came back from dropping Johnny off. I put the car away and then waited with the Spencers on the porch until Arthur's man arrived, half an hour later. He introduced himself as Leonard and said very little else. He was a burly black man, and he wore a nondescript blue suit, beneath which he also wore a shoulder-harnessed pistol. Arthur told him he was to stay at the house with us until further notice, and he nodded without the slightest expression.

Not long after the Spencers left, the phone rang; Liz picked it up in the kitchen. I heard her say that Mother was in bed. She mentioned a bit of what we'd learned from Isabel, and then, there was a long silence. "*When?*" Liz said, at last. "All right, I'll tell her when she comes out. Yes…it might be good…change of scenery…yes. I'll tell her." When Liz hung up, I was standing behind her in the kitchen. "Mom's parents," she said. "They're driving out to Southampton, tonight. They want us to join them for a few days."

CHAPTER 22

❀

Driving east on Old Montauk Highway, we passed the Sacred Hearts of Jesus and Mary Catholic Church, and saw people filing in for eleven o'clock mass. Bells rang in the bright June air.

"This is Southampton Village," Mother said to Leonard.

"Yes, Ma'am."

"The street we're on becomes Jobs Lane," she added. "Then, you'll see Main Street. Just turn right."

"I will," he nodded.

"By the way…"

"Ma'am?"

"Call me Mary…please…"

"Oh," he muttered, embarrassed. "Yes, Ma'am. I will."

A few minutes later, at the corner of Jobs Lane and Main, he paused for some crossing traffic, and we watched people going in to services at the Presbyterian Church. Then, Leonard turned and drove another mile until South Main Street ended at Gin Lane. He made the hard left, following Mother's direction, and drove us along the beach road toward the "old town" section of Southampton, Long Island, where Mother had spent her summers as a child.

As we came to the Brents' property and slowed down, we could see a wide marsh lake just north across the road, and a row of beautiful homes, each with a wide back lawn that came down to the reeds at the edge of the lake.

At the front edge of the Brents' property there was a green wall of thick hedges, 20-feet-high and broken at the midpoint by a white, wooden gate, which had been left open for us. Leonard turned in and followed the white gravel driveway through the maze of tall hedges that guarded the path until, finally, the great house appeared before us in the warming Atlantic sun. It was covered in brown wooden shingles, and had a roof that swooped and curved like an ocean wave, from which four redbrick chimneys rose. Porticos at the east and west ends of the house had matching rows of white, Doric columns. And the many window frames were painted white.

Mother's parents had been watching for us, and as Leonard pulled the Buick up to the front of the house, they came out and hurried down the wide, beveled front steps. There were silent embraces all around. Mother introduced Leonard and Isabel to her parents. Rose Coughlin, the housekeeper who lived up on the third floor, appeared from one side of the house with her husband, Frank. After a few polite words with them, we followed our grandparents inside, while the Coughlins took care of putting the luggage into our second-floor bedrooms.

After a quiet lunch, Liz got the three children into bathing suits and took them down to the beach behind the house. Leonard followed them out. Then, as Mother talked with Grandmother in the parlor, I sat with Grandfather in the solarium. I answered his detailed questions about Father—and the rest of it—and when I'd finished telling him what Isabel had told us, he couldn't speak. He simply stared out through the solarium windows at the pale sky above the ocean.

At some point, Grandmother Alice peeked in and said, "Mary and I are going for a walk...on the beach."

"Tell Arthur's man," Grandfather demanded.

"His name is Leonard," said Grandmother.

"Yes," he muttered, turning from his wife and staring out the window again. "Just tell him."

For several more minutes, we sat in the sunny solarium. Then, he asked me to take a walk with him as well. We stepped out onto the veranda, and felt the cool ocean breeze mixing with the warmth of the brilliant sun. We walked down through Grandmother's English-style garden, and from there to the flat green lawn that ran out about 60 yards toward the beach. At the far edge of the lawn, there were dunes, from which sea grass grew thick, and curved in one direction from the wind.

We walked over the dunes and down onto the wide, white beach. Liz and the children were playing in the waves, riding them in and tumbling onto the wet sand, as white foam dissolved around them. I could see Leonard watching them from a spot 20 or 30 yards up the beach. He seemed concerned, alternately glancing at the children, and then east at Mother and Grandmother walking in the distance.

"It's all right, Leonard!" said Grandfather, as we neared the ocean. "We'll stay here, with the children. Why don't you go with the women!"

A relieved smile came over Leonard's face. He nodded, and walked rapidly after Mother and Grandmother Alice, now tiny dots disappearing on the white strand.

I stood with Grandfather at the edge of the water, as the children squealed and laughed. When Liz warned them to watch for the undertow, Isabel came out of the waves and stood in the knee-deep surf very close to Liz. A moment later, she grabbed my sister's hand.

To the east along the dunes there were four more houses, with generous space between them, all designed like the Brents' house. I noticed a man standing behind one of them, now, pointing at Leonard who was walking past. "Hey! Who are *you*?" he shouted. I could hear the mixture of surprise and alarm in his voice. Leonard must have heard him, too, but he ignored the man and kept walking east, trying to catch up to Mother and Grandmother. "Are you *deaf*?" the neighbor called out.

Suddenly, Grandfather took a few steps in that direction and raised his hand high above his head, calling out to his neighbor. "Wendell! Wendell! It's all right...all right," he shouted, as the neighbor turned and looked. "That man is with *us*," Grandfather assured him. "It's all right, now." At that, the neighbor glanced again at Leonard, who was already past the edge of his property, moving quickly. The neighbor raised his hand in a tentative wave to Phil, and then returned to his house, where his equally curious wife stood waiting in the back doorway for some explanation.

"Those are all pretty new," said Phil, pointing to the four neighboring houses. I looked at them and nodded. "*Our* house went up in Eighteen Eighty-eight," he said, "and there were going to be two more along there. Stanford White liked to put up small clusters of homes on beachfront like this. He put a group of houses on the bluffs out in Montauk, and another one at East Hampton...on the Great Pond. He did *our* house while he was working on opening the Shinnecock Golf Club, but he couldn't finish the others. Ran into some money problems, and had to hightail it back to the city to work on some big commercial jobs. So, our house was out here by itself for a while...bounced around among a few owners and...was almost torn down, at one point. Your grandmother and I bought it in Nineteen-eighteen." He paused, and watched the children in the waves. "We had this whole beach to ourselves for years, and you know, the dunes and the water were much farther from the house back then…until the hurricane, in 'Thirty-eight. *That* changed the whole beach-front. The waves came right up to our back door at the height of the storm. We were lucky not to lose the house. People back west toward Dune Road and the old Southampton Bathing Corporation were hit the hardest…*terrible* storm. Anyway, a few years later, some hot shot developer threw up those houses you see there, now. Didn't even use a real architect…just imitated our house…old Stanford White's design."

"They look pretty nice," I said, staring east along the dunes.

"Yeah, I guess they do," he sighed. "Eighteen Eighty-eight…same year I was born. That's a long time ago…and Annapolis seems a long way from here, now. But at least, there's the ocean…"

"It's beautiful, Grandpa."

He frowned, and then nodded. "Those children sure love it…don't they? Gives me a good feeling to see that…reminds *me* of what the Maryland beaches were like, when *I* was a kid." He paused, watching Liz and the children bob in the waves. "Your father always liked it, here," he said. "Always seemed to, from what I could tell. Used to come here, with your mom and you kids…way back…when it was only Liz and you. Your mom would bring y'all out here and it always made your dad smile." He paused again. "*Those* were happy days," he sighed. "And Joe loved it…well, he loved your mother anyway…*anything* that made *her* happy."

Tears flowed from my eyes. I looked down at the sand and swallowed hard, forcing back the impulse to sob. I didn't want to lose control—not yet. Suddenly, I felt my grandfather's hand on my shoulder, and I raised my head again, and we both stared out to sea.

I awoke just before eight on Monday morning, and the house was quiet. I threw on some blue jeans and a shirt, and headed down toward the kitchen, but stopped in the solarium, which was already catching the brilliant white sunlight. I walked toward the large ocean-facing window and stood there, shading my eyes, feeling the prismatic intensity of the light, suddenly realizing that Mother and Grandmother were already outside, working in the garden. They wore big straw hats with wide brims, and they were kneeling in the dirt, digging, pulling out wild beach grass, sweating.

"What're you *doing?*" said Liz, coming up behind me. A moment later, when she joined me at the window, I pointed toward the women. "That looks interesting," she said. Then, she went out through the veranda door and walked down to the garden. I saw Mother look up and wipe the sweat from her brow, as Liz approached. Mother's lips moved, and the expression on her face changed, like a cloud quickly passing in front of the sun. Then she stood up, handed Liz her gloves and trowel, and pointed to a spot on the ground. Liz knelt and started digging. Grandmother glanced over and smiled at them. Mother walked to the nearby wheelbarrow and reached in for another pair of garden gloves and a digging trowel, and went back to kneel with Liz.

And as they worked, a sudden memory—the first memory of my life—enveloped me like the warm sunrise. I saw my mother sitting right outside this very window, reading a long letter which, I always assumed, was from Father. In the memory, Mother wore a bright blue dress and sat on the veranda in a brown, wicker chair, like the ones in the solarium. Liz was a little girl leaning against the side of the chair. And as Mother finished reading each page, she handed it to Liz, who placed it down neatly on Mother's blue lap. I remembered that an old-fashioned automobile had been parked on the grass behind the house near the garden. White sunlight glinted brightly off its thick, black paint, and black figures on its orange license plate were indecipherable, all except for the date, which was clear at the bottom—1942. I was five years old, then, and Liz was six. Father would have been away with the Marines, maybe already on Guadalcanal.

As clear as this memory was, it was possible that I'd imagined or dreamed it, because Mother could never recall it in the precise description I would give her. She could only recall that she'd spent time out here during the war, and so would have read many letters from Father in those years. And my sister's memory of that day was no better. But now, standing at the solarium window, and watching them in the garden with Grandmother Alice, I decided it didn't matter—maybe our lasting memories are always solitary visions of people we love.

At about eleven o'clock, Grandmother Libby arrived in the blue Ford, without Grandfather Hank. For a while, we all walked in the garden together, and then Grandfather Phil sent Liz and me to town with Leonard, for some Crutchleys crullers. When we returned a short time later, with the familiar white bakery boxes imprinted with dark green lettering, we placed them on the kitchen counter and Rose Coughlin began arranging crullers on platters.

"They're all in the parlor," she said to Liz and me. "I'm makin' tea for the grownups, now…you can have that, hot or cold…and I think I've got some lemonade, too."

We asked for iced tea and joined the Brents and Grandmother Libby and Mother in the parlor. They'd been talking about Father but stopped when they saw us coming in. Liz and I sat down and waited in the silence. I could hear the children running from room to room above us on the second floor, and then Frank Coughlin telling them to "quiet down or go outside and run." After a while, Rose brought the tea and crullers in and people helped themselves.

At last, Grandfather Phil broke the silence. "I guess…he thought he could change things," he said. "I used to say to him…Joe…you can't change the world. You need to just live the best way you can…follow your conscience, and think about others more than yourself. You do *that*…you'll tend toward the right, more often than not."

Grandmother Libby nodded and smiled weakly. "Well," she said, "he was a person who wasn't ever satisfied, Phil. He *wanted* to do more than care for life's unfortunates, which is what he'd seen *me* do, when he was boy. He *did* want to change things…the injustices at the root of poverty…the ignorance beneath the injustices. He was a good man…a good son." She paused and sighed. "You knew he saved Donald and Grace from drowning, when they were all kids?"

"I think I heard something about that," Phil said. She smiled. "Would you *tell* us the story?" he said, sipping tea.

Libby glanced at Mother, who nodded gravely. Then, after a brief pause to think, Libby said, "well…if it's all right." She paused again and scanned our faces, and took a deep breath. "This was at our place in Garrison," she began. "Donald and Grace used to play down at the edge of the river…they had a little raft that Hank had tied to a tree with a long piece of rope…and they'd sit on that thing…for hours. One day…the rope snapped…and the raft went out into the river, on the currents, with Grace and Donald on it. I was working in the kitchen, and hadn't a clue about this, but apparently Joe'd seen the rope break from an upstairs window. He started calling out to me: 'Get help! Phone help…State Police. Donald and Grace 'er in trouble!' I remember the words exactly. He came down from the third floor, barged through the kitchen…almost knocked me down. 'Raft's on the river!' he shouted, running out the back door and down the hill. I watched from the kitchen window for a moment, and saw him dive in and swim out…then I saw the raft and realized what he'd meant. I was frantic, then. I reached for the phone to call the police and Joe swam out ahead of the raft…it was amazing how he got out ahead of them just in time…they were starting to gather speed in the current and…he'd have never caught them again." She paused to sip some tea. "And then, the raft was gone around a bend with Joe holding on. I tried to be calm, while I told the police what had happened. They said they'd go take care of it. And I spent the next several hours on tenterhooks. Well…the State Police and some West Point cadets finally found them, huddled against the riverbank…miles downstream. They had to use ropes to pull them up. The bank was so steep there, you see, the children couldn't get up, and the police could only go so far down in the trees and then the slope just dropped off…sheer rock to the water. When they got the kids up, Joe told the police that he'd managed to hold onto the raft and gradually work them back to shore against the current. Thank heavens he was such a good swimmer…excellent swimmer…always *was*. Of course…the whole time…Hank was…staying in Brooklyn. I called him later that night, after I'd put the children to bed. Joe was asleep, on the couch in the living room. Exhausted, he was. Hank rushed up to Garrison, next day, and there were stories in all the local papers…even a few of the big New York City papers. I guess the police called the press about it. Reporters called our home for days afterward, to get 'quotes' from us, they said. The story wouldn't die down and…Hank wouldn't go back to Brooklyn until it did. He loved the attention we were getting." She paused and replaced her cup on its saucer. She looked away quickly and sniffled back a tear. Then, she sighed and looked around at us with an embarrassed smile just like Father's. "The whole thing's sort of a family legend, now," she said. "Donald and Grace used to tell the story at family gatherings; I must have heard it a hundred times. Hank told it more than anyone else, especially if he'd been…well…you know. But the whole thing made Joe uncomfortable…*hated* for people to talk about it. One time…Hank got very angry with him…said he should be *proud* of what he'd done, saving his brother and sister like that. And Joe just turned to his father and said, 'what if I hadn't looked out the window at that very moment, Pop? What then…would it be a great story *then*?'" Libby looked at Mother who was wiping her eyes with her handkerchief. "I'm sorry, Mary…I shouldn't have gone on with that…"

"No…no," Mother said, as Grandmother Alice gripped Mother's hand. "I wanted to hear it. *That's* Joe." Libby frowned and nodded.

"How is *Hank* doing?" Alice suddenly asked.

"He's at home," Libby answered, sourly. "Rarely comes *out* of the house, now. Sits there, drinking in the parlor and staring out the windows at Prospect Park. When he gets good and drunk enough, he starts to mumble Joe's name, and I can't stand it. I have to go upstairs to my room or leave the house entirely. By the time I come back, he's either asleep, snoring in his chair…or *he's* gone out…to some Seventh Avenue saloon."

Later, we all went down to the beach. There was a cool weather front moving east along the shoreline, bringing a bank of steel blue clouds with it. We ignored the weather, walking east along the strand for miles before heading back. It was starting to mist as we reached the house. And then, after a light supper of sandwiches together, Grandmother Libby said her good byes and drove home to Brooklyn in the dark rain.

Leonard drove Mother and Liz to Sacred Hearts every day, so they could pray for Father. I couldn't bring myself to go with them. On Tuesday, Grandfather Phil had to take the train into New York to do some work at his office, but by Thursday noon he was back. He went with Mother and Liz to pray after lunch on Thursday. And when they returned, they said they'd also gone to visit the Sacred Hearts cemetery where Mother's sister, Lily, was buried. Lily had been born in the summer of 1927, when Mother was 10, but had died in her sleep at just a few months of age. On Friday morning, even Grandmother Alice, who was Episcopalian, decided she would go with them to Sacred Hearts Church.

Friday was the Coughlins' day off, and they'd driven back west to visit their daughter and her husband in Rego Park. So, when the group returned from church, Grandfather announced that he was taking us all out for dinner that evening. "I'll call the club and reserve a table," he beamed. The children didn't really know what to make of this, but they got the idea that it was a celebration. And as they smiled and clapped their hands, begging Liz to take them down to the beach before "the party," I noticed Mother and Grandmother glancing at each other with grim expressions.

It was a long, warm Friday afternoon, with very little breeze down at the beach. At about four-thirty, Grandfather turned to me and said, "I think we'll need two cars tonight."

"Right," I said.

"You and Leonard decide who wants to drive the Buick," he said. "I'll drive my rig, and we'll divvy up."

It was decided that Mother and Isabel would go in the Brents' Chrysler; Leonard allowed me to drive the Buick while he sat across from me, and Liz sat behind us with Mary and David. When we arrived at Grandfather's club for our early dinner, we got out of the cars and two parking attendants took charge of them. I thought I heard one parking-lot boy whisper something in a nasty tone to the other one, but I wasn't certain.

We filed into the old clubhouse behind Grandfather, and he led us to the edge of the dining room, where a tall maitre d' dressed in a black silk dinner jacket waited near an antique mahogany secretary, on which menus were stacked.

"Hello, Louis," said Grandfather.

"Mister Brent," the maitre d' replied, with a nod, as his eyes furtively glanced at our group. I noticed an odd buzz among the patrons inside the dining room, now, and suddenly, I understood the problem—Leonard and Isabel. I glanced over at Liz, and she stared knowingly at me.

"Our table ready, Louis?" Grandfather asked. But the man seemed frozen. "Reservation for *nine*," Grandfather reminded him.

Finally, the man spoke. "Mister *Brent*," he said, in a cautious and respectful whisper, leaning toward Grandfather submissively and then straightening up again.

"Speak up, man," said Grandfather. "What's the problem?"

But the man simply frowned, reached down and grabbed some menus, and then turned and walked into the crowded dining room. We followed him to a corner, near a large window that looked out onto the golf course flowing down from the rise on which the clubhouse sat. I could see the Great Peconic Bay off to the west and beyond it the sun, low in the sky, starting to set. It was just six o'clock. Our long table had been set with nine places, and the maitre d' stood by with the menus cradled in one arm. As we took seats, he walked around behind each of us and placed a menu down on our dinner plates. Then, after a respectful bow toward Grandfather, he returned to his station. By now, everyone in the dining room had stopped talking and eating. Every head had turned in our direction.

Grandfather continued acting as though nothing in the world was amiss. "The Del Monico steak is *particularly* good here," he said, looking at his menu. "The bay scallops, too…they're Peconics," he smiled, nodding out the window. "And whatever the fish is today, will have been brought in this morning from Montauk."

Slowly, other people went back to their meals and I gave Liz a relieved glance, thinking that we'd dodged trouble. But within minutes, people at three different tables suddenly got up from their dinners and left. And I began to notice that, though the room seemed filled with waitresses—bright and friendly college-age girls—none of them was coming anywhere near our table. Grandfather raised his hand several times to the nearest one, but he couldn't get her to look in our direction. Finally, he stood up and politely intercepted the girl. I heard him say that his guests needed table water, and that when she brought it we'd be ready to give her our dinner order. She frowned at him and nodded her head. Briefly, she looked at our table, and then broke into tears and ran out of the dining room.

Grandfather returned to his seat at the head of our table and sighed. He turned and stared briefly out the window at the lovely golden sunrays settling over the golf links. Then, he turned back and looked at us with deep embarrassment.

Grandmother Alice leaned in from the opposite end of the table and whispered, "it's *all right*, Phil."

Leonard started to get up. As he did, he looked over at Grandfather and said, "Mister Brent...sir...maybe I should just go outside and wait."

"You will *not*," said Phil, angrily. And then, "*please* sit down, Leonard...I beg you."

Leonard frowned and sat back down, as Isabel lowered her gaze and stared at her empty bone china plate with its blue and gold piping. We waited for another fifteen minutes without service until Grandfather decided to put an end to our predicament. He apologized to everyone, and asked us to get up and leave. As we rose from our seats, Grandmother Alice took Isabel by the hand and walked quickly toward Leonard, and she whispered something to him, as they walked together out of the silent dining room.

Mother stepped toward her father and embraced him. "What's this...what's this?" he said, with great surprise.

"Dad," she said. "I love you." Then she kissed him, and walked out with David and Mary.

"You better go on," he suddenly said to Liz and me, as he stood near the table and stared around at his silent fellow members.

Liz and I left the dining room, ignoring the apologies of the maitre d' as we passed him. Moments later, we were standing outside with the rest of our group; the parking lot boys were retrieving our cars.

"Where's your grandfather?" said Grandmother Alice abruptly turning to Liz and me.

"Still inside," I replied.

"Go get him," she said.

I started back up the steps and felt Liz right behind me. Inside the lobby, we could see all the way into the dining room, where several waitresses were changing the china and silver settings on our table—changing everything, even the brilliant white linen tablecloth. Suddenly, we heard Grandfather's voice coming from a small room across the lobby. Liz and I walked toward it, and as we drew near we could see that it was the club manager's office. We stood outside the half-opened door and waited.

"Be *reasonable*, Phil," we heard a man say. "You know how the membership feel."

"I've never seen any reference to something like this…in writing," Grandfather replied, angrily.

"*Phil*," the man said, in a patronizing tone. "In *writing*? This is the sort of thing one is expected to know…and I thought you did. Among people of a certain taste, and background, a thing like this is…*understood*."

"Is *that so*?" said Grandfather. "Well…this has nothing to do with taste…not even good manners. This is pure stupidity."

"Have it your way, Phil," said the man. "But I have a whole membership to consider."

"Yes, well…there'll be no further scenes," said Grandfather. "I'm submitting my resignation from the club."

"Now, Phil…"

"You'll hear from my attorney on Monday, about settling my account and my bond."

"Please, Phil…don't do this."

"I'm sorry…whatever I may have overlooked in the past, I *can't* maintain a membership here, now…"

"This isn't *like* you, Phil."

"Maybe you're right," said Grandfather, with a rueful tone.

"Isn't there anything I can do, Phil?"

"Yes…you can feel free to give me a call, when the membership decides to change these…restrictions."

When Grandfather came through the door and saw us waiting for him, an embarrassed look came over his face. But we stood close to him, Liz on his one side and me on his other, and we walked together out of the club.

Leonard took the wheel of the Buick for the ride home, and he followed the Chrysler closely. At the corner of Main Street and Jobs Lane in the village, we saw Grandfather Phil abruptly turn and park against the curb. Leonard parked next to him, and as Grandfather got out of his car Leonard rolled down his window. Grandfather pointed to the row of stores along the street and said, "I'll get us some dinner, here at Stern's." Then, he walked quickly to Stern's cigar and newspaper store and went inside.

"What's Grandpa doing?" said David.

"Getting us some dinner," Liz said.

"In *there*?" he replied, skeptically. "Looks like a *candy* store."

"It *is*, buddy," I said, turning toward him. "But there's a little restaurant in the back, and they make great things…"

"*What* things?" he scowled.

"Delicatessen things," said Liz. "Stuff like that."

"Oh," he muttered.

About fifteen minutes later, Grandfather emerged from Stern's front door followed by Leon Stern, a balding man, slightly younger than Grandfather, dressed in a white shirt and a long white apron, which was wrapped tightly around his middle and tied behind him. They each carried a large cardboard box, overflowing with paper-wrapped sandwiches and boxed salads. I jumped out of the Buick and hurried toward them, taking hold of Grandfather's box.

"Thanks, Tom," he smiled.

"Hello, Mr. Stern," I said.

"Tom," he replied, smiling and nodding, in lieu of putting out his hand. As he lugged his box toward the Chrysler, Grandmother Alice got out to help him. "Thanks, Missus," he said, when she opened the trunk and guided Mr. Stern's box down inside. After some small talk with Grandmother, he came back toward the Buick. I'd already put my box into the trunk.

"How've you been, Tom?" said Mr. Stern.

"Fair," I replied, shaking hands with him.

"I appreciate all this, Lee," said Grandfather. "I know you want to close up."

"How long we know each other, Phil?" said Mr. Stern, waving his hand.

"Too long," laughed Grandfather.

"And how long you lived in this town?"

"Thirty-five years," Grandfather replied.

"So only *now* you realize this…about this club?" Mr. Stern's voice had a gentle, scolding edge.

"Yes…well," Grandfather replied, embarrassed. "Sometimes we forget, Lee. We may think because *we've* been accepted somewhere…that the world's basically okay." Mr. Stern snorted and shook his head. "You go to a place for years…never hear a bad word uttered about any sort of people," said Grandfather. "But then, you see how they react just because a guest's skin is a different color. They'll never say that, of course…just don't challenge it…don't bring a guest unless they're as white you and me."

"And even *then*," snorted Mr. Stern.

Grandfather froze, understanding Mr. Stern's point. "I never thought you cared about a club like that, Lee," he said.

"Me?" said Mr. Stern. "I'm not a golfer." He paused, and gave Grandfather an odd look. "But, if I *were*...then..."

"Lee...I'm sorry," said Grandfather.

Mr. Stern put his hand on Grandfather's shoulder. "We're friends, Phil...always *have* been. I'm just saying...a thing like this can't be right, if it's wrong." And then, Grandfather sighed and lowered his head, embarrassed.

It was just dark when we reached the house, and we quickly tore into Mr. Stern's packaged delicacies. After a small sandwich, Grandfather went to his study and made a phone call; I could hear enough of what he said to know that he'd called Arthur.

"Yes," I heard him say, "Tom told me the whole story. Well...she's fair...it's been good to have her and the children out here this week." Then, I heard Grandfather relating the incident we'd just had at the club. After a long silence, I heard him say, "well of course, Arthur...I just never thought...well...no, that's not true. I *did* know the rules. They didn't need to be posted. And what *I've* done is allow myself to look the other way. Maybe everything that's happened has...made me angry enough to be more honest about it. I've been thinking about Joe a lot, this week, Arthur. How he used to like to play golf here with me...except, now that I think of it...there *was* always some reason he had to hurry off afterward...so he wouldn't have to go inside, and have dinner with me in that dining room. I suppose I knew why...all along...but I never raised it with him. Honestly, I don't know what I would have done. If he'd made a big stink, then, it *would* have been out in the open, wouldn't it? Then, I'd *have* to address it. And he was too polite to put that pressure on me. I knew Joe's views...I guess I just thought...well, he's from this younger generation, going overboard again with things. But this sort of thing is more than just...*unfriendliness*, Arthur. It's dead wrong...morally. I'm so ashamed of myself." Then, after another long silence, he said, "yes...well...I've been giving that some thought, too. Perhaps we could pool our ideas, and come up with something useful. Do you think you could come out here, tomorrow? We could discus it over lunch. Yes...I want to help...whatever I can do...for Joe's sake. Yes...what...dangerous? Of course it is. But, should we do *nothing* about Joe? Tomorrow, then."

CHAPTER 23

❀

The Spencers got to Southampton just before lunchtime on Saturday. Rose Coughlin brought them into the parlor, where we'd been waiting, as Mother and Grandmother Alice discussed a memorial service for Father. But after brief greetings and kisses, the Spencers sat down, and Grandfather Phil got to the more pressing issue.

"I think we're all agreed that we can't jeopardize the girl," he said. "And *that* prevents us going to the authorities with proof about Joe, even if we believed they'd listen. So…what *else* can we do about these people?"

"Block their bid for St. Nicholas Avenue," said Arthur, firmly.

"Exactly," said Phil.

Mother's face looked tense. "But…do you think you can match the size of *their* proposal?" she asked.

"Arthur isn't going to match it," her father said. "He's going to *block* it."

"But *how*, Dad?"

"By turning *some* technical aspect of their bid against them," he replied.

"Such as?" she asked.

"Their *offer*, for a hundred and twenty-five million dollars," Arthur said. "It's more than twice what *our* group proposed…but it's a *phony*…"

"That's *right*," said Phil.

"Artificially inflated to warn off other bidders," Arthur continued. "Stannard and O'Leary and their partners will never have to come up with that kind of money."

"How is this possible?" said Mother.

"Mary, I wasn't sure," Arthur said, "until I saw the pictures of Bob Moses and Charles Stannard shaking hands in all the newspapers last week…but…"

"It's about *federal money*, Mary," said Grandfather Phil.

Arthur nodded. "I've been doing some research this week," he said. "I believe they're using federal housing funds to underwrite an inflated bid. Joe and I applied for Title I housing assistance too...but we'd been getting the run-around from the City...our bid was *never* going to be approved...we were dangled out there, just to make it look like a bidding process."

"But they don't *plan* public housing," said Liz, interrupting. There was silence among the adults, then. "Isn't that right?" she added. "The papers say they're building TV studios, and offices...and *luxury* apartments!"

Arthur stared at Liz for a moment, and then he answered her. "St. Nicholas Avenue is a Title I site, and Moses is just turning it over to Stannard. Now...Stannard plans slum clearance...*urban renewal*. He'll remove blighted housing...just like *we* would have done...*that's* a legitimate qualification for Title I money..."

Liz was still confused. "But he has to build *new* affordable housing...doesn't he?"

"Sure," Arthur said. "But to qualify, I believe he's only had to submit a proposal saying he will...*somewhere* in that neighborhood." He paused and Phil nodded in agreement. "I've seen public housing put up *ten blocks away* from a qualifying site," Arthur added. "And Stannard could do that here, too, by incorporating an adjacent block as part of the St. Nicholas Avenue rehab zone. Title I sites come with a lot of transferred power...condemnation...eminent domain. And I'm afraid that...after Moses turns them over, he doesn't always pay attention. Look what's happened at the Manhattantown project over there between West Ninety-seventh and a Hundredth Streets. The developers who got *that* site haven't built new housing or *anything else*. They've displaced *many* tenants, and they're still collecting rents from others...and the place is a mess, a worse slum than when they started. A fifty-four-million-dollar project that the developers just milked. It's been so bad that it's being investigated by reform-liberal activists, like Hortense Gabel...and *even* the U.S. Senate...meanwhile, millions of dollars in Title I money earmarked for that site has apparently vanished."

"Are you saying...they'll just be moving all the poor people *off* St. Nicholas Avenue?" Liz muttered, in amazement.

"Wouldn't be unheard of," said Arthur. "But child...they probably won't do just *that*. More likely...they'll wait till the last minute, and announce that affordable housing doesn't work...anywhere *near* St. Nicholas Avenue. They'll cite design changes...traffic flow impact...whatever they have to. By then, the federal money will be allocated…and they'll just work out some other deal with the federal housing authorities…the City, the State. They'll agree to make good, and build low-income housing *somewhere*…maybe in the city, farther east or uptown…or in the Bronx…or Brooklyn…I know Jackie Robinson's been pushing *hard* to get housing projects built out there."

"Or Newburgh?" I interjected.

"That's right," said Phil. "Stannard mentioned Newburgh at his press conference, last week."

"But it all gets done at a much *lower cost*," said Arthur, "because Newburgh, or the parts of Brooklyn and the Bronx that they're probably looking at are *less desirable* properties than St. Nicholas Avenue. So…the Stannard Foundation gets a bargain in the deal!"

"How do they get *away* with this?" asked Liz.

"No one will hear much about it, until it's too late to stop it," Arthur replied. "Meanwhile, low income people will be pushed out of St. Nicholas Avenue…and kept out…which is probably what the City wanted, all along."

"The commercial tenants coming *into* that neighborhood certainly do," said Phil.

"What you're basically saying is…these developers are using public housing money as a…commercial loan," Mother said in disgust.

Arthur nodded.

"So then…what if we got this promoted in the press?" said Phil.

"That's the problem," Arthur said. "So far…every paper in the city except the *Post* has basically *ignored* Manhattantown…even *with* all the investigations. And besides, we'd need *definite proof.*"

"But if we could *get* some and give it to the *Post* and say…okay, now that's *two* Title I projects that look fishy. *That* sort of publicity *would* give O'Leary and Stannard fits," said Phil. "Maybe some other papers *would* pick up that story, if the *Post* ran it. The federal government wouldn't like it, nor the City. The Mayor would be embarrassed and…neighborhood people would be up in arms. Moses might take the site back from Stannard, then."

Arthur looked at Phil, and smiled. "Isn't this the kind of fight you told Joe and me to keep out of…last week?" he said.

"A lot has changed in a week, Arthur."

"But, Dad. Is it *worth* doing?" Mother said. "It seems…complicated."

"I know a few experts on Title I and public housing, Mary," said Arthur. "These guys know how the City and State commissions work. Let me make a few phone calls…see what they say. If they think it's possible…I'll head back to Manhattan this afternoon and start."

"And *I'll* work with some of my own contacts, when I get back to New York on Monday," said Phil. Mother still seemed unconvinced. "Mary, if the newspapers *did* report that O'Leary and Stannard are misusing public funds," her father said, "their political support would back away. And once *that* happened…some district attorney might get enough backbone to go for a *murder* investigation. The newspapers sure would. We *have* the proof…an eyewitness."

"I don't know," Mother said.

"*Mom*," I interjected. "Dad once told me that they have trials, where the key witness is *never* identified…because they've been threatened. It's usually a *mob*-thing, he said. They testify behind a screen or something."

"The boy's right, Mary," said Arthur.

Mother stared around the hushed room. She could see her father nodding at her, encouraging her. Finally, she looked at Arthur and spoke firmly. "Make your calls." Then, she stood up and looked at Grandmother Alice. "I'd like to talk more about the memorial service, Mom." She asked Hazel to join them, and the three women left the parlor together.

Grandfather Phil took us to his study, where Arthur used the phone to call a number in Hastings-on-Hudson—the residence of Allen and Esther Rosenthal. When he finished his brief conversation, he hung up and turned to Phil. "They're *in*," he said, with a grim smile.

"Good," said Grandfather. "Let's have some lunch."

Eventually, the women rejoined us for sandwiches, and it was decided that Mother would go back to Garrison that afternoon in the Buick with Leonard and the children. She planned to call St. Mary's Church about the memorial service, and asked Liz and I to represent her at the meeting with the Rosenthals that afternoon in Arthur's office.

"I want *you* to help Arthur, in any way you can," she said. "Do *exactly* as he says. That's what your father would want. But no more secrets."

We agreed, and quickly packed our bags and loaded them in the trunk of Arthur's Oldsmobile. As Laureen and Hazel got in the car, we said goodbye to our grandparents, thanking them for the week. We hugged the Coughlins. Finally, I looked around and said, "where are the kids?"

"Leonard's letting them have one last dip in the ocean," said Grandmother Alice.

"Oh," I said. "And Mom?"

"She may be with them," Grandmother frowned. "I'm not sure."

"I need to ask her something," I said.

"Better hurry up, boy," Arthur scolded, from the open door of his car.

"I will…just two minutes!" I ran back into the house, looking in the parlor, and the kitchen, and even Grandfather's study. But there was no sign of Mother. Finally, I walked to the solarium and saw her standing on the veranda, beyond the big window. She was looking out past the garden to the lawn and the dunes. Next to her was a wicker chair that someone had dragged out from the solarium. She glanced down at the chair, suddenly, and then looked around at the wide veranda as if remembering something. A moment later, she gazed out toward the ocean again, and abruptly sat at the edge of the chair. She seemed stunned, as she lowered her head and leaned one hand against her forehead. I decided to ask her some other time about speaking at Father's service. I hurried back to the Oldsmobile.

It was just about three o'clock when Liz and I pulled away from our grandparents' summer home with the Spencers. And then, during the long drive to New York, Arthur told us about the Rosenthals.

Allen had been a prodigy, a kid from Queens who'd finished high school at 15 in 1933, and won a scholarship to Harvard. But his classmates, pampered and narrow-minded sons of the Cambridge aristocracy, were unfriendly. This sparked a rebellious streak in Allen, and he left Boston with his bachelor's degree after three years. He then enrolled at Columbia, earning a doctorate and a professorship in economics before his 22nd birthday.

His wife, Esther, who'd gone to Vassar, was a poet, and was four years older than he. She was the daughter of Jacob and Helen Strauss, of the fountain pen Strausses, who lived in an elegant, Emery Roth building just off Riverside Drive in the West 90s. The Strausses also owned a Westchester estate near Bedford where, every summer, they entertained artists with progressive reputations—people like Paul Robeson, Orson Welles, Duke Ellington, Aaron Copland, and Lillian Hellman. These friendships, and Allen's own radical views, had led to his resignation from Columbia in 1951, "about five minutes before being asked to leave by the campus loyalty committee," Arthur said. So Allen and Esther now lived in a stone cottage in Hastings, supported by her considerable inheritance, and dedicated to progressive politics and social activism.

Two men watched from across 125th Street as we entered Arthur's theater at five-thirty. Hazel went home to make dinner, while the rest of us settled in to wait for the Rosenthals in Arthur's private office. Finally, at six o'clock, a short man walked in with a tall, graceful woman.

"Allen Rosenthal, everybody," said Arthur, shaking hands with the man. "And Esther." Arthur seated her in a chair near his desk. Then, he joined two of his business aides leaning against the desk-front. "Set the stage for us, Allen," he said.

"Sure," said Allen, striding to the middle of the room in tan cuffed slacks, a red cotton shirt with short sleeves, and brown penny loafers. He had a street-wise smile and wore glasses with heavy black frames and thick lenses, behind which his intense brown eyes focused suddenly. "Liz and Tom, right?" he said. We nodded from our seats on the couch with Laureen. "Esther and I are awfully sorry," he said. "I didn't know your father as well, or as long, as Arthur did...but I know one thing...he was a *mensch*...the world needs *more* of his kind." Esther nodded, staring at him with a magnetic concentration. She wore a flowing, blue skirt and a burgundy gaucho jacket, and her black hair was parted in the middle, held tightly behind her head by a gold, Aztec broach. Her bright red lips parted slightly, in a smile. "Now, *this* theater we're in represents a rare victory over Robert Moses," said Allen, turning toward Arthur. "You're looking to beat him a *second* time?"

Arthur frowned. "We're concerned with Stannard and O'Leary...the two people I spoke to you about...*they're* developing this project...*not him*."

Allen sighed. "But it's important to understand how difficult this is gonna be, as long as Moses *approves* their project. Most of the public and mainstream press think of Robert Moses, even now, as the brilliant social reformer he was, once...the mastermind of wonderful public works...parks, beaches, swimming pools, highways and bridges...*and* affordable housing. That's why this is so difficult...*for me*, too. It's a tragedy, really...because of what might have been, had he kept faith with what Belle Moskowitz and Al Smith taught him about public works years ago. *They* were his conscience...they reminded him to think of *people*. Even *FDR* did that...and *they* hated each other...but they *worked* together...on the basis of public works for *people* and *social change*. But he's so powerful, now, that he answers to no one...and so...there *is* no conscience. *That's* the heartbreaker. The thing is...he still thinks of himself as a man who does great, good things for the general public. He thinks he's still that reformer from the 'Twenties and 'Thirties...but he's a reformer gone mad with power, now. His public works are more and more spectacular...but less and less about people. He thinks people don't know what's good for them...only *he* does. And that's all he wants to know. So now...what he builds is mostly about his own vision...about himself, really. It's a waste of public money and disdainful of the public, *especially* the poor..."

"Focus on the financials," said Arthur.

"Sure," Allen nodded. "The first thing about *that* is...his projects are too expensive. He charges the public to build them...charges the public to use them...forever. He levies tolls on bridges and parkways...at the beaches and parks. None of that money goes back into paying off the construction debt...it goes straight back to his Triborough Bridge and Tunnel Authority. And he doesn't even use the money to build *new* projects. It buys influence...to make sure the projects *he* wants...and only those...are built."

Liz leaned forward and raised her hand, as if in a classroom. "How *are* the projects paid for, then?"

"Construction bonds, that the Bridge and Tunnel Authority issues or...sometimes he gets the City or the State to do it...the bonds are then sold to big investors...and the general public. Wall Street investment banks...like Stannard's...underwrite the bond issues; big law firms do the contracts; brokerage houses handle the dispersal and trading of the bonds...all for hefty fees...and only the firms Moses picks get a piece of that action. It doesn't stop there. He pays high rates of interest to investment banks that underwrite the bonds. He lets certain banks buy the bonds at an inside price, and lets them sell off at inflated prices in the secondary market. The public pays for all this through increased taxes...and tolls and fees. Moses takes no public money for himself, you understand. This is *influence peddling*. You see...elected officials and agency appointees are often owners...or silent partners...or board members at the banks and mortgage companies that get all this favorable treatment...the insurance firms, the real estate development companies..."

"Like the O'Leary companies," I said.

Allen nodded. "*Their* firms are chosen because they've got the right political influence at some level...zoning authority...access to public lands...the ability to raise taxes...and approve public bond issues. And they're willing to sell their influence...and cooperate with what Moses wants to build. He rewards them for playing ball..."

"And uses his press contacts to smear those who *won't*," Arthur said.

"That's right," Allen said, in disgust. "I'm afraid the political smear is a common thing, now, in business *and* politics, and you know, Democrats do it just like Republicans do. You make an accusation...doesn't matter if it's true...the papers report it, people believe it or over-react to it, and suddenly...it's a fact that can never be changed. The smear is what works if favors don't, but by and large, things normally operate on favors. And that's true for Moses. He gives favors to certain institutions with influence in the City, like the Catholic Church, which has a lot of real estate interests…buys and sells a lot of land…does a lot of construction. And of course…though he doesn't particularly like them…he does favors for the investment banks, too…the old-line WASP banks." Allen paused, and sighed wearily. "So…*this* is the system we're up against…what ordinary people are *always* up against."

"What about Title I," said Arthur, "public housing money?"

"Well, Arthur, as you know, *federal* money for the large public works that Moses likes to do dried up before the war. The Feds are spending heavily on veterans, now; helping them with college and low-interest mortgages for homes, out in the nice clean suburbs. But in New York and many other big cities, there's still a housing shortage. So about five years ago, the Feds came up with Title I…a new section of the old Federal Housing Act…basically diverting millions of dollars into state and local hands, to clear slums and build affordable housing…*not* the kind of projects Moses loves. But ironically, Title I is the single *largest* source of federal assistance coming into local government, now. And *he's* in charge of it."

"We applied for Title I at St. Nicholas Avenue," Arthur said.

"*That's* the kind of project it's *meant* for," said Allen, who suddenly frowned and stared down at the floor.

"What *is* it, Allen?"

"Arthur," he replied, looking up again. "Just before I came over, I was able to reach Horty Gabel…"

"Oh? How *is* my old friend?"

"She has some bad news for you, Arthur. You know that she's been pushing hard to get the City to re-open the Planning Commission study of Title I sites…the study that looked at Manhattantown, and was so edited and whitewashed when it came out a few months ago? Well…the City is *refusing* to re-open that study. And now, she can't get the *Times* or any other paper…except the *Post*…to even write about the fact."

"So, what are you saying?" Arthur asked. "You told me on the phone that we could *do* this…"

"I know…"

"Don't you think we can prove Title I money is being used to move low-income people off St. Nicholas Avenue?"

"Oh, I *think* we can *prove* it," Allen sighed. "I just worry about…how many people are gonna say, 'yeah…*so what*?'"

In the wood-paneled dining room of the Spencers' three-story brownstone, on West 155th Street, Hazel passed bowls of vegetables and potatoes to her guests as Arthur sent a platter of roast beef around from his seat at the head of their table. Allen and I sat across from Liz, Laureen and Esther.

Allen suddenly asked what seemed a casual question. "So…Arthur…seen anything of the Robesons, lately?"

"A bit," Arthur said. "They sold the Enfield house, last year. Paul spends a lot of time at his brother Ben's parsonage, now…"

"The Zion Church," said Allen. "On a Hundred and Thirty-sixth…right?"

Arthur nodded. "Hazel and I have been to see him…we went to the rally they gave for him, last month. He still can't get out of the country to do concerts in Europe…the government refuses to give him back his passport. Of course, he can't get a booking here in the States any more. So…he's broke."

Allen frowned and shook his head. "This all started with that Peekskill concert for the Civil Rights Congress…in 'Forty-nine…remember?"

"I do," Arthur said, nodding gravely. "The CRC was on the Attorney General's list of 'subversive' groups."

"Bunch o' local yahoos rioted the concert," Allen said, glancing first at Liz, then me. "Including *some* Catholic organizations…I'm sorry to say." Liz and I nodded.

"Don't forget the American Legion," said Esther.

"Or the Klan," said Hazel.

"Really?" I said, surprised. "*They're* in New York?"

"Well," Arthur smiled, wearily, "they've had a pretty strong chapter in *Peekskill* for years."

"Some say *they* were the instigators," Allen added. "The mob sure acted like it…burning crosses…carrying racist signs…yelling foul things about Negroes and Jews. They set up roadblocks and trapped people as they left the concert…attacked the buses and cars, demolished and torched the stage, started fights. Paul's manager barely got him outta there in one piece…they drove him over to my parents-in-laws' place in Bedford. That was about a month after Jack Robinson's HUAC testimony." Allen turned to his wife, who nodded. "Robinson basically disavowed Paul," said Allen. "That was all those racists up the river had to hear."

"It's not the way Paul felt about it," Esther said, contradicting her husband. There was a long silence, then. I glanced at Liz, but she stared through me, while Laureen hung her head and gazed into her dinner plate.

Arthur broke the chilly silence. "Esther's right. Paul *had* made that statement in Paris, about American Negroes never fighting for the U.S. against Russia. Jack Robinson couldn't defend that, when he appeared at HUAC...he *had* to distance himself...let's be fair. Jack had *served* in the Army."

"Sure," Allen said, with a frown. "But *you* know as well as *I* do...Paul's problem was...he wouldn't shut up about discrimination...and lynching. People didn't want to hear about it...especially after the war. He made an unwise remark...and everybody jumped on it. Every notable Negro person ever called before HUAC had to disavow Robeson and that statement, or be called a Communist, too..."

"Jackie defended Paul in the papers...*after* the concert," interjected Hazel. The other adults nodded silently. "Didn't he say something about Paul having the right to sing anywhere...believe whatever he wanted?"

Esther nodded and said, "I believe Jack's *exact* words were, 'if Congress wants to investigate something, they should investigate those *rioters.*' He *also* said...in America...'anything progressive is called Communism...to discredit it.' But...it is true...Jack *could* have made stronger statements at HUAC, in Paul's defense."

"I'd say Jackie and Paul are more alike, than not," offered Hazel. "I think *they'd* say the same."

The table was silent, for a moment. Then, Esther leaned forward with an intense expression. "It always disappointed Paul," she said, "that he never got credit for putting *his own* athletic reputation on the line, in the early 'Forties...when *he* lobbied major league owners about breaking the color barrier in baseball...hardly anyone even knows about that...now. They've even rescinded his All-America status..."

The conversation stalled again, as Laureen and Liz stifled odd giggles. Suddenly, Allen cleared his throat and sat back in his chair. Esther gazed off into space. Hazel seemed embarrassed. She got up and began clearing the table, and Arthur rose to help her.

Allen abruptly changed the subject. "You two kids should come with us this summer." He paused to glance at his wife as she lit a cigarette, inhaled, and casually blew the smoke up toward the ceiling. "Esther and I are going to Alabama and Georgia...to work with ministers and church groups, for public school integration. Laureen's coming..."

"I've already asked Liz," said Laureen. Liz nodded.

"Oh, good...that's good," Allen smiled. "How about *you*, Tom?"

"And do what?" I asked.

"Like I said…discuss school integration strategies…maybe even voting rights. Negroes *and* poor whites are prevented from voting in southern states…by the poll taxes and outright intimidation…*lynching*…still happening." I nodded. "In *my* opinion," he said, "young people like you should be present when these things are discussed. It's *your* future, after all. I think your father would agree."

"Maybe," I said. "I *know* he'd agree with what I told my sister…sounds *dangerous*."

I couldn't sleep. I sat up, turned on a small bedside lamp, and checked my watch. It was three o'clock in the morning. I snapped off the lamp, reached down to the end of the bed for a borrowed bathrobe and stood up, as I wrapped it around myself. Sitting again at the edge of the bed in the dark, I thought about Mother.

Liz and I had called home to check with her after dinner, and she'd assured us that she and the children were "quite safe" with Leonard there to protect them. "He goes outside and walks the property, every now and then," she said. "He's an awfully nice man…he's watching television with the children now."

We reminded her to be careful speaking on the phone in detail about anything important like that. No one mentioned Isabel, but we hinted that Arthur and Allen had decided to proceed with the plan, even though Allen had made clear how difficult it would be. But our call seemed to comfort Mother. It was Liz and I who felt a million miles from home.

We'd rejoined Laureen at the table and listened, as Arthur and Allen drank coffee and discussed ways of getting a copy of the Stannard-O'Leary group's St. Nicholas Avenue bid. At one point, Allen suggested having someone break into O'Leary's private office to search his files if Arthur's men failed through legal means. "Easier than getting into Stannard's bank, I think."

"Are you *serious*?" Arthur asked.

"I'm serious about *helping* you, Arthur. What…you think they wouldn't do the same to us…or worse?"

Arthur sighed, and nodded. "Let's just see what my boys can do at City Hall."

When the Rosenthals left at about eight forty-five, Liz and I followed the Spencers into their vast front parlor, where three different sofas and four armchairs were arrayed beneath a dizzying, high ceiling. There was a Dumont television set in one corner, and a big Philco radio in a more prominent place against one wall. Another wall was lined with bookshelves, and had a fireplace dead center, with a facing of white marble tiles. There was no consensus about whether to watch Caesar or the Dorseys on television, so Arthur decided we'd listen to the radio for a while. He tuned it in to a small Harlem station, and when he heard a female voice, he smiled and sat down in a big armchair close to the Philco. "Hazel Scott," he said. And as we listened to her play the piano, Arthur told Liz and me the story of how, a few years earlier, she'd been one of the biggest names in show business. She was the wife of an outspoken Harlem congressman, and was a vocal civil rights activist herself. She'd refused to disavow her friends or her beliefs in a 1951 HUAC appearance, and ever since, she'd been blacklisted in main stream movies, TV and radio.

By eleven, everyone had gone off to bed—Arthur and Hazel up on the second floor—Laureen in a big suite of rooms on the main level in back—Liz and me in adjoining guest bedrooms near the front.

Now, I rose from the edge of the bed, walked to the door and slipped out into the dark, quiet hallway. I crept along on creaky floorboards past the dining room table and into the parlor, and then to a full-length window that faced 155th Street. Standing between long, green velvet curtains, I gazed out on the silent street, lit at each end by a dim lamppost. I sat on the window's deep box ledge, and stared at nondescript shapes of cars parked along the curbs. After several minutes, I began to feel calmed by the silent blackness. Then, a burst of light flashed inside one of the parked cars. It quickly went out but was followed by a long, red-orange glow that faded and came back every few moments. Someone was sitting in the car, smoking a cigarette.

I heard the floorboards creak in the parlor. Peering back between the curtains, I saw a figure moving deftly across the room toward my window.

"I couldn't sleep either," whispered Laureen. "Shove over." She moved between the curtains and got up onto the other side of the window ledge. For a few moments we sat in silence, facing each other in our bathrobes, with our legs drawn up to our chests.

Finally, I whispered, "so…what were you and Liz laughing about…at dinner?"

"Nothing," she said."

"Come on," I said. "It was something about Esther…right?"

After a long silence, Laureen sighed. "She and Paul Robeson…supposedly, had a love affair."

"*Really*? When?"

"Oh, years ago…it may not be true."

"But *you* think it *is*?"

"I suppose," she sighed. "She didn't know Allen, then. He was in Italy…in the Army…"

I stared out the window. "How long have your folks *known* the Rosenthals, anyway?" I asked.

"Oh, they've known Allen for…maybe ten years…they've known the *Strausses* since before the war. They all care about the same things…believe in the same things…mainly. They do favors for each other…*that's* what's important."

"What sort of favors?"

"A few weeks ago…Allen asked our dads to hire some blacklisted actors for a stage production at the new theater," she said. "Allen raises money for blacklisted actors and writers…he tries to get them work. He and my dad have even talked about financing a low-budget movie…with blacklisted actors, and a blacklisted screenwriter and director." She laughed softly, "even the composer." She paused and glanced out through the window with me. "Two years ago," she whispered, "during all that opposition about the theater…Allen and Esther and her parents helped organize the neighborhood groups that supported our side."

"Oh…*right.*"

"Daddy and Mama like them a lot…like with *your* mom and dad…they *love* your mom and dad…like family."

"I know…"

"That's why Daddy blames himself…"

"For *what?*"

"Everything…"

"Listen," I said. "My father lived the way he wanted…and my mother let him…even when she didn't agree with him…it's *our* life…your parents aren't responsible…"

"I know…it's what your mom told 'em…"

"If you want to find somebody to blame…look elsewhere." I stared through the windowpane and suddenly saw two cigarettes glowing inside the car parked against the curb below.

"Tom…"

"What," I muttered. She didn't respond. Finally, I turned toward her, and she leaned forward and kissed me on the cheek. I smiled and started to look out the window again, but she held my chin with her fingertips, and for a moment, we stared at each other in the shadowy window box. Then we kissed.

The church bells of Harlem were ringing when I awoke, startled to see the bright sun shining and well-dressed people walking to Sunday services on the street below. There was a space at the curb where the smokers' car had been.

I heard voices upstairs in the Spencers' bedroom. Quickly, I slipped out of the window box and tiptoed back to my room.

Liz was sitting on my bed with her own borrowed robe wrapped around her and a sullen expression on her face. "Where have *you* been all night?"

"Couldn't sleep," I said.

"Neither could Laureen…apparently."

"*What?*" I snapped.

She didn't answer. Abruptly, she rose from my bed and went back to her room.

I washed up and dressed. I made my way out along the hall to the dining room, where the table was already set for five. Arthur was sitting in his chair with his head down, mulling over the *New York Times*, and sipping a cup of coffee. He was dressed in a suit and tie. I could hear Hazel out in the kitchen.

"Good mornin'," Arthur nodded.

"Good morning," I replied, sitting down.

He rustled his newspaper and read on in silence. Soon, Liz joined us and Hazel appeared from the kitchen, offering waffles or pancakes. I chose pancakes, but Liz asked for "a little cold cereal if you have it…any kind is fine."

"You girls eat like birds," said Hazel, archly. Liz offered to help, but Hazel waved her off and spun back toward the kitchen. Soon, she returned with six tiny boxes of cereal and a large pitcher of milk balanced on a tray, which she placed down near Liz before disappearing into the kitchen again.

Laureen arrived and mumbled, "mornin'." She slid into her seat next to Liz, and kept her eyes averted from everyone, especially me.

"Good mornin', daughter," Arthur said, without looking up from his paper.

Liz stared at me with narrowed eyes, her lips pressed tightly together.

Suddenly, Hazel emerged from the kitchen with a covered platter, which she laid down in the center of the table. "Hot pancakes!" she sighed. Then, she headed to her own seat. A moment later, she spoke to Laureen without really looking at her. "Get yourself some breakfast, child." I reached forward and lifted the cover off the platter of steaming, brown pancakes. Hazel muttered to her daughter, "cereal's there, too."

"I'll just have a pancake," Laureen said, with a brief smile at me.

Still not looking up from his paper, Arthur muttered, "sleep well, Tom?" Again, Liz stared angrily.

Laureen rose abruptly from her seat. "I'm not hungry," she said, hurrying toward the parlor.

At a few minutes past noon, Arthur walked Liz and me to his car, and then we headed downtown to catch a train at 125th Street.

As he drove, he glanced at us. "You kids understand our strategy?" We nodded. "When you get home," he said, "ask your mom to look through your dad's papers. Look for any scrap of information you think bears remotely on this thing we're doing…anything about our St. Nicholas Avenue bid. Look for references to Title I, Moses, Stannard, O'Leary, and Gerry Moran." We said we would. "Good," he replied, looking at his watch. "Now…before you catch your train, there's one stop I'd like to make." Abruptly, he turned left on 145th Street and headed east for several blocks, and then turned south on St. Nicholas Avenue. For a moment, we thought he was taking us to see the bid site, but then he turned east again at 136th and drove slowly along the block. Finally, he stopped in front of an old church building that had a narrow walkway beside it. "This is it," he said. We all got out and walked toward a little building behind the church.

Arthur rang the doorbell and waited. We heard faint footsteps inside, and then an elderly black woman opened the door a few feet and peered out. "Mr. Spencer?"

"Yes, Ma'am."

"Come on in," she said, stepping back and pulling the door all the way open. "He's waitin' for you…in the parlor." She pointed toward a dark hallway. "Through there."

Liz and I followed Arthur into the dim passageway, which brought us quickly to a small sitting room with darkly upholstered furniture. The shades were drawn on two small windows near a couch on one side. And in a corner, a man sat in an armchair. He was a massive black man, with long legs and arms and a barrel chest. His handsome face seemed warm and inviting, though he looked tired. And as we drew closer, I could see that his hair was graying and thinning. "So *these* are Joe's children," said Paul Robeson.

CHAPTER 24

From the platform above 125th Street, we could hear the distant rumble of the northbound 1:05. Other travelers edged forward. Arthur put his arms around us.

"When you get home, tell Leonard to call me," he said.

"Mom likes him," said Liz.

Arthur smiled weakly and glanced down the track. "I want to say something, now." He paused and we waited. "My Laureen...she's..."

"Arthur," I quickly said, trying to stop him.

"...Just an impressionable young girl..."

"I know, Arthur..."

"And I'm worried about this..."

"It's *my* fault..."

He sighed in frustration. "Will you let me get a word in, boy? I'm talkin' about this *trip*...with Allen and Esther..."

Liz glared at me. Then, she looked at Arthur and said, "she asked me to go with her."

"I haven't decided if *she's* going," he said.

"Oh." Now, Liz was confused too. "Why...because she's too young?"

"She's too young, all right. But...what I really want to say...I just hope none of you kids feels obligated...to make *your parents'* mistakes..."

"You have to stop blaming yourself," I said.

He shook his head. "I keep wondering what Joe'd want me to tell you kids...what advice..."

"Arthur," Liz interjected. "Why did you have us meet Mr. Robeson?"

"Why...to see the truth, for yourself. It's a hard road."

"When someone wants to tell the truth, and people prefer a lie?" she said. "Of course it is. A man like that is *dangerous*...people are afraid of him..."

"Afraid?" Arthur smiled weakly. "Maybe they were *once*." Moments later, the train lumbered slowly along the platform, with bell clangs and hissing air brakes, and finally it stopped with a gasp. Arthur stared gravely at Liz. "All I'm saying is...you have your own lives...you kids. Whatever you do, don't live someone else's without thinking twice about it." He paused again and stared at me, as the train doors clambered open. "Boy," he said, "ain't nothin' free...not in *this* world. Make sure you know what you want." He smiled again and let us go. "And *be* careful!"

We hurried into the nearest car just ahead of the closing doors, and found two seats together as the train moved and quickly gathered speed. We pressed our faces against the window, twisting to see the station platform as Arthur walked to the stairs that led down to the street. We waved, but he didn't see us. We were already too far away. Liz fell back into her seat near the window. I watched her for a moment as she gazed out, saying nothing. The last tenements of upper Manhattan rushed by. Then, we were in the air above water, clattering on the Harlem River trestle, heading northwest to the Hudson.

The conductor came through, and I gave him a five-dollar bill for two tickets home. As he made change, I casually asked a question. "If we got off *before* Garrison, could we get on again...with *these*, I mean?"

"Same day only," he said, punching our tickets. "Where would ya' be gettin' off then?"

"Peekskill," I replied. I could feel Liz staring at me now.

"Ah! It's a nice town, that...I've many a friend there." The conductor pulled a schedule from his pocket and examined it. "Two trains more ta' Garrison from Peekskill this evenin'," he said. "Er's one at six...and at nine..."

"Thank you," I replied, as the conductor nodded and moved on. Liz glared at me. I leaned toward her and whispered. "There may be a way to get inside O'Leary's office." She shook her head in disbelief. "Just *think* about it," I whispered.

"*No*," she said, coldly.

"We'll find more in O'Leary's files than Dad's," I said. "And *not* just about St. Nicholas Avenue." She sighed angrily and turned away, but I persisted. "You heard Allen say how hard Arthur's plan would be. *He's* the one who mentioned O'Leary's office."

"Are you crazy?" she hissed.

"If we wait till dark," I replied, "there'll be nobody around…it's…Sunday night."

"*Why* are you doing this?"

"You know why."

The train whistled twice as we approached the next station. The clacking tempo of the wheels slowed. Finally, she looked at me and said, "it's a can of worms, Tom…it's family. You don't *want* to know."

"*Dad* did," I argued.

She sighed and looked away again. "So…this is still about trying to make it up to Dad," she whispered.

We neared Peekskill, and I could see the Hudson Electric stacks bleeding exhaust into the sky above the river. Out across the bay, the merchant ship graveyard glistened in silent, brackish water beneath the sun. I looked at my watch. It was two o'clock. We'd be reaching the station in ten minutes.

Liz slept beside me. But as I watched her peaceful face, her head rocking slightly with the movement of the train, my own nerves pulsed like electric currents beneath my skin. I leaned back in my seat and forced myself to breathe slowly, hoping for the slightest calmness. Finally, I tried closing my eyes, but there was no peace—only Robeson's face and his haunting voice.

"My dear children," he'd said, leaning forward in his armchair to shake our hands, as Arthur introduced us in the cramped parsonage sitting room. "I'm so sorry for you…Joe Gannon was a friend…the best of men. I've been anxious to sing for your father and Arthur…at their new theater. I just don't know what to say now…"

"I wanted these young people to meet you," Arthur said. "To help them understand…" Arthur suddenly stopped and hung his head, staring at the worn, dark carpeting. "God *damn* that place," he muttered.

"*Misguided* people," Robeson said with a tired, whispered sigh. Then he shook his head, as his Shakespearean voice rose: "Wake up America! Peekskill did." He paused, bowed his head, and whispered again. "That was their battle cry."

Arthur looked up and explained. "He means the riot, the concert in 'Forty-nine."

"Was the Klan really behind that?" I asked.

"Oh, yes," Robeson said distractedly, as if sifting through his memories. "Their mark was on that day."

"Tell us about it," I said.

He pressed his lips together and frowned. "Why would you care...now?"

"Because it's something we should *hear*...and never forget," I said, feeling constricting anger in my voice. "My father wasn't murdered by strangers...they were people from our family's own background...maybe some of the same people who threatened *you*." Robeson stared at us with a grave expression. "My father never saw it coming," I said, angrily. "But, that's him. I don't forgive as easily as he did, and I *don't* have his faith in people's...goodness."

"No?" said Robeson, sounding surprised.

"Why should I?"

"You should *never* lose hope, son. Your father didn't die without friends. Yes, he believed in something unpopular...but we're still *many*...those of us who know this Negro problem isn't just some subversive...unpatriotic notion. It's the whole *country's* problem...and 'til it's resolved, we'll never be what we claim to be." Robeson glanced at Arthur and asked, "how can I help these children?"

"We *aren't* children...not anymore," I blurted. "Just tell us the *truth*."

"Truth about what?" he said.

"What sort of cause it really *is*, that my father died for!" I said. He stared at me quizzically, and the cramped room was silent.

"*Tom!*" Liz whispered, shocked.

"I don't mean to criticize *you*," I said.

"Then, what *do* you mean?" Robeson asked.

"It's said you're a Communist," I replied, feeling my anger, understanding only part of it. "Maybe you are...maybe you're not. I don't care, but lots of people do...I guess they don't know what else to think...they need simple answers, to understand a person like you...or my father...whoever doesn't fit the mold. *But*...there was *some* reason why Jackie Robinson felt he *had* to deny a connection with you...publicly...with your beliefs." I paused, and Robeson lowered his head in embarrassment. "Was it that statement you made about the army...or not? I know my *father* wasn't a Communist, but if he believed the same things you do, maybe it's not so hard to understand why people may have *thought* he was."

"Tom," Liz interjected, "this isn't fair." Then, she looked at Robeson and said, "sir, he's just upset...he doesn't mean to be disrespectful."

Robeson shook his head and waved his hand to quiet her. "It's an honest question," he said. "Son...I can see you're troubled...but the men responsible for...what happened to your dad...don't judge the country by them. I wouldn't even judge Peekskill by them. I hope you find a way to see them punished. I'll help you…in whatever way I can, believe me. Now, Jackie…I've no quarrel with him…got a great deal of respect for him. What I've said before…I still believe…he's entitled to his views, just like I am mine. That House Committee insulted us both…and the whole Negro race."

"So, why do people say his testimony *encouraged* the riot at Peekskill?" I said.

He glowered and shook his head. "No. That's just folks blamin' one colored man for what happened to another." He looked hard at us for a moment, and then pointed to the nearby couch. We sat down. "All right," he sighed. "I'll tell you what I think…and what your father thought. *Most* of those people up there you're talking about…they're just working people. That's all. But they've been hoodwinked into believing there's only *one* way to have this dream of being an American. Now…used to be a big food company…had a plant up there; made yeast, I think it was." He glanced at Arthur who nodded. "During the war, they employed about twelve-hundred local people," Robeson said. "But by 'Forty-nine…half those jobs were gone. That's a lot of jobs in a little town, and there were hard feelings over it. The men who ran the company were concerned…some of the workers they still had on were talking about starting a union. So now…here *we* come from the city, on Labor Day no less, to do a concert on the old golf course up there. Didn't help that I was known as such a strong unionist. I've done movies and plays about unions…about exploiting men's work…a lot of the folks with me were unionists, too. I can *say* that our focus that day *wasn't* unions…it was raising money and awareness about civil rights…for American Negroes…but I can't deny who I am…I carry *everything* I believe wherever I go. And that's what those company men used…"

"Used it how?" I said.

"They *simplified* everything…deflected animosity from the company onto me…and the people who came with me. They divided us from those local working people, who *should* have felt a natural solidarity with *us*. It was those company men who didn't want a Labor Day concert…they'd gone to the editor of the Peekskill newspaper, where they did a lot of their advertising you know, and they got him to write hateful editorials about Paul Robeson…the Communist. 'Outside agitators are coming to disrupt our clean, honest way of life. Communists are coming to enslave us.' And it worked…because those poor people already felt hoodwinked…out of work, and angry about it. By the time we got there…they were ready to kill." He paused and sighed. "Arthur, you can blame the Klan, and those *other* groups, if you want…but I put most of the blame on that newspaper, and those businessmen. People can be fooled into doing some strange things when they're afraid. I guess there aren't many things more frightening than losing your job."

Liz got off the train with me, after all. We took a taxi into downtown Peekskill, and the cabbie dropped us in front of the bus terminal at about two-thirty.

"We better call Mom," Liz said. "She'll worry."

I nodded. "I'll do it."

"And say *what*?" she replied.

"I don't know…that we're helping Arthur…something…"

She shook her head as we walked to the Arcade Cinema and bought tickets for the matinee double feature. Before going in, I glanced across the street at the O'Leary Building. It seemed deserted. But when I looked at Liz for vindication, she wasn't paying attention. She was gazing back at the bus terminal.

The first film was already playing as we struggled to our seats. As my eyes adjusted to the black and silver glow of the almost empty movie house, Liz leaned back and closed her eyes.

"I'm gonna use the phone out in the lobby," I whispered.

"Good luck," she muttered sarcastically, without looking up.

I went back to the lobby and dropped a dime into the public phone near the men's room. I heard only one ring.

"Hello?" said Mother, urgently.

"Mom…it's me."

"Oh," she said, sounding relieved. "I'm glad you got me. We're just leaving. Leonard is taking us to Beacon…I'm seeing Father Hanlon about the…"

"Memorial service," I said.

"Yes. When will you be home…where are you *now*?"

"We're in New York," I said. "Arthur asked us to help him do research on public housing…we're at his office, going through some of his files." There was silence on the line. "He gave us a list of things to look for…said it would save him time."

"Is he with you?"

"Yes…he's meeting with some people, though."

"Let me speak to Liz."

"She's using the ladies' room…downstairs."

"Oh…I don't have time to wait. *When* will you be home?"

"I don't know…depends what we find, I guess."

"I don't want you home late," she urged. "Tell Arthur I said that. Call us when your train gets in to Garrison. We'll come get you."

"All right, Mom."

"We should be back from St. Mary's by…five o'clock, probably," she estimated.

"Can *I* speak about Dad…at the service…Mom?"

"We can talk about it…just get home early…do you hear?"

"Yes, Mom."

When I got back inside, Liz was asleep. For a while, I watched the famously patriotic actor onscreen imitating people like my father, the real heroes of the Pacific War, which he'd spent in Hollywood, shamelessly avoiding the draft. By some weird alchemy, he was forging a reputation as a patriotic saint by questioning other men's loyalties, now. I turned away in disgust, and looked at my sister. Her eyes were still closed as her head lay back, and the reflected movie light on her peaceful face was the color of moonlit snow. I leaned back in my seat, and finally slept.

We left after the second show, at about five thirty, but lingered for a moment on the sidewalk, watching the Arcade staff empty wastebaskets and push carpet sweepers in the lobby. The ticket booth was already dark, and suddenly the candy counter lights flickered off, as the staff prepared to close for the night.

I checked my watch, and glanced across the street at the quiet office building. "We have to kill more time," I said.

"You hungry?" she asked.

There was almost no traffic on Main Street, now. Everything looked shut down, even Penney's Soda Shop, where Liz and I sometimes got burgers and shakes. But I noticed a light flickering in a window up the block, between the O'Leary Building and the American Legion Hall. It was a seedy tavern, called Coppie's Bar & Grill.

"We could get a hot dog at the bus terminal…or try *that* place," I said, pointing toward the flickering light.

Liz shrugged. So we crossed the street and walked up to the dreary, red brick tavern building. There was a wooden front door, flanked by dirty windows—a blue, fluorescent Pabst Blue Ribbon sign glowed in one; a red Reingold sign flickered in the other.

Liz opened the door and I followed her into the dark, smoky tavern. There was a long wooden bar on the left. Behind it, scores of liquor bottles stood in descending rows, each capped with a curved silver spout like a shiny beckoning finger. Invisible lights beneath the shelves gave the bottles a weird glow. And above the far end of the bar, a television played an old Hopalong Cassidy movie. Two men were sitting halfway down the bar smoking cigarettes, chatting with the bartender. A woman sitting at the near end, a few steps from the door, stared at us. Tables and booths on the right were fenced off from the bar by a four-foot partition of cheap, paneled wood, with a wide opening at each end. Two young women sat in a booth near the back, listening to an old Perry Como record on the big, red and gold Wurlitzer:

Till the ennnd of time…long as stars are in the blue…

The staring woman got up, suddenly, and walked toward us. She was tall, with bleached out, frizzy-red hair and a tired face coated in thick, tan makeup. She must have been around 40, but it was hard to tell exactly.

"How old're you kids," she demanded, as the bartender watched closely.

"I'm eighteen," Liz said.

"What about *him*?"

"My brother's *almost* eighteen…"

"Oh, yeah? Yuz look about fifteen ta' me…I'm not servin' yuz any liquor."

"We just want a coke," Liz said. "Something to eat…we're waiting for a bus. The terminal's too crowded…we couldn't get near the lunch counter."

"No?" said the woman, with a skeptical frown. Then, she glanced at the bartender. "Hey, Coppie! These kids say they want cokes…somethin' ta' eat…girl says she's eighteen." The bartender, a tall man in his 50s with dyed and thinning black hair slicked down, waved his hand and nodded. "Awright," the woman said, pointing to the tables. We chose the nearest one and sat down. "I'll get ya' cokes," she said, pointing to the red plastic menu stuck between the salt-and-pepper shakers. "We're outta the fish sticks. Try the pot roast."

She went to the bar, and we could see her from the waist up as she leaned over to order our drinks. The other two men suddenly laughed and turned on their stools, staring at the young women in the back booth. One man whispered something to the other, and they both smiled in a vaguely unpleasant way. The men noticed Liz and smiled at her, too. She rolled her eyes, and I laughed as we examined the simple menu and quickly agreed on something that had to be cooked now. When the waitress returned and slapped two glasses of Coke down on the table, I said, "two steak sandwiches, please…with fries."

"*Well-done*, please," added Liz.

"Mmm-humm," she muttered, turning to shout the order.

But the bartender had heard me. "Comin' up," he barked, waving the waitress off. He stepped out under the television, and disappeared behind a swinging kitchen door. The waitress shuffled back to her stool, lifted a burning cigarette from an ashtray, and took a drag. The Reingold sign flickered in the window behind her, as she stared into space.

> *…So take my heart in sweet surrender…*
> *And tenderly say that I'm…*
> *The one you love and live for, till the ennnd of time.*

The bartender returned from the kitchen and called out, "five minutes!" I waved.

Moments later, Liz tapped my forearm and nodded toward a young man who'd just come from the men's room and was sitting down, awkwardly, on the last bar stool beneath the television. "Boy…is *he* drunk," she whispered.

He was a sullen figure, sitting with his back to us and leaning on the bar. Suddenly, he raised his hand and pointed toward the bartender. "Hey! Coppie! What I gotta do…getta drink?" The bartender glanced up, sourly, from his conversation with the two other men. Then, shaking his head and muttering under his breath, he walked slowly down to the young man, leaned over, and whispered something. Moments later, the young man yelped. "I *know*!"

"So…don't you think you've had enough?" the bartender said. "Go home…get some sleep, Mike. We'll call a cab…I'll call your mom…tell her you're on your way."

"No…no…NO!" the young man blathered, as the other two men and the women in back murmured.

"Well, I'm sorry," said the bartender. "I can't serve you any more…lemme know when you want the cab." He walked back to rejoin the other two men, who shook their heads in commiseration.

I leaned over the table and whispered to Liz. "I've seen that guy, before. He was my bus driver…that morning…he saw everything, just like *I* did. Isabel…her grandfather…everything. I asked him to stop and go back to help them…but he wouldn't. He *knows* O'Leary, too."

"Oh, Jesus!" the bartender suddenly shouted, over the sound of shattering glass. Everyone looked. The drunk had just hurled his empty glass against the wall behind the bar, and shards fell down on rows of clinking, wobbling liquor bottles.

"Yoo can' talk a' me like tha," the young man bellowed. "Whoo you thing you are?"

"Calm down, Mike," Coppie said, rushing back to the young man.

"Or else wha'? Gonna call a' police? Go 'head. Wanna call ya' boys…have 'em chuck *me* inna rivah?"

There was no more murmuring in the bar, nothing except Tony Bennett's voice in the jukebox.

> *I know I'd go from raaags…to riccchhhes…*

"Calm down," Coppie demanded.

"Gimme 'nutha drink, then…"

> *If you would only saaaay…you care…*

"You're done," Coppie said. "Go home and sleep it off. I'll buy ya' one t'morrow…Jesus Christ, whatta mess!"

The waitress suddenly rose from her seat, walked to the young man, and put an arm over his shoulders. Leaning close, she spoke in a low, calming voice as Coppie watched from behind the bar. It seemed at first that the young man was listening. He nodded with exaggerated politeness as she whispered in his ear. Then, he erupted, screaming over the bar. "FUCK YOU…Coppie!" The startled waitress stumbled back. "Ahm not some niggah! Wha'…you wan' my seat?"

"Go home, Mikey," Coppie demanded.

The young man struggled off his stool. Once on his feet, he needed to grip the bar to stay up. "Hap-py now?" With his free hand, he pointed somewhere in the direction of his barstool and said, "go 'head…call a' police. Call a' congressman, why-you're at it. Tell 'im his mother n' father can 'ave *my* seat. I don' care…don' hafta throw *me* offa bus. Ooops." He giggled sarcastically, and awkwardly raised a hand to his mouth. "Shushhhh." Then, he glanced down the bar at one of the two men staring in disgust. "Hey, buddy," he shouted. "Betta get up…congressman needs *two* seats for 'is mother n' father!"

"Shut your goddamn mouth, Mikey!" Coppie ordered, waving his arm at the other men. "You guys…help me get him outta here…Delma, call a cab!"

The waitress quickly reached over the bar and retrieved a black telephone with a long extension cord. She placed the phone on the bar, lifted the receiver and dialed, as the young man collapsed in a heap. The young women in the back booth gasped.

"Goddamn drunks," Coppie muttered, when he noticed Liz and me watching it all.

The young women got up and started for the front door. "Money's on the table, Coppie," one of them said.

"Hey…girls," one man shouted, standing over the drunk. "Where ya' goin'?" The women ignored him and moved quickly past Liz and me, and they were gone in seconds.

As the front door slammed shut behind them, the disappointed man grumbled. "Shit."

Coppie glowered at Liz and me. "What's everybody *staring* at?"

We looked at each other, then, as he stepped beneath the television and came around to the front of the bar. The three of them hoisted the drunk off the floor, and walked him past the jukebox, down a narrow hallway beyond the rest rooms. When they were out of sight, we heard what sounded like a face being slapped hard.

"Cab's comin'!" the waitress shouted, holding one hand over the receiver.

"Tell 'im to come 'round the back," the bartender grunted from the hallway. We could hear him struggling with the other men to drag the drunk out the back door.

The waitress mumbled something more into the phone and hung up. "I'll check ya' steaks," she smirked, shuffling toward the kitchen. "Should be well done, by now."

By seven thirty, a few bright stars had emerged in the darkening sky above the deserted city. Liz and I stood again beneath the Arcade Cinema marquee and looked across Main Street.

"Tom. Let's just go home." I looked into my sister's piercing eyes and suddenly understood why she'd gotten off the train. "You don't have to do this," she said, grabbing my arms and shaking me.

"I'm gonna try the side door," I replied. "In the alley…will you stay here?" She pressed her lips together and shook her head hopelessly. "I'll come to the windows in front, and you'll see I'm okay," I promised. "You let me know if anything's up."

"How do I do that?" she said.

"A *signal*," I replied, as she frowned, skeptically. "I know…we'll use baseball signs." I put out my hands. "That's the 'safe' sign…it means the coast is clear…and the 'out' sign is your thumb…it means trouble…somebody's gone into the building after me…or you see somebody in an office."

"A night watchman, for instance," she said, pointedly.

"That place is deserted…look." I nodded confidently toward the darkened windows along the front of the O'Leary Building. "You can see everything from here. The front entrance and all four floors…see?"

She nodded. Suddenly, the nervous expression on her face dissolved, and she smiled, almost against her will. "You're such a jerk."

"I know it," I said, smiling back at her.

"When are you gonna grow up?" she asked. I shrugged. She grabbed my hands. "Tom…don't go in there."

"Wait for me," I said. "I'll be back."

I crossed the street, moved quickly along the right side of the office building to the back of the alley, and came to a thick metal door with a small window embedded with wire mesh. I peered inside at a dim vestibule leading to an elevator. I tried the door handle. Then, I reached into my back pocket for the table knife I'd stolen from Coppie's. I inserted the blade in the doorjamb, and worked it for several minutes, managing to push the simple handle bolt back enough to release the door. I listened for alarms. When I heard nothing, I glanced back at Liz, and then stepped inside. But the door wouldn't lock when I pushed it shut, now; I'd damaged the bolt.

A small menu on the wall beside the elevator said Andrew O'Leary's office was Suite 402. I went up in the elevator and stepped out on a long, dark hallway with office doors along both sides. There were dim security lights along the walls, and a red EXIT sign glowed above a safety door at the far end. At the midpoint of the hallway, I came to a landing from where stairs descended to the third floor. A wide archway beyond the landing opened out to a large room filled with desks and chairs. I could see the dark outlines of telephones and typewriters on the desks, and beyond them, a wall of glass—the fourth-floor windows facing the street. I crossed the landing and walked past the desks to the windows. I saw Main Street, and Liz, beneath the marquee on the other side. She seemed to be watching the street-level windows. I wrapped my knuckles on the windowpane, louder and louder, until she finally heard the sound and looked up. She raised her hand. I waved back and returned to the hallway.

Suite 402 was the last office on the right, near the EXIT sign. It was mildly surprising to find the door unlocked. I stepped inside, and the door closed automatically behind me. I found a switch near the door and turned on a fluorescent ceiling light. Straight ahead, there was a large desk with a phone, a typewriter, and wilted flowers in a cheap glass vase. A removable nameplate, held by metal runners to the desk front, said: *Miss Conway*. Against the wall on the right, there was a long couch covered in dull brown cloth. A coffee table overflowed with golf and boating magazines, ashtrays, and a large cigarette lighter with a silver cap and a crystal base. There were two doors on the left. The one nearest the desk was labeled with large, black letters: **Andrew O'Leary, President.**

This door was unlocked. I pushed it open. Light from the reception area shone in on a simple, windowless room with a desk and chair, and a file cabinet. There were two phones and a large shaded lamp on the desk. I walked in and turned on the lamp. Now, I noticed an antique ship's clock and framed photos on the desk—a formal portrait of the O'Leary family, alongside a smaller photo of them waving from the deck of their cabin cruiser, *The Patriot*, moored in a slip at the Highland Yacht Club. On the wall, there were more framed photos of O'Leary with celebrities and other politicians.

The ship's clock suddenly chimed—a quarter to eight. As I moved quickly to the file cabinet, the desk lamp fluttered and grew brighter, then dimmer, and fluttered again. I heard a low hum in the wall behind the outlet, where the lamp was plugged. Finally, the hum subsided and the lamplight stabilized. The top drawer in the cabinet opened when I tried it. It was empty. I riffled through a dozen green folders in the middle drawer, but found only standard contract forms and sales brochures for small housing developments. The bottom drawer held stacks of "makeup dummies" for newspaper ads.

The desk lamp fluttered again. And the humming in the wall resumed as I stepped out and stared at the other door, which was made of thick, hard wood and locked with a dead bolt. I took the knife from my back pocket and placed it on Miss Conway's desk. Then, I took the cushions off the couch and threw them on the floor in front of the bolted door. I stepped back several strides and leapt in the air. There was a loud thud and a slight cracking sound as my feet hit solidly against wood and I landed on the cushions. I stood up and examined the door. It was still solidly in place, but a small superficial break spidered between the knob and the deadbolt. I repeated my leap, again and again, until the tiny fissure became a gaping wound in the oak. Finally, after several more leaps, I broke through with a loud crack.

My back throbbed as I got to my feet and quickly retrieved the knife. At the broken door, a small, jagged piece of wood still held the deadbolt in its locked position against the doorframe. I reached in and hit the switch. Bright fluorescent lights fluttered and came on in a windowless, rectangular room. I saw a row of black, metal file cabinets lining each wall and a long aisle between them. I stepped into the room and walked down the aisle, checking each cabinet, finding it locked, reading each label: Hollywood, Radio & Television, Broadway, Newspapers & Magazines, Colleges, Labor Unions, State Department, Judges, Congress. I found files with labels reading: *Red Channels* and *Counter Attack*, the blacklist publications. And at the very back of the room, I found a cabinet labeled *Special Projects*.

I inserted the knife in a seam, and worked feverishly to pry open the top drawer, but succeeded only in bending the knife blade and the drawer frame. I felt the cheap knife handle cutting into the heel of my hand, and I was covered in sweat. My back ached, but I struggled on, levering the drawer. Finally, the blade snapped with a ping. I took a breath, dropped the useless handle-butt on the floor, and stared helplessly at the file cabinet. But when I realized that the drawer had slipped out a few inches, my heart pounded. I pulled the drawer all the way out, and thumbed through hanging files with plastic tabs labeled for big commercial real estate deals. Toward the back, I found folders labeled for St. Nicholas Avenue, and in one of these, the formal bid by O'Leary Realty Corp. for $150 million on behalf of a consortium of banks and private investors. I placed the heavy document on top of the cabinet and searched on. At the very back, I found a file marked *Gerry Moran*. It held numerous letters from O'Leary to Moran, dating to the late-1940s. Each letter involved a different person Moran had been paid to name as a subversive in HUAC testimony. From the letters, it appeared that each of these people had had real estate dealings with O'Leary. Closing the folder, and hanging it back in place, I noticed something that lay flat at the bottom of the drawer. I pushed several folders apart, reached down and removed a scuffed, old file.

When I opened it, pieces of rotted paper floated into the air like burnt ash. I carefully read page after page of yellowed documents involving a real estate business group called *The Highland Association*. And as I read, it became clear that the main purpose of this group was to keep "coloreds" from buying choice land or housing in the Highlands. There were familiar names in the membership roster, men known to our family, but not friends, exactly. I'd met many of them at church in Beacon and back in Park Slope, usually introduced by Grandfather Hank. They were men who passed out collection baskets on Sunday mornings with him, who wore white carnations in the lapels of their neat Sunday suits, and always smelled of mint and tobacco and sweet, cheap shaving cream. Finally, I realized why Hank Gannon's name appeared more than any other in the dusty pages—he'd founded *The Highland Association* in 1937.

Then, in an envelope, I found a newer and more terrifying document. It was three pages of amateurish, single-space typing on onion paper, held with a paper clip and folded twice—the minutes of a confidential meeting—exactly what I'd come to find.

"What the…fuck!" Andrew O'Leary stood in the broken doorway, examining the damage, wearing khaki slacks, a short-sleeved shirt, and a straw fedora. As he touched the jagged wood with his fingertips, the muscles in his forearm rippled and his hand closed in a fist. Glancing briefly at the couch cushions strewn across the reception area, he laughed coldly. "Lovely speech you gave the headmaster," he sneered. "Now what…breaking and entering?"

"We *have* her," I said.

He looked at me straight on, and his smile hardened. Now, I wished I hadn't admitted it so readily. "You've got nothing," he said, "except someone else's property in your hands. You've broken into my goddamn office, son. The place is prob'ly plastered with your fingerprints. I heard how you broke in the hospital…but I'm not as patient as Charles Stannard. You're on *my* turf, now…I deal with things direct…"

"Oh, really?" I laughed. "Like you dealt with my father? You needed a *crowd* to stop him, you cowardly fuck." His face was without emotion, flat and merciless. "And *everybody's* gonna hear about it, soon enough," I said.

"From who," he snapped. "Some colored girl?"

"Why hide her, then?" I said. He stepped toward me with his fists clenched. I smiled, and took a step toward him. Abruptly, he stopped, with a surprised, animal glare in his eyes. "Don't like *these* odds?" I sneered. His glare turned pensive, as I held up the meeting notes typed on onion paper. "When *this* starts going around to the right people, who won't ignore it, *Congressman*…and you see it in the papers…that'll wipe the smile off your face."

"You keep shaking that thing at me," he spat, "I'll put it up your ass!"

"I'd love you to try it," I said, smiling again, in a way he clearly didn't like. "You're not dealing with your son, now, or your wife…*or* my father. *Please* try something."

"I don't think you'll show that to anyone," he said. "You know why? It's more embarrassing to *you* than me. I'm just a businessman…that's all that paper says about me. Or Stannard. But, your grandfather?" He laughed again. "I know him a long time. I know a lot more about him than even you, prob'ly. Believe me…he's no angel…especially when it comes ta' coloreds n' Jews. *He's* the one that agreed to get your father to pull out of St. Nicholas Avenue…and testify about Moran…*and* Spencer."

"My father wasn't gonna do *any* of that."

"Whatever you say, kid. It was your *grandfather's* idea, not mine. It's all there…and the old drunk thought we'd actually cut him in on a project like St. Nicholas Avenue!" He laughed sarcastically. "So, go ahead…be my guest…rummage around all you want. Everything you'll find is true…and neither that note nor anything else in there's gonna hurt *my* reputation. Whatever lies that girl's told you…well, we'll just see. Lemme tell you somethin' about most people…they're realists. They don't see things like your old man…don't care; never will. People want rules…law n' order…"

"*Rules*," I scoffed.

"That's what they want…even if they intend to bend 'em a little. What they *don't want* is troublemakers, questioning everything all the time. And troublemakers that end up dead…most folks assume they deserved it." He paused, looked again at the broken door, and sighed. "Anyway…you stay right there…I'll go call the police. You can explain your theories ta' *them*, when they arrest ya' for breakin' and entering…and when they confiscate what you've got, there, they'll just hand it back to me." He laughed coldly, turned and disappeared into his office. I heard him dialing his phone. "Yeah…police?" he barked. "Chief Walton there? Well, call him at home. Yes, now! This is Andy O'Leary…that's right. I'm reporting a burglar…in my office building, yeah…Main Street." I raced out of the file room and stood in his doorway, watching him lean against his desk with the phone pressed against his right ear and his back to me. A burnt electrical smell filled the room, and the lamp on his desk fluttered wildly. "That's right," he said into the phone. "Alley door…west side of the building…asshole broke the lock, and he's in my private office…stealing private papers…I want this kid arrested and charged…what? Yeah, a kid…a teenager. I don't know why…yes, he's still here. Send some cruisers right over. No…I already know who it is…he's…his name is…"

I leapt into the office and my feet landed squarely against his back. He grunted as the air blew out of his lungs. The receiver flew from his hand, and I heard picture frames shattering. I looked up from the floor. He was bent over his desk, struggling to turn and kick me. But his false leg was caught. I jumped up as he reached for the desk lamp and yanked it, cord and all from the wall socket, swinging at my head in a violent roundhouse. I ducked, and he growled, as his lunging swipe missed me. The lamp slipped from his grasp and crashed against the opposite wall. I launched a hard right fist at his face. It landed square on his nose, and broke it. Blood spurted. He screamed and fell back against the front edge of his desk. Then, he sprang forward and gripped me in his arms like an angry bear. He punched me hard in the kidneys. He wanted to kick me, but his legs were helpless, and I punched again and again at his stomach with both fists until his arms fell off me and he sagged, heaving for air.

I stepped back and punched his face with all my strength. The shock of nerve damage jolted my right arm, as his body flopped over the desk and tumbled onto the floor behind it with a loud pop. His false leg had been dislodged and torn through his pants. It lay at my feet with its shoe on, and a bit of khaki trouser cloth wrapped around it. My hand throbbed. As he struggled up on one leg, holding the back edge of his desk, blood dripped from the center of his face. I saw, now, that he'd pulled the socket plate off when he'd yanked the lamp. White-blue sparks of raw electricity were exploding from the exposed wall, lapping against his wooden desk. Suddenly there were flames. He started coughing. My eyes stung from the smoke. The torn, hanging cloth of his pants caught fire and he screamed, frantically slapping at the flames. The electric sparks now shot under the desk to the opposite wall, and a barrier of fire began to separate us. I heard an explosion somewhere in the building. The walls and the floor trembled. O'Leary's good leg was burning now, as he slumped back against the wall behind his desk and slid to the floor.

I raced to the file room for the onion paper document, which I quickly folded and shoved in my back pocket. I knew the police would be there at any moment, so I grabbed the bid document from the cabinet top and walked out to the coffee table. I rolled a magazine and lit it with the crystal table lighter. Then, I hurled the lighter into the file room where it shattered. As the odor of fluid filled the air, I tossed the flickering magazine in and jumped back as a whoosh of flame shot from the door. The file room was ablaze, now. I heard O'Leary groan in his office. He was somewhere on the other side of his burning desk. Suddenly, he screamed. The flames grew higher, hotter, consuming his office. The screams grew louder and the heat was intense. Finally, the screams stopped, and the anger I'd felt for days and weeks was gone, replaced by unexpected guilt.

I hurried to the hallway door and grabbed the knob. It scalded my hand. I pulled back and searched the smoky floor for a couch cushion. I found one and placed it over the doorknob and awkwardly turned it. As the door opened, flames shot wildly down the hallway and I fell to the floor. Smoke and heat consumed oxygen. Flames and smoke billowed over me in the open doorway. The heat was intense. I could hear the elevator rumbling—I had to get out ahead of the police. I could barely see the red glow of the EXIT sign to my right. Holding the cushion and the bid document in front of me, I jumped up and raced to the EXIT door, lunging against the push bar.

The door flew open on a hot gust that carried me onto the upper landing of an iron stairway outside the building. A loud rush of heat and flame scorched the air. Finally, the safety door slammed shut and I scrambled down the iron steps and then fell forward, sliding on my stomach, down the remaining steps to the ground. I got to my feet, stunned, and walked along a narrow space between buildings and squeezed out onto Main Street.

Police cruisers were parked haphazardly in front of the O'Leary Building. I could hear sirens in the distance. There were people on the sidewalk in front of the building, but I couldn't see their faces. I couldn't see Liz. I walked quickly across the street, half-hidden in darkness, as people watched fire lapping behind the office windows. My legs and arms and back ached as I headed quickly to the cinema. I realized that I'd lost the O'Leary bid document, but I cared only about reaching Liz, now. I couldn't see her in the flickering shadows under the marquee when I reached the Arcade. I looked for her against the glass doors, and then turned to look across the street, searching for a glimpse of her in the growing crowd. I started toward them. I could see Coppie and his two buddies. I saw other people I didn't know. I saw cops. I stopped in the middle of Main Street as fire engines blasted their horns and came toward us. I looked toward the tavern again and saw the frizzy-haired waitress out in front, staring at me, smoking a cigarette. A loud explosion drew a sickening roar from the crowd. I looked up and saw flames shoot high into the black sky above the building, ripping through a hole in the roof. A sea of endless fire engulfed the upper floor.

The fire engines stopped near the cinema, behind me. "Start working the adjoining buildings," shouted one fireman as others raced to unspool the hoses. Moments later, the roof fell in with an explosion that drenched the sky in flame. People cried out on the street. Awestruck firemen dropped their hoses and gazed. Policemen pushed the crowd away from the burning building, but I was running toward it.

"Liz!" I screamed.

Instantly, thick arms grappled me at my chest and an angry voice shouted. "Whatta you crazy? You can't go in there!"

CHAPTER 25

The cop finally let me go with an angry, frustrated push. He walked back to his partners, and I waited at the edge of the crowd, as firemen struggled against the tide of flame consuming the collapsed building.

"It's a total loss," the fire captain said, watching his men spray cold water on the roofs of adjoining buildings, where it turned to hissing steam. A dank haze began rising into the night, and the street was littered with flecks of ash and charred pieces of wood.

"At least it was after hours...nobody inside," said a man, staring at the blaze.

The fire captain turned to him and said, "you didn't hear?"

"Hear what?"

"Just before the fire...someone called the police about a burglar..."

"In that building?"

"Yep."

"Did they catch 'em?" the man asked, as the fire captain shook his head. "You think somebody's still *in* there?"

"Don't know," the captain muttered.

A tap on my shoulder distracted me, and I turned to look; it was the waitress from the bar. "Where's ya' sister?"

"What?" I said.

"You heard me."

I glanced at the fire again. "Leave me alone..."

"Yuz both was in the bar..."

"You must be thinking of somebody else...Ma'am."

She shook her head and smirked. "I saw you sneakin' around the Arcade...I don't know what yuz're up to, but I don't forget faces. It was you...and ya' sister...waitin' for a bus, yuz said...pretty late for a bus..."

"You're mistaken!" I snapped, glaring at her pasty face in the garish light. Then I walked away and stood in another part of the crowd. Once or twice, I glanced back and saw her talking earnestly to Coppie and some other men. They looked in my direction several times, but never came toward me.

Hours passed before it was certain that the fire crews had kept the flames from jumping to other buildings. When I remembered to look at my watch, it was ten-thirty. The building was a smoldering pile of collapsed masonry and charred glass, now, though occasional bursts of flame brought gasps from the people gathered on the slick, wet street. The air was filled with acrid soot, and a black stream of water rushed along the curbside. Finally, people began drifting away, and by eleven o'clock only the most ardent curiosity seekers were left. The firemen pulled in their hoses and prepared to leave. The police sent out for coffee.

"Time to go home, son," said the cop who'd grabbed me, earlier. I looked at him and nodded.

Another cop whispered. "Who's that kid? Looks familiar."

"Think anybody's still alive in there?" the first cop said to his partner.

"Wadda you kiddin'?" the other cop sighed.

I felt sick, now, thinking of what I had to tell my mother. I looked at the hopelessly ruined building one last time, and then turned in a daze and walked across the street, as the cops talked among themselves. I walked quickly past the deserted bus terminal, beneath the glowing red sign of the Hudson Electric Company. And then I started to run, beyond the end of the pavement to the edge of the city, running west toward the darkness of the river. When I reached the intersection for Route 9, I ran north along the shoulder of the winding highway, out of the Peekskill flats and gradually up the long, dark face of the mountain. There was no moon. Thickening haze obscured all but a few bright stars and the smell of burnt wood and rubber hung in the cold, quiet air.

The headlights of a northbound car flashed behind me. The car quickly passed and disappeared up the highway. A southbound car exploded into my eyes and sped past with its horn blaring. Suddenly conscious, I realized I'd been running for some time. It was too dark to see my watch, but I could see the blinking light at the east entrance of Bear Mountain Bridge a mile away, and I knew it had been an hour, or more.

My body was winding down. My skin tingled, as if melting from the outside in. I pushed on to the top of the mountain road, and finally reached the blinking light as another northbound car came up from behind. But it didn't pass. It slowed, and came alongside me, matching my pace. Its ceiling light came on, and I glanced inside at an elderly couple. The woman rolled down her passenger window and the man peered out at me from behind the wheel. "What's the trouble?" he asked.

Then, the woman spoke. "You're Joe and Mary Gannon's boy…Tom!" I stopped, and their '39 Packard sedan pulled up next to me.

"Yes, Ma'am." I breathed heavily, with my hands on my hips, suddenly feeling the deep ache in my legs and back, and the numb pain in my right arm.

"What in hell 'er you doin'?" the man asked, sounding amused.

"Everett!" the woman whispered, scolding him.

"Better get in," he said, ignoring her. "We'll take you home."

I stared up the road into the darkness. "It's only about five miles more," I said. "I'm all right."

"Well, you don't look it," she said. Then, she opened her door, climbed out and pushed her seat forward. "You get in there, now."

The old man smiled. "Better do as she says, boy."

I got in, and collapsed in the back seat. As we started up the highway, they introduced themselves as Everett and Ann Thomson. They said they were old friends of the Wilsons, and said they'd known Father ever since he'd spent his first summers in the Highlands as a boy. I was surprised when they said they'd been to my parents' wedding.

"Your mother made the prettiest bride," Mrs. Thomson sighed, wistfully. "She's got those movie star looks, you know…and oh my…but your father loved her."

Mr. Thomson nodded in agreement.

"So, what happened?" I said.

"Happened?" she asked.

"Why haven't we met, before?"

There was a long silence. Finally, he answered me. "Had a bad argument with your grandfather…Hank."

"When was this?" I said.

"Oh…you were just a baby…"

"Over what?"

"Well…never mind about it," he said, with an edge in his voice.

Mrs. Thomson glanced at her husband. "You know, Tom," she said, "it made us heart sick when we heard…'bout your father bein'…lost an' such."

Abruptly, she stopped, and there was no more conversation. They didn't even press me about what I'd been doing out so late.

Minutes later, we reached the front of my family's property, and Mr. Thomson pulled over and stopped at the edge of the driveway. "Take care, now," he said, as I got out.

"Tell your mother we said 'hello,'" Mrs. Thomson added, getting back in.

"I will," I said. "You were kind to stop for me."

"Nonsense," she said. Then, she rolled up her window and their old Packard continued north.

I walked up the gravel drive to the darkened house, and used my key to get in through the front door. I stood at the edge of the living room, feeling relief and fear, looking up into the dark stairwell. I got ready to climb to the second floor, so I could look inside Liz's room, almost hoping I would find her safely asleep in her bed.

But then, I noticed the glow of the kitchen light around the dark edges of the hallway door, and my heart beat rapidly. I hurried through the dark living room to the hallway and pushed into the kitchen. There at the table, with his sleeves rolled to his elbows and a long hand of solitaire laid out before him, was Leonard. A pot of coffee warmed on the stove and a cup rested in front of him.

"Heard ya' come in," he said, with a glance. My eyes were drawn to the big, bulky pistol hanging in the shoulder holster against his left side. "Where's your sister?"

"She…she didn't come home, earlier?" I said, with one last, crazy hope.

He frowned and shook his head. "Thought she was with *you*…"

I glanced at my watch. I stepped to the sink and looked out the windows into the overpowering darkness. I poured a cup of coffee and sat down across the table from him. For a moment, I stared into the black liquid in the cup, and then I watched him laying down cards, working out his hand. Finally, I heard myself start to tell him what I'd have to tell my mother. But I realized he wasn't listening. He was staring past me. I turned and saw Mother, standing in the hallway door, waiting for me to finish.

When fire and police investigators examined the building rubble, early on Monday morning, they found Liz's body in the elevator, at the bottom of the collapsed shaft. She was quickly identified by the contents of her wallet, and a policeman immediately called the house. Mother answered in the kitchen. I hurried to the living room and picked up in time to hear the cop say that Liz hadn't been burned, that she'd been trapped inside the elevator car, and probably suffocated.

There was a pause, before Mother spoke. "And her body…it wasn't…"

"It's like she's asleep, Ma'am," the cop said. "Like she fell asleep." Then, I heard my mother sob as she dropped the phone. A moment later, I heard the back door slam.

It took until much later in the day for O'Leary's body to be discovered, burned almost beyond recognition. We learned this when the police called again and asked Mother to come down to the stationhouse to speak with investigators, and to make an official identification of Liz. After Arthur and Hazel arrived, without Laureen, Arthur drove Mother down to Peekskill. Hazel and Leonard sat with the children in the living room, watching television. I waited in the exile of my bedroom, staring at the ceiling.

I heard Mother and Arthur return several hours later. Before long, I was summoned downstairs and taken into Father's den. Arthur closed the door, and the three of us were alone in the little room. Mother stared in furious anger, as Arthur explained what the police had told them.

"Their theory is…Liz went to meet someone in the office building. They asked us who we thought that might have been." He paused and glanced at Mother. "Naturally, we said we had no idea…that we're shocked by the entire situation." He paused again. They both kept their eyes set firmly on me. "The police mentioned O'Leary's phone call…said he reported a break-in…said they don't have a name, but they're sure it's a male teenager…they're still looking for his body. Then…this Chief Walton…he asked your mother…whether her daughter was…"

"What?" I said.

"Having an affair," Arthur replied.

"With *who*?"

"Congressman O'Leary."

"That's enough, Arthur," Mother snapped.

"We got up and walked out on 'em, then," said Arthur. "Now, they're not saying what they really think. They tried to upset us…see what we'd say." He kept staring at me. "Are you sure he didn't get your name out, when you heard him make that call?"

"I'm pretty sure," I said. "What's the difference, now?"

Arthur sighed. "What were you thinkin', boy?" I reached into my pocket and pulled out the folded, crumpled pages of onion paper that I'd taken from

O'Leary's file. I handed it to him. "What's this?" he grumbled, as he unfolded the document and skimmed it.

"It's…it pretty much says everything," I said.

"You should look at this, Mary," he said.

"Later." She waved her hand and stared at me.

"I found a copy of their St. Nicholas Avenue bid," I added, "but I lost it during…I saw a file about Gerry Moran…he worked with O'Leary…for years…naming people as Reds, like they did to Dad…and there were other things…about a group Grandpa started…"

"*What* group?" Mother snapped.

"Some real estate investors…developers," I said, "who want to keep colored people out of the Highlands…as far away as possible." I looked at Arthur and at my mother. "I saw a lot of names I recognized…from church…friends of Grandpa's…you know the ones…from around Peekskill…*even* O'Leary. He and Grandpa weren't exactly strangers."

"This is…*unbelievable*," muttered Arthur, as he read the document.

"Grandpa thought he was getting a share of St. Nicholas Avenue from O'Leary and Stannard," I said. "*But*, he had to convince Dad to name Moran…and Arthur…as Communists." Arthur stopped reading and looked up. He and Mother stared at me, waiting for me to say something more. Tears welled in my eyes. "She was supposed to stay outside…on the street," I whispered. "She was supposed to be the lookout, and that's all…she should have waited there…"

"But she didn't…did she?" Mother said, glaring.

Arthur glanced at her and said, "she probably saw O'Leary go in. Maybe she saw the fire from the street…whatever it was…she knew Tom needed help…"

"Why did you do this?" Mother asked, pointing to the document in Arthur's hands. "It couldn't have been just…*for this*." She kept shaking her head in solemn disbelief. "Don't tell me you risked your sister's life…and your own…for this. Don't tell me that…because you couldn't possibly think any of this was important enough…that a *million* of these men were worth your sister's life."

I couldn't respond. How could I tell her that my reasons had been so much more selfish than that? The look on my mother's face said no answer would ever matter.

CHAPTER 26

By Wednesday, June 16th, the Highland papers were filled with accounts of the fire. Several papers said police were looking for "a third individual," who might explain the "mysterious circumstances" of a male and female body found at opposite ends of the rubble. But all of that seemed to exist in another world when we arrived at St. Mary's just before eleven for Liz's funeral, which Mother had decided to combine with Father's memorial service.

She'd gone ahead with Arthur and Hazel, so Leonard and I took Laureen and the children in the Buick. After I'd parked behind the church, we got out and stood for a moment in the dusty, crowded parking lot. The air was humid and warm, without sun. Laureen kissed me on the cheek, and then she and Leonard took the children inside, while I went to where the hearse was parked in front of the church. I waited there with Arthur, Jack Wilson, and Jimmy Pauling, as attendants pulled the casket from the hearse and placed it on the waiting carriage.

"It's Jeff Lloyd," Jimmy suddenly whispered, pointing to the tall, handsome young man approaching us from the parking lot.

Jeff had been the captain of our football team, two years earlier. He was at Georgetown, now, and already their varsity quarterback. I didn't know him very well, but I'd seen him play during his last season at St. Paul's, and he was a marvel of physical grace. Also an excellent student, he surely was on his way to a brilliant career in business or politics. But as he approached, dressed in a smart blue suit, his light brown hair neatly slicked back, I wondered why he would have come all the way from Washington.

He reached his hand out and smiled, as if we'd been best friends for years. "Tom," he said.

"Hello, Jeff," I replied, tentatively, noticing the fatigue lines in his handsome face, and the dark, bulges beneath his eyes. "Thanks for coming," I said. He frowned, shifting his feet awkwardly, before nodding to Jimmy. "Jeff Lloyd," I said, "these gentlemen are close friends of the family...Mr. Arthur Spencer..."

"Sir," said Jeff, extending his hand to Arthur.

"And Mr. Jack Wilson," I added.

"Pleased to meet you too, sir," Jeff said, shaking with Mr. Wilson. A moment later, Jeff folded his hands nervously in front of himself and said, "how can I help, Tom?"

"Well...we're about to go in..."

"I was a friend of Liz's," he blurted. "Did you know that?"

"No," I replied, as he nodded emphatically. "I'm sorry, Jeff. She never spoke of you."

Then, he smiled broadly and his handsome face shone like a sun. A tear fell from one eye, and he smeared it away with a hard wipe of his long fingers. "She was...a special person," he said.

An uncomfortable silence followed; then, I pointed to the casket. "You know what? *You* take *my* spot."

"Oh, no," he replied, nervously. "I didn't mean...I couldn't..."

"Go ahead, Jeff," I urged, stepping back. "Something tells me she'd want you to." Reluctantly, slowly, he moved toward Liz's casket and positioned himself at my corner. "Good," I said. "That's good."

Arthur nodded at me. And then we waited in the humid air, under the seamless gray sky. When it was time, they hoisted Liz's casket off the carriage and started into the church. I followed closely behind them, and as we moved slowly up the center aisle, I could see our pastor, Father Hanlon, waiting near the altar.

I glanced to the left and right at the packed congregation. A large group of Liz's friends and teachers from The Mount had come, and I could see them sitting together in shocked silence. Nearby sat Edith Neumann and Doris Dickinson. Elaine Wilson and Johnny were sitting with the Thomsons and another couple, a young man and a young black woman. Andy O'Leary Jr. and his mother sat near a large group of boys from St. Paul's. All the members of the track team were there, with Coach Bunning. Jimmy Pauling's mother, and many of the other mothers from school, had come. Georgie Keller and Penelope Potts sat with Georgie's parents, close to Father Stevens and a few other professors. Anne Drummond was there, too, several rows behind them. She seemed stunned. Father McHenry was even farther back. Sister Paul and Sister

Gertrude had come from St. Raphael's. And there were many people from Arthur's theater and real estate offices sitting with the St. Nicholas Development Corp. investors. They'd come in a chartered bus, organized by Arlene Baker, who sat with her head down and a white handkerchief pressed against her nose.

When we reached the end of the aisle, the casket was placed on the bier just outside the open altar railing. Father Hanlon thanked the pallbearers, and they went to their seats. I walked across the front of the church past Mother, and she stared straight ahead, as Arthur sat down beside her. Hazel was on Mother's right side. Then came the Rosenthals, Laureen, Isabel, Leonard, Mary and David. And at the very end of the first row, a space had been left for me. Father's parents and Mother's sat directly behind her, separated from each other by Donald and Grace Gannon. I saw some of my parents' old friends from Park Slope, as I reached the end of the front row and sat down. David's hand brushed mine briefly, as he struggled uncomfortably in the crowded pew. At last, his body grew still and he leaned with all his weight against my shoulder.

Father Hanlon finished praying at the casket, and then walked back inside the railing and stepped up into the wooden pulpit. He waited, as people coughed and sneezed and wept and scraped their shoes against the floor. Finally, he spoke.

"Man is terrified by death…the *unexpected* death of a noble daughter…the disappearance and presumed death of a good husband and father…both still very young…how can we hope to understand such things?" He paused and looked straight down at Mother. "Mary, we pray for your dear husband, Joe, and your daughter, Elizabeth. We pray for *some* understanding. Each person, here, offers this prayer…and surely Our Blessed Lord will not overlook these many voices." He paused again. The church was quiet, now. People seemed to be holding their breaths. "Christ tells us that each person follows his own path to the Father…Almighty God…and that we are all just pilgrims…that this life is only a journey. We know that Christ himself took the very journey that he asks of us. In his humanity, he traveled the path of earthly sorrow that ends in death…but his assurance is that we are reunited, at the journey's end. We must accept that, on this journey, some go ahead…leaving behind those they love and who love *them*. That their paths have crossed briefly with our own…is perhaps the closest thing we have to understanding the meaning…and purpose…of this journey. The memory of our departed loved ones is what we carry until *our own* journeys end. These memories do not diminish…they grow stronger with time, and remind us of an *eternal* life. Our prayers…affection…sympathy, are with you, Mary, and your children…Thomas, David and Mary. Let us pray for the strength that will help us acknowledge the pain in our hearts…we must accept this loss as part of the life that God has given us…and for which love is the only response…the only answer. We *must* love and continue to love…all living beings on this earth. If we do not…then we *are* lost, journeying in darkness…blind…dead…before our time. In the name of the Father and of the Son and of the Holy Ghost…"

"Amen!" the congregation thundered.

Father Hanlon then read a brief passage from the New Testament, the story of Lazarus. When he was finished, he closed the book, took a deep breath, and looked out onto the congregation. "Who speaks for Elizabeth and Joseph Gannon?" he asked.

I stood up and walked across the front aisle, through the railing, to the base of the pulpit. As the priest stepped down and made room for me, I climbed the wooden steps and looked out over the sea of silent faces. At the very back of the small church, I recognized a few show business people who were in trouble with the authorities, according to the newspapers. These must be the people that Arthur and Father and the Rosenthals had been trying to help, I thought. And as I stood there, I knew I would never question my father's judgement again about such things. If he believed these people deserved compassion, had been unfairly treated, then I would believe it, too. After all, if they were truly disloyal people, what impulse had brought them here this morning?

I fought back a sudden wave of dizziness and nausea, as the main door at the rear of the silent church opened and quickly closed again. Heads turned. It was April, standing nervously inside the door in a simple black summer dress. Standing with her was Martha Bradley, also in black. April looked at me briefly, and then walked with Martha along the rear aisle. They found seats, and heads turned toward the front again.

"My mother asked me to say something to you, about my sister and my father," I began. "There is…there's so much about them…even in their short lives…that would be worth knowing…that, it's difficult to find…to know…the right thing to say." I paused for a breath and to wipe sweat from my nose. "But, I'll try." I could see that my mother was sobbing, now, her body shaking, her ravaged face hidden behind her black veil. No longer numbed by anger, I began crying, too, and couldn't stop.

There were nervous murmurs around the church, and then commotion in the front pew. I looked down and saw Laureen, holding Isabel by the hand, struggling out of their seats into the center aisle. They stopped near the casket, and Laureen looked up at me for a moment. Then, she turned to face the confused congregation, and began to sing. Isabel immediately caught up to her, and their voices sang together.

> *This little light of mine, I'm gonna let it shine…*
> *This little light of mine, I'm gonna let it shine…*

A collective sigh seemed to lift the congregation as other voices joined in.

> *This little light of mine…*

Gradually they built to a thunderous wave.

> *I'm gonna let it shine…*

Even Father Hanlon started singing, as he stood near my sister's casket.

> *Let it shine, let it shine, let it shine.*

I stepped down from the pulpit and stood next to the priest. Now, from the back of the church, I heard an unmistakable voice. As the singer stepped out of his pew, and stood at the rear of the church clapping his massive hands, his great black smile beaming, his oceanic voice filled the room and thundered in the rafters.

> *Ev'ry where I go, I'm gonna let it shine…oh…*
> *Ev'ry where I go, I'm gonna let it shine*

Liz's casket was carried out to the hearse, and then the driver went ahead to the cemetery—in a clearing, a few hundred yards from the church, beyond a thin line of trees overlooking the valley. We followed, walking quietly past the parking lot, as two FBI men watched from their car and four policemen from Peekskill stood nearby.

We walked through the trees and into the clearing. From there we followed a simple, gravel path that wound through a maze of gravestones. Soon, we could see the hearse backed up with its rear door open, near the grave. The casket waited on the grass near a fresh pile of dirt.

It took a few minutes for everyone to reach the gravesite, and to gather in a silent semicircle. Then, Father Hanlon began the final prayers for Liz. Insects hummed in the humid air and birds thrummed quietly in the thick forest on the north end of the clearing. I prayed for my sister's forgiveness, and my father's, as a gust of wind rose from the river and faded. I prayed without hope.

As the priest prayed, I heard another car crunching into the parking lot back through the tree line. A moment later, a man got out, accompanied by two more policemen. The man spoke to one of the cops in the group near the FBI men. Something in the cops' body language suggested animosity toward him, and toward the cops who'd come with him. The man started through the trees and the two cops stayed right behind him. When they reached the edge of the clearing and saw our silent group standing around the grave, they stopped and watched. The man removed his hat and bowed his head, and suddenly, I realized he was the young bus driver, who'd been drunk at Coppie's Bar.

Father Hanlon finished his recitations, and then went to Mother and embraced her. He shook hands with Arthur and Hazel, paid his respects to my grandparents, and said some words to my brother and sister and Isabel and Laureen. As he nodded at me, I stepped away from the grave. Mourners began approaching the casket, pausing to say prayers of their own, or simply lowering their heads in silence before moving on. Many stopped to say something to Mother before heading back to their cars. The young bus driver started to leave, and I watched him walk unsteadily back through the tree line toward the parking lot, stumbling once, the two cops holding him up.

I saw Jeff Lloyd speak to Mother and then leave, after a final wave to me. As the Wilsons spoke to Mother, the Thomsons stood close by and glanced in my direction. The old couple seemed troubled, and they soon left with the Wilsons, and with the younger couple who'd been sitting next to them.

I noticed Miss Drummond standing with Father McHenry, talking seriously. Father Stevens saw them, too, and as he walked toward them, Miss Drummond turned to look. Suddenly, she shook her head and he stopped before reaching them. His body seemed to stiffen as she turned her back on him again. And as she continued talking with McHenry, the headmaster walked back toward the parking lot alone.

Mrs. O'Leary and Andy Jr. approached Mother, nervously. The women spoke quietly for a moment, as Andy looked on. Then, Mrs. O'Leary walked up to me with her son and stared into my eyes fiercely. "Tom...I just told your mother...and I want to tell you...I appreciate everything your family has tried to do for my Andy."

"Mrs. O'Leary..."

"You stood up for him in school," she replied, with determination. "Andy told me it was all a misunderstanding, but that doesn't change what you thought you were doing…for him. I'm just concerned there's been trouble made for the teacher over it." I nodded, as she continued. "I spoke to Father Stevens. He showed me that thing my son signed his name to…which my own husband made him sign…I was appalled." Andy lowered his head. "I told the headmaster, 'I won't allow my son's name to be used against Father McHenry.' He said he'd remove Andy's signature, if I wished, but…he's already fired Father McHenry…whatever did or didn't happen in history class that day was 'the least of it,' he said." She shook her head in disbelief.

"I'm sure Father McHenry appreciates it," I said.

"I felt so awful…especially after Andy told me how this teacher's been trying to help him. Were *you* aware of that?"

"No, Ma'am…not until recently." I looked at Andy and he looked back at me.

"Your father, too," she said.

"My *father*?"

"Yes," she said, with a sad, embarrassed bow of her head. "He…he confronted my husband, once…they almost came to blows." She turned her face and wept in shame.

"Mrs. O'Leary," I whispered, suddenly remembering the argument between her husband and my father, outside Wilson's

"Now…it's over," she said, turning back to look at me, taking a deep breath. "And I'm burying him. It'll be quiet, and private. And that'll be the end of it." Andy grabbed his mother's hand. "I'm just…I'm very sorry…for your losses," she muttered. And a moment later, they walked away.

Miss Drummond was speaking to my mother, now, and Father McHenry caught up with the O'Learys and headed toward the parking lot with them.

"We came to say goodbye, Tom," said Edith Neumann, suddenly standing close by with Doris. "Our station wagon's packed; we'll be heading for Maine."

"All right," I said. "I'm glad you came…"

"I've just told your mother that I won't be back at the house," Edith said. "We wanted *you* to know."

"We're very, very sorry," said Doris, reaching out her hand and holding my arm.

"But, we'll see you in the fall…right?"

They stared at me, silently. Then, Edith shook her head. "I've put my house up for sale, Tom…and I'm selling the shop…Doris has let her apartment go…"

"I don't understand," I said.

"I'm not coming back to school, next fall," said Doris. "They've asked me to leave."

"But why?" The women smiled at me, then. They seemed embarrassed to say what I instantly knew. "Oh…no."

Edith reached for my hand and said, "will you come see us, sometime?"

"I'd like that," I said. "Send me your address?"

She nodded, and said she would. Then, they turned and walked away together.

Allen and Esther Rosenthal finished talking to Mother and approached me. Esther put her hand on my shoulder and leaned forward to kiss me on the cheek. "I'm sorry, Tom," she said, as she stepped back. I smiled feebly and nodded.

Allen seemed deeply troubled, even angry. Suddenly, he lunged at me and wrapped his arms around me in a hard embrace. As he held me close, he whispered in my ear. "What did you do?" I was dumbstruck. I could hardly breathe, as he squeezed me. "We would have found whatever we needed," he whispered, harshly. "You didn't have to do that." Finally, abruptly, he stepped back, but kept his hands gripped on my shoulders, as he looked into my eyes and shook me. "You stupid kid."

Then, he lowered his head and sighed. As he released his grip on me, his body seemed to slump. He turned and walked toward the parking lot with his head down. Esther lingered, and touched my shoulder again, briefly, before following her husband back across the clearing.

More and more people drifted away from my sister's grave. Only a few were left, now, to pay their respects and say something to my mother.

"Are you all right?" asked Arthur.

"Don't worry about me," I sighed. He frowned. "Arthur, tell me something…do you know that old couple who came with the Wilsons? Their name is Thomson."

He nodded. "I've met them…I know who they are. Their family's lived up here for generations," he said. "They sold your grandfather the property in Garrison, back in the late 'Twenties."

"Oh?" I muttered, as Arthur nodded. "And that *other* couple with them?" I asked. "The young man and the…*colored* woman?"

He smiled, and nodded again. "That fella's the Thomsons' son…their youngest, I believe…the woman's *his* wife. Why?"

"No reason…just curious. They seem like…nice people."

Arthur nodded. "We'll be waiting…at the cars," he said. Then, he started back toward the parking lot with Hazel and Laureen.

I turned once more toward my family, gathered at my sister's grave. April and Martha approached Mother. I couldn't hear them, but my mother treated them warmly, grabbing April's hands. When they finished speaking, April turned to face me. Father Hanlon put his hand on Mother's wrist—a silent urging for her to leave. April kept staring at me. Martha stood with her and stared at me, too. It was clear that April had been crying, but not even this could keep me from walking away.

At about three-thirty, I descended the hill behind the house in the warm overcast. Many mourners had come and gone, and several were still inside the house with Mother, but I needed to get away. I walked into the trees above the river, stepping over fallen logs, moving through the thick undergrowth along the path my father always took when he came down to swim. I reached open space on the last small rise, where the pitch was steep and covered in tangled onion grass. With a final leap to the base of the mountain, I stood in the cinders near the railroad tracks. I crossed over the rails and walked onto the giant rocks and boulders below the track bed. Just beyond the rocks, the river lapped against the muddy shoreline in casual waves.

I sat on a giant boulder and prayed again for my father and my sister. An oil tanker's horn moaned somewhere up the valley, and its sound passed over the river like a whisper in the sunless heat. The river was full of whispers. It overflowed with them. Each wave that lapped at the mud beneath my feet was another whisper escaping into the sullen air.

"Tom." I looked up at the water. "Tom!" The voice called out again, insistently. I turned and saw April standing on the rise above the tracks. The onion grass covered her feet, and her black linen dress clung to the perspiration on her stomach and her thighs. She held her shoes in her right hand. She reached out her left hand. "Won't you help me down?" I turned away from her again and looked out over the water. "I'll come to *you*, then."

"Oh, fuck," I muttered, as I got up from the rock and walked angrily back over the tracks and stood in the cinders below her. I reached up and held her hand, as she slid down the onion grass on her bare feet, and landed softly against me. I stepped back and walked across the tracks again. She followed, stepping gingerly over the cinders and rocks. I sat down on the boulder, and she sat next to me with her feet out in the shallow water.

"You're so angry with me," she said, staring at the river. I nodded, silently, and she sighed heavily. "Are you really as perfect as all this, then?"

"Far from it," I said, angrily. "Listen…I'm in no mood for lectures, right now. My family's been through a lot."

"I know…"

"*What* do you know?" I snapped. "Can you even admit to yourself what *your* father's been doing to people?" She looked away from me, and stared down river. "The misery and the pain he's caused? For what…power…more money? And the thugs and creeps he consorts with? It's corrupt, April…I can't even begin to tell you the things I've learned about him…and it doesn't matter how many mansions and gardens and butlers and lawn parties there are…"

"All right, now, *you* listen," she said fiercely. "Those are things *you* seem to pay an awful lot of attention to."

"Oh…excuse me," I said, with sarcasm. "I get it."

"Do you?"

"Yeah. I do."

"It's about time, then. If you understood *anything*, you'd know that whatever my family is…is mine. Leave them to me…"

"Then leave *mine* to me," I said. "What's left of it…and leave *me* alone…"

"No…I won't. I won't allow you to do this so…dishonestly."

"*Allow* me?" I said, laughing bitterly.

"So, you've discovered there's evil in the world…and it's close by…"

"I discovered that long before I met you…"

"Fine. And what are you going to about it? Sit here and cry?"

I looked down into the shallow water at our feet. Suddenly, my anger seemed to elude me. I tried holding onto it, but I couldn't. "I don't know," I muttered.

"But you're *quite* sure of what *I* should do," she said. "Go ahead…tell me…what am I supposed to do, Tom?"

Finally, I looked up into her green eyes. "Tell your father you know what he is…*who* he is…what it's cost my family…and many others."

"And what makes you think I haven't done that already?"

I looked away again, but I felt her hand reach for mine and hold it, tightly, squeezing it, pressing it against the rock on which we sat, until I could feel her pulse beating, steady as the tide.

An hour later, we climbed over the tracks and up onto the onion grass rise, and then we walked slowly back toward the house. Halfway to the top of the hill, I saw Laureen standing on the porch, looking down the lawn at us. I waved. For a moment she stared, silently, and then she turned away and went into the house. The screen door slammed behind her.

I walked April to her small white, Italian sports car, which was parked below the front porch. She looked at me and said, "it feels like...we have to start all over again." Then, she got in the car, started the engine, and rolled down her window. I bent down and kissed her. "Will you call me soon?" she asked. I nodded.

She put the car in gear and drove out to the highway. She put her hand out the window in a brief, tentative wave, as she turned south. Then, I looked around and noticed that most of our visitors had finally left. It was almost five o'clock.

I turned toward the house and saw Mother watching me from the living room window beneath the porch. Her expression was blank. I hurried up the front steps and through the door, but when I got inside she wasn't there. I stood in the living room and peered down the hall into the kitchen, but saw only Grandfather Hank sitting with his back to me, a half-bottle of whisky on the table near him.

Suddenly, he muttered. "It's *your* fault, as much as *mine*." I could see no one else in the kitchen with him, but he kept talking. "If *you* hadn't taken him on those goddamn visits, when he was a boy...all that goddamn social work...takin' my son to those hovels in Manhattan...for what...to show him the poor downtrodden...wastin' their lives?" His voice was bitter. "It's *you* filled his head with foolishness...made him believe he's responsible for everyone *else* in the world."

"You horrible man...you poor, wretched excuse of a man." Now, Grandmother Libby walked into view, and stood over him at the table. She looked down at him with a stern expression and said, "this is the end of it, then."

"Agh!" he growled, reaching for the bottle and putting it to his lips.

Grandmother shook her head and walked to the sink. Standing there, with her back to her husband, she stared out the windows. "I want you out."

"What's 'at?" he muttered, angrily.

"You heard what I said, now. I won't be under the same roof with you again."

"You don't know what you're sayin', woman...besides...the church don't allow it..."

"You'll go back to Brooklyn by yourself..."

"And where will *you* go?"

"Never mind me...I'll stay with Mary...and the children. They can use my help...you've done enough."

"How many times must I explain this to ya'?" he pleaded. "Did ya' think I wanted *this* ta' happen..."

"There's nothing more to be said. You pack your bags...or I'll pack mine...it doesn't matter which." Then, without looking at him, she walked to the back door and stepped outside. I heard the door slam behind her.

"Libby!" he called. But there was only silence. He reached for the bottle again and held it to his lips, gulping feverishly until finally, gasping, he thrust the bottle down on the table. For a moment he sat there, rigid. Then slowly, his body began to shake and his head drooped, and as he shook violently, he fell forward onto the table with his arms slung out in front of him. His head lay on the tabletop, now, and he was crying.

I felt a hand on my arm. It was David. "Hey," I whispered, as he pulled me toward him.

"Mom's lookin' for you," he said, gravely.

"She is?" He nodded, with a morose frown. "What's the matter, buddy?"

"They're in the den," he replied, blankly. "They said they want you, right away." Then, he looked into my eyes with great concern.

"Have you seen Laureen?" I asked.

"She's up in Liz's room...Mom said she could have Liz's records. Isabel's up there with her...Mary too." Then, he turned away and went out through the screen door onto the porch.

I walked to the den and found Mother standing with Arthur and Leonard, next to my father's desk. Phillip and Alice Brent sat on the couch with Hazel.

"Close the door," Mother said. "Sit down." I sat in the big armchair near the door, and I could feel all the eyes in the room staring hard. "We've just had a call from your friend," Mother said, "Agent Valeriani." I was surprised. "He called to warn us...the Peekskill Police have a warrant for your arrest...for the murder of Andrew O'Leary."

I nodded. "Did he say when they're coming?"

"Probably tonight," said Arthur.

I nodded again, as Mother spoke sternly. "He thinks they have very little evidence. Even if you'd left any fingerprints, they'd be hard to find in that burned out rubble. Apparently, somebody saw you and your sister in town before the fire, and again later...leaving the burning building." I nodded. "Valeriani said the police figured the rest of it out...they'll *try* to make it stick, anyway."

"We can fight this, Mary," said Arthur, "no matter what the cost…"

"There'll be no discussion of cost," interjected Grandfather Phil.

"We'll get the best lawyers," Arthur agreed. "And private investigators…we'll organize a campaign with the newspapers…elected officials…we'll find a way to fight this…it won't stand…"

"How long will this take?" asked Grandmother Alice.

"Can you guarantee we'll *win*?" Mother added, in an ominous voice.

At first, there was no response. Then, tentatively, Arthur said, "there's *another* way to deal with it." Everyone listened. "I could make…arrangements…to get Tom out of the country…"

"My god," muttered Grandmother Alice.

Mother stared at me as Arthur continued. "I can have him taken to Canada, and then Europe…France is probably best…extradition would be difficult…"

"You wouldn't seriously consider this, Mary," said Grandmother Alice.

Mother stared at her for a moment. Then, she spoke to Arthur. "How far would he get before being stopped? The roads are probably being watched."

"Mary…I'm not talking about *driving* him to Canada," Arthur said. "I can have a fast boat come and get him, right down in back. I can have it here in an hour…maybe two." Arthur glanced at Leonard, who nodded in agreement. "I'll have people with him all the way…to ensure his safety…and money…and a place to stay arranged in Europe. *Then,* we can worry about these charges…they just won't have Tom in jail, while we fight them over it."

The room was silent, as the reality of what was being discussed settled in on everyone. It was an outrageous idea, and I didn't know what to think about it, but it hardly mattered. Whether I stayed or left, my life was over. I'd already accepted that, welcomed it. I looked at the confused faces of my family, and could see that even these earnest adults didn't know what the right thing was to do. Finally, I decided to let one person in the world make this choice. I looked at my mother. "What do *you* think?" I asked. "Tell me what to do."

She breathed in, deeply, and looked around at the others. "I've given enough of my family to this thing," she said, as her parents hung their heads. "I'll give no more."

I finished packing the one small bag that Arthur told me I could carry. I looked around the bedroom, and David watched me from the edge of his bed.

"You know any French?" he said.

Suddenly, I couldn't help laughing. Then he started to laugh. I noticed the history books piled neatly next to the dresser. Pointing to them, I said, "could you help Mom take those back to St. Paul's for me?"

"Yeah," he muttered.

"Thanks, buddy," I smiled, just as Grandmother Libby appeared in the doorway. "How's…how is Grandpa?" I asked, as she walked in.

"Sleeping it off," she said. "I've called Grace and Donald…told them to come back and get him…take him to Brooklyn."

"I'm sorry, Grandma…"

"No, no," she said, waving her hand. "None o' that, now. I want to give you something…to take with you…and I want you to keep it. Never let it go…no matter what happens."

"What is it?" I asked.

She handed me a white business envelope. "I've had this for two years, now," she said, as I opened the envelope and looked inside. I saw a newspaper clipping, neatly folded. "Few things ever made me so proud as this," she added, pointing to the envelope. I removed the clipping and unfolded it. And I smiled when I saw it was the *New York Times* story, about Father's court victory in the Harlem theater project. The photograph next to the article was almost as I'd remembered. It showed him smiling—but somehow younger looking than in my memory—a boyishly happy smile. Arthur hugged him tightly with one arm, and they both seemed to be laughing, as if someone had just said something that couldn't have been funnier. And the other Harlem businessmen who'd been in on the deal stood bunched together with them. You could see the bright future in their smiles. "It's my only copy," she said. "Take care of it."

"I will," I promised, looking once more at my father, and then folding the clipping and putting it safely back in the envelope. She kissed me hard on the cheek. Then, she turned and walked out quickly.

I opened my bag and slid the envelope down to the very bottom where it would stay flat and protected, beneath the soft weight of my clothes. I zipped up the bag, and then David and I left our bedroom and started down the stairs. On the second floor, I looked into Liz's room one last time. Laureen was sitting on Liz's bed, with record albums strewn across the coverlet. Isabel sat at the foot of the bed with Mary.

I looked at David and held up my bag. "Would you take this down for me?"

"Sure," he said.

And as he headed down, I looked at Laureen again and walked into the room. "Everything's so rushed," I said, tentatively. "I didn't want to leave, without saying…something…"

"I know," she said.

"Laureen, I'm sorry…I…love you…"

"Like a sister," she frowned. "I know." She pushed some of the albums down toward the foot of the bed, and patted her hand on the space she'd made. "Can you sit…for a minute?"

I walked to the edge of the bed and sat. "I can still feel her," I said, breathing in deeply, looking around the room. Laureen nodded. I glanced at Isabel and Mary and struggled for words. "I don't know what came over me, Laureen, but I…"

She put her hand out quickly and covered by mouth. "It's *my* fault," she said, "not yours."

"It's *nobody's* fault," I said.

"I know what you want, Tom. You *love* her."

"Well…I don't know…"

"Of course you do. Anyone can see it. It's not *her* fault what her parents are. Give her a chance to be who she is." She paused for a moment. "Will you write to me…when it's safe?" I nodded. "My father will know when."

"Take care of yourself," I said, leaning forward and kissing her cheek.

"You too."

"Be good to your parents," I said. "They worry about you."

Suddenly, she stopped smiling and looked behind me. I turned and saw Arthur standing in the bedroom doorway.

"It's time, son," he said. "You have to hurry now." Moments later, as we all walked down the hill behind the house, Arthur gave me his last directions. "Here…take this." He handed me a tightly packed brown envelope. "There's three thousand dollars in there. When you get to France, you can change some for *francs*, at almost any bank or currency dealer. Change a little at a time…don't attract attention to yourself. In a month or two, if you're still there, your Grandfather Phil will wire you another three thousand. Now, here's the address of a small, out of the way hotel, where you're already booked." He handed me a folded piece of paper. "It's in Paris…it's what they call a *pension de famille*…a boarding house…you can stay there, indefinitely."

"Arthur, I've made so many mistakes…is this *another* one?"

"If you're gonna start all that…I'm gonna get angry," he groused. "Now listen. There'll be two men on the boat with you, besides the captain. They'll take you as far as they can by water. Then, a car will meet you to take you the rest of the way, over the Canadian border, somewhere up toward Nova Scotia. From there, you'll take another ship…a tanker…to Le Havre…on the English Channel side. The men will leave you there, and come back. You'll be on your own, then. You'll have to get to Paris from there yourself. There are trains, or, you might get one of the bateaux that go up and down the Seine between Le Havre and Paris. In that envelope, you'll find a passport and a map and a dictionary, and some directions…information about boats and trains."

"All right."

"Now don't try to contact us," he said. "*Any* of us…or anyone else…do you hear?"

"Yes."

"We know where you are…we have the address and phone number…*we'll* contact *you*, when we think it's safe."

"I understand."

We were through the tree line now, gathered together on the onion grass rise above the tracks. In the shallows of the river, just beyond the rocks, a long wooden powerboat puttered. There were two young black men standing on the rocks, waiting for me. An older black man stood behind the wheel, watching us, keeping the boat near shore.

Arthur grabbed me and held me tightly. Then, he stepped back and I turned to my mother. We hugged.

"Be careful," she said. "We'll work to get you back as soon as we can." I nodded.

I hugged the Brents, then, and Grandmother Libby. I kissed Isabel goodbye, and Laureen, and little Mary. Even Leonard hugged me. Suddenly, I looked at Mother and said, "where's David? I don't see David."

"He's upset that you're leaving," she said. "He stayed up at the house."

"Oh, no," I said, turning to Arthur. "Do I have time to go back up and…say goodbye?"

"'Fraid not, Tom," he said, grimly. "You gotta shove off."

I looked at the people gathered with me on the rise. "I love you," I said. "Tell David he gets my first letter." Then I jumped down to the cinders, and walked quickly over the tracks and the rocks. With the help of the two young men, I jumped onto the boat deck. It was seven o'clock, the end of a sunless day. "Can I stay on deck?" I asked the young men.

"As far as Albany," one said. "We get to Albany, you go below."

"All right."

The captain shoved off and the engine growled as the boat swerved and edged out into the darkening river. I stood on deck and waved to my family and our friends, as they waved back from the rise above the tracks. Fifty yards from shore and heading upriver, I could still see everyone waving from the rise. On top of the hill far above them, the windows of our house glowed in the gathering dusk. Suddenly, I saw someone running along the shoreline, keeping pace with the boat. "Tom! Tom!" It was David, running along the water's edge, calling out to me. "Tom! Be careful, Tom!"

And then, briefly, the sun dipped below the cloud line on the western horizon far beyond the cliffs, and rays of gold light appeared over the river. I could see everybody, still waving, a hundred yards away now, standing in the beautiful, unexpected sunlight. And on the shoreline, David had stopped running. He was standing with his right hand shading his eyes against the golden glare, and his left hand stretched high above his head.

CHAPTER 27

This house was built for summer. Its autumn chill has crept overnight into my aging knees, and the living room seems so much smaller than my memory of it. The furniture is new and differently arranged though there's still a telephone near the front door. And a wide-screen television that our son, Joe, installed for Mother fills the corner, where the old black and white used to sit. But I resist the impulse to switch the thing on just to feel connected. This morning, I'd prefer the phone to ring.

I gaze out the porch windows and see a figure moving across the north side of the property in dreary rain—a man, carrying something that looks like rolled white paper, almost three feet long. He cradles it against his chest and leans forward, as if protecting it from the encompassing weather. I look at my watch. It's only eight o'clock.

I open the front door and step out onto the porch. The cold September rain pours over the edge of the roof and clatters down onto the runny gravel below, and the figure coming toward the house wears a shabby Marine-issue overcoat and an old, blue baseball cap.

"Johnny?" I call out. "John Wilson…is that you?"

He stops and stares up at me from thirty yards away. "Tom?"

"Come on up here…get out of that rain!"

He smiles and walks quickly the rest of the way to the house, jumping over the larger puddles and stepping up on the porch. As we shake hands, I look into the leathery face of a man in his fifties, who was a boy when I saw him last.

"Christ," he says, "this is some storm."

"Will you come inside and get dry?"

He shakes his head. "Can't stay long…gotta get to the VA…they're still fiddling with this thing." He points to his right eye, which is glass. "I'm sorry…I won't be at the church, today…"

"It's all right, John. Still having trouble with the eye?"

He nods. "Thirty years and eleven operations later…they never rebuilt the socket right…keeps getting infected…damn thing falls out." He shrugs, and laughs ruefully. "Should've gone with the black patch…whadya' think?"

"Like the Hathaway Shirt man," I say.

"I guess," he says, holding up the white object he'd been carrying. "These are for your mom…magnolias…"

"Really? How'd you get them?"

"From Japan…that's where they grow this time o' year…in hothouses…got 'em over the Internet…amazing, huh? Thought I was outta luck…but they came into JFK yesterday, before they shut it down again. Oh…and they're white…"

"Her favorites," I say, taking the package from him.

"Yeah. So…this is the first you're back…"

"Since my sister's funeral," I nod. "Haven't been…able to…legally…"

"Yeah," he shivers.

"I was about to make some coffee…won't you come in?"

"Naw…thanks though…"

"Did you walk through the woods?"

"Sure…only takes about a half-hour…you *must* remember *that* at least…"

"Of course I do, John…but…I mean…the rain,,,"

"Yeah, well…car's in the shop. Damn roads around here still don't have enough lights on 'em. Got a little close to the shoulder the other night…nipped a tree. So…you been livin' in France…"

"Paris…yes…"

"Yeah…your mom always got real excited when she went over ta' see you…and your kids." I smile and nod. "You know, *my* parents passed away a few years ago," he adds.

"Mom told us…I'm sorry, John…"

"Thanks," he sighs. "Anyway…"

I touch his forearm briefly. "Is there any way we can help?"

"With *what*?" he says, with an irritated frown. "Oh. You mean drinkin'." I stare at him and he turns away, looks out under the porch roof toward the back of the house. The rain falls steadily. He's thinking hard about something.

"So…your mom told you about that, too," he mutters, before turning to look at me again. "Don't worry about it."

I hold up the wrapped flowers and say, "*this* is very nice."

He takes a deep breath. "You know…she called me almost every day."

"Really?" I smile.

"Yeah…she'd invite me over…have me sit here on the porch with her…or we'd go inside if the weather was lousy…and she'd always make tea." He laughs and I smile. "Yeah, tea," he says, "and she'd sit an' talk with me. She'd always ask…you know, 'how are you *feeling*, John?' An' I always knew what she meant…drinking or whatever…but she'd never say it. I guess she figured I knew what she meant."

"I'm sorry, John…it's none of my business…"

"She loved to talk about the old days, too…when you all moved in here." I smile, ruefully, at the painful memory. "My dad knew your dad from when they were kids, I know," he says. "But your mom would always say how welcome my folks made you feel in those days."

"It's true…that's how we *all* felt…"

"So anyway, we'd have our tea, and sometimes we'd watch the TV…you know…the stock market channels…the Mets…the Yankees…Oprah…your mom loved Oprah." I laugh. "Or talk," he says. "Mostly, we'd talk…about anything…even 'Nam…she wasn't upset by it like *my* mom was…she knew a lot, your mom…a lot more than most women generally know about war…"

"More than most *men*, probably…"

"Maybe so…all I know is, I told *her* some things I'd never told anyone, not even my *own* father n' mother…like that Vietnamese kid, who stabbed me in the eye. How I had to kill him…with my bare hands, when he jumped in my bunker that night, and my weapon jammed…we struggled, ya' know…and…while I'm wringin' his neck…he knifes me. The tighter I squeezed his throat, the more he turned that knife in my head…broke all the bones around the eye. Jesus, I thought he'd never die. I told your mom all about that. It never fazed her…"

"Well, she probably heard a lot of things from my father," I say, "about Guadalcanal."

"I guess. *My* dad had his *own* stories…from Bataan. I know for a *fact*, he told my *mom* about it. But she just didn't want to hear any o' *my* story. I could tell…so I just clammed up or whatever. My *dad* asked me to tell him about it, once. I started…but I could see how angry he was getting…upset…ya' know. I never brought it up again."

"Did you *want* to talk about it?"

"Would've been nice...if they *tried* to listen or whatever...they just couldn't..."

"You were their son, John." He presses his lips together. "How about the VA?" I ask. "Other vets? They have discussion groups, don't they?"

"Yeah...group therapy..."

"How *is* that?"

"Awright. It's just...I don't know...you have to like that sorta thing, I guess. I mean...these are the things that happened when I was over there...and this is how I felt about it. That's all I wanna say...but they make it seem like you're crazy...I mean...these *are* the things that happened...I didn't make 'em up, for chrissake. Ya' know?" I nod. "It's ancient history now, anyway. Who cares? I'm just saying...your mom was easy to talk to...she had a special way...great woman. That's my verdict, anyway."

"Mine too, John. So...what are you doing these days?"

"Oh...little o' this...little o' that. I tend bar a few nights a week...in Beacon...still do some landscaping in the summer time. I work with a guy's got his own truck an' all...we do awright...I don't need much...house is free n' clear...I get the government allotment for the wound...and when the eye falls out, the VA puts it back. What else do I need?" We laugh together for a moment. "You been teaching, right? That's what your mom said..."

"That's right, John...in Paris, mostly...a little bit in London, too..."

"College, right?"

"Yes."

"Yeah...you kids...you were always smart..."

"Well...I don't know..."

"I'm sorry I didn't do better in school...but...well...I kinda lost interest if I'm honest. It was tough when I got back from 'Nam...that was 'Sixty-nine...I know you weren't here, but you prob'ly read stuff in the papers...things were bad here, then...people were crazy. I'd done *two* tours in 'Nam." He points to his glass eye. "This happened on the second tour. Then, I spent almost a year in a Marine hospital in San Diego. So finally I come home, and one day I go downtown...Cold Spring...to have a beer...I'm wearing my uniform...and this kid with long hair and some girl he's got hangin' all over 'im...college kids or whatever...they're comin' up the street. And they just keep starin' at me, so I say 'hello' and they stop, and the kid looks at me for a second. Says...'what're *you* lookin' at, you murderin' pig'...and the girl...she spits at me..."

"Christ."

"Right on Main Street…near my pop's old store…it's a Starbucks, now. Bet you didn't know that."

"No."

"Yeah…anyway…I was shocked, I'll tell ya'. I said to myself, 'if that's what they're teachin' kids in college these days, I don't need it.'"

"What did you do?"

"What was I supposed to do?" he snorts. "Fight the kid? Come on." He frowns sarcastically. "You must've seen that anti-war business…even in the Paris papers."

"Yes…there were big demonstrations *there*…in 'Sixty-eight…"

"Yeah. Well, I might've even agreed with that kid by the time I came home…about the war an' all. I'm still not sure we shoulda been over there…but you know…the government asked us to go…so we went…thinkin' it was the right thing…what people wanted. But…I guess they weren't really sure. I say they shouldn't a' sent us, if they weren't sure." I nod. "One thing I *do* know," he says, "they shouldn't a' *blamed us*…they shouldn't a' spit at us, Tom. We were just kids, ourselves…am I right?"

"You're right."

He sighs and looks out over the rain swept landscape. "So, listen…I better get going…"

"Do you need a ride to the VA?" I ask, as he smiles and shakes his head. "There'll be plenty of cars here, later," I add. "You're welcome to use one."

"I'm fine thanks, Tom…a buddy's gonna pick me up. You gonna be around long?"

"A few days…I have to speak with my brother and sister about the will…decide what to do with this house."

He nods. "Doesn't your wife's family have a place across the river, too?"

"They used to," I say. "After her father died, her mother signed the property over to the State…for back taxes…she moved to Newport…died a few years ago. Bob Moses turned the place into a golf course…"

"Oh, now I remember…Highland View State Park…"

I nod. "We stayed *here*, last night. Got in from Paris on Monday, and we'd *been* staying at a hotel in the city…but our reservation was only through Wednesday. And…after…what happened Tuesday morning…all the hotels were suddenly booked solid…we couldn't extend our stay. They kicked us out of the room yesterday, and we couldn't get another…anywhere. So here we are. It's pretty confusing being here…after so long…"

"Yeah," he says. "And Christ...what a time to come back. Did you know anybody in those buildings?"

"No," I say.

"They say people are still stranded...all over the country...all over the world...most of the flights are cancelled...I read there's a lotta people still haven't heard from family members...and friends...even now."

I nod. "Our youngest daughter...Lizzie...we haven't heard from *her*, since Sunday."

"Where is she?"

"Africa," I say, and he looks confused. "She's a doctor," I explain. "She's been working in northern Rwanda...there's been terrible fighting there again. And AIDs..."

"Jeez."

"We spoke with her before we left Paris...we told her Mom wasn't doing too well...just 'a matter of days,' the hospital said. So, she was supposed to catch a flight on Tuesday morning and be here Wednesday night. We haven't heard from her...we've called her cell phone over and over...we can't get through."

"Oh, Tom, I'm sorry. There haven't been any hijackings over *there*...have there been?"

"None that we know of. It's just pretty dangerous where she is...you know? I wish we'd hear from her...she has the phone number here. And *our* cell phone number...we don't even know if she made it to the airport..."

"Well...I'm sure she'll be awright. You'll hear from her." I nod at his kindness. "I'll say some extra prayers today," he adds.

I thank him again and we shake hands. He walks down the porch steps onto the flooded gravel and starts back across our property. Once or twice, with his hands in the pockets of his overcoat, he looks up into the nothingness of rain and sky. I watch him until he disappears into the woods. Then, I step back inside the house and shut the door behind me.

"Darling? Who was that?" My wife is calling from the bedroom, where my parents once slept.

"The Wilsons' son...Johnny...*John*! He brought magnolias for Mother!" My wife is walking out of the bedroom and coming along the hallway toward the living room. I hold up the wrapped flowers. "See?"

"That's awfully nice," she says, kissing me. "Any calls?" I shake my head. She grabs my hand. "Let's make coffee."

We'll be riding to church with our son, Joe, and his son, Hank. Joe's 34 now and Hank is five. Joe and his wife, Wendy, work for the same law firm in Manhattan, and they have a rambling waterfront home in Old Greenwich, Connecticut. Wendy is a beautiful Chinese-American girl from San Francisco. She was with a client in Palo Alto when the planes stopped flying on Tuesday, and she's still there, now, waiting for the airport to open.

Our middle daughter, Alice Mary, is five years older than Joe. She's a software developer and lives in Burlington, Vermont. She'll be coming today without her husband, Bob, whose absence has nothing to do with airports. They've been having some trouble lately. Alice Mary and our oldest, Connie, a sculptor who lives alone in Lenox, Massachusetts, drove to Boston yesterday. They stayed last night at Isabel's apartment in Cambridge, and they'll all drive down to the church together this morning.

My brother and sister, and their families, are driving up from their homes on Long Island to meet us here at the house.

"It's still raining pretty hard," Joe says, peering out the living room windows. "You and Mom better take my umbrella."

Smiling at my son's chivalry, I ask, "where's Hank?"

"In the car. Come on out, whenever Mom's ready." Then he opens the front door and steps outside, but leaves the door ajar. I hear familiar voices now. I look out and see Joe, standing next to David's car, telling him something. David's wife, Penny, sits quietly beside my brother. Their three children sit behind them and listen. I can see Mary and her husband, Irv, and their son, in the car behind David's. Irv has his window down and his head is out, so he can hear what the other men are saying. The idling cars exude trails of blue exhaust.

I turn from the door and call to April. "My brother and sister are here! Joe's ready to go!"

She calls back faintly from the bedroom. "What about the girls?"

"They'll meet us at church!"

"They know how to get there?"

"Of course! Yes...I gave Alice Mary the directions again last night!"

A moment later, April comes to the living room. She holds Mother's magnolias in one arm. I grab her other hand and we step out and close the door behind us. I hold the umbrella over her and we hurry down the porch steps. "Watch the puddle," I say, as we head toward Joe's Lexus. I wave to my brother and sister and their spouses. They all wave back. Joe is already at the wheel of his car and his son is sitting, quietly, next to him. I hold the umbrella up, as

April gets in the back seat with the flowers. I follow her in but I keep my arms extended, shaking the dripping umbrella outside the door.

"Here…gimme that," Joe says, as he pops the trunk and jumps out of his seat. He grabs the wet umbrella and throws it into the trunk, as I pull my door shut.

As Joe jumps in behind the wheel again, Hank turns to us and says, "ready Grandpa?"

"Ready, Teddy," I say, to make him laugh.

"Ready, ready Teddy…ah' ma' ready Teddy," he sings. "Ready, ready, ready to…rock n' roll, yeah!"

"Who taught him that?" his father mutters, as he puts the car in gear and we start.

"Who do you think?" April sighs, with a brief smile at me. Then, with the magnolias cradled on her lap, she stares out the window to her right. I reach for her hand and feel the elegant bones and the finger tendons flexing, and her pulse ticking like a clock. I feel that I'm waking from a dream, as if forty-seven years have not passed, and we're still sitting together in silence on a boulder near the river, with our damaged lives still to be lived.

She'd come looking for me when a week had passed and I hadn't called her. She pleaded with my mother to know where I was, and Mother promised to help her contact me when it was safe. But the situation remained difficult throughout that summer.

Arthur and Grandfather Phil worked diligently, but even with their money and influential friends, they failed to attract support for my case, or to change the authorities' focus on it. Mother had never wanted to involve Isabel in murder accusations against O'Leary. And then, the strangest of ironies had occurred. I was accused of murdering *him*—and our only real defense, that O'Leary had murdered my father, was no defense at all. It was a motive that would make the case against me. Agent Valeriani had been our only good source of information inside the investigation, and so in August, when we learned he'd been fired, it was clear that I wouldn't be coming home any time soon. Mother arranged to have me finish school in Paris that fall.

April's first letter got through to me in late October, but it said that she wouldn't be in Paris for several more months, because there were "certain details" she needed to address. When she finally arrived, just before Christmas, there was something different about her. The second she stepped off the plane at Orly, I could see it. It was an unseasonably warm day and she wore a gray suit and white gloves, but no hat. Her golden hair was long again, and she was a beautiful woman.

We got a table in the airport café, and she told me that she'd turned eighteen in November and was now "independent." She used that word, and even her voice seemed different. She said that her inheritance had become effective and irrevocable. There'd been a terrible argument with her parents, and even threats of disinheritance from her mother, but April's own attorneys had put a stop to that talk.

"So," she said, as she reached her hand across the table toward me. "Here I am."

We sat in the café and talked for hours about the future, as if we could see what it would be. I told her that whatever else happened, I needed to live my life in my sister's memory and in my father's. She answered this by squeezing my hand. And then we went back to my *pension*.

For the next two years, we lived in separate apartments on the same street. She enrolled at L'Ecole Nationale to study painting, and I was admitted for the literature degree at the University of Paris with a recommendation from Father McHenry, who'd gotten a teaching position there. During my third year at the university, we discovered that April was pregnant with Connie. So we asked McHenry to marry us, and then we moved into a large apartment on a cul de sac street near Rue St. Germaine, a few blocks from the Bois de Bologne.

The cars move slowly north on 9D, between Garrison and Beacon. Rain drums the roof of the Lexus and washes in waves across the windshield. The wipers struggle and the windows are cloudy. Joe increases the speed of his defroster fan. Tiny crescents emerge at the base of the fogged windshield, and grow into lateral horizon lines that meet.

"That's better," he says.

April asks him about Wendy—things she already knows, but which he tells her again anyway. I know this is a shorthand language between mother and son, the assertion of some invisible, molecular connection that calms me, too. Hank is humming to himself. I think we're all trying to keep from worrying about Lizzie.

Joe starts talking about my mother, now, but I listen only vaguely, because I'm lost in my own thoughts of her. My son and his wife were very close with Mother. They spent time together in Garrison and Greenwich, and I imagine the comfort this must have been to her—this reassuring glimpse of her family's future in the inscrutable world. Several years ago, as Mother's health grew weaker, and she became less able to get out and around, Joe and Wendy bought her a computer. They helped her install Internet access and sign up for an email service, thinking she'd enjoy online chats with her scattered children and senior friends. To everyone's amusement, she quickly discovered how to trade stocks through an electronic brokerage she'd found while "surfing the World Wide Web," as she put it. She was soon managing a growing investment portfolio, and sending stock tips to her children.

It was around that time that Wendy became pregnant. And in her seventh month, Joe sent me a letter saying that after considerable thought and discussion with Mother, he and Wendy had decided to name their son after my grandfather.

"It doesn't say that what he did was right, in any way," Joe wrote. "Only that the capacity to forgive defines a family. My great-grandfather was a man filled with the hatreds of his time and background. But he started from nothing and worked hard for his family, educated his children if not himself, and then gave your family his favorite house. Dad, I just think that the past should be allowed to be the past. P.S.—Wendy loves the name, Hank. So if you have any objections, you'll need to deal with *her*. And good luck!"

I was surprised when I laughed at this. More oddly, I felt relieved—such a graceful act of hope, I thought, the terrible sins of one generation absolved by another's refusal to carry them forward.

I hear Joe's voice. "Dad, are you listening?"

"Uh…yes, what were you saying?"

Everyone laughs at me.

"I want to make sure you're satisfied with the way things have been done." He's referring to Mother's will, which she's left with him to file, and which names me as executor. A considerable amount of money has been left for Mary, and for the grandchildren. The Brents' summer home in Southampton was left to David. It's up to me to decide what will happen to the Garrison house.

"I *am* satisfied," I say, looking at the rain washing across our windshield and the wipers beating it back.

"Because I had the feeling, when I spoke to Uncle David…he *wasn't*."

Glancing forward, I see my brother driving his car with Penny next to him, and their children sitting behind them. He married relatively late in life, and I'm pleased that he seems as happy as he does, now, after a troubled youth. He met Penny in AA, in his mid-30s, and she's been good for him. They've been good together. Their children—Billy, Andrew and Tara—are 17, 15, and 10—and they're bright, spirited kids with open hearts like their father's.

"He'll be all right," I say. "I'll talk to him."

"You can understand," Joe adds, sounding like a lawyer. "He's been sober all this time, now, and he's got that good advertising job…and he was *so* close to Grandma. I'm sure he doesn't begrudge her naming *you* as executor, so much as…well, he may wonder if she thought he still wasn't dependable enough."

"It isn't about that," says April, suddenly. "Your grandmother named your father for one reason…to *involve* him…get him here."

Joe nods as he drives. "You think Uncle David realizes that?"

"I'm sure he does," she says.

"I'll talk to him," I say again.

We negotiate a long turn in the highway, and for a few seconds I can see ahead, into Mary's car, which leads our little convoy. My sister is saying something to Irv, and he nods, as he patiently steers. Their 11-year-old son, Michael, sits quietly behind them. I can see his brilliant red hair above the rear seat. He looks straight ahead without moving, a disciplined sort of kid; he loves to read more than anything.

Mary was married once before, briefly, to an alcoholic newspaper reporter who beat her up. It took her a long time, after divorcing him, to rebuild her self-confidence. But when she did, Irv Ross came along, to her great fortune. Irv has his own accounting business, and they told me this week that they're opening a vineyard on some land they bought, out on Long Island's north fork. I know they would have liked more children, but there just wasn't time. This new wine-growing venture seems to have tickled them, though, and they're planning to spend Christmas and Hanukkah out there this year—two full weeks. They want April and me stay with them, but I'm not sure if I can come back to the States again.

"Almost there," Joe says.

April turns, and nods at me. I make another call to Lizzie's number with our cell phone. Again, the recorded message we've been hearing for two days: "The subscriber of this number is either busy or outside the calling area. Please call back later, or leave a message, after the beep." I press the OFF button and slip the phone back into my jacket pocket. I cling helplessly to the thought that the same message would play, whether she was in Boston, Chicago or Los Angeles. April turns away, and gazes out her window. The rain seems to be slowing.

St. Mary's Church looks well preserved, sitting at the crest of the hill where it's been for almost a century. Its brightly painted white clapboard almost vibrates in the mist, and the proud steeple with the black iron cross at the tip is like a sword against the dark sky.

As Joe drives up in front of the church, behind Irv and David, I see the main doors are open. There's a soft orange glow inside. I'm glad to see the hearse is already here. The casket has been removed and taken inside, by prior arrangement with the funeral home.

We emerge from our cars. I hug my brother and sister and their spouses. We greet their children with kisses and smiles. Their youth is reassuring. I see other cars in the rear parking lot, which I notice is paved with black asphalt and marked with bright, white lines. There are other mourners coming toward the church from the lot. These people seem quite old. I don't think I know any of them. I imagine they must have known my mother. Perhaps, some are the funeral-goers that every parish has.

We approach the front doors, where Connie, Alice Mary, and Isabel are waiting, just inside. We embrace and kiss each other, and continue into the church together. Once we're seated, I notice that the pews have been remodeled. Even the confession box on the other side near the back has been stained with a brighter tint, and doors have been added on each side, where velvet curtains had been.

My mother's casket sits just outside the closed altar railing. Beyond the railing a pair of three-foot-long, white candles stand in bronze candlesticks. Father Collins, the priest who is to perform the service, sits silently on the left side of the altar. We don't know him very well.

Finally, everyone seems settled, but the priest continues sitting quietly in his large, wooden chair. Its burnished arms and ornately carved back cradle him. The seat is cushioned in Cardinal-red velvet. He wears richly detailed silk vestments—purple and white—and his hands are folded over a large, black missal in his lap. He gazes down in meditation. He's establishing a mood, I think to myself, an extended moment of silence that distinguishes the world outside this church from the one he will assure us has welcomed my mother. An altar boy sits quietly on each side of him, dressed in black and white, and remarkably free of nervous tics. They must be the best, most disciplined altar boys in the parish, hand picked, a sure sign of respect for my mother who, after all, gave so much of her time and money to this church for so many years.

At last, the priest rises. Trailed by the well-mannered boys, he walks slowly across in front of the altar, bows, and steps down toward the railing. Standing on its other side, he offers a brief blessing to the shrouded casket. I notice that the white and purple shroud cloth is spotted with raindrops.

It is to be a simple ceremony. "No eulogies or pomp of any kind," it said in my mother's will. She wants her family to spend what little time there is, today, with each other. That's what the will says, and that's what I told Father Collins, who greeted this request with surprise, initially, and then a cool compliance. He finishes his blessing and then walks up toward the altar. On the back of his garment are the cross, the ancient symbol of Christianity, and the Latin letters, IHS—*In Hoc Signo.*

I suddenly remember what they taught us in grammar school—that Constantine the Great dreamed of Christ, on the eve of a battle to recapture the eastern territories of the Roman Empire, in 312 AD. And in the dream, Christ assured Constantine of victory if the battle and the empire were dedicated to Him—a worldly command that always seemed at odds with the Jesus I'd read about in the New Testament. Still, we were told that the emperor saw a vision of the battlefield, and above it a giant, flaming cross. And from the rolling clouds in the distance, the voice of god, exhorting Constantine: *In hoc signo, vince.* "In this sign, conquer."

The rain starts up again. I can hear it tapping the roof as the brief service begins. I look at my watch. It's eleven-fifteen. An organist intones the ponderous chords of a medieval hymn. Sweet incense is sprinkled on coals in a golden burner, held by the priest from a two-foot chain. I wonder of this is my mother's idea of simplicity.

As the priest swings the incense burner back and forth, blue smoke fills our nostrils and rises above the altar, drifting into the old rafter beams high above us, signifying the dissolution of all earthly things. The rising smoke is also meant to symbolize our prayers reaching the heavens. But my prayers are for the living, as much as for the dead. The dead are saved already; the tears of the living are eternal.

Following the service, I linger in my seat, watching the empty altar. My family seems to understand that I need this moment alone, and so they've gotten up and started toward the door. I close my eyes; and my sins are there. I can see them.

With a sigh, I rise and move out of the pew, noticing an elderly black woman who seems to be waiting for me in the center aisle. Her face is warm and her dark eyes pierce mine as I reach her. "Mr. Gannon?" she whispers.

"*Tom* Gannon, yes."

"My name is Florence Evans," she says, reaching out her hand to me.

"Yes?" I say, holding her hand.

"I wanted to thank you, sir, for all that you've done…"

"That *I've* done?"

"Your foundation…the Gannon Foundation."

"Oh."

"With your help…*two* of my daughters have gone to college, Mr. Gannon…and *one* is in law school now."

"That's wonderful," I say. "I'm very glad to hear it."

"I knew your mother, a little…from church."

I smile. "You say…your name is Evans?"

"That's right."

"Yes. I think…I recall the name…from our files."

"It's wonderful work that you do, sir."

"Yes…well…it's *all* in my sister's name, actually…and my father's. It's *their* foundation; we formed it in *their* memory."

"Well, it's generous of you…and your family. It's *god's* work."

"Thank you, Ma'am. I hope you're right."

She smiles. "Your mother was a good person, and *they* must have been very special people, too…your sister and dad."

"Oh…yes," I say. "They taught me everything worth knowing…just about…"

We follow the hearse by car from the front of the church toward the parking lot; I see that trees no longer stand between the lot and the cemetery. We cruise slowly through the lot, and along a private driveway, to a paved road that encircles the cemetery and soon brings us to a spot where we can get out and walk a short distance to the gravesite.

Mother is to be buried next to Liz. On her other side, there's a small stone in memory of Father. And though they never lived together again, after Liz died, Libby and Hank Gannon are buried here, too, in another section of the cemetery.

The priest's prayers are simple and brief. He wishes us well and walks back toward the church. We stand, now, at our mother's grave, praying our private thoughts as the soft rain taps against our umbrellas. Two cemetery workers wait, nearby, in a green pickup truck. The man from the funeral home nods to April, and she steps forward to place John Wilson's white magnolias on the rain-spattered casket.

I wait a minute more in this dreary rain before I turn to the funeral director and say, "okay, that's it."

"No last statements?" he asks.

I look around at the faces of my family. There is love and sorrow in their eyes as they stare back at me. White vapor swirls as they breathe the cold air beneath their umbrellas. "No," I finally say. "It's been said."

He signals the workmen. They slide out of their truck but linger, at a respectful distance, as we start back along the short gravel walkway to where we left our cars in a row on the loop road. I remind everyone to come back to the house in Garrison for something to eat. I see their silent nods, as they open the doors to their cars and get in out of the rain. Engines start, doors slam and windshield wipers squeak. Headlights come on, though it's minutes before noon.

I help April back into the Lexus, as Joe and Hank slide into their seats in front. Suddenly, I see my old classmate, Andy O'Leary, standing near his car some distance away on the loop road. He's almost completely bald, but somehow taller and thinner than I might have expected. After all this time, I'm able to recognize his face. It looks just like his father's now.

"Give me a minute," I say to April and Joe, closing the back door of the Lexus. Then, my umbrella aloft, I hurry to Andy and reach out my hand. "How are you, Congressman?" I say. He smiles and we shake, firmly. I hold the umbrella over him and we stand close. "I didn't notice you inside."

"Just got here," he says. "It's been a busy morning to end a terrible week."

"I know. Andy…I really need to thank you for your help this past year." He waves me off. "I mean it, now. I'd never have been allowed back…"

"There *was* a lot of red tape…I'll give you that," he says. "The case was inactive, but it took a year to get them to close it…officially…I'm just glad we finally did. I promised your mother. My staff had to really press the state attorney though. I guess it helped that I used to work there…anyway, you're free and clear now. It's over." I laugh at this, ruefully, and I think of Lizzie. I want to be wherever she is. "It's over, Tom," he repeats, reading uncertainty, but about the wrong thing, in my expression. "Stay as long as you want. You're a U.S. citizen."

I want to tell him about my daughter. "Andy," I start to say.

He shakes his head. He thinks I'm trying to thank him. "No need," he says. "I owe *you*…"

"For what?" I frown, skeptically.

The other cars are driving past us, now, and heading back toward the parking lot and the church driveway, which will take them down to the highway. I glance back at the Lexus, and I see Joe and Hank and April waiting for me.

"From when we were kids," he says. I stare down at the raindrops hitting the puddles along the loop road. "I can still see you standing up in class, and hauling off on old McHenry," he says. "Thinking you were defending me. You were pissed off *that* day."

"McHenry was a good man," I say. "I still miss him."

He nods in agreement. "And then…when you told off Stevens, and my old man. Now…*that was somethin'* I wish more people had stood up in those days…and said what needed to be said…I don't mean *about me*…I mean…about what was going on, and what we were being told. It was all…"

"Bullshit," I say, and he nods. "So how *is* everything, Andy?"

"Well…I *thought* this term would be about getting the river cleaned up…we've been negotiating with Hudson Electric on that…and we need to get the nuclear power plant down river caught up to the latest regs. Of course, there's *always* cutting taxes. Voters are very concerned with that. At least they were…before Tuesday…"

"Yeah."

"Priorities changed like *that*," he says, snapping his fingers. "It's all about security now. The federal government is making all kinds of promises…there's talk in Congress about developing a whole domestic security program…it's a good idea, but it's gonna cost money. We'll have to see. We have concerns, here, at the local and state level…people want answers Meanwhile, something good has actually come out of this nightmare, too. People want to know what they can do…how they can help…make things safer. So, I've been out talking with voters across the district this week…visiting church and community groups…went to three different breakfasts this morning, already…business groups. And I imagine I'll be going to some more funerals soon." He pauses and stares out across the cemetery clearing. "Thirty-seven residents of this district worked in the towers…thirty-two of 'em are still missing. Plus…we lost eleven police and firemen that day."

"I'm sorry, Andy. It's terrible…people seem so…stunned…"

He nods. "Because they don't know what to think. What we need is information. People want that…that's why I'm forming a committee to look into ways we can organize and educate ourselves in this district…I'd like to reach out and ask for people to contribute their knowledge and expertise…maybe *you*, too."

"What can *I* do?" I say. "I haven't been here…for almost *fifty years*."

"*That's okay.* You're an American…with a foreign perspective…objectivity…*and* you're a historian."

"Why would people listen to *me*?"

"*I'll* listen to you…I'll encourage *others* to listen…because *you* understand that most of the answers to what we're facing…can be found in history." He pauses, and seems to be considering something frightening. "*Tom,*" he says, "if we fall into the trap of thinking that this attack…as *horrible* as it is…is something truly unique in the history of the world and mankind…we're gonna be ripe for manipulation. I mean…have we forgotten War World Two…the Holocaust…the evils of mankind throughout history? The evil in the world *always* has to be fought…but with intelligence…wisdom. But…the sort of thinking that says, 'hey…*anything* we do now *has* to be right.' That's dangerous. There are some crazy ideas floating around Washington, now, about invading countries…"

"Don't you think we should do *something*?"

"*Yes*…against the people who *did this*. But…you don't know the crazy talk that's going on down there. Tom, Americans love the simple answer to things. But there *are* none in this case. The fact is…these hijackers come from countries that are supposed to be our allies in the Middle East and Asia…allies and business partners. And this Al Qaeda group…it's been allowed to take root in Afghanistan. *That's* where we need to start, but we have to keep our wits about us. Or else…crazy ideas might start to seem reasonable…like fifty years ago. Remember?" I nod. "People thought they were gonna be blown up by Russian and Chinese atom bombs…so suddenly, we were hunting for spies and traitors in our midst. And we kept it up, long after we found them all. It was madness."

"I know."

"I don't want us to turn on ourselves again, like that. The sort of ideas that come from fear are *always* wrong, and it seems there's always a few unprincipled people willing to exploit our fear. *That's* the biggest danger I see. So…maybe you could help me with some *sensible* ideas…some speeches, maybe. We could promote our ideas with the media…"

"If you think it'll help…"

He nods. "I want to develop a communications program in my district…that *we* run, locally…something that gets everyone involved…educates them about the *real* external threats…and deals with homeland security, too…but protects our rights." He pauses. "I'm trying to get at least one veteran involved from each of the major conflicts…you know…World War Two,

Korea…Vietnam…the Persian Gulf. My thought is…they've all had what you might call *crisis experience*. People are shell shocked from this attack…but our veterans already *have* that experience. I'm thinking, maybe *they* can help the rest of us keep things in perspective…remind us what it means to go to war…keep our emotions in check, as we decide how to fight this *terrorism* thing. These veterans have a lot of wisdom and experience…and people will listen to 'em now. We could set up town hall meetings…talk to local media…that sort of thing. The more voices…the better. You know?"

"Yes," I say.

"I've got several people who've already agreed to work with me…but I'm still looking for someone from the Vietnam era. So many of those guys are still so…disaffected. I'd love to get someone to head up that part of the committee…but not a hateful or bitter type veteran. I need a patriot from that time, if there *are* any."

"There are…"

"It's got to be a person who's had war experience…first hand. I'm putting some funds aside to pay them, too…won't be a lot, but it'll be something. That's important, I think. It's fine to say citizens should volunteer and…*this week*, I'm sure we'd get a lot of volunteers. But I'm serious about this…long term. This attack could change us…and I want to make sure it's not a change for the worse." I nod in agreement. "I don't suppose you know anyone who could fill a position like that," he says.

"Matter of fact…I think I do."

"Yeah?"

"He's an old friend," I say. "He came to see me at the house this morning. He's a neighbor. A decorated Vietnam vet…wounded in combat…saved his whole platoon from being overrun by surprise one night. He killed the lead scout…hand to hand. He's a good man. As I understand it, he's got some time available."

"What does *that* mean?"

"He's a good man…this sounds like the job for him."

"All right," Andy says with a nod. "Who is he?"

"John Wilson…his family lived in the house next to ours for years. His father and my father grew up together…"

"Wilson, huh? All right. Have him call me."

"I will," I say, glancing back at the Lexus. I look at my watch; it's twelve-fifteen. "Andy…why don't you come by the house…we're having something to eat…it's just family…we can talk some more about this…maybe I can get John to come over, so you can meet him."

He looks at his watch and shakes his head. "I'm late for a lunch meeting already. Have Wilson call me next week. And…can *you* call me…*separately*?" I nod in confusion. "There's another thing I need to ask you, Tom, but this isn't the time."

"Jesus, Andy…don't stand on ceremony *now*."

He stares at me for a moment. Then he glances around, as if making sure that no one will hear him, but there's no one nearby, only April and Joe and Hank, waiting patiently in the Lexus. "I always *assumed* that you were there," he begins, "in my father's office building, the night he died. And I appreciated that you admitted it…man to man…when your mother asked me to call you last year…"

"I should have said something sooner, Andy, but back then, she made me promise I'd never admit it to anyone outside the family. She said refusing to go along with the prosecutors was the only justice we'd probably ever get. She said it might not feel like justice…because we had to take it ourselves…but we had to be strong enough to live with that…and with *our own* sins…however wrong it felt." He nods, listening. "You see, there were some serious mistakes that I'd made…family things…and the more I tried to make up for them…the worse the mistakes got. So I came to this decision that…whatever my mother said or wanted…from then on…no matter what…*that's* what I'd do…whether it seemed right to *me* or not. But I guess I just figured…it was time…and well, it was *you*."

"I understand," he says. "I appreciate your trust. It always seemed unfair to my mother and me that they were charging *you* with murder…"

"Well…Andy…I…"

"After all, you were only trying to get out alive…and you ended up…losing your sister and all." He pauses. "Of course…we'd heard the rumors…that my father was somehow responsible…for *your* father's…disappearance…"

"What's your question, Andy?"

"Do *you* think my father murdered your father?"

"Yes…we had proof."

"And you never brought it to the authorities?"

"We didn't *trust* the authorities…and it would have jeopardized someone else we needed to protect…the witness."

He sighs heavily, and stares down at the ground. "I'm sorry, Tom…it seems like you ended up paying a price…living in exile all this time…knowing my father had done this terrible wrong to *your* family…"

"I wouldn't call my life an exile, Andy…not really. I deserve nothing, and I've been amazingly lucky…married to the girl I loved…my children have all done well. I'm a fortunate man…all in all. But…I've decided that that's just another part of my punishment." I think of Lizzie, and he stares at me, quizzically.

"You should understand something, Tom…maybe it'll help. The truth is…I never lost another night's sleep after my old man died…and I don't think my mother did. He was a frightening, brutal man, who had a lot of hate in him…and that destroyed our feelings for him. I *hated* him…for the things he would do to me…but I could have *killed* him for what he did to my mother. And…I'll admit something to *you*…if it had gone on much longer…I probably would have. I would have taken one of his shotguns and blown him in two."

"Andy," I say, with sympathy.

"So, now…just tell me again, so I'm clear. You said, you didn't even try to help my father get out that night…right?"

"That's right."

"Okay. I understand. All I'm saying is…don't feel guilty about it."

I shake my head and frown, looking around. "There's one other part of this I've never told anyone…not a soul…not even my mother, though I always thought she suspected," He stares at me urgently. "You told me something, once," I begin. "I don't know if you remember…you once said that Sunday night was your favorite night of the week." His face drains of color at the memory. "At first, I didn't understand you…all of us kids hated Sunday nights, because it meant the weekend was over and school was back in session the next morning."

He nods. "Those damn Monday quizzes."

"But here you said, that you *looked forward* to Sunday nights."

"I said that, huh?"

I nod. "You said it was the *one* night of the week you knew your father wouldn't be home, because he almost always went to his office on Sunday nights, when it was quiet, so he could catch up on his work for the following week."

"That's true," he says, "but I don't remember saying it to you…"

"You just tossed it off once…maybe you weren't paying attention to yourself. But I heard you…and after I thought about it, I realized what you meant...the *way* you said it...it seemed like such a relief." He nods with silent pain. "And *that's* what I remembered...when I went there, that Sunday night..."

"You...expected him to be there?"

"I *wanted* him to be. And he was."

"Christ, Tom."

"I'm sorry, Andy."

"Don't forget, we need coffee," April says.

"There's a Starbucks in Cold Spring," I say. Joe nods and we head south on 9D.

"Was everything all right with Mr. O'Leary?" April asks.

"He says there won't be any problems...any more," I sigh.

"That's great, Dad," says Joe.

April squeezes my hand and I reach inside my jacket for the cell phone. I dial Lizzie's number again, and I glance at April's impassive profile as I press the phone to my ear. I hear nothing this time, not even the recorded message. I hit the OFF button and slip the phone back in my pocket.

"If we don't hear something soon," April says, "we're flying over there...the first available plane." I nod and the car is silent as Joe drives to Cold Spring.

Ten minutes later, we're moving slowly down Main Street into the business district. I see the houses along High Street are still there, though they seem smaller, but I'm amazed at how unchanged the rest of the village looks at first. There's still a boat ramp and a white gazebo at the bottom of the hill near the edge of the river. And then, I notice that the stores have different names on them. Many have been rebuilt; designed to recapture the look of small town America, circa 1910.

I see a bistro in the space where Sposato's Hardware Store used to be. Jensen's Sweet Shop is a wine importer. The old Post Office Theater is still a movie house, somewhat refurbished, but now devoted to foreign and independent American films. It says, *You Can Count on Me* on the marquee. And the space that once held Edith's Dress Shop has been extended on both sides, and has become a fresh food emporium with a big green awning over a wide front door.

Joe pulls the Lexus up against the curb in front of Starbucks. He starts to get out.

"No...no...no!" I say, reaching forward and tapping him on the back. "I'll get this." I turn to April. "What kind should we have?"

"Whatever you think," she says, blankly. "One pound should be decaf, though."

Little Hank suddenly turns in his seat. "Can *I* go, Grandpa?"

"Sure. If it's okay with your dad."

Joe is laughing. "He compares them…"

"Compares what?" I ask.

"The different Starbucks," Joe says. "He's intrigued, for some reason, by how each one is just a little different from the others…you know, how they put them in whatever old spaces are available…old banks…taverns…soda fountains…"

I nod, and look at Hank. "All right, kiddo…let's go see." He smiles broadly and whips his body around in the front seat. His father hits the lock button, and Hank pushes his door as I get out from the back.

We meet on the sidewalk in front of the car, and I grab his little hand. We wave to Joe and April and then walk together toward the coffee shop, which I can see is busy. The Starbucks people have remade the Wilsons' old storefront, but have kept the original glass and wood-frame door. I grip the polished brass door handle and push, almost expecting to smell newsprint and tobacco. Instead, we're welcomed by the rich aroma of coffee and the sounds of youthful conversations and soft jazz.

"Cool," Hank says, and I smile at him. This kid is priceless.

I choose a pound of French Roast and a pound of Mocha Java decaf from the shelves, and we get on line. Hank is looking all around, examining the walls and ceilings. He's watching the groups of young men and women sipping lattes and mochaccinos, chatting on cell phones, working laptops, reading the *New York Times* and the *Wall Street Journal*.

Over the sound system, I suddenly hear Billie Holiday—it's a recording from the early '50s. I immediately remember the first time I heard it with Liz, on our grandparents' big box radio.

> *Smooth road…clear day,*
> *But why am I the only one…travelin' this way?*
> *How strange the road to love…should be so easy,*
> *Can there be a detour…ahead?*

I think of the Spencers, suddenly. I remember getting word from Mother that Hazel had died of a heart attack, the year after I'd left for Paris. I think of Arthur, who lived on until 1968 and then died of cancer, early in the year, before Martin Luther King's murder. I was always glad that life had allowed him the small satisfaction of never knowing that. He'd proudly witnessed Johnson's signing of the great civil rights act, and had seen King become a prominent world figure—things that might have seemed implausible only a few years earlier. But the last years of Arthur's life were mostly melancholy. He'd never fully recovered from the loss of his wife so soon after what had happened to my father and Liz. And then he lost Laureen, too, in 1958. She was killed in Mississippi, where she'd been working on voter registration in the all-black neighborhoods of Jackson. One night someone had come up behind the car she was sitting in, out in front of the Baptist church, and shot her in the head with a rifle. No one was ever charged. Whoever it was also shot the white man who was sitting in the driver's seat, Allen Rosenthal.

The line shrinks ahead of us and we're standing next to the newspaper rack. A few copies of today's *New York Times* are still left. I glance absently at a front-page story about the many nations that have condemned terrorism this week. Another says that the Justice Department has identified the 19 men who hijacked the planes that were used in the attacks. I see a small story about discussions to find the proper way to rebuild downtown Manhattan.

They never did build television studios up on St. Nicholas Avenue, I suddenly remember. Charles Stannard's bank pulled out shortly after O'Leary's death, and the deal more or less collapsed in the autumn of 1954. City Hall lost interest in the site and the surrounding neighborhood, and had already moved on to a different slum clearance project, where Broadway and Amsterdam Avenues cross between West 62nd and 66th Streets. It took several years to clear the 15-acre complex of tenements there. And then in 1959, President Eisenhower went to the groundbreaking ceremony for Lincoln Center. The City had its new arts and entertainment complex at last, and over time, several of the major TV networks built their vast, modern studios nearby.

We come through the front door and I see everyone sitting or standing around in the tiny living room. Some have drinks in hand. Most of the children are sprawled on the floor. None of the food has been brought out. David is standing in front of the big screen TV, lowering the sound in a vaguely suspicious way. Connie and Alice Mary stare at us with odd expressions.

"What's up?" I say.

There is silence, and heads turn away.

"Answer your father," April commands our daughters.

Finally, Connie speaks up. "CNN just reported...a field hospital was overrun by rebel troops, three days ago in north Rwanda...where Lizzie is..."

April's voice is flat. "What else did they say?"

"They don't have many details," Connie replies. "The story's just coming out...some of the government forces defending the hospital retreated and escaped...a few of them got to Kigali today...and spoke to a reporter."

"They said there were a lot of casualties among the government troops," adds Alice Mary, who starts to cry.

"Tom," David says. "The rebels went through the hospital and killed all the patients they could find...in their beds...they took some of the hospital staff outside, and executed them on the spot...but there's a lot of confusion still...about the details."

"Turn it up," says April, suddenly, in a forceful voice. David turns the volume up again, and April sits at the edge of the nearest couch. I look at the screen and see the president and his wife coming out of a church. The announcer is saying that they will fly immediately to New York, so the president can visit the site where the towers were.

"Most of the news channels are covering memorial services in Washington," says Isabel. "The Rwanda story was a brief...a thirty-second news break. That's all."

April sits, stoically, and stares at the screen. I look at Isabel and nod. Then I walk through the crowded living room, down the little hallway and into the kitchen. I put the bags of coffee down on the old counter next to the sink and, briefly, I stare out the windows. The last part of the rainstorm is moving across the valley, now, churning the river black as it comes east. The western sky is losing its black overcast. The sun may even shine tomorrow, I think.

I feel a hand pressed on my back. I turn and see Isabel standing there. "What can I do?" she asks.

"Pray, I guess."

"I've *been* praying, Tom. I meant...what can I do to comfort you...and your wife?"

I sigh. "I don't know...is anybody hungry? Put out the food, maybe. We ordered a lot of salads and cold sandwiches...there's some soup, too, I guess..."

She smiles. "All right...I don't think anybody's ready to eat yet...but I'll check..."

"What are you doing tonight?" I ask.

"The girls and I were planning to drive back to Boston...but now...I don't know..."

"Do you have Saturday classes?"

She nods. "A morning seminar…but I can have one of my assistants handle it…I may do that…if there's *any* chance we'll hear something about Lizzie…I'd want to be here…with you all."

I remember the first time I ever saw Isabel—a little girl with a blue dress sitting with her grandfather in the old Peekskill bus terminal—now, a tenured professor of American studies at Harvard. "I guess, when you're the head of the department," I say, "you can make executive decisions…"

She smiles and steps toward me, and we hug. "I owe so much to your mother, Tom."

"So do I." I step back and look into her warm face. "Everyone in this house owes something to her. I'm glad you're here…that we're *all* here." She agrees, with a nod. I turn and glance back through the hallway at the crowd of family members gathered around the TV. "Anything yet?" I shout.

"Nothing!" David shouts back. "We'll tell you!"

Suddenly Mary's husband appears. He stops at the edge of the hallway near the kitchen door and he glances around, as if looking for something but not wanting to seem impolite. He's a tall, lanky guy, a good man with a good heart. I liked him from the moment I met him, years ago, when he and my sister came through Paris on their honeymoon.

"Whadya' need, Irv?" I say.

"A little white wine…for Mary?"

"All the booze is on the counter, there. Help yourself…"

"Thanks, Tom." He walks across the kitchen, and I pat his arm as he passes.

"Looks like the rain's stopping," mutters Isabel, staring out the windows.

"Think I'll get some air," I say.

I leave the kitchen from the back door, and walk down the old wooden stairs onto the sodden grass. My feet sink into the mud an inch or so, at first. But the footing seems better as I walk farther down to where the hillside is so steep the rainwater has run off. I look across the river and see the military academy. Lights are on behind most of the windows. I check my watch. It's two in the afternoon, but it's as dark as dusk in the valley. Last night, the academy lights never went out. I could see them all night from our living room.

"Hey, Dad!" It's Joe's voice. I turn and see him standing on the top step, just outside the back door. He has little Hank with him. "What are you doing?" he shouts.

"Just walking," I say.

"Wait up!" They hurry down the steps and out onto the grass, and quickly catch up to me. My son has his mother's personality, not mine. I'm glad about this. And somehow, he's followed the example of my father without ever knowing him. His clients are the richest media tycoons of New York, and their high tech counterparts in Northern California, but I know his heart is increasingly taken with *pro bono* cases for Asian and Middle Eastern immigrants, struggling for citizenship, starting small businesses. I hold Hank's hand, and for a moment, we all gaze out at the dark river below us. "I promised I'd take him down to the water," says Joe, suddenly. "If the rain let up."

"Oh," I say, releasing Hank's hand and trying to smile.

Joe takes his son's hand and says, "are you all right, Dad?" I force another weak smile, and nod. Then, he points to the thick underbrush and trees above the riverbank. "We'll just go down through there," he says.

"Be careful," I say. "It's slippery as you get close to the edge."

"We will," they say together.

They start to walk down the slope with their backs to me, now, and as I watch them, I think of Liz, and my father. I imagine I can hear them speaking to me. I look out over the river and I watch it flow away into the valley. It isn't the rain that keeps the river filled and flowing, I suddenly think, but the tears of the living that flow forever. I look down the hill for Joe and Hank, but they've already disappeared into the trees.

Suddenly, I hear a cheer go up inside the house, and I turn and gaze back up the hill. Now, I hear April's voice in the distance. "Tom! Tom!" I start toward the house and I see her standing on the edge of the porch, waving down the hill to me. "It's Lizzie...it's Lizzie! She just called..."

I stop and shout toward the river. "Joe! Hank! Hurry up...Lizzie's on the phone!"

I turn and run up the sodden hill toward the house. Twice, I nearly slip and fall on the wet grass. The hillside is steep. My knees are aching, and I'm a little short of breath as I reach the hilltop and see that April has already gone inside. I rush around to the front steps and up onto the porch. I hurry through the front door and see my wife holding the telephone. She's crying uncontrollably, and smiling at the same time. "Here he is," she says into the phone.

"She made it to the airport at Kigali," says David.

"She escaped the hospital with some patients, and a news photographer from Reuters," says Mary. "A woman," she adds with great pride. I smile and nod as I watch my wife listening to the phone. Her weeping is subsiding. She's still smiling.

"The news photographer led them out of the jungle," says Alice Mary. "Lizzie said she's an amazing person. They've been trekking through the jungles for days."

"I'll put your father on now, Dear," April says, looking up at me and handing me the telephone.

I hear voices. I glance out the windows beneath the porch and see Joe and Hank hurrying up the final few yards of grassy hillside toward the house. I put the phone to my ear. "Lizzie?"

"How are you, Daddy?" Her voice is a million miles away.

"How am *I*?" Tears rush from my eyes. I can't stop them. My hand is shaking. "I'm great, Liz…I'm happy…I'm…when are you coming home?"

"There's supposed to be a plane out tomorrow, and I'm on it. It goes to London, first, and then I'll get a connection for New York. I should be at JFK Sunday night, your time…"

"Day after tomorrow!" I say.

"That's right!" my daughter says.

"She'll be in New York by Sunday night," I say to everyone in the room. They smile and nod at me. They know these details already. Suddenly, Mary and Irv's son, Michael, tells my sister he's hungry. Everyone laughs. We can't stop laughing, now. Even Michael is laughing, though he's not quite sure why. Joe and Hank are coming through the front door.

"What's so funny?" I hear Lizzie say.

"We're just happy," I tell her. "Everyone's happy."

I stand on the porch in darkness, listening to the river. My family is inside the suddenly warm, old cottage. There are children sprawled on the living room floor, some watching television, others playing a game on my mother's computer. Everyone has eaten, and the adults are speaking in low voices, planning what we'll do with Lizzie when she gets here on Sunday. For the moment, we've pushed away the sadness of my mother's passing, and the grief that hangs over all of America tonight.

My mind rushes with memories of my Grandmother Libby, and the Brents, and the steadfast Spencers. I remember the Wilsons and Edith Neumann, the Rosenthals, Agent Valeriani, Sister Paul, and Father McHenry—their many acts of courage and kindness. I pray for Hank Gannon and I shudder, thinking of Andy O'Leary's loyalty to me, and his forgiveness, which, like so much else in my life, is undeserved. But I understand my punishment—to have been granted everything I once thought was important, to be the beneficiary of my family's love, and my children's, and my wife's admiration—to be the least worthy member of this family, left with the responsibility to tell its story.

I look down the valley and see headlights flickering across Bear Mountain Bridge. And two miles to the north, the Wilsons' house lights are glowing above the dark treetops. John must be back from the VA, I think; I'll call him in a minute.

I remember the winter day we moved in here—Liz and I discovered an ancient radio our grandparents had left behind in the third-floor hallway, upstairs. It was a massive box radio, with its own table stand, and it took a minute for its tubes to warm up when we turned it on, but it pulled in a strong signal. And because of the great heights, here, we found that we could get broadcasts from cities so distant and unfamiliar that they seemed like alien planets.

During that winter so long ago, Liz and I would head upstairs after dinner most evenings and turn the thing on, twisting its large glowing dial with great anticipation until we caught something we liked. Then, we'd lie back on the floor in the hall, close our eyes, and travel. On some nights we heard big bands out of Chicago, and on others, French jazz records that a station in Montreal played, or Hank Williams tunes from New Orleans. They played a lot of Hank Williams, then, because he'd recently died. And sometimes, we'd find a station that played "rhythm and blues," what white people called "race music" back then. It was hard to find, but Liz and I loved it because it seemed to make the grownups uncomfortable.

"That's pure sex, put to music," I said to Liz one night.

"Whadda *you* know about sex?" she smiled. And then, she said, "listen *closer*."

I remember the night we were listening to a country music show from a concert hall in Baton Rouge, and a white teenager nobody had ever heard of came out and sang the old Rogers and Hart song, *Blue Moon*. He wailed it in a slow, falsetto voice, the way black singers sometimes sang rhythm and blues, and the audience seemed stunned. Liz turned the volume up as loud as it would go, and halfway through the song Mother called up the stairs to us from the living room. "*Who* is that singing?"

"Some boy...from Mississippi," Liz replied. "A white boy."

"Really," Mother said.

And there were nights when we'd all sit together in the living room, and watch the old black and white television. But when summer arrived that first year, Father started rousting his children out for walks along the back hillside after dinner. Sometimes Mother joined us, but more often she stayed behind and watched. We could see her, too, a silhouette moving in the kitchen windows, whose soft glow made it seem as if the moon had come to rest on the hilltop. She'd play her old Frank Sinatra records as she worked in the kitchen light, and we could hear the music in the silent summer air.

> *I sit and daydream...I've got daydreams galore...*
> *Cigarette ashes, there they go on the floor...I'll*
> *Go away weekends, leave my keys in the door...*
> *But why try to change me now...*

And Father would describe the skies as a great map, illuminated by celestial road lights. He'd point out the North Star and the bright summer evening stars, showing us how they rose and set in precise patterns each evening, and how the change of seasons affected where you'd look for them. "You're never really lost, if you know the heavens," he'd say to us.

David and Mary would start to lose patience. They'd giggle and roll down the hillside, or fight with each other, or race back to the house, determined to win control of the television. Father would smile at Liz and me, then, and tell us one of his stories about the mythic figures in the stars—obvious tragic lessons it seemed to me, then. But I was protected by assumptions. I couldn't see, in the stars or in myself, how little the future is changed by what we know of the past. All time flows together like a river, unbroken. And we are all drawn along in its inevitable wake—those who came before us and those who will follow are with us now. My father wasn't searching for answers, gazing into the endless night skies with his children around him. I realize, now, he'd have settled for hope.

I look down at the hillside, illuminated once again by the kitchen's reflected light. I listen for the voices of my father, and mother, and sister. But I won't hear them on the hillside, or in the river, or the trees, or the subtle night wind. If I listen closely, I'll hear them inside myself tonight. I've become the voice that speaks for them, and for these memories of distant hours, and days and years—all like a single moment to me now. In this moment, my family is whole again.

Acknowledgements

Timothy Harper helped me enormously in editing this book and revising its structure. I received generous comments and useful suggestions along the way from Phil Carolan, Kathleen Lynch Gaffney, Procter Lippincott, Dr. James Lynch, Joann Mulqueen, John Mulqueen, Andrew Nibley, Marybeth Michael Nibley, and Quan Tran. Patricia Bosworth offered inspiration and encourage ment, Kevin Daly conceived a brilliant jacket design.

Many thanks to Tim Harper and Walter Boyer, Dave Logan and Jonny Harper at BooksByBookends, Ridgewood, NJ, for their invaluable help to me in bringing this book to life.

And for her taste, judgement, encouragement and support, I am indebted to my wife, Angela K. Crooke.

Author's Note

While this book is a work of fiction, it is set in an historical context, which I have tried to render as accurately as possible in the broadest sense. I depended for this on a number of historical and biographical works, but wish to acknowledge two primary sources. For an understanding of the ways in which building development, politics, money, power and prejudice merged in New York City in the years following World War II: *The Power Broker: Robert Moses and the Fall of New York*, by Robert A. Caro (Vintage Books, 1975). And for an understanding of the House Committee on Un-American Activities, the McCarthy Senate investigations, and the many personalities drawn into their wake: *Naming Names*, by Victor S. Navasky (The Viking Press, 1980).

Nevertheless, it should be stressed that all names, characters, places, and incidents in this book either are products of the author's imagination or are used fictitiously. Any resemblance to actual events or locales or persons, living or dead, is entirely coincidental.

About the Author

Robert Crooke is co-author of *Between Ocean and Empire: An Illustrated History of Long Island,* and his poetry has been published in the *West Hills Review,* the literary journal of the Walt Whitman Birthplace in Long Island. He contributed original dramas for a radio series affiliated with the former *Chicago Tribune/New York Daily News* Syndicate. He began his career as a sports reporter and columnist for the *Long Island Press,* and for 13 years he served as the North American press spokesman for Reuters, the news and information company. He and his wife live in Bridgewater, CT.

0-595-33565-9

Printed in the United States
24196LVS00003B/79-144